SHARP FOCUS A First Daughter Mystery

ALSO BY SUSAN FORD WITH LAURA HAYDEN

DOUBLE EXPOSURE: A First Daughter Mystery

SHARP FOCUS A First Daughter Mystery

SUSAN FORD WITH LAURA HAYDEN

THOMAS DUNNE BOOKS
ST. MARTIN'S MINOTAUR ✹ NEW YORK

THOMAS DUNNE BOOKS.
An imprint of St. Martin's Press.

www.minotaurbooks.com

Library of Congress Cataloging-in-Publication Data

Ford, Susan 1957–
    Sharp focus: a first daughter mystery / Susan Ford with Laura Hayden.—1st ed.
        p. cm.
    ISBN 0-312-28499-3
    1. White House (Washington, D.C.)—Fiction. 2. Children of presidents—Fiction. 3. Women photographers—Fiction. 4. Washington (D.C.)—Fiction. I. Hayden, Laura. II. Title

    PS3606.O747S53 2003
    813'.6—dc21

                                                          2003041289

First Edition: July 2003

10   9   8   7   6   5   4   3   2   1

To my family

ACKNOWLEDGMENTS

With gratitude and love to my parents, husband, and children for giving me the time and encouragement to do this.

And for all the First Children, thanks for the adventures and excitement—past, present, and future.

Thanks to the men and women of the United States Air Force and their families, who put up with far-flung assignments, an endless supply of cardboard moving boxes, and indecipherable office symbols. Special thanks to the Public Affairs departments at Wilford Hall and USAFA for their help.

Lastly, thanks to Denise Little for being the best editor/collaborator/mentor/friend/amusement park groupie a girl could have—and to Mel Berger and Ethan Ellenberg, those superb agents, for their supreme patience and support.

CHAPTER ONE

U.S. AIR FORCE ACADEMY PUBLIC AFFAIRS
USAF ACADEMY, CO 80840

ACADEMY ANNOUNCES GRADUATION GUEST SPEAKER
U.S. AIR FORCE ACADEMY, COLO.—Elliot J. Cooper, President of the United States of America, is scheduled to deliver the commencement address to the class of 2003 at the 45th U.S. Air Force Academy graduation beginning at 11 A.M., May 28, in Falcon Stadium . . .

"Good God, Diana. What are you trying to do? Kill me?" I whispered to the woman who was strapping me into the seat.

She tightened the harness. "Not at the moment, but I may change my mind if you don't sit back and let me get on with it," she said.

My favorite Secret Service agent, Diana Gates, was in the process of restraining me in what looked to me like a death trap. It was the Secret Service's job to protect me and my family. But I was having some doubts about their intentions right now.

"Are you absolutely sure this is safe?" I asked.

"Nope," Diana said. "But the Air Force is—and they should know." She gave one last pull on a piece of canvas webbing and stepped back, ready to let the professionals take over.

Several Air Force cadets stepped forward at her signal to check over every detail of the tiny aircraft I was sitting in, as well as the straps holding me in it. If I hadn't been so busy worrying about my future survival, I'd have appreciated the view a lot more.

BRING ME MEN—that's what it says in big silver letters on the ramp leading up to the Air Force Academy cadet area. When I'd seen the words, I'd had to hide a smile. The phrase sounded more like the secret plea of a high school girl than a military slogan. Now I was surrounded by an assortment of those very men—trust me, the Air Force's finest are easy on the eyes—and I was literally all tied up and too apprehensive to enjoy it. That was despite the fact that I knew that the men checking my straps were every bit as concerned about my future survival as I was. My dad was, after all, technically their boss.

My name is Eve, and I'm the First Daughter. My father is President Elliot James Cooper, Commander in Chief of the Armed Forces and Leader of the Free World. I just call him Dad. And because of Dad, I was about to take part in something that the Air Force considered a high treat.

It's not that I mind flying. I like it—in large jets with even larger wings. With bathrooms. And engines—I like having engines. Lots of them. The more, the merrier.

But I was now immovably attached to a flying machine that looked like a child's toy, not an aircraft. And it was completely engine-free. My confidence in the theory of drag and lift shrank accordingly.

Diana moved closer once the fly guys gave her the high sign. "You ready?" Despite the fact that Diana had her game face on—that official Secret Service blank stare—I'd gotten to know her well enough to realize she was suppressing a small, unauthorized grin.

But Diana's expression didn't keep my attention for long. No, right now I was far more interested in the yellow glider I was sitting in, attached to its tow plane by a rope.

Not a steel cable, but a rope.

A thin rope.

Somehow, that didn't seem right to me.

Diana's attention was elsewhere, scanning the tarmac, as she remained on the lookout for danger. In this crowd it was unlikely to materialize, but it was her job to watch. The glider I was sitting in was parked on the run-way of the U.S. Air Force Academy, just north of Colorado Springs, right on the edge of the Academy's eighteen thousand acres of beautiful Colorado landscape, and we were waiting for clearance for takeoff.

The local Air Force personnel wanted to make sure the time I spent with them was memorable. As I sat in that glider, my face frozen in what I hoped was a pleasant expression, trying not to hyperventilate, I knew they'd succeeded. I was just scared enough to have this moment indelibly engraved on my brain for the rest of my life.

I was here because Dad was to be the main speaker at this year's Air Force commencement celebration. It's traditional for the President to make the obligatory "For God and Your Country" speech to one of the three service academies each year—working in due course through the Air Force Academy in Colorado Springs, West Point in New York, and the Naval Academy in Annapolis. It was no secret that Dad was thrilled that the Air Force Academy had been first up in the rotation for him. He'd done a tour in the Air Force as an officer, and had stayed active in the reserves for a long time. He might not be an Academy grad, but some of his best friends were. And those blue-suiters do tend to stick together.

I'd been thrilled too. I grew up and went to school in Colorado, and had taken the opportunity to come in early to catch up with some old friends. As a consequence, I beat Dad to the Academy by a good six hours.

Dad was due to arrive in *Air Force One* later today at nearby Peterson Air Force Base, much too late to do me any good. Right now I was the only Cooper in sight. The glider ride was mine. The things I do for the press and my country . . . it always amazed me.

But I needed to look less scared than I felt, because the press was watching. I didn't want to let Dad down.

At the edge of the tarmac, the light of flaring camera flashes threatened to blind me as the media took advantage of the photo op. Diana's vision was, I hoped, in better shape than mine. I wouldn't be able to spot a threat right now unless it was the size of a city bus.

"Do I *have* to do this?" I asked, even though I knew I did.

Diana didn't even look at me. "No. But Captain Perky will be so disappointed if you don't."

"Durkee," I corrected. That was the name of the crackerjack military media liaison who had been my guide for the VIP tour all morning. The captain was probably my age, but the severity of her uniform and her haircut made her look older—or at least much more mature. She also knew her facts and figures cold. She was the reason I knew that the Academy grounds covered eighteen thousand acres.

"Whatever," Diana replied. "Don't worry. People go up in these things every day."

"It's not the going up that bothers me." I said. "It's the coming down. Straight down."

"We've been told the glider has been thoroughly inspected. That shouldn't be an issue," Diana said. In this context "We" meant Diana and the new agent who'd been assigned to me from the White House detail for this trip, John Kingston. Evidently, the higher-ups in the Secret Service thought it was wise to match Diana with someone who was impressively large. Trust me, Kingston was huge. He looked like an agent, all right—a free agent signed by the Washington Redskins, rather than a Secret Service agent.

Lord knows, the Skins could use someone with his heft and reflexes this year.

Big as John Kingston was, Diana was just as capable of protecting me. Diana was fast, tough, and smart. I'd learned that back in February when she got me out of a nasty situation—one that could easily have resulted in both of our deaths. I always felt safer when Diana was around.

But in a few minutes, I'd be on my own. The glider could hold only one person besides the pilot. That would be me. Just me. No protocol officers. No journalists.

No agents.

It was a naked kind of feeling.

I was probably being paranoid. Here, smack in the middle of the Air Force Academy, should be a very safe place to be the President's daughter. And there was a Secret Service agent in the tow plane—I wasn't going to be completely alone while I was up in the air.

On the other hand, this particular Air Force base was the biggest tourist attraction in the state. Visitors came and went in large numbers through more than one open gate. And Dad's speech had been scheduled for months, with the time and location widely publicized, as was the fact that he was bringing his daughter along. Anybody looking for a newsworthy target for trouble would know exactly where to find us. And if I needed help while I was in the glider, that Secret Service agent in the tow plane wasn't exactly within walking distance of me.

So that naked feeling was all too real. I hadn't been "by myself" in public in months—since before the election last November. The protection had been even more intense since the day Dad stood on the Capitol steps and repeated the oath of office. From that moment on, any time I stepped outside of our private residence (and I'm not talking the entire White House, just parts of it), I had a security tagalong. Here it was, the end of May, and I'd finally gotten accustomed to the comfort factor of their presence.

I glanced at the pilot who was to be my sole companion in this brief foray into the wild blue yonder. He looked like a typical cadet, with his short dark hair and his chiseled, freshly scrubbed face. His smile could only be described as *Top Gun* cocky.

A fighter pilot-in-training, I bet. Dad had warned me about guys like that.

I knew enough from the tour so far to realize that the patterns of silver rickrack on his uniform meant that he was a "firstie," which was Academy-speak for a senior. His name badge read "Taylor 'The Jokeman' Dobbs." Fulfilling the promise of his nickname, he immediately stepped off on the wrong foot.

"Hello, pretty lady," he said with a wink to Diana. "With agents like you on duty, the security checks will be a pleasure. Can I volunteer for a strip search?" I *think* it was supposed to be a joke.

Rule number one: Never joke with Secret Service agents while they're on duty. That privilege is reserved for my dad, and even he doesn't try it too often.

Rule number two: Never put the moves on a female agent while she's on the job.

I half expected to see "The Jokeman" fly across the tarmac and end up with the dusty imprint of one of Diana's black dress flats centered on his back.

But Diana was too professional to lose it over something so insignificant. She merely gave the cadet a glare that made him shrivel up and shrink down like a salted slug.

All the better to fit into a small glider . . .

Deflated now, he turned his attention to me, trying to resurrect his Tom Cruise smile. "Have you ever ridden in a glider before, Miss Cooper?"

"No." That was the truth. "I'm looking forward to it." That was a whopping lie.

"You couldn't have picked a better day. The weather is perfect for a good soar."

Falling on my months of experience in the public eye as the First Daughter, I conjured up a pleasant expression. "Then, shall we?"

I repositioned my camera free of the harness, reminding myself that I'd gone through worse to get a good photograph. Prior to my father's election, I'd been a professional photographer based in Denver. I'd worked part-time for the NPS wire service, covering everything from the beautiful bodies walking the world's catwalks to not-so-beautiful bodies found dead in abandoned cars, and I liked to think I was pretty good at what I did, even if I was currently unemployed. This flight promised to give me a unique perspective on the academy—at least, visually.

I mustered up a smile for Diana. "Banzai . . . ," I mouthed. I'd been informed that this particular glider was used as a trainer, so all the dials and the controls I could see had corresponding duplicates in the rear seat, which would be used by the pilot during this flight. I prayed that "The Jokeman" wouldn't do anything stupid while we were in midair, like say, "Here, you try it. . . ."

John Kingston, my other agent, leaned over, checked the straps holding me in my seat, and gave me a reassuring smile. "Don't worry. I fly gliders as a hobby. Before I went up the first time, some guy told me that it was a lot like another very popular leisure activity." He winked. "The first flight's the toughest, then you fall in love with the sensation. And nerves on your maiden voyage are perfectly natural. He was right. I survived mine. You will too."

"Really?" Surprised by the length, not to mention the content, of what amounted to an epic speech from the normally silent agent, I gave John a once-over. Kingston weighed somewhere between 250 and 275 pounds— nearly all of it bone and muscle. If John could do this, then maybe I wasn't going to fall out of the sky today.

Maybe . . .

Kingston gave me a thumbs-up, then stepped back as the pilot got ready to take off and two other cadets closed the canopy.

I could hear the engines revving on the tow plane, but we weren't moving yet.

Then I felt a slight lurch as the slack was pulled out of the towrope. The little glider jumped forward. A few seconds later, we were rolling down the field behind the tow plane. At first it was really noisy in the cockpit; then suddenly the sound level lessened. I pressed my face to the clear canopy and looked down, realizing that although the tow plane was still on the ground, we weren't.

I wondered if this was what it felt like to ride a kite.

Then the tow plane lifted off and we started gaining altitude. Despite his nickname, Cadet Taylor "The Jokeman" Dobbs got down to some serious business.

"This part of the flight may be a little bumpy," he said. "But things'll smooth out once we're on our own." He had to raise his voice to be heard over the rushing wind and engine sounds of the plane ahead of us. "In the meantime, I can tell you a bit about the Academy."

Dobbs kept his spiel serious and straightforward—a quick summary of the history of the Air Force Academy, which pretty much jibed with what I'd gotten from my briefing before the trip. It was established in 1954, it was the newest of the service academies, it served roughly four thousand cadets, and so on.

I'd worried a bit about what Dobbs might be like after I saw his nickname, but as it turned out, I didn't have to. Like all the other cadets I'd met today, he performed his job well and with a certain amount of flair.

Despite his moniker and my initial negative impression, I found myself liking him. Yeah, he was cocky, but he was also really competent. After all, the U.S. government spends millions and millions of dollars training the students at all the service academies to be all they can be. I was dealing with the end result of that training: the very fit, very well mannered, and very bright people I'd met today, from the youngest cadet to the highest-ranking officer. They were, taken singly or as a group, an attractive bunch. Including "The Jokeman."

I was drawn to these military types. Some of that was probably because of Dad—who is the finest man I know. Dad spent years in the Air Force. Because of Dad, I knew that a big part of a military education centered on when and how to kill our country's enemies. The people at the

Academy were warriors. But I don't think that the element of danger was the attraction for me. I think what called to me was their sense of purpose, and their willingness to commit themselves to the cause of serving our country. It was sobering to realize that several of the people I'd met today were likely to lose their lives in the course of their military duties.

That thought had planted itself in the back of my mind as I talked to the men and women at the Academy, especially the cadets. We all had one thing in common: understanding and respecting duty and sacrifice. I'd learned about both recently, my sense of responsibility had put me in a situation where the price for doing my duty could have been my life.

Consequently, I felt a great deal of respect for cadets like "The Jokeman" and their willingness to offer up their lives for their country. Of course, I hoped it would never be necessary—that they would serve out their careers productively and peacefully, retire full of honors, and bounce grandbabies on their knees.

All of that was going through my mind as I listened to Dobbs point out the highlights of the panoramic view of the Academy visible through the canopy. Dobbs interspersed his facts and figures about the Academy with the theories behind the science of soaring. I listened to him explain thermal lift, slope lift, and all the other reasons why, once released from the mother ship, we wouldn't plunge like a rock straight down toward the earth and end up as a small, greasy spot on the Terrazzo. Maybe he had a point. I took a deep breath and tried to relax.

"See that small yellow handle in front of you?" As I'd said, we were in tandem seating, with me in front, Dobbs in back.

"Yes."

"Pull it," he ordered.

I reached out automatically, then hesitated. The President of the United States hadn't raised a fool for a daughter—and this guy's tag *was* "The Jokeman." "What happens if I pull the handle?"

"That's the tow release." He chuckled. "It's time for this baby bird to leave the nest."

Oh, great. I swallowed hard, wrapped my fingers around the handle, and paused. "I've never done this before. What if I do something wrong?"

He laughed again. "Don't sweat it. You can't mess this up. And if we don't release right, the tow pilot will simply let go of us from his end. So don't worry. Just do it."

I took a deep breath and pulled.

There was a small mechanical clunk, and I watched the end of the towrope come into sight. Suddenly, we were on our own—high up in the sky without an engine.

I wasn't frightened. Much.

We were banking hard to the right. Common sense suggested that the maneuver made sure we wouldn't run into the tow plane ahead of us. But I wasn't brave enough to look down not quite yet. My camera slipped in my lap and I grabbed it instinctively, still keeping my eyes straight ahead.

In a matter of seconds, the engine noise of the tow plane faded away, leaving us aloft in a majestic silence broken only by the quiet swoosh of air over the glider's surface. Intrigued, I finally looked at the ground below. Although we no longer had an umbilical cord tying us to the plane, we seemed to be flying successfully without it.

I tried telling that to my heart, which was wedged in my throat.

But after a few dozen thundering heartbeats, I began to enjoy the feeling of freedom as we soared through the sky. Soon I found myself leaning against the canopy to look out at the quiet, almost pastoral scene passing below us. Trees, rocks, houses . . . I remembered my camera, which I was holding in a death grip. I was pleased when my hands didn't shake as I raised it to the glass and took several shots. But as much as I was used to seeing life through the viewfinder, I realized that I couldn't spend the whole glider ride taking pictures. After getting enough exposures to fulfill my "I've done this and I have the pictures to prove it" checkbox, I tucked the camera beside me on the seat and enjoyed the unobstructed view through the clear canopy.

And what a view it was.

As we danced along the air currents, the tension in my shoulders drained away and I felt a sense of serenity I hadn't experienced since the election.

After a few minutes, Dobbs spoke, breaking the silence. "I love flying gliders. There's something really tranquil about being up here," he said in a soft voice. "Life down there"—he tipped the glider slightly to the right so I could see the cadets milling around the Terrazzo—"can be really stressful. It's no secret that it's tough being a cadet. The Air Force expects the absolute best from us, twenty-four/seven. When things get tough, that's when I really yearn to get up here and escape, if only for just a short while.

To get away from everyone, the noise, the responsibilities . . . Yep, I like gliding, and I do as much of it as I can get away with."

As much I sympathized with his apparent need for an escape valve, I wasn't sure I wanted my pilot contemplating it at this particular moment. Neither of us could afford to go AWOL, no matter how attractive the idea was. Dobbs had a graduation to attend later today. And Dad expected me to be where I was scheduled to be, or he'd worry.

"Flying . . . er . . . soaring . . . isn't just about freedom," I said. "It requires a sense of responsibility, doesn't it? And a lot of concentration, skill, and theoretical knowledge, not to mention actual practice." I looked at the controls in front of me, then at the mountainside looming not very far away from the glider's wingtip. Places to land on those steep slopes appeared to be nonexistent. "Make that lots and lots of practice." My tentative sense of comfort vanished in direct proportion to the closeness of the craggy mountainside.

"I see you're noticing our beautiful Rocky Mountain landscape," he said. "I can also see your white knuckles, even from back here. If this is a little too close for comfort, I can back off."

"Thanks," I said. "I'm probably just being silly." The hillside receded a bit as the glider responded to subtle changes in the flaps. "I'm new at this."

"I'm not, and I normally wouldn't get quite this close. The winds can be tricky. But not today, for some reason. This is the calmest I've ever seen it around here, and I thought I'd take advantage of it. Don't worry, I've got hundreds of hours under my belt in this thing," he said.

"I'm not worried." At least, not much, I thought, staring at my hands and willing them to relax.

"Flying is a lot like driving a car," he continued. "When you're first learning, you've got to be really careful. Then, eventually it becomes second nature, and you can let go a little. Haven't you ever taken a long drive out to the countryside? Just to breathe in the fresh air, enjoy the scenery, get away from the big-city traffic and stress?"

"Sure."

"Times like that, driving isn't work. It's fun. But despite all the fun, you're still behaving responsibly and driving safely. Even if you concentrate on the cows and the trees and the wind in your hair, you're still paying attention to what you're doing on the road."

I thought about the last time I'd driven a car. It had been too long, but Dobbs was right. I loved the feeling of flying along in my car, happy, content, enjoying the scenery, achieving that nirvana where freedom and control worked hand in hand, seamlessly.

"I know exactly what you mean," I said. I made a silent promise to myself that as soon as we got back to D.C., I was going to break my ancient Mustang out of storage and take her out for a spin in the country, even if I had to have a Secret Service agent in the passenger seat and a follow-up car behind me to do it.

Of course, that scenario had its good points. The Mustang could be cantankerous. I was suddenly hit with the mental image of two agents in a black government-issue sedan towing me in my Mustang behind them. A sign on the towrope said "Your Tax Dollars at Work." I couldn't help it; I laughed at the thought.

"You okay?" Dobbs sounded as if he was fairly certain I wasn't. "You know, the air is a little thin up here. We were at sixty-five hundred feet before we even took off."

"I'm fine," I said. "It's not the air. Or lack of it. I was just thinking about taking a drive in the countryside once I got back to D.C."

I couldn't begin to explain to him why that was funny, nor did I want to try. The narrow boundaries my new role placed on my life weren't his problem or his business.

But I could certainly enjoy the moment at hand. Suddenly, any lingering fears I had of heights or of flying without an engine vanished, and I let myself wallow in the beauty of the scenery below us and the freedom of being up in the glider. I felt better than I had since the day Dad won the primary.

Maybe I needed to take flying lessons.

Now *that* would give the Secret Service fits. They were having a hard enough time with my baby brother Drew's learning to drive. I almost started laughing again.

Evidently Dobbs realized that I didn't need him to live up to his "Jokeman" nickname. He continued to wax philosophical about the wonders of flying. He pointed out red rock formations in the distance, a herd of grazing deer on an athletic field, and what we both believed might have been a bear running across a clear spot on one of the mountain slopes.

I was indeed having a good time, just as everyone had predicted. But after fifteen minutes or so, I realized we were getting closer to the ground. An unexpected sense of sadness flooded me. I'd enjoyed both the flight and Cadet Dobbs's low-key company.

"Time to land?"

"I'm afraid so. All good things must come to an end."

And so they did.

He steered the glider into a long swooping curve, lining up on the runway, and we descended slowly as we approached the asphalt.

Finally we touched ground—a perfect landing. Just as we came to a final stop, the Secret Service agents flanked the glider, waiting to reclaim their protective-custodial duties.

I started talking before the canopy was completely open. "You were right," I said to Diana as I got out. "It was fantastic." I turned around and shook Dobbs's hand with honest enthusiasm. "Thanks so much. Not in my *wildest* dreams would I have thought I'd have liked it that much. It was so peaceful, so relaxing, so much fun. . . ."

The cocky Jokeman grin came back, as if, once his feet touched the ground, Dobbs became a different person.

"So . . . you up for trying some aerobatics next time?"

I thought about the state of my stomach in the presence of loop-the-loops, barrel rolls, and other equally unsettling maneuvers. "Thanks anyway. I'll take a pass on that. But the ride . . . it was fantastic! I really enjoyed myself."

After that, my entourage and I climbed back into the official cars for our next stop on the Grand "Distinguished Visitor" Academy Tour. The written itinerary sheets I'd seen abbreviated that as "DV." I found it tough to think of myself as distinguished.

Before Captain Durkee could resume her narration about the Academy, Diana leaned over and whispered, "You're still smiling. You must have enjoyed yourself." She gave me a quick glance. "When you get home, are we going to have to figure out how to protect you while you take flying lessons?"

"I'm tempted." I laughed at the look on her face, then shook my head. "Don't worry. It was fun and I'd love to go again—as a passenger—but, no, I'm not going to sign up at the nearest flying school as soon as we get back to D.C."

She looked relieved.

"Good." That came from Kingston. His concise contribution to the conversation caught both Diana and me off guard.

I studied his face. "Why? You said you flew gliders as a hobby. You must like it."

He spared me a quick glance. "It's not that." He turned back to looking out the window for threats. "I've been riding with Drew since he got his learner's permit. One novice driver in the family is enough."

That explained everything. I'm twenty-five, and all grown up—for the most part. But my brother Drew is only fifteen, deep in the throes of adolescence, and still quite capable of in-line-skating his way into the Oval Office during an important meeting to show Dad his latest trick. He's learning to drive, and I think he takes a secret glee in scaring his Secret Service agents to death as he hones his skills. Just before we left for Colorado, I'd heard tales of Drew taking a wheel-screeching right turn on red that had given more than one agent new gray hairs.

Since my mother died, I've served as a mom substitute for Drew. That's why I'm unemployed and living in the White House instead of out on my own, making a living, like my brother Charlie, who's a year younger than I am. Heck, Charlie's not only on his own; he's a dot.com tycoon. My overachieving brother has a very satisfying life in Vermont, where he runs an Internet software business that he built from scratch. It survived the tech-sector meltdown in style, and these days Charlie's raking in the cash. Charlie has always been independent to a fault. I am too, but Drew and Dad need me. At my father's request, I gave up my job and moved in with Dad when he was elected.

I'm not some kind of substitute First Lady. My aunt Patsy is Dad's official hostess. I'm Dad's unofficial sounding board and Drew's unofficial mother figure. The last year was hard on Drew, and the pain isn't going to end anytime soon. I've been doing my best to make things easier for him, but being a teenager is tough enough under ordinary circumstances. Add in a cross-country move to D.C., plus the transition from normal kid to presidential offspring, and tough doesn't begin to describe Drew's last few months. Despite everything, I know Drew will weather the storm. Of course, I'm Drew's sister. I love him. The Secret Service is merely stuck with him. That includes hair-raising right turns on red and everything.

I reached over the back of the seat and patted Kingston's massive arm. "You have my sympathies. They don't pay anyone enough to ride along with Drew behind the wheel. One terror source in the family is enough, don't you think?"

Kingston almost smiled.

Captain Durkee took up her monologue on the academy, interrupted by the glider flight, again. "Our next stop will be the Cadet Chapel. It took five years just to design the chapel. Construction began in 1959 and the building was completed in the summer of 1963. Within the one structure, we have three religious facilities: a Protestant chapel that seats twelve hundred, a Catholic chapel that holds five hundred, and a Jewish chapel that seats one hundred."

I tuned out her facts and figures, turning my attention instead to the building itself. I'd seen it earlier while we were touring the Cadet area, and of course I'd seen pictures of it all my life. But until we stepped out of the car and stood in the circular driveway in front of it, staring up at the gleaming spires pointing into the sky, I hadn't realized how truly beautiful it was.

Before we went inside, Captain Durkee pulled us over to the side of the chapel so that she could point out some of the building's unusual architectural features. Once again, I put on my official First Daughter smile and listened politely.

"As you can see, the main structure is joined to the foundation using a unique pin-hinge connector. We get such high winds up here that—"

We heard a shout behind us.

Then another voice joined in. "Oh my God . . . look!"

Diana and Kingston reacted fast. They had me down on the ground sheltered between two of the cars before I could think. But then we realized the person who'd shouted was pointing toward the mountain. My agents got off me and started dragging me toward the nearest door leading into the chapel, but I dug in my heels. It was evident that this wasn't about me. The object of everyone's concern was a glider in the distance, skimming much too close to the craggy mountainside.

The glider wobbled from side to side. One wingtip skimmed perilously near a tall tree on the heavily wooded hillside, much closer than "The Jokeman" had dared to take me on my flight. The tiny flier coasted by the top branches with absolutely no room to spare. Then the glider's flight path straightened out, and it appeared as though the pilot had regained control of his craft.

Before we could offer a gasp of collective relief, the glider banked sharply to the left. . . .

And crashed into the mountain.

CHAPTER TWO

KOAA-CHANNELS 5 AND 30 NEWS FIRST MIDDAY

"Tragedy struck the Air Force Academy today, only hours before the 2003 graduation commencement exercises were scheduled to begin. A glider lost control and crash-landed near the Stanley Canyon Trail. El Paso County search and rescue teams responded and, working with Academy security forces and medical teams, airlifted two crash victims . . ."

Despite the accident, graduation eventually went on as planned. But the decision to go forward was hardly a casual one.

After being given ten or fifteen minutes to collect my wits and for the Secret Service to confer with the military, I was spirited away to a bunker hidden beneath what appeared to be the shopping district of the base.

It seemed an odd place to put that kind of thing. Go figure. . . .

We sat in a cramped conference room, everyone sitting around a large table except for me and the lowest-ranking officer in the room, Major Fairchild, who introduced himself as the "superintendent's Exec." We were isolated at a tiny side table. I'm sure the small slight was intentional. The military honchos wanted me to be aware of my place in all this—which was out of the way, and well out of their command structure.

"Gentlemen, I need answers. Now." The assembled officers didn't wilt under Lieutenant General Donald O'Toole's glare, but I almost did. Even though General O'Toole had been a family friend for years, I barely recognized him, operating as he was now in full military mode. Those three stars he wore on each shoulder evidently weighed about a ton apiece at this moment.

I was the only person in the room not wearing a uniform, and judging by the cool looks I'd gotten from the gathering officials, they'd noticed.

I was definitely out of my comfort zone. Diana, John, and even Captain Durkee (who met the dress code) had been politely asked to stay in the hallway. Evidently Major Fairchild had been appointed my keeper for the duration of this meeting. If he, too, resented my presence, he had the good manners to hide it.

Perhaps in reaction to the cold looks aimed at me, General O'Toole said, "I spoke briefly with the President to inform him of the incident. He has asked that Ms. Cooper be allowed to sit in on our discussion, and to act as his liaison until he arrives."

That announcement caught me by surprise, but it explained a lot. I'd just figured I'd been stashed down here because someone had decided it was where I could get in the least amount of trouble. Apparently, that wasn't why I was here at all. My father trusts my instincts. No doubt he'd ask me later what the men in this room said and did—I'd just been promoted to be his independent observer.

I also appreciated that General O'Toole referred to the request as coming from the President rather than from my father. It was a subtle difference, one that probably placed me higher in the food chain. But O'Toole's underlying message to his men was still the same.

Translation: *Shut up and deal with it. She's the boss's daughter.*

The general turned to a man sitting on his left. "Your report, Colonel?"

The man started to speak, then caught himself. He turned to me and gave me a curt nod. "Louis Handleman. OSI," he said.

Major Fairchild leaned over and whispered, "Office of Special Investigations."

That one I knew.

Handleman continued. "We've cordoned off the crash site and will maintain security until the FBI arrives." He glanced at me again. "Because of our high-profile guests, we are operating on heightened alert. At this moment, we have no indication that this was anything other than an unfortunate accident. But because there's been a fatality, we're preserving the site as a crime scene until we learn otherwise. We have a team of investigators from the NTSB's South Central field office in Denver scheduled to arrive within the hour."

"Have we identified the victims?"

"Major Anthony Gaskell."

The general looked even more stricken. "The AOC for the 23rd?"

"Yes, sir."

So far I'd been able to reason through most of the military jargon, but "AOC" defied my guesses, even in context. I turned to the Major sitting next to me. "What's an AOC?" I said in a low voice.

He whispered back, "It stands for Air Officer Commanding. Each cadet squadron has an officer assigned to act as a leader or mentor. Major Gaskell was the AOC for Cadet Squadron Twenty-three. He was also an experienced instructor pilot and one the best fliers on this base, certainly the person most capable of handling any emergency in-flight situations."

The general leaned forward. "I understand the fatality was a civilian passenger?"

The wing commander nodded. "Yes, sir. A young female, listed on the log as Ashley McCurdy." He turned to the man sitting next to him. "Father?"

The chaplain was dressed in the same uniform as the others, with only the addition of a small cross to signify his different duties. He sat up a bit straighter once identified. "The Red Cross has made the initial contact with Miss McCurdy's family, who live in Albuquerque. I've spoken to my counterpart at Kirkland Air Force Base, who happens to be a good friend of mine, and he's already headed to the family's residence and will act as our official liaison with the family, to offer counseling and provide information on the ongoing investigation, as soon as we can release it."

"Thank you, Father." The general turned to another man in blue. "George? A medical report?"

The man turned toward me and gave me a curt nod of acknowledgement. "Colonel George Franklin, 10th Med Group Commander." He turned back to the general. "Fort Carson provided helicopter rescue support and both passengers were airlifted to our hospital. The initial rescue response team attempted to resuscitate Ms. McCurdy both on the ground and in the air, but they were unsuccessful. The preliminary assessment is that she most likely died on impact. However, the pilot did survive and is currently undergoing emergency surgery."

"What are Major Gaskell's chances of survival?"

"Fair to good. He suffered a severe concussion, several broken bones, and internal injuries, including a possibly ruptured spleen."

The general turned back to the OSI guy. "I know that when the response team reached the scene, they reported that Gaskell was unconscious. Do you know if he regained consciousness at any time in the ER prior to surgery?"

The investigator shook his head. "No, sir. He didn't. I had a man posted in the ER in case Gaskell did wake up so we could get as much information from him about the crash as we could. But we never got the chance to debrief him." He turned to Colonel Franklin. "Any idea when we will be able to talk to him?"

Franklin shook his head. "It'll be another eight to twelve hours before the surgery is completed and he gets out of the recovery room. By then, he should be able to talk."

The general pounced on this bit of implied good news. "Then you do expect him to recover?"

"Yes, sir."

A sigh of relief went around the room.

"Major Trichey is heading up the surgical team," Franklin continued, "and they're doing what they can for Gaskell. I suspect they'll recommend that he be seen by an orthopedic specialist."

"Keep me posted as to Gaskell's condition. Now, as unfortunate as this accident was, we have to determine how it will affect today's graduation plans. We only have about an hour to come to a consensus and make any changes to the graduation ceremony that we deem necessary."

Ah, yes, the graduation ceremony. I'd figured it would go on, and that Dad's speech wouldn't be canceled. I was right. However, the brass considered literally every aspect of the ceremony before making that decision. Another general's exec (not the major sitting with me) was sent out to determine if the crash site was visible from Falcon Stadium, where the ceremony was to be held. And then, while we all waited for the answer, the military men debated whether, if the wreckage could be seen from the stadium, they should keep the ceremony there as scheduled, or move it to their inclement-weather standby, the Field House.

When the exec called in from the stadium with his report, they put him on the speakerphone.

"Well, Major?" General O'Toole prompted.

"I've walked along the top row of seats on the west side of the stadium, where the guests sit. I've gone from the north end to the south and I can't see the crash site at all. Of course, the guests will be sitting on the west side of the stadium, facing east, so that's a plus. I even went to the east side of the stadium, where no one will be sitting. I still can't see any signs of a crash."

"What about the view from the press box?"

"Still okay. No line of sight, sir. Too many trees. Also no line of sight from any of the parking lots. The hillside rises too sharply and masks the mountains in the distance. Unfortunately, there are unavoidable lines of sight from the interstate, but the distance from the interstate to the site is far enough so that you can see no real detail beyond a splotch of color. Otherwise, there are no lines of sight from the public routes from just beyond the gates to the stadium. I don't think the view will be a problem for either our cadets or their families and friends."

The group released another collective sigh of relief.

I was surprised at how upset these men were about the crash, and how determined they were to protect their cadets from being confronted by evidence of the tragedy. In their line of work, you'd think that accidents would be common enough occurrences to harden them. Although I'd been around the fringes of the military during some of my life because of Dad's many years of reserve duty, as well as around all his military aides since he took office, I'd allowed myself to expect a stereotypical stiff-upper-lip, get-on-with-the-business-at-hand reaction from the officers in this room.

I was wrong.

It was evident that they cared deeply, both about those involved in the crash and about the cadets under their care.

The officers continued their discussion. Now that the location was set, should they make any changes to the program itself in acknowledgment of the tragedy? In the middle of that discussion, someone knocked on the door. Captain Durkee stuck her head in the room.

"Excuse me, sir."

"Yes, Captain?"

"Ms. Cooper has a call."

I felt every set of eyes in the room zoom in on me. The looks might not have been openly hostile, but I wasn't currying anyone's favor with the interruption.

Captain Durkee added nervously to me, "It's the President . . . um, your father. On line two."

The exec reached over, retrieved the phone, and handed it to me. Unfortunately, it was still on speakerphone.

My dad's voice boomed across the room. "Sweetie girl, are you okay?"

I cringed as the affectionate nickname from my childhood was broadcast to everyone in this room, knowing that their level of respect for me probably dipped to an all-time low. I stabbed the speaker button, and suddenly Dad's voice was in the receiver only.

"Eve?"

"I'm fine, Dad." I moved to the far corner of the room, trying to speak as quietly as I could and still be heard.

"Are you sure?" he prompted. Like most fathers, he knew that a "fine" from his child could cover a range of reactions, from "I was a basket case but now I'm doing better" to "I remain totally oblivious of everything around me, as usual." In reality, I'd been a little shaken up by actually seeing the crash, but I had myself pretty much back under control.

"Yeah," I said. As long as I didn't think about it too hard . . .

"So, have they come up with a reason for the crash?" he asked.

"The investigation is just getting started, but so far, no. From what they tell me, there's nothing obviously wrong," I said.

"How about the weather? It can get windy pretty fast around there, I've heard."

"No, the weather's fine. It's not windy at all. It's a perfect day for a glider ride. At least it was when I went up."

There was an uncomfortable pause.

"When you what?"

I swallowed hard. They hadn't told him? Oh, great. Now it was up to me to tell him. "When I went up. In a glider. This morning. They had a cadet take me up for a glider ride." The fatherly presidential silence that followed my remark was deafening. I rushed ahead, hoping to short-circuit any of Dad's concerns. "It was fine. I really enjoyed it. The weather was perfect, the pilot was great, and the flight was totally uneventful." I shivered, the memory of that perfect flight now tainted by images of another glider, broken and in pieces. "Totally," I echoed, trying to sound convincing.

Dad sighed. "Oh, Eve . . ."

I felt as if I'd done something wrong. And I certainly hadn't meant to. I'd been on my best behavior. "Dad, I wasn't taking unnecessary risks. I was being polite, going along with the program. The Academy decided it'd be the perfect entertainment." I realized that my comments probably left the people in this room holding the bag—which was the last thing I wanted to do. "And I was glad they suggested it. They were right. It *was* fun."

Dad chewed on that for a minute before speaking. Then he said, "Tell me that someone has at least double-checked to make sure that you didn't fly in the glider that crashed."

Oh, now there was a new and cheery thought. Since I'd seen a number of gliders both on the ground and in the air, I hadn't stopped to wonder if the glider I'd ridden in earlier was the same one that crashed.

"Eve?"

"Well . . . I don't know."

"Then ask someone. Now."

I resisted the urge to ask "Why?" and turned to the nearest uniform—a Colonel Someone. "Dad wants to know if anyone has checked to see if this was the same glider that I flew in earlier."

Judging by the looks on the faces around me, no one had. General O'Toole turned to his exec and gave terse directions to check on it, then turned back to me. "Tell your father the President that I'm having them look at the flight records right now."

"They're checking, Dad. You don't really think . . ."

"Damn it, Eve. . . . You're more than just my daughter. You're the President's daughter. We both know there are a lot of sick people out there who are desperate to be remembered for something, anything, including killing a President's daughter."

"Oh," I said in a small, scared voice. I found myself unable to swallow around the boulders in my throat.

"Sweetie?"

I managed to push a "Yes?" through the rock slide.

"Don't let this get to you. It probably has nothing to do with you and I'm just being overprotective. That's a parent's prerogative. You've got the best protection in the world. You have your Secret Service detail, plus I'm sure the Academy will beef up their security around you. And once I arrive, I'm not letting you out of my sight. Okay? Does that make you feel better?"

Actually, it made me feel about five years old. But now wasn't the time to discuss that. And he had a point. "Yes, sir." I thought about Diana and John Kingston, standing on alert in the hallway. I trusted them.

"Donald O'Toole is there, isn't he? Let me talk to him."

I held out the phone to General O'Toole. "Dad wants to talk to you."

Even though they were old friends, General O'Toole straightened in his chair. "Yes, Mr. President? No, sir. Yes, sir. Absolutely, sir. We suspended all flights the moment we got word of the accident. Yes, sir. Yes, sir, I'll do that personally. No, sir. No, sir. No, sir. . . . Thank you, sir."

The general held the phone out to me. "He'd like to speak to you again."

"Yes, sir?" I said to my father. That "sir" was a reflex—I swear I wasn't trying to make fun of General O'Toole. I realized belatedly that Dad was probably one of the few people the general responded to with the obligatory "sir."

"I've just told Don that as long as he can personally guarantee that your safety will be their top mission, my participation in the Academy's graduation ceremony can go on. I don't want to disappoint almost a thousand young men and women who, despite today's tragedy, deserve a chance to celebrate this very important accomplishment in their lives. But I won't do it at the cost of your safety. I hope everyone there understands that."

"I'm sure they do. And, honestly, I feel totally safe. I'm sitting in an underground bunker surrounded by the Academy's top brass. I'm probably safer here than I would be at home." I really didn't think that, but it wouldn't hurt to let the "Academy's top brass" hear someone tell their boss how great they were. "I can't wait to see you."

"Me, too." He paused for a moment. "Eve, play it safe, okay?"

"I will, Dad. Promise."

"Now let me talk to Don again."

I handed the phone back to the general, returned to my neutral corner, and listened to the Top Brass hammer out the last details with Dad on the speakerphone.

The graduation ceremony would be held in the stadium, not the Field House. I silently agreed that it would be a pity to waste the beautiful Colorado day. During the invocation, the chaplain would call for a moment of silence for fallen comrades and safety in the skies, but everything else would go on as originally planned.

Someone suggested that the Thunderbirds, who were scheduled to perform, should start their flyover in the "missing man" formation, where one plane drops out and leaves a noticeable gap, but that idea was—forgive the pun—shot down. Dad stomped on it. He defended the right of the team to perform its regular routine, based on their prearranged script, the weather, and the winds. It was safer that way. As Dad put it, the last thing they needed at the Air Force Academy today was another crash to spice up the ceremony.

The Academy fliers seconded Dad's views strongly—and were apparently surprised at his unswerving support for leaving the Thunderbirds' performance unchanged. It made me wonder a bit about their experiences with previous dignitaries. Maybe not all their "DVs" were as reasonable as President Cooper.

The meeting finally adjourned, and I said good-bye to Dad on the phone, knowing I'd see him in person soon enough. *Air Force One* was about to land at nearby Peterson AFB, which, unlike the Academy, had a runway big enough to handle the big Boeing 747-400. And even with the security measures and the press to slow him down, I knew Dad would find a way to be by my side as soon as he could.

Sure enough, less than an hour later, I watched Dad's limo pull up, along with the rest of his convoy of Secret Service cars, police, military escorts, and press pool vans. I'd been shifted after the call from the command post, where the initial "Do we or don't we" powwow had taken place, to the press box at Falcon Stadium. It was where all the DV types were being wined and dined prior to the graduation ceremony. The elevated location gave us a clear view of the surrounding area, including Dad's arrival at the academy.

And the exec had been right. You couldn't see the crash site at all.

As Dad stepped out of the presidential limousine, he made the obligatory greetings and shook the necessary hands, but by the time he hit the reception area, his mission was evident; he was trying not to be rude, but he wanted to work his way over to me.

Fast.

I decided to help the process along. Ditching my untouched glass of Diet Coke on a handy tray, I moved through the crowd toward him, trailed closely by Diana and Captain Durkee.

"He looks worried," I said in a low voice to Diana.

"Can you blame him? After what happened?" Her poker face revealed something to me that most people never had a chance to see. A sliver of emotion. "This might be my last assignment to your detail. I strapped you into that glider."

I stopped short, and the other two women almost plowed into me. "Oh, come on. You're not worried, are you?"

Diana didn't answer.

"The Academy personnel fly these things all the time, and they looked it over and did the normal preflight check, right?"

"Yes."

"And after everyone else checked the glider, you had our guys check it over, right? Including John, who has flown gliders and knows them?"

She nodded again.

"I'm still here, without a scratch on me, so you evidently did your job right. Absolutely nothing bad happened while I was up there." I put a hand on her shoulder for a moment in silent support. "Pardon the saying, but they'll remove you from my detail over my dead body. And trust me, I'm still alive and kicking."

I looked over at Dad, who had been caught up in a knot of blue-suiters. "After all, let me point out that all this talk about potential threats and possible sabotage is merely speculation right now. Plus, don't forget I have some pull with the big boss."

"I still don't like it," Diana said darkly.

"Don't worry," I chided. "I don't throw my weight around often, so when I do, Dad listens because he knows it's important." I plotted a potential path through the milling crowd. "And the sooner I see him, the sooner I can tell him how I feel."

Perhaps motivated by those words, both Diana and Durkee did a magnificent job of helping me cut my way through Dad's well-wishers and get to his side.

His face lit up when he saw me alive, well, and unscathed. He hugged me. "You okay, sweetie?"

It felt wonderful to be in my father's arms. Damn the photographers— I gave in to the comfort of it for a moment before I pulled away. The media were watching—it was time to look official.

"I'm fine," I told him. "Diana's been taking good care of me." I nodded at the Secret Service agent, who'd carefully stopped two steps behind me and was surveying the room. "But it's been quite an adventure today."

"So it has." He stooped a little until our faces were on the same level. "Are you sure you're okay, doll?"

"I'm fine," I repeated, punctuating the remark with a kiss on his cheek. "My security detail is absolutely top-notch, and I know I'm in the best of hands with them at my side. You don't have to worry about a thing. Now go be presidential." I knew his actions for this day had been orchestrated down to the minute and that I was using up someone else's allotted time. I'd done what I needed to do—I'd reassured him that I was safe and sane, and that I would remain so.

I pointed to the nearest empty sofa. "I've been touring all day and my feet are tired, so I'm going to sit over there by the window with Diana and my military escort and simply enjoy the view until this thing starts. You can find me there if you need me. Okay?"

He rewarded me with a quick kiss and allowed his handlers to pull him away to his next scheduled duty.

Looking at the scenery visible through the press-box window was far better than staring at the blank walls of the underground bunker. My view was of the playing field and, far beyond that, a wide plain dotted with buildings and edged by a band of dark forest. When I asked, Captain Durkee supplied the name: the Black Forest. It fit. But Durkee apparently felt that the events of the day meant she could stop playing tour guide and just be herself. We ended up just shooting the breeze until show time. I learned she was a southern belle who had lost her accent after an Academy stint (majoring in foreign languages—Durkee spoke fluent Russian, Japanese, and German) and a tour in Germany. Before too long, we managed to forget all about crashing gliders and commander-in-chief fathers and started talking about movies and television shows we liked.

It was almost like being normal again.

Then it was nearly time for the graduation ceremony. We left the press box and moved to take our places in Falcon Stadium. I was surrounded by Secret Service agents and military security as we moved through the passageway and toward the DV seating area. The only surprise lurking for me there was when I discovered that Michael Cauffman had hitched a ride with Dad. He had been hanging out on the field among the throng of photojournalists, jockeying for position for pictures.

Michael is the official White House photographer, a job I wish I could have claimed for myself. But then again, while he was elbowing his way to the best position on the stadium floor, I was comfortably seated in a VIP box. Nobody was going to chew on me if any pictures I took today weren't properly photogenic. And I did have an absolutely perfect vantage point to get some great shots. . . .

Being First Daughter does have its privileges.

I pulled out my camera and gave Michael a pointedly sweet smile.

He pretended not to notice.

We have a sort of friendly rivalry going. I'm only the tiniest bit jealous of his success in his career, and that's not enough to prevent us from being friends. Because of his official status, Michael gets opportunities to go to places and meetings that other photographers would kill for. Then again, as First Daughter, I have some photo ops that no one else in the world would have, including Michael.

The friendly rivalry for getting great shots keeps us both on our toes.

All sense of competition aside, our game of one-upmanship means that we're building a pretty decent friendship, not to mention fabulous portfolios.

Of course, Michael doesn't really need a fancy portfolio—he already has a job. Me, I'm still unemployed, mired in my somewhat undefined role as a member of the presidential family, the adult child who hangs around the White House with no discernible or official responsibilities. So far, neither Letterman nor Leno has skewered me in public as a freeloader, but I figure it won't be long until they do.

I raised my camera and snapped a couple shots of Dad as he spoke with General O'Toole. He and the general went way back, having served together when Dad was first in the Air Force. Although Dad was smiling, I could spot a bit of nervousness dancing in his eyes.

I wondered if he was worried about my safety or his speech. I was pretty sure it was his speech. It's not that he hates this part of his job, but he does dislike dealing with the sense of anticipation and the anxiety that go with giving a major public address. I could understand it—every public word Dad spoke, good or bad, could end up in endless rotation on CNN or MSNBC.

An aide leaned over and whispered something to the general, who turned to Dad and gave him the high sign.

Time to get this show on the road.

The Academy ceremony started with pomp, circumstance, obligatory military tradition, brass bands, lots of marching, and everything else patriotic you might expect at a military graduation.

I followed along in the official program, waiting for Dad's turn to speak. Through the camera lens, I could see the barely perceptible movement of his head as he counted off his customary three-second pause before starting his speech.

His voice rang out loud and strong. "Secretary Delancie, General O'Toole, General Ballinger, General Edwards, General Hernandez, Chief Walsh, Academy staff and faculty, distinguished guests, officers, cadets, and graduates, thank you all. It's a real pleasure to return to the United States Air Force Academy. I only wish I could have gone to school here myself." He leaned forward with a slight air of conspiracy. "But don't tell my alma mater that. They might drum me out of their alumni association."

The crowd laughed.

Early into his talk, Dad acknowledged the glider accident. He expressed his sorrow, and made some stirring extemporaneous remarks— something about honoring not only those who serve their country, but those who stand by those who serve. A ripple of applause turned into a roar and then into a midspeech standing ovation. I could tell that took Dad by surprise; after all, he was speaking from the heart and off-the-cuff at that moment, not reading from his prepared speech.

Blushing slightly, he waited until the din died down; then he continued. He didn't let the accident dampen his obvious enthusiasm for the

Academy and the Air Force, and his words rang true with his usual zeal for the military.

He ended his speech with, "I am grateful to each one of you for giving these years of your lives to your country. We are proud of you and counting on you. Personally, I would have been proud to serve with each and every one of you. To each man and woman in the 2003 Bong class, good luck, and Godspeed."

Say what? *Bong class?* That threw me for a loop. I knew better than to think it meant what it sounded like it meant. I found the answer in the program. Each class at the Academy selects a leader of the past to be their inspiration for the future. This class had selected the great American ace fighter pilot Major Richard Bong as their inspiration.

Ahh . . . Now it made sense. And I'm sure that the cadets chose their leader of the past without even once thinking about that very reaction on the part of today's audience . . . Yeah, right. . . .

Back to my story . . .

The crowd loved Dad. So do I, for that matter. We all joined in another standing ovation. Afterward, he assisted in awarding all 964 diplomas, one at a time, shaking each graduating cadet's hand and saying something to each of them. What I liked seeing was the cadet's reactions to Dad's private words—their smiles broadened, their straight spines grew impossibly straighter, their salutes snapped with extra precision. I could see that Dad's presence meant something important to them.

After the last diploma was awarded, the class stood at attention and waited for the fateful words to be spoken: "Class of 2003. Dismissed."

With magnificent accuracy and exact timing, the Thunderbirds skimmed over the field, streaking across the sky at the same moment that almost a thousand cadets tossed their white hats into the air. When I could tear myself away from the spectacle of the Thunderbirds' midair acrobatics, I watched my dad. His face was lit up like a kid's at Christmas. He loved planes and he loved flying. And, unfortunately, thanks to his job, he probably wouldn't get behind the controls of a plane for at least another three and a half years.

Oh, the sacrifices we make . . .

After all the ceremonial hoopla, a select group of special guests at the ceremony and high-ranking officers rode over to General O'Toole's house, where we all congregated in the living room, sipping iced tea. The general lived in a large, rambling house that his wife told me predated the Academy itself. It certainly looked nothing like the housing area we'd just driven through, which was full of small, identical houses lined up like little soldiers.

I watched the general and Dad play "Top that story." It was an old game, but they were playing it quite consciously today. I knew what was happening; both of them were trying to avoid the subject of the crash. They wanted to keep the visit light and friendly.

But when a stone-faced aide slipped into the room and waited by the door until he could get the general's attention, we all knew he had news about the accident.

From the look on his face, bad news.

The general beckoned for the man to come closer. "Yes, Captain?"

The aide cleared his throat. "We have the preliminary investigation report."

The general shot Dad a questioning look, as if wondering whether he should discuss the initial report here or adjourn to someplace more secure. Maybe he also didn't want to expose any security shortcomings of the Academy in front of his commander in chief.

Dad gave him no choice. "Go ahead, Don. I'd like to hear this too."

The general looked at his aide. "And?"

The man braced himself and gave his report. "Major Gaskell is out of surgery and listed in fair condition. He's still unconscious, so he hasn't been debriefed. But the NTSB team has started their initial investigation of the crash site and they say they can't rule out sabotage of the craft. They've found evidence pointing to that possibility but say they won't be sure of anything until they can analyze the wreckage more closely."

Okay, up to this point, I'd been able to keep it together, but the aide's speech really shook me. Dad and the general looked a little green around the edges too.

I had forced myself to stop dwelling on the thought of the crash, and the fact that I'd been up in a glider only an hour or so earlier. I'd made it through the morning by refusing to believe that I'd ever been in any sort of danger. That this was an accident. That it had nothing to do with me. The aide's word "sabotage" shredded that nice illusion to bits and threw the bits into a gale wind.

Never mind that I was in the middle of a military academy. That Dad was the commander in chief of the United States armed forces.

The Big Boss, so to speak.

That I should have been completely safe.

I had been hanging on to that point of view like a lifeline—until just this moment, when the words "they can't rule out sabotage" ripped it away from me.

I've known since long before Dad was elected about the dangers of being the President. Anybody who has sat through public-school history knows that heads of state get assassinated sometimes, including too many American Presidents. I understand that there's risk involved in what Dad does. After Dad decided to run for office, I did some research. I wanted to see what we were getting into.

Four United States Presidents have died from assassins' bullets while in office: JFK, William McKinley, James Garfield, and Abraham Lincoln. An additional ten sitting Presidents have had attempts made on their life— including nearly every single modern President. Assassination threats serious enough to trigger an in-depth investigation by the Secret Service come in about once a month, on average. After I did the math, I figured out that all of that translated into roughly one-in-ten odds for my father to leave office feetfirst, and nine-in-ten odds that somebody would at least try to take a shot at Dad while he was in office.

If Dad gets through his term or terms unscathed, things look a lot brighter. Only one president so far has had a serious assassination attempt made after he left office. Somebody shot Teddy Roosevelt in the chest in 1912, while he was in Milwaukee on his way to make a speech. Teddy's eyeglass case and the folded speech in his jacket pocket slowed down the bullet enough to save him. Teddy insisted on making his speech before going to the hospital to get the surface wound attended to. He told the crowd that day that he'd never been gladder in his life that he was short-sighted and long-winded.

These days, I can thank the White House curator, Carl Wallerston, for feeding me presidential trivia. The man loves history almost as much as he loves having a captive audience.

So, simply put, any idiot can take it into his head at any time to go after a politician or a public figure, and Dad's job makes him a target for that kind of thing. There are too many idiots in the world. I pray for Dad's safety a lot.

But, except for one time when somebody tried to take out Mary Todd Lincoln by sabotaging her carriage wheels, all those threats to the President have never translated into attempts on the lives of other presidential family members. It made no sense that someone would go after me and not Dad.

As I said, I had been hoping this would all turn into a tragedy that had nothing at all to do with me. I couldn't deny that I'd experienced a sense of relief when I learned it hadn't been Cadet Dobbs who'd been involved in the crash. I figured that meant that the crashed aircraft probably wasn't the same glider I'd been in earlier.

Right?

The general's face grew gray.

My dad leaned forward in his seat. "Don, what is it?"

General O'Toole held out the report to my dad, then shot me a pained look. "According to the flight records, the equipment that Eve flew in is indeed the craft that crashed shortly thereafter." He turned to face Dad, no longer in the role of friend, but in the role of subordinate, delivering bad news. "Sir, since the investigators can't rule out sabotage, they believe it's entirely possible the glider was meant to crash—" The general paused and drew in a deep breath.

"With your daughter in it."

CHAPTER THREE

COLORADO SPRINGS GAZETTE

Academy spokesmen have offered no official reason why one of their gliders crashed shortly before graduation. One passenger has been confirmed dead, but the victim's name has not been released pending notification of the family. An Academy spokesman has confirmed that the pilot, name also withheld, is not a cadet, but an officer instructor.

I knew I was getting "the Stare" before I could even see it. But when I finally got up enough courage to glance in Dad's direction, the mixture of emotions on his face brought me to a complete standstill. The last time I'd seen him look like that, we had just learned that we were losing Mom.

Shock, concern, fear, love . . . Somehow I ended up in his arms, and we just stood there for a moment.

I once heard somebody say, "Sometimes you just have to hug your kids."

It works both ways. Sometimes kids have to hug their dads. . . .

"I don't know what I'd do if I lost you," Dad whispered. "You're my little girl."

"I'm not going anywhere, Dad."

He broke the bone-crushing hug. "I know, I know, but I worry anyway. And when something like this happens, I worry even more."

"Nothing happened, Dad." I suddenly realized how callous that sounded. "Not to me, that is. And nothing's proven. We're still not sure that anything was supposed to happen to me."

"No matter, I think you need to come home. Forget the vacation—"

"Dad . . ." I fought the instinct to roll my eyes like I've seen Drew do a thousand times. "I'm an adult. I'm twenty-five years old." I lowered my voice after I looked around at the crowd of people who were trying not to eavesdrop on what should be our very private conversation.

Dad's face grew even more resolute. "Eve, I'm serious. I really think you need to come home with me and make plans for a vacation another time."

Color me stubborn, but I'd been cooped up with the Coopers for too long. I love my family, but I'm not too sure anyone realized how much privacy I'd given up by forsaking my professional career, my nice apartment, my friends . . .

. . . and then I realized this was not the time to play the "Independent Grown Child" card. Sometimes you look into your father's eyes, no matter if he's a head of state, head of a company, or simply head of the janitorial staff. When he says, "You're coming home with me," you listen.

And obey.

This was one of those times.

I held up one finger. "A compromise."

He raised an eyebrow. "What?"

"I go home, but I don't hide. It makes *you* look bad if I hide. At home, I go about my usual business and I simply postpone my planned vacation in Colorado until after we learn more about what happened here."

"We'll discuss this later." Dad leaned over and kissed me on the forehead. An insidious man, our President. He can make me feel like an independent grown adult and like a ten-year-old, all at the same time.

So, evidently, my plans for a real vacation were going to vanish. It was, I suppose, a small price to pay in light of what could have happened. I slipped away into a nearby hallway and made hurried calls to the friends I was planning to visit. I offered apologies, but without giving out any real details. I simply promised to tell them more later, when and if I could. I hoped and prayed that the wire services wouldn't report on the crash at all. Or at least that they would not draw attention to the "irony" that I'd been up in that same glider only minutes before it crashed.

But wishing that stuff was just a waste of time, don't you think? The news media are insatiable.

There was no way the Academy could keep a lid on the crash itself. The glider's fragments and the sign of its impact with the ground might not have been visible from the stadium, but I imagine the wreckage could be seen from a variety of other locations both on and off the Academy grounds. And there had been enough photo coverage of me on the airfield, preparing for my first flight, to mean that someone would put one and one together.

I could already imagine the photos, nestled somewhere on page 2—or maybe, if it was a slow news day, on page 1 below the fold—a grainy picture of me wearing my best "I really don't want to be here" smile, being stuffed into the glider. Next to it, a clear photo of the crashed glider. The cut line would read something like "First Daughter's Near Miss."

They say a picture is worth a thousand words. That's true, but it doesn't allow for the modern media. These days the right picture can generate a billion words. CNN and the other 24/7 news channels would probably grab a story like this one just like a drowning man would reach for that seat cushion that doubles as a flotation device. I only hoped that the Academy had a good, solid news blackout on the accident report.

As we rode in the motorcade across town back to Peterson Air Force Base, where *Air Force One* sat on the tarmac, Dad remained uncharacteristically quiet. Someone from the protocol office had tried to be good. He'd left us a stack of photos commemorating Dad's visit to the Academy. I hoped he'd pulled the shots of me in the glider. Heck, if I'd been thinking, I could have beat Dad to the pictures and done it myself. Too late. Dad lined up a row of candids of me in the glider, growing a little paler with each shot he pulled out of the stack.

He looked at me. "Do you realize that if things had gone just a little differently, these might be all I had left of you?" he said.

So much for our tentative truce.

"It didn't happen that way," I pointed out. "You can make yourself crazy worrying about things that might have been."

Silence fell again.

Riding along with us, Michael Cauffman sensed the terror in the air and tried to distract us with tales of some of his adventures during the graduation ceremony.

He leaned forward in his seat, his look of nonchalance almost believable. "Sir, I have a question."

Dad looked up, still worried. "Yes?"

"Okay." Michael got ready to launch into his story. Habit had Dad listening—though not with his usual intensity. "So I knew the cadets always toss their hats up when the flyover starts. I wanted to get a shot of you, sir, on the dais in the background, and of the cadets and their hats in the foreground. I thought I had found the perfect place for shooting that image. I was kneeling against a low wall—I had to get close to the ground to get the right angle for shooting into the sky."

"Uh-huh," Dad said.

His thoughts were clearly elsewhere. I knew exactly what Dad's thoughts were dwelling on. So were mine.

Michael continued, even though he could tell he was losing his audience. "I got my shot. But no one told me about the kids."

That got my attention back. "Me, either," I offered.

I'd been taken by surprise by the rush of children who flooded the field only moments after the cadets hurled their hats into the air. Judging by the dedicated (actually, more like ferocious) looks on the kids' faces, and the looks of mild amusement on their parents' faces, it was evidently considered a grand tradition to collect the discarded headgear.

Michael was right. We needed a distraction. A conversation of any sort was far better than the alternative: tense silence. I don't like it when Dad gets quiet. He was very quiet while my mother was sick, and ever since then his silences always worried me terribly.

Since I needed to play along to keep the conversation going, the children's antics seemed a safe enough topic. I asked Michael's question for him. "So exactly why were they doing it, anyway?"

"I don't know," Michael said. "I was hoping that your father could tell me."

"It must be something compelling," I said. "You'd figure one hat would be enough, but I saw some kids carrying off four or five of them."

Michael laughed. "Yeah. I saw that too. I had the distinct feeling the little halflings weren't picking up extras to selflessly give to their younger brothers or sisters either. When that crowd of kids ran over me it reminded me of a military invasion—if the invading force was very short and light on weapons. Who knew little kids could pack such a wallop?" Michael rubbed his arm. "They bowled me right over. I went down like a load of rocks. When I got back to my feet, I realized they weren't just collecting the hats, but looking inside them." A sparkle entered his eyes. "And pulling out money."

I have to admit I'd paid little attention to the kids once they rushed the field and started their hat cleanup. I'd been more interested in the Thunderbirds and their air show. "Don't the cadet dress uniforms have a place for stuff like that? I mean, do cadets have to keep their pocket money in their hats? Hats they have no chance to recover once they're thrown?"

Dad turned away from the window toward us. "It's an Academy tradition. Once the cadets graduate, they become lieutenants, and the white wheel caps they've worn at the Academy aren't authorized headgear for them once they're officers. So they tuck money inside the brim for the kids." Dad's voice went flat. "It's supposed to be for good luck."

Dad paused. He gave me the sort of look he wears when he's yelling. But this time, he wasn't yelling. His voice was barely a whisper. "We can't rely on luck, Eve. You know that. What happened today was awful. But it could have been so much worse." He turned his attention to something beyond the window. "Much, much worse," he said almost to himself.

I knew what he meant, but I wasn't sure what to say. We'd had this discussion a million times before—about the inherent dangers of his elected position, not only for him, but also for the rest of us. He knew that I wasn't going to do something foolish, but that I also wasn't going to become what Aunt Patsy refers to as a "hothouse rose"—a pretty thing grown under glass to keep it safe, and regularly fertilized with a load of manure.

I wanted to live, if not a normal life, at least a life that took advantage of some of the opportunities of being First Daughter, without being hemmed in by the position's responsibilities. The trick, for both Dad and me, was in finding a happy medium he and I could live with, somewhere in the public venue required of the First Family.

"I know, Dad," I said. "Things could have turned out badly for me on that glider ride. But they didn't. And it's not like I was going off on my own, taking insane chances." I swear I wasn't whining, even if I did sound like Drew trying to excuse his latest misadventure. "I'll admit I wasn't all that anxious to go at first, but it turned out to be really . . ."

My voice trailed off. Somehow, it didn't seem appropriate to admit that I'd actually enjoyed myself. Not after that poor girl had died on the mountainside.

"Really what?" Dad asked.

I thought about lying.

Really . . . different. Well, at least that was true.

Really . . . scary. Even if it was a bit frightening at first, that was definitely the wrong direction to take, considering what happened afterward.

Really . . .

"Really what?" Dad repeated.

I sighed. The truth won out.

"Fun. Exciting."

There was a moment of silence; then Dad smiled a little. "Flying *is* exciting. I feel that way every time I get behind the controls of an aircraft. I love it."

With the ice finally broken and the subject of the accident behind us, we were able to be more open with each other. Michael, clever young man that he was, remained quiet while Dad and I had a nice father-daughter chat, rehashing the events of the last few hours.

I'd finally accepted Michael in the role of family confidant. Michael and I had become close shortly after Dad became President. We were thrown together when the two of us found a body in the Rose Garden. As a bonding experience, something like that puts a blind date to shame. Now we hang out together a lot. In the last few months, Michael and I'd danced around what could have been a more personal relationship.

But then something had happened. These days, what I felt for Michael was almost like brotherly love. I think the same thing had happened to him. In fact, I was beginning to suspect that Michael had a strong streak of matchmaker in him. Recently, he'd introduced me to some of his friends, and not only had I been welcomed, but I'd seemed to fit in.

Michael's friends were mostly media professionals, all of them bright and funny and interesting. Lately we'd gone all sorts of places together. Sometimes, the group broke into couples. I'm not talking about folks slipping away into a handy bedroom, but something a little more old-fashioned. Certain people tended to pair off when we were together, whether into natural conversation groups, or picking a dance partner, or looking for a shoulder to cry on. Generally speaking, since there was never an equal number of males and females, it was a matter of fluid group dynamics in action. But sometimes it was something more.

Michael and I ended up together occasionally. After all, we had a lot in common—photography, the White House, a warped sense of humor. Not to mention that he hangs around with my family a lot. But more often, as time goes on, I end up talking the night through with Michael's best friend, Craig Bodansky.

And Michael's generally the one that throws us together, then wanders off, wearing an insipid smile. See what I mean about that matchmaking streak?

So my relationship with Michael is evolving. These days, he's a buddy. A really good friend—and I need a few of those. I decided after a couple of months of hanging around with Michael that I prefer him as a friend, rather than a potential lover. Those early flutters of attraction have grown into something stronger, but not at all sexual. In fact, even the thought of kissing Michael . . .

It would be like kissing Drew. . . .

But back to us in the limo.

The father-daughter chat Michael witnessed didn't change anything— Dad was still concerned about my safety, and I was still worried about Dad's. The glider was still crashed on a Colorado mountain. But we were at least able to talk about it, rather than dodging the subject. After we'd gone through it all one more time, Dad and I disengaged carefully from that conversation, both of us agreeing that treading lightly until we knew what was going on was a wise thing to do.

The adult thing to do.

For both of us.

But I knew Dad never forgot that he'd put his whole family in a fish-bowl existence when he'd decided to run for President. He regretted that. After today, he regretted it even more.

After all, having the public interested in our personal lives was bad enough.

Having the public want to *end* our personal lives was terrifying.

Once we cleared the runway, our flight home was uneventful. Dad had a mountain of paperwork to review and unending affairs of national importance to address. Michael and I sat together, neither of us really needing or wanting to talk. Sometimes it's nice to have a friend like that.

In fact, Michael was so comfortable with not talking that he took the window seat and slept almost all the way home.

Lucky stiff.

I wish I could have slept.

I couldn't. It didn't help that somewhere in the back of my mind, I couldn't stop equating flying with soaring, aeronautical theories aside. And soaring was now pretty closely linked in my mind with crashing. Although I didn't expect anything to go wrong on the trip home (*Air Force One* only has engine or hijacker troubles in the movies, not in real life), I couldn't relax enough to get comfortable, much less fall asleep.

But by the time we got to Andrews Air Force Base and then took the motorcade back to D.C. and finally got home, I was exhausted. Going to sleep was no problem at all. In fact, I fell asleep the moment I hit the bed. I slept soundly until around four in the morning.

That's when I ran into the side of a mountain. . . .

Not really, of course—though it felt like it at the time. It was odd. I don't usually have bad dreams, and if I do, they're usually so nonsensical that I don't get too torqued about them.

But this nightmare was a doozy.

I was riding in the cockpit of *Air Force One* and the pilot turned around and said, "Here. You try." Then he walked away.

So there I am, trying to fly this huge plane, and I have no idea what to do other than grab the yoke and hold on tight. Lightning flashes and thunder rolls. The radio crackles and suddenly I'm being told if I don't turn the plane around, we'll get shot out of the sky. A jet flies along beside us and I can see it's an Air Force Thunderbird. The pilot makes a frantic "Look ahead!" gesture to me and then veers away. I looked into the distance and see a large mountain dead ahead of me. And no matter what I do to the controls, no matter what direction I try to steer, we continue to fly straight and level, right for the mountain.

Suddenly, I'm no longer in the pilot's seat. I'm sitting on a big cloud, watching an even bigger television. Another woman—no . . . a girl—is sitting where I sat only moments before. It's like watching a horrible action movie. She's screaming; the mountainside looms closer. I find myself yelling at her, telling her to grab the yoke and turn it.

But she never tries. She just sits there, screaming, crying, and praying for someone to save her.

And nobody does.

The movie camera pulls back and I watch in horror as the plane hits the mountain.

Kaboom . . .

I didn't scream when I woke up, but I did leap out of bed, land on all fours, and crouch there like a dazed, confused animal for a few moments, breathing heavily.

I remember looking around and thinking, This isn't my home.

Yes, it was. . . .

I was in the White House.

Even in a dream state that's a shock.

I sat there, trying to catch my breath and control my thundering heart rate.

Damn nightmare. . . .

I knew going back to sleep was out of the question. I threw on a robe, stumbled to what Drew has been referring to lately as my "snack kitchen," and nuked some water for herbal tea, my universal cure-all for bad dreams, sleepless nights, and undue stress. I was suffering from all three. Once the tea was ready, I wandered through the solarium and out onto the roof level, cup in hand.

In the White House, sometimes you wonder if you'll ever be alone. Between the staff, the ushers, the aides, the security personnel, and the authorized visitors (hopefully no unauthorized ones), there are only a few places that could be described as really private in the house. But during the wee hours of the morning, the White House is at its quietest—national and international emergencies excepted, of course. Luckily, the world had been nice and quiet lately, and Dad had been getting his full quotient of shut-eye.

Day or night, winter or spring, the place in the White House I like the most is the roof. It's quiet. Most important, it's off-limits to almost everyone outside of the family. No affairs of state or even states of affairs are discussed out there. Aunt Patsy actually threatened to needlepoint a sampler, to hang over the French doors from our private quarters out to the roof, that said, "Abandon Politics, All Ye Who Enter Here." We've reserved the porch as a place where we try to pretend we're just a normal family, doing normal family things.

For example. . . .

The day before the big annual White House Easter Egg Roll, we had some distant cousins come to visit us. Drew and I ended up sitting with the little kids out on the roof, dyeing Easter eggs. The kids made an ugly mess, but that was okay. We'd spread newspapers around to catch the worst of it. The roof was the only place in the White House where the sight of a mess like that wouldn't have sent Mr. O'Connor, the head usher, into a state of apoplexy. (We don't make jokes anymore about Mr. O'Connor having a heart attack, since his twin brother died of one in the Rose Garden in February. But that's another story, one that I won't go into here.)

The mess on the patio wasn't any trouble at all. Drew and I simply wadded up the newspapers and mopped up the remaining spilled colors after the kids left. We counted ourselves lucky that the ugly mess was confined to the porch. But that kind of messy, drippy, silly activity was exactly the sort of thing we would have done in any other house we'd ever lived in—it was a normal way for us to celebrate the Easter holiday, with family members around us, pursing our own traditions, not White House ones.

The porch made the White House feel a bit more like home, which has been one of Dad's private agendas.

So now I stood out on what I had started to think of as our family balcony, trying to ignore a small sprinkling of pink glitter Drew and I had evidently missed in our cleanup efforts. Resolutely, I turned my head away from it and ignored the urge to get a towel. Instead, I watched another splotch of glittering pink, this one the first faint glow of daylight edging the eastern sky.

There was a little touch of chill in the early-morning air, but otherwise it promised to become another warm, lazy May day. It was almost summer, and it was starting to feel like it.

In the distance, I watched a small airplane making a final approach along the Potomac to Reagan National. I shivered, not sure whether it was the chill or the eerie sight of the small plane alone in the sky. It reminded me of another small plane, presently adorning a mountainside in Colorado. Memories can be tricky things to deal with right before dawn.

"Eve?"

I turned and saw Aunt Patsy standing in the doorway. She took a sip from the steaming mug she held in both her hands. I knew she was slurp-ing hot chocolate. Just like my Dad, that's her preferred morning beverage. Coffee's got its place, but not in the Cooper kitchen.

"You're up early," she said.

"Nightmares."

She placed her mug on a nearby table, walked toward me, and wrapped me up in a wonderful hug. "I'm sorry, sweetheart."

I put my head on her shoulder and drank in the comfort. "What about you?" I said. "You're usually not up this time of morning."

"I had nightmares too," she confessed. "When Elliot called me and told me what happened, all I could think of was that it could have been you . . . My little girl, taken from me much too young. It's hard for me to handle that." Aunt Patsy sighed a mother's sigh.

Although Patsy's not my mother, she's the next best thing—an aunt who loves me like her own.

I was twelve when my mother died of lung cancer. It was one of those terrible, not-fair things that sometimes happen to wonderful people. She was a nonsmoker. Secondhand smoke killed her.

But even though I lost her so young, I'm lucky. I remember my mother—her face, her voice, her perfume, the sense of acceptance and love I always got from one of her hugs. I wasn't sure Drew had those memories.

I also remember the day that Aunt Patsy arrived in our lives as a full-time member of the family. She arrived on our doorstep when things were awful, not to take Mom's place, but to be there for us because we so des-perately needed her. Just as I needed her now.

Patsy and I stayed there together on the porch like that for a few moments, soaking in the comfort of loving arms to hold us. When we finally broke apart, my aunt tucked a loose strand of my hair behind my ear. That was something my mother used to do. I felt a tear run down my cheek—I turned away and wiped it off before Patsy could notice it.

"Want to talk about it?" Patsy retrieved her hot chocolate and settled in a chair.

"Not really," I said. "But you deserve to know. I was flown around in a glider, then an hour or so later I watched a glider crash into a mountain. Somebody died. That was upsetting enough. But then I learned it was the same glider I'd been riding in. . . ." I shivered a little. "I read the preliminary report. The investigators are being cagey, and they won't commit to anything, but I think they believe there was something wrong with the glider."

"Your dad says the crash might be a setup—one that was aimed at you. You think. . . . ?" Her voice trailed off.

"I don't know. No sane person could possibly think that eliminating me would cause a ripple effect that would bring down the U.S. government."

"I'm not so sure about that."

"But I'm nobody. They elected Dad. I'm just the White House window dressing that came with him. I'm not important."

Aunt Patsy made a rude noise. "Horse apples. You're the First Daughter. Like it or not, that makes you a somebody."

It was my turn to make a rude noise.

She persisted. "You're underestimating your importance to national security. Your death would be hell on your father. You're Coop's first child and his only daughter. If, God forbid, something happened to you, he'd be devastated."

"Devastated. . . ." I echoed.

"Yes," she said with surprising passion. "It would absolutely destroy him. Eve, you know how much your father loves you."

"Sure, but—"

"But nothing. You're his baby. And in so many ways, you're his last link with Carolyn. You remind both of us so much of your mother. . . ." Patsy paused to wipe her eyes, which looked a bit teary in the dim light. "If Coop lost you, especially in a politically motivated attack, he'd be so demoralized I'm not sure he could remain an effective president. He'd never be able to stop blaming himself for putting you in the public eye."

That was a sobering assessment. Even worse, once I thought about it, I suspected Patsy was right.

I swallowed hard. "Really?"

"Yes." She gave a curt nod. "Really."

I sat down. Sure, I knew my father loved me, but I'd never considered a scenario where some jerk took me out to get at my dad. All my sweat-inducing assassination scenarios had always involved somebody going after Dad.

But Patsy had opened a gate that I couldn't now close. The key word there was "blame." Dad *would* blame himself. That blame would eat him up from the inside out. But blame was a sharp-edged sword that cut two ways. . . . I felt my knees grow rubbery, and I plopped down in the nearest chair.

Patsy sprang to my side. "Eve, are you all right? Your face just went white."

I was able to keep my voice relatively calm. "This is all my fault."

"What's your fault?"

"That girl's death . . . I rode in a glider. That glider crashed only minutes later, and it killed her. If the glider was indeed sabotaged, and if that sabotage was meant for me, then I am responsible. I was the target, and the man who was injured and the girl who died in that crash were bystanders put in harm's way in my place."

"It wasn't your fault."

I looked up at Patsy. My aunt didn't look any happier than I felt.

"Don't you see?" I swallowed hard. "Because of me, Ashley McCurdy is dead."

CHAPTER FOUR

CNN NEWS CRAWL

Glider crash at the U.S. Air Force Academy killed one civilian passenger and injured its military pilot. CNN has learned that President Cooper's daughter, Evelyn, had used the glider only minutes before. The National Transportation Safety Board and the FBI have been called in to investigate the crash. An anonymous government source has told CNN that sabotage could have been involved. The NTSB has declined to confirm or deny this.

The newspapers and morning news shows all had their pet theories about the crash, crediting everybody from domestic anarchists to foreign terrorists to a disgruntled suitor. Little did they know that my love life had been so slow in the past year that I didn't have any suitors, disgruntled or otherwise.

As to the other sources of ill will, your guess is as good as mine. . . .

But I couldn't just sit around and pretend nothing had happened. I had to acknowledge the tragedy and do it in some sort of public forum. So I decided to write my own press release. By necessity, it would need to go through the proper White House channels before being released to the public, but the important point was that I needed to instigate it rather than have others fashion it for me.

It was the adult thing to do.

I stumbled through the first draft and tried to cover the salient points: how upsetting it had been for me to witness such a tragedy and how my heart went out to the victims. I wished Major Gaskell a speedy recovery and sent my sincerest sympathy to the family of Ashley McCurdy for their untimely loss.

It was a lot harder to write than I had expected.

I was trying to polish a second draft of the release when I was interrupted by a call on my private line. I stared at the phone, almost afraid to pick it up. As it rang a second time, I prayed that none of my friends had been coerced into giving the press access to my unlisted number—one of my last bastions of privacy.

I picked up the receiver. "Hello?"

"Eve? This is Megan Lassiter."

I released a mental sigh of relief. A friend, not a reporter.

"Hey, Megan, long time no see. I was just thinking about you the other day. You still working at the Pentagon?"

"Yes." There was moment of silence. "Eve, I need to talk to you."

"Shoot."

"In person." She paused again. "It's important."

I'd met Megan when we were in graduate school in Denver. She was a friend of a friend. We'd ended up hanging out one night, and we'd discovered that we had a lot in common, including an ex-boyfriend. Okay, so she'd gone with him for a year and I'd only dated him a few times, but we both had horror stories about the guy. Nobody appreciates a horrible guy story like another woman who has dated that same guy. We'd laughed and cried together and become fast friends, joined by the bond of shared torment. They say misery loves company. . . . Well, it worked for Megan and me.

When Megan joined the military and was spirited off to a bunch of far-flung places, we tried to keep in touch, but despite our best efforts we grew apart. The calls and e-mails dropped off. The last time I'd heard from her, a couple of months ago, Megan had mentioned that she'd moved to the D.C. area. She'd been assigned to the Pentagon. I'd been meaning to reestablish contact with her before the military bundled her up and moved her someplace else. So I was glad that she'd called. But she sounded really strange, kind of abrupt and uncomfortable.

"Well . . . uh . . . sure, Megan. It'd be great to get back togeth—"

She didn't even let me finish. "I'm at the Pentagon. I'm coming over. I can be there in twenty minutes." She hung up.

Megan could be a bit no-nonsense at times, but this was far worse than usual. Whatever was bothering her, it was enough to have her in a real twist. It was probably a bit selfish of me, but I figured a good dose of worrying about someone else's troubles might help distract me from my own problems. I was almost looking forward to seeing what had her so worked up.

It was yet another case of misery loving company. . . .

I made all the appropriate calls to clear Megan through the various security checkpoints and allow her access to my private quarters, and sure enough, in a scant twenty minutes, I got a call that she'd arrived. I met her as she emerged from the elevator to the family quarters.

I'd never seen Megan in her Air Force uniform before. Between its severe lines and her brisk manner, I felt as if she were some stranger rather than a good friend. She marched toward me, her heels clicking in an imperious rhythm.

Whatever was bothering her, it was bad.

Real bad.

Her greeting was a brusque "We need to go someplace where we can talk." She glared at me. "Privately."

I swallowed back a "Nice to see you too" and motioned for her to follow me to my part of the private quarters. It was off-limits to aides when I was there, and the only bugs hiding in the vases were of the real insect variety.

At least, that's what I'd been told. . . .

We barely made the third-floor hallway before Megan whirled around, her hands bunched into tight fists. Her cool, carefully controlled features dissolved into a hot cascade of tears.

"My God, Megan. What's wrong?" When I reached out to hold her, she jerked away as if my touch were repugnant and so was I.

"Ashley McCurdy was my . . . sister," she spat out, anguish and fury dripping from every syllable.

What? I gaped at her, unable to say a word. My heart literally skipped a beat, and then it wedged itself firmly in my throat. *Her sister? Oh my God.*

Tears rolled down Megan's face and spilled off her chin, leaving dark blotches on her light blue uniform shirt. "Ashley's dead and it's all your fault."

Her words hit me hard. It'd been bad enough to wrap my mind around the idea that a stranger had died, quite possibly in my place. But now . . . to learn that it was no stranger, but the sister of a friend? I hadn't thought the burden of guilt could get any worse. I'd been wrong. . . .

"Your s-sister. I—I didn't know," I stuttered. "N-no one . . ." I reached behind me, groping for a nearby seat. Finding one, I sat abruptly, my knees unable to support the growing weight of my anguish.

Megan stood over me, angry and tense. It was as though she were waiting for something from me.

"Your s-sister . . ." I repeated. "I'm so sorry." I couldn't help it. I started crying too.

Her face softened slightly. "You didn't know," she whispered.

"No." I forced myself to stand. "I had no idea . . ." I reached out again, and this time Megan didn't jerk away. I wrapped my arms around her and we stood there, each sobbing into the other's shoulder.

"I had no idea she was your sister. The different last names. . . ."

"She was my half sister," Megan managed between watery gulps. "Mom got remarried and had Ashley when I was eight. I loved her so. . . . I keep thinking of her crashing into that mountainside."

It was all I could do to not think about it myself. I remembered what I'd felt like when Mom died. I knew how painful it was to lose someone you loved, so I had some inkling of what Megan was going through right now, and the thought was doing a good job of turning me into a total basket case.

After a few more sobs, Megan stepped back, dried her tears, and faced me. Judging by the look in her eye, she was holding her abject sorrow in check just now with an overwhelming need for justice.

Or worse, revenge. . . .

"You can't bring her back. So what *are* you going to do about it?" she demanded.

"M-me?"

"Yes, you. You have connections. Authority. Influence." She looked around. "For God's sake, your dad is President and you live in the White

House. I need your help. I want to know who did it. The military is stonewalling my family and me. They say it's a Secret Service operation. The Secret Service refuses to tell us anything. They say it's a matter of national security. I don't care. I just want to know who did this, who killed my sister." A harsh light entered her eyes. "I already know why."

As upset as I was, I couldn't let that go unchallenged. "Why?"

She seemed taken aback by my question. She sputtered a bit, then finally said, "They were trying to kill you."

"Maybe." I said. "But why?"

She glared at me as if I were the world's biggest (and soggiest) dummy. "Because of your father, of course."

"Why?"

Now Megan was openly confused. "Can't you say anything but 'why'? Because your father is the freakin' President of the United States and killing you would . . ." She slowed down. "Would be the most devastating thing they could do to destroy his presidency outside of . . . assassinating him." Her look of accusation faded to one of infinite pain.

"Yes."

It was her turn to sag to the closest seat.

"I'm so sorry that Ashley's gone," I said softly. "I want to know who did this every bit as much as you do. Especially if they were coming after me and my family. But Ashley's death is not my fault. Not really. I did nothing wrong. I wasn't being careless. I didn't act rashly. My only sin was in being my father's daughter." The truth of that washed over me. For the first time I realized it *was* the truth. "I was a victim. Just like Ashley."

Megan sniffed. "Her only crime was to be in the wrong glider at the wrong time."

I nodded. "Exactly. It was an accident—and nobody could have predicted it. The Secret Service wasn't expecting trouble. We'd had the usual crackpot threats, but nothing serious for a couple of months. If my agents had had any inkling something like this could have occurred, that glider would have been grounded—and so would I. But nobody had any reason to be concerned. Both the Academy officials and my security detail checked the glider over completely before I got in. I don't see how they could have missed anything."

"But maybe they did."

"Maybe they did," I echoed. "But they didn't mean to."

We'd reached a stalemate in the guilt-versus-blame department. Finally the heat of emotion drained from Megan's eyes and she buried her face in her hands. "I'm sorry, Eve. I . . . I needed someone to blame."

I patted her shoulder. "And I was handy." I felt the tension drain from my body as well. "I understand." And I did. Perhaps more than she'd ever know. "Apology accepted." We sealed the truce with a hug.

With the dam broken, we were able to return to my sitting area, grab facing chairs, and sit down and really talk. In reality, Megan did most of the talking, about her sister, her family, all the regrets that haunted her, how cheated she felt because Ashley's young life had been taken too soon, the struggles that Ashley had had, her triumphs, her failures. Most of all Megan mourned the sister she'd never see again and the woman Ashley would never get to become.

Megan needed to talk and cry and reminisce. I let her. As she started telling me stories about Ashley, about silly things they'd done together, fights they'd had, the good times and the bad, I couldn't help but think about Drew again, and Charlie, too. I couldn't imagine life without either one of them. If something bad ever happened to either of my brothers, I'd go on the rampage too, looking for someone to blame.

As a fellow big sister, I understood all too well the responsibilities and demands of the position. In fact, I cried right along with Megan. Sometimes I played another role, one I was also familiar with: the comforting mother substitute. I've played that role all too frequently with Drew. The kid complains that between Dad, Patsy, me, and Charlie, he has four parents.

So while Megan fell apart, all I could do was be there for her. Nothing could change what had happened, but maybe I could help her deal with it emotionally.

By the time Megan was ready to leave—it was about an hour later—she'd been able to put aside the animosity she'd arrived with (for the most part, that is), but her original request was the same:

"Do something, Eve. You've always been able to cut through the BS and find the kernel of truth. Do it now. For me. I remember Denver. I know you can help."

She was talking about a time back in Denver when I'd been in a ticklish situation, thanks to a photo I'd taken on the job. That photo had ended up being a key piece of evidence that helped to convict a killer. The killer had known about the photo—and had come after me to keep me from testifying. It all worked out—the police caught him before he got me. But things had been a little tense in my life for a while, and in the end I'd had a hand in catching the killer.

My part in that case was a well-kept secret. My identity had been kept quiet by both the police and the court. It hadn't come out even during Dad's presidential campaign, despite the fact that one of his opponents (a lesser man than my father—in both political know-how and morals) had turned over every rock he could find, looking for any dirt he could on Dad. And when he found none, he turned his attention to Patsy, Charlie, and me. He even went after Drew—though the kid was hardly old enough to have done something awful. But even a nosy politician looking for trouble never uncovered my involvement in that murder case, thanks to some very tight-lipped Denver cops and prosecutors.

But that was all before we'd moved into the White House. Quite frankly, I'd just as soon not talk about that case again, ever. Especially not with Megan, and especially not now.

"Let's not go there," I said. "I'll do whatever I can, Megan. I promise."

After she left, my first instinct was to head directly for the Oval Office, but then I remembered that Dad's schedule today was packed with meetings—even more than usual. So instead, I went to Peter Seybold's office. As head of presidential protection detail, Mr. Seybold oversees Dad's security, and also the security of his family. He and I had been forced to establish a somewhat professional relationship after the body in the Rose Garden incident that rocked the White House in February. These days, three months after that bit of trouble, he seemed to view me less as a First Nuisance and more as a Necessary Evil.

Okay, maybe his opinion of me was a bit better than that. After all, Seybold did credit me once in private with what he called a "pivotal role" not only in figuring out who killed our head usher's brother, but also in finding a way to clear my father's name. Seybold said I'd possibly saved Dad's presidency from a major scandal in its first weeks.

Okay . . . maybe Mr. Seybold didn't exactly say that last part, but Dad sure did. He'd been the one who proudly claimed to anyone who'd listen that I'd kept him in the Oval Office by ferreting out and exposing the truth.

And, trust me, lots of people listen to the President.

Of course, it's Dad's job to be inordinately proud of his kids' accomplishments, big or little, so I suspect the White House staff took his stories with the proverbial grain of salt. I don't expect the same sort of blind faith and lasting loyalty from Peter Seybold.

As I headed to Seybold's office, I paused to look out the window, and spotted Megan as she walked out through the North Portico. She left the grounds and made her way through the usual group of reporters that hung out near the security kiosk at the fence, ignoring their questions. Then she paused and appeared to call out to one of them. A man scurried over toward her, and the rest followed him, like lemmings. There was a sudden explosion of strobe lights.

My heart settled somewhere in the vicinity of my toes. Well, there was nothing I could do about that now.

I couldn't make out who the guy was. I just hoped it was someone from the *Post* and not the *National Intruder*. At least Megan and I had parted on decent terms; she'd be more likely not to skewer me now. It would have been a nightmare if the press had interviewed her when she first arrived.

I figured CNN would tell the tale soon enough . . . but I had a duty to prepare the troops.

By the time I reached Seybold's office, I'd put away my fear of raging headlines and savage sound bites and turned my attention to the problem at hand.

Telling him about Megan's visit . . . and its aftermath.

As I entered his office, he gave me a bland, measuring smile. It was the kind of look a bomb specialist might give a suspicious package. "How are you, Eve?" He consulted a file folder on his desk, closed it, then looked up at me with something that bore a faint resemblance to compassion. "I suppose that yesterday's events were quite taxing for you."

Nothing gets by this guy, I thought with less charity than I should have had. I offered him a politely guarded look—something like the one he'd given me. "Yes. I didn't sleep well last night. It's not every day that I witness a fatal airplane . . . er . . . glider crash. Especially one that might have been meant for me. These little irritations have a way of affecting my dreams."

"Just so. Sit, please." He indicated a chair by his desk, then started shuffling the rest of the papers on his desk back into their respective files. Once he'd finished, he repositioned himself in his seat, rested his arms on his blotter, and laced his fingers. I knew that posture. It was a sign that the introductory pleasantries were over. "From what I've been told, the investigators have been unable to determine whether the crash was due to a simple mechanical failure, pilot error, or something less innocent."

Less innocent. I found the phrase almost amusing. Did it mean the same thing as "slightly guilty"? "That's what the early report said. I haven't heard anything more today, but that seemed to be the party line as of yesterday."

He lifted one somewhat bushy eyebrow and speared me with an "Are you accusing us of not doing our job?" look. "The party line?" he repeated.

"Let me rephrase that," I said, backpedaling as fast as I could. Suddenly, I found my chair to be inordinately uncomfortable. "I don't think . . . I mean . . . I know you'd tell me if . . ." Stymied by my inability to dance around the topic any more, I plunged into something that I knew Seybold appreciated: the unvarnished truth.

"It isn't just the fact that a girl died that's bothering me right now. I have a connection to the victim. And that connection is apparently talking to the press right now." That got Seybold's attention, big time. I drew a deep breath and spilled the story of Megan's visit and its subsequent sequel with the press corps outside the White House. I tried to be succinct but thorough, but I was unable to prevent way too much emotion from creeping into my voice at times.

"I had absolutely no idea Megan even had a half sister, much less that her sister was the Ashley who"—I stuttered over the word—"d-died in the crash. They have . . . had different last names. I didn't know." It was a pretty lousy excuse, but the only one I had at the moment.

Seybold tented his fingers, tapping his fingertips lightly together. It irritated the hell out of me. "And your friend thinks that it's *your* responsibility to investigate?"

I shifted in my seat; the chair had grown entirely intolerable by now. "Not precisely. She feels it's my responsibility to find out who is responsible. I don't think she cares who does the investigating. But she does want her and her family to be kept informed. And if the official investigators don't keep her briefed on the latest information—and she believes that she is being stonewalled already—she wants me to tell her what's going on. She feels that her family's grief and need for resolution will get lost in the political shuffle. She believes, and I think she's probably right, that everyone involved in investigating the accident is much more concerned about my security, and my dad's security, and maintaining good public relations, than they are about recognizing and respecting her family's need for closure."

"She's right. Your security is our first priority, and I'm willing to take any necessary steps to maintain or regain it. But does your friend honestly believe we'd sacrifice her family's peace of mind if what we discovered proved to be unflattering toward you?"

Unflattering? Now there was one I hadn't thought about. "What do you mean, 'unflattering'?"

Seybold leaned back in his chair and laced his fingers behind his head. "For example, what if we discovered that the injured pilot was your former lover who was trying to get your attention? Or worse, what if he was attracted to you, and when he was unable to get your attention, he decided to commit suicide despite the fact that he had a passenger. Or what if, during your earlier flight, you had played around with the glider's controls and caused some sort of system failure that compromised the following flight?"

The man had a nasty mind, and he was really picking up speed now. The more he spoke, the wider my mouth gaped.

"Or perhaps the passenger coerced the pilot into flying too close to the mountain because she wanted a closer look at you. Or perhaps *she* was your spurned lover, who had decided to end it all because you—"

"Stop," I said. "I get the picture." For a brief moment, I wondered if dear Mr. Seybold was making this all up, or whether there was someone out there painstakingly investigating all those possibilities, no matter how absurd.

"None of those apply," I said. "I only did what the pilot told me to do. The only control I touched was the thing that disconnected us from the tow plane, and that's because the pilot instructed me to do it. I was too afraid to touch anything that looked like it might make the glider fly. And, more important, I had never even met either of the pilots before. In fact, I'd never met Megan's sister Ashley"—I shuddered—"and I haven't been *anybody's* lover in so long that it's getting frightening." I realized what I'd just said. "For the record, that's not an offer. But I seriously doubt Megan's worried about anything like that."

"I agree." Seybold tented his fingers again. "It's more likely that she's afraid we'll determine it was a case of sabotage, a botched assassination attempt, and in light of that, she'll be forced to accept that her sister died needlessly in your place. In her eyes, it would then become *your* duty to make sure the sister's death didn't go unpunished. That's especially true if we can't or won't identify the true culprit—assuming there is one—due to security reasons. Megan would be compelled to place the guilt for her sister's death on you by default. So, are you guilty?"

Trust Peter Seybold to lay his hands right on the soft spot.

And dig in a bit.

I suppose, to do him justice, that's why he's so good at what he does. He examines all the angles. But that didn't make it hurt any less.

"No." I shook my head. "Not exactly." I stared at the folders on his desk, blinking back a stray tear. "But it is my duty to find out what happened. Exactly," I continued in a hoarse whisper.

He reached down, produced a box of Kleenex, and slid it across the desk to me. "You can't let her blame you, Eve. You've done nothing wrong. It was probably an accident, and one that had nothing to do with you. According to the NTSB, ninety-nine point nine percent of all glider crashes are due to pilot error, compounded by meteorological events. Plus, you must consider . . ."

I listened to his litany of possibilities. It was a relief to hear him explain why I was probably innocent. But I did remember my pilot remarking that we couldn't have picked a better day to go up, because it was perfect gliding weather. Didn't that eliminate one of the NTSB's major factors in glider crashes?

After Seybold finished his long-winded explanations, I shot him a smile that was only somewhat drippy. "Thanks. You've made it a little easier for me to accept . . . to honestly believe . . . that I did nothing wrong." I took great pride in the fact that I didn't start bawling again. "But no matter what caused that crash, a friend of mine is hurting. I can't just sit here and do nothing."

He graced me with his small, rare smile. "You could. You could simply leave it up to those of us whose job it is to protect you." His voice softened. "We're willing to protect you from saboteurs, as well as character assassins." But the uncharacteristic softness didn't quite reach his eyes. "But you can't leave it totally to us, can you?"

I snagged a tissue, blew my nose as discreetly as possible, and stood.

"You know the answer to that."

CHAPTER FIVE

NATIONAL TRANSPORTATION SAFETY BOARD—
PRELIMINARY REPORT

*Accident occurred Wednesday, May 28, 2003, at USAFA, CO.
Aircraft: Schweizer SGS 2-33A. Injuries: 1 fatal, 1 serious.*

*This is preliminary information, subject to change, and may
contain errors. Any errors in this report will be corrected when the
final report has been completed.*

*While soaring along the mountainside, the pilot descended
the glider to about 20 feet above the trees. As he made a turn
away from the mountain, the glider encountered heavy sink and
descended. A wingtip caught a tree and the glider spun around and
nosed into the trees and into a rock ridge, where it came to rest.*

The media was kind, or I was lucky. Apparently I had figured in
Megan's interview as a family friend and a witness to the crash, rather
than as the intended victim of it. CNN ran a tiny bit of that interview,
along with some footage of the glider crash shot by the parents of one of
the cadets. I was avoiding watching TV right now so that I didn't have to
see that tape, which was currently in heavy rotation on the news channels.
Seeing it live had been bad enough.

I was relieved that the interview was so innocuous. Summer was
coming, and I wanted a bit of peace. Maybe it's strange, but I'm still

stuck in the mental mode that says the advent of summer should bring with it a freedom from responsibility. I guess it's a leftover from those formative years in school, where summer holidays automatically meant more freedom. It's funny how things stay with you like that. Artifacts of the past.

I certainly envied Drew's giddy sense of glee at having survived his last day of school. And, to add fuel to his celebratory fire, he'd finished his freshman year relatively unscathed. That meant he could put behind him his lowest-of-the-lower-classmen status, and plan as a sophomore on doing unto next year's freshmen what had been done to him.

So when Drew came bouncing into the kitchen, papers and books exploding from his arms in all directions (someone I knew and loved had waited until the last possible moment to clean out his locker), I understood his sense of glee, even if I was too mired in my own troubles to share in it.

"Let's do something!" he demanded. He piled his papers on the table, and I spotted at least one note, dated March 12, that was supposed to have been signed by a parent. Drew tended to believe in the out-of-sight, out-of-mind theory of the universe. At least this time it hadn't had any permanent repercussions.

"Do something like what?" I said.

He rummaged through the refrigerator and pulled out a can of root beer. "I don't know. Go swimming or go play tennis or something."

I mulled over the possibilities, realizing that I didn't really want to go outside and face an uncertain public and the overly attentive press corps. I still needed to get a handle on this whole situation before I did that. I'd already dodged several phone calls from journalists I knew pretty well and might even trust, not to mention a slew of requests for interviews from everyone from the wire services right on up to the networks. But I'd made it plain that I didn't want to talk about the crash. That's why I was issuing the press release.

I released a sigh that made him stop in midswallow.

"What's wrong with you?" he demanded.

Ah . . . to be young and oblivious. He had to know all about my misadventures in Colorado. And, to his credit, he wasn't the sort of kid who had desensitized himself to real violence with the video version.

He drained his root beer in a way only teenage boys can. Then, unlike most kids, he managed to cover the resulting belch. "You still messed up about the glider thing?"

Out of the mouth of babes . . .

"Yeah, I'm still messed up," I admitted.

"Then you need some distraction. Let's go somewhere. A movie. A drive . . . just somewhere outside."

Outside. Right now, the outside world didn't sound the least bit appetizing. Not with a jungle of journalists waiting outside to pounce on me. Of course, I had to venture out sometime. I couldn't imagine myself becoming housebound for long. What I needed to find was a suitable distraction close to home to satisfy Drew's need for activity and my need to stay out of the limelight.

Luckily, I had an epiphany.

I rubbed my hands together. "What about the White House bowling championship of the world?"

The offer seemed to satisfy his requirement for both entertainment and competition. "You're on," he said with an evil smile.

According to Carl Wallerston, the White House curator who delights in knowing stuff like this, Harry Truman had the first bowling alley put into the White House, but that one was eventually dismantled. The room we were about to enter dated back to the Nixon era. It had proved popular enough with White House inhabitants to keep intact ever since, and had been kept up-to-date with the latest in bowling technology. It even had fancy score-keeping machines that rewarded you with triumphant cartoons for making spares and splits.

Two lanes, no waiting.

Once there, I allowed Drew to completely stomp me in our first game. I'm a fair bowler, but I was having a hard time keeping my concentration centered on the game, and not floating back to sudden, unwanted visions of a glider crashing into the trees on the side of a mountain. In my imagination, I could hear the sounds of shattering wood, whining metals as the cockpit distorted against the rocks, and the victims' screams of terror, none of which I'd heard in person.

As I said, my imagination is a bit overactive. . . .

But, lucky for me, Drew's exuberance and competitive drive finally dragged me away from my unwanted thoughts and my rampant imagination and back toward the frivolous championship at hand.

Somewhere around the sixth frame of the second game, he started throwing gutter balls. Since Drew's not the type to dull his competitive streak in order to let his sister win, I knew something was brewing.

I stopped the proceedings. "Okay, what's wrong?" I had visions of him suddenly confessing about how much my misadventures had actually affected him.

Not so . . .

He scuffed the toe of his bowling shoe against the lane markers. "We were supposed to end the year with a big freshman-to-sophomore dance at school. But now we can't have it."

"What happened?"

"There was some sort of explosion in the auditorium and the place caught on fire. The sprinkler system kicked in and put out the flames, but it flooded the auditorium and the gym. Now the gym floor is warped and we can't have our dance there."

"An explosion?"

He shrugged as if it were *no big deal. . . .*

But it was a *very big deal* to me. Especially after what I'd been through.

I gave him the most encouraging smile I could muster. "Would you excuse me for a minute? I just remembered that I have to make a call."

By virtue of necessity, the bowling alley is long and narrow. I couldn't use the house phones if I didn't want Drew to overhear my call. Even the longest phone cord was too short to be pulled out to the hallway.

I stuck my head out the door and waved over John Kingston, my Dawg du Jour. "Do you have a cell phone I can use?"

He nodded and reached into his jacket, then hesitated.

"It's not long-distance or anything," I assured him. "I'm just calling Mr. Seybold to verify something."

John pushed a couple of buttons, then handed it to me. "He's on my speed dial," he rumbled in explanation.

I gave him a weak smile of thanks, and tried to hear the rings over the thundering of my heart. My voice remained relatively unshaken as I made it through the secretarial gauntlet and was transferred directly to the man himself.

"Yes, Eve?"

"Drew just told me that there was an explosion and a fire at his school." My overactive imagination galloped ahead unchecked, and I was inundated with visions of bombs wrapped around gas pipes, their timers' red numbers flashing a countdown.

"Yes, there was indeed an explosion of sorts." Only Peter Seybold could make that statement in a calm, flat voice.

"Of sorts . . ." I echoed. "Exactly what does that mean?"

"It means there was a small leak in the school's natural-gas line, which comes into the building right behind the back auditorium wall. We, along with the District fire investigators, believe the electrical timer which controls the school's outside lights probably created enough of a spark to ignite the gas vapors."

My mind's eye created a ball of fire covering the entire building.

"Was it bad? Was anybody hurt?" I found my voice sinking to a whisper. "Did they think someone did it on purpose?"

"No, no, and definitely no." Seybold's voice softened. "Eve, don't worry. There was absolutely no sign that this was anything other than an unfortunate accident. The fire damage was actually very minor. The real damage occurred because the sprinkler systems ran unchecked for too long. I understand that the wood floors in several rooms will need to be replaced due to water damage."

"You're sure?"

"It's my job to be sure, Eve. I promise I won't keep anything from you or your father." There was a click and silence on the other end.

I held the phone out to John. "Thanks. I appreciate the loan."

He stuffed the phone back into his jacket pocket. "No problem. Everything okay?"

I nodded. "Yeah." I started back inside and then paused, turning to John. "Do you like him? Mr. Seybold, I mean?"

He shrugged his massive shoulders. "He's my boss. Don't have to like him."

"But you respect him? Think he's doing a good job?"

John nodded with unusual resolution. "He's good."

From anyone else, I'd consider this faint praise, but I already knew from past experience that John wasn't given to superlatives. His assessment might lack some frills, but I understood what he meant.

I stepped back into the bowling alley, feeling about twenty pounds lighter.

Drew crossed his arms and glared at me. "Happy now?"

"About what?"

"To find out that the fire in the auditorium was nothing more than an accident." He made a face. "Who'd you call? My principal?"

"I called Mr. Seybold."

"Oh. Him." Drew leaned forward as if afraid we'd be overheard. "I don't like that guy."

I leaned forward in pseudo-conspiracy. "I'm not sure I do either. Let's get back to the game."

Having discovered common ground, we fell back into bowling, playing the "You know who else I don't like?" game as well. Eventually we worked the discussion around to the lack of a venue for the freshman dance.

"So they couldn't find any other place to hold the dance?"

Drew made a face. "I don't think they even looked. They don't understand how important it is to us. It's a major thing to survive your freshman year. We were going to use a *Survivor* theme and everything."

Drew had only started private school in January, but he'd quickly insinuated himself into the class structure and seemed to be making good friends. I was quite pleased that he had found a sense of connection with the other students without too much strain.

"Can you and your friends try to find an alternative place by yourselves?"

He made yet another face. "Mr. Lendon, the headmaster, didn't like any of the places we mentioned."

I had a feeling I wouldn't have either, but I had to ask. "So what sort of places did you guys suggest?"

He lowered his voice and did a fairly accurate imitation of his headmaster. " 'Nice try, boys, the Altamont School isn't willing to pay five thousand dollars to rent a ballroom at the Willard.' "

I gaped at my brother. "The Willard? Are you crazy? That's the last place in the District that wants to host a bunch of wild freshmen for an end-of-school bash."

Drew stiffened. "We're not wild. Mr. Lendon says we're mature enough to have a party there, but we can't do it because we haven't raised enough money." He ducked his head. "Jason's dad said he'd cough up the difference, but Mr. Lendon won't allow it. He says if we didn't earn it, we can't spend it."

That sounded like sterling good sense to me. I'd already learned to appreciate Mr. Lendon's stunning good looks after watching him participate in Drew's school musical back in February. Both Patsy and I had figured that all of the senior girls and half of the female staff were probably in lust with him. Later on, we found out our guess was on the low side. I'd been told that Mr. Lendon's leadership ability was on a par with his looks. It seemed those reports were correct. I was quite relieved to learn he was seeking a way to make a bunch of ritzy private-school kids understand the value of an honest buck.

Drew sat down and started retying his shoe. "So, you got any ideas about where we can find a place big enough to have our party? Within our budget?"

"How much money do you have?" I wondered, if I suggested Chuck E. Cheese, would Drew think it was kitschy, or simply be insulted? Then again, I didn't know if there were even any Chuck E. Cheeses in the D.C. area. I had a sudden craving for pizza, good, bad, or cardboard.

Drew quoted a sum that would have been sufficient to buy decent, maybe even hearty, snacks for a hundred or so kids at a gymnasium dance, but not enough to cover the rental of anything other than maybe the meeting room at a Denny's.

I was pretty sure they had those in the D.C. area.

"That's not much," I admitted. "Don't any of the kids' dads have a gym or maybe a corporate meeting area or . . ."

The light of sudden inspiration flared in Drew's eyes.

And I didn't like the look of it. "What?"

"A place with a large party room, plenty of parking, good security, great food?" A big grin split his face. He did his best Rod Serling imitation. "Picture, if you will, a large, well-furnished room with an eastern view. Music blares, teenagers dance. Food is served. Welcome to . . . the White House Zone."

Here? I started to make a mental list of all the reasons why he couldn't have a party here. They might make a mess. What if a couple of idiots decided to have a food fight? There are important, expensive paintings on the White House's important, expensive walls. Most kids his age didn't have the proper respect for the historical value or significance of the building. . . .

Then it hit me.

Why not? This was our house, right? Granted, not solely ours, but hadn't Dad been talking about ways to make the house our home? As long as there were reasonable rules and enough adults in attendance to forestall any inventive mischief, why couldn't Drew have his party here? It wouldn't be the first kids' party in the White House.

I pulled him closer. "Okay, if you want to use the East Room, here's what you do. First, talk to Mr. O'Connor. Find out what it'd take to use the room for your party, what rules you'd have to follow, what promises you'd have to make, and what dates it's free."

"What if he wants to know if Dad said it's okay?"

"If he asks you that, explain that you haven't discussed it with Dad yet. You wanted to investigate all the facts and figures to see if it was logistically possible before asking permission from Dad. Tell him that you want to be well armed with information when you ask Dad—if you're even able to ask Dad—if you can come to an agreement you think you can stand with Mr. O'Connor and can answer all of Dad's questions, then you have a shot at it." I raised a finger in warning. "And you'll have to be prepared to take no for an answer, if that's what it comes down to. But first . . ."

"First, what?"

"We have a championship to finish."

He grinned. "Okay." He paused for a moment, then looked down, color flooding his features. "Thanks for the plan of attack."

"Anytime. Now stand back. I'm up and I feel lucky."

I promptly blew my next four throws and ended up losing Game Two by an embarrassing margin. However, I promised to beat Drew's butt without mercy in the third game. And in my quest for that goal, I even got some strikes in the first few frames. I'd just thrown what had hopes of being a good ball when I heard a voice behind me.

"First Daughter, first strike?"

I waited until the ball completed its journey and hit the head pin solidly, resulting in the dreaded seven-ten split. Then I turned around and addressed Michael, who stood there grinning.

"I had three in a row until you showed up. You're bad luck, Cauffman."

"Three strikes and you're out?" he said, laughing.

"Wrong game."

He shrugged. "No matter. I was just checking to see how you were doing."

I shrugged in response. "I'm okay."

"And," he continued, "to see if you wanted to go out with the gang to-night and celebrate."

Drew sidled up next to us. "If anyone should be celebrating, it should be me. Today was the last day of school." He pulled himself to his full height, which was now eye to eye with me and only a couple inches shorter than Michael. "Congratulate me. You're looking at a sophomore now, pal."

"I know. And you carry it off well." Michael grinned at my brother, then reached over and ruffled his hair as if to say, *And I'm still taller than you, even if she isn't.* "That's the reason why we bigger"—he shot me a quick glance, as if to gauge my height, or lack thereof—"make that older and wiser kids want to celebrate. One of our gang is a teacher who is just as glad as you are that school is over and summer has started."

I chose to ignore the implication that I was short. At least I had been described as wiser, and that was entirely acceptable. "I thought Julie said she was going to pick up a slot teaching summer school."

Michael shook his head. "Nope, she's had a change in plans. She said she'd tell us all about it tonight, somewhere over her third beer. So, you coming?"

"I don't know. . . ."

"Oh, come on. You're not going to let this glider business turn you into a hermit, are you?"

"Well, I'd considered it."

"C'mon, Eve. You're tougher than that. That was a once-in-a-lifetime coincidence. It's not going to happen again. You're back on your home territory and you'll be with friends."

Just an hour earlier, I'd been telling myself that I didn't want to go out with Drew and face an uncertain public.

"Well . . ."

He glanced at Drew. "And what sort of example are you setting for the kid here?"

Drew chimed right in on cue. "Yeah, what sort of example?"

I threw my hands in the air and officially gave up. "You're right. I admit it. You're right."

What had happened to change my opinion so quickly?

Had bowling actually given me a little needed release from the tensions of the day?

Oh, yeah. Sure.

Or maybe the prospect of facing the public or, worse, the press was a little easier to swallow when sitting safe within a circle of friends who would provide a nice buffer between me and the rest of the world?

Or was it the fact that I was starting to get some warm, fuzzy feedback from Michael's best friend, Craig Bodansky, whom I found to be funny, smart, polite, and good-looking, and I wanted a chance to further pursue that budding attraction?

Sometimes I tend to overanalyze a situation. No matter what the labyrinthine path my reasoning took, the answer was still the same: "Okay. Count me in."

I plucked the bowling ball from the return, hoisted it, and made a hearty attempt to pick up the seven-ten split.

It rolled. We waited. "Goal!" Michael and Drew said in unison as the ball perfectly bisected the gap between the two remaining pins.

Drew looked at the scoreboard and made a quick calculation. "You might as well give up. I'm so far ahead of you, you can't win even if your last two frames are strikes."

Maybe there was a glimmer of hope that he'd actually earned an A in math this year. Or at least . . . passed. Only his report card would tell the tale. . . .

"I'll leave you to complete your humiliation in private." Michael adjusted the camera bag he had slung over his shoulder. "I have a meeting to photograph. Pick you up around seven?"

"I'll be ready. But I'm hiding in the backseat. I don't want some eager-beaver paparazzo hiding in the bushes with a long lens to get a wretched shot of me and sell it to the gossip rags."

"Deal." Michael shot me a thumbs-up and departed.

I went ahead and finished the game, losing to Drew with my usual lack of grace. But despite the loss, my spirits were lifted considerably by the prospect of going out tonight and pretending I was just like everyone else.

It's an art to maintain a sense of normalcy when you live in the White House. To their credit, my Secret Service detail has grown adept at staying in the background and not overtly cutting in on my fun. They've gotten to know me well enough to realize I try not to put myself in inherently insecure situations, get slobbering drunk, make a play at one of them, or try to duck out on them for fun.

Not like somebody else in the previous administration with the initials Willa McClaren, who thought that giving her agents the slip was great sport and who honed her craft as often as possible.

Of course, that doesn't mean that the agents relax their guard around me or anything remotely similar to that. But I think they secretly appreciate the fact that rather than attend some large, loud concert full of stoned metalheads (where I would stick out just as badly as the agents would), I'm more likely to go to a quiet bar in a good neighborhood with a small circle of friends who respect my need for privacy and good jazz.

"What we appreciate most is a venue with a more easily securable perimeter," Diana said once. Of course, maybe it helps that one of the places that we tend to go to turned out to be a Secret Service agent hangout. At first I worried that I was encroaching on their off-duty territory, but, as Michael, Craig, and the others have said, it's a free country, and the place does have the best buffalo wings in town.

Plus, I have a distinct feeling that none of the agents would openly complain about my choice of location.

At least not to me.

And, I have to admit, I feel extraordinarily safe when we're there.

That said, we ended up going to a completely different watering hole that night, which was just as well. If the press was lying in wait for me, they probably had all our usual haunts under surveillance.

As it turned out, a friend of Craig's had just bought a restaurant-bar combo in the suburbs of Virginia, and Craig persuaded everyone to try the new place for a change. I'm not sure whether he recommended it because of his insight into the journalistic mind, or whether it was just happenstance, but I was grateful for the suggestion. Once there, we realized that our little entourage—agents included—didn't blend into the scenery quite as well as we did in other places.

Because of its location in a shopping center bordering a residential area, this particular restaurant-bar attracted as many families with children as it did groups of adults. But we didn't stick out completely. Since Craig knew the owner, he'd called ahead and had been able to reserve a large table in the back corner of the restaurant portion for us, and a smaller table for the agents.

It's nice having friends who simply accept my limitations and make allowances for them without question or comment.

K. O. Riley's was an interesting place, filled with World War II patriotic decor, from old "Buy War Bonds" posters to covers of popular magazines from the thirties and forties. I couldn't help but laugh when I saw the *Hellcats of the Navy* lobby card, complete with action shots of a young Ronald Reagan and an even younger Nancy Davis. My laughter actually had nothing to do with the Reagans—the Reagan family and the Cooper family had a lot in common, and we had always enjoyed meeting each other whenever we turned up at the same political functions. But as a recent birthday present, a friend of Dad's had created a parody of that memorable image, inserting Dad and Patsy's pictures instead of Ron and Nancy's and changing the title to *Hellcats of the White House.* Dad liked it so much that it had a place of honor on his Oval Office desk.

Once seated, we all ordered the house specialty—the place served huge platters of nachos. As we waited for the food, Harry Mitchell—who was Michael's ex-roommate, an amateur pilot, and an irrepressible flirt— was the first to broach the subject of my recent misadventures.

"Hey, Eve, crash any planes lately?" He elbowed me in the ribs. "They say the best way to forget a fall is to get right back on the horse. Wanna fly with me?" His broad wink gave the words a whole different meaning than their face value implied.

Craig caught him in a "You're a complete idiot" glare. "Shut up, Mitch."

I appreciated Craig's intervention, but Harry wasn't hard to control. I leaned closer to him and said in a clear voice just loud enough for everyone at our table to hear, "Fly with you? I hear you can hardly get off the ground."

Harry colored slightly and everyone else laughed, perhaps a bit too enthusiastically. That was probably a low blow on my part. Harry had always cut a wide swath through the ladies. But I wasn't about to be part of his parade. And at least he'd had the nerve to bring up the subject. I figured that every person at the table had spent time trying to figure out the best tack to take, or whether to bring it up at all.

Was I still upset by the incident?

Yes.

Did I need to continue to wallow in the memory of it?

No way.

I lowered my voice. I didn't want to risk the remote chance that any loitering journalists might overhear me. "Okay, gang, some ground rules." Everyone huddled nearer to listen. "What happened in Colorado was . . . unfortunate and unpleasant. The military says it was merely coincidental, at least as far as I'm concerned. I don't know if that's true or not. I do know I'm not going to forget it anytime soon. But tonight I need an escape back to the ordinary." I glanced over at my two Secret Service escorts for the night, Diana and the massive John Kingston. "As ordinary as my life can be, considering the circumstances. So, can we talk about something—anything—else?"

"You bet." Craig lifted his glass of dark beer. "Here's to maintaining a low-key life in the glare of the public eye. Skoal."

All the others raised their glasses in a toast, echoing a quiet "Skoal!" I looked over and watched Diana lift her glass of tea in a similar salute. I knew she couldn't overhear us, but she knew me well enough to guess the gist of our huddle.

We received and polished off the nachos in record time, lingered over our drinks, and eventually wandered en masse into the bar. There we discovered that, rather than darts or a live band, the big entertainment tonight was a video trivia competition. We commandeered another corner table and a small portable console that allowed us to compete against the other patrons at the bar as well as a national audience in the ongoing trivia contests.

Michael insisted we call ourselves "the First Team" and proceeded to type in our names for all the world to see.

I looked over at Diana and she rolled her eyes. *So much for staying low-key.*

It took about ten seconds for everyone at the bar to notice our group. I figure about half of them recognized me right off, and the rest of them thought I looked familiar enough to either stare or start whispering to their tablemates. I refused to speculate on what they were thinking or say-ing, and why. I just hoped no one was going to yank out a cell phone, call a reporter, and rat me out.

This was my personal, private time, and damn it, I wasn't going to let anyone ruin it for me.

So we ignored the stares. And we had a good time. Not a great time, but a good time. And—guess what? We came in second in the trivia tour-nament. Michael knew where the Mississippi and Missouri Rivers' conflu-ence occurred: Missouri. I figured he'd paid more attention than I had to his geography lessons. As it turned out, he'd grown up in that part of the country. Not surprisingly, I was well read in presidential trivia. Between our various areas of expertise, and thanks to good luck when it came to getting the right questions, we ended up winning a round of drinks as well as ball caps emblazoned with the bar's logo. And when the bar owner asked to take a picture of me, I said yes, but insisted in my best gracious manner that it ought to be a group shot with the whole winning team.

We all proudly sported our new hats as we grinned into the lens.

Craig was our designated driver for the night, and it wasn't until we'd dropped off the others and it was just the two of us left in the car that I realized he'd figured out an almost logical route that didn't make it appear too obvious that I was to be the last delivery.

Smart man.

Cute, too.

He pulled up to the South Portico, stopped the car, and dutifully trot-ted around the front bumper in order to open my door for me.

Diana and John pulled behind us and climbed out of their car, but Diana demonstrated her usual sense of propriety and quietly shifted so that she and John stood more in the shadows than in the light. They could still see me, but I didn't feel that in my private moment I was being observed like a lab rat about to do something interesting. Craig and I had the luxury to pretend for a moment or two that we were truly alone.

Craig tilted his head slightly. "Did you achieve the level of escape you needed to feel back to normal?"

"Define normal." I laughed, then added, "I do feel better. Thanks."

"No, thank you, for allowing me to offer some support to a friend."

At first I thought he meant his buddy, the new owner of the bar. Then

I realized he meant me. I could feel the heat rise in my face and wondered if the darkness successfully hid the fact that I was blushing.

Blushing furiously.

He continued, oblivious of my state of confusion. "I was worried about you, but it looks like you're handling this well." He reached out and took my hand. "I don't want you to spend all your time worrying that something bad is going to happen to you."

What was I supposed to say? *Me, either?* Something about the blood rushing to certain parts of my body was robbing me of my usual ability to engage others in sparkling conversation.

So I did the next best thing.

I kissed him.

Now, lest you think I was the aggressor, taking advantage of some poor, unwilling male, allow me to assure you that Craig met me halfway. Maybe even more than halfway. In any case, it was apparent that the thought of kissing me had crossed his mind. It was a good kiss—long, sweet, and definitely not like kissing either of my brothers.

Far from it.

When we finally broke apart, he shot me a devastating grin, then winked. "I had a great time, Eve. Good night."

"Me, too. Good night, Craig."

He walked around the front of his car and opened the door, giving Diana and John a discreet wave of acknowledgment and maybe thanks for giving us a bit of privacy.

Brilliant conversationalist that I am, the only thing I could think to say was "Drive carefully."

"I will." He paused. "Sweet dreams?"

"Sweet dreams," I echoed, hoping that tonight's potentially sweet dreams would replace last night's sour nightmares.

I took the elevator to the third floor, pausing to ask the agent if my father was in. "Yes, ma'am." The young man added, "I believe it's an all-star night."

Unfortunately, all-star nights have nothing to do with Hollywood. (I'm still waiting for George Clooney to personally deliver his next blockbuster movie for an exclusive White House showing. So far, no show . . .)

Dad's an amateur astronomer. All-star night, in current White House parlance, meant he was on the roof with his telescope. Dad turns to the stars primarily for two reasons—either he's very happy or he's very upset.

I was betting on the latter. . . .

It was a temptation to go straight to bed. After all, I'd had a couple of drinks. Even on a full stomach, alcohol makes me sleepy. But I'm a dutiful daughter, and I know it's better to get things out in the open rather than let things fester.

So much for my happy buzz. . . .

I trudged down the hallway to the solarium and through the French doors leading to the roof porch. If I was lucky, something else had happened in the world to upset Dad, and he was stewing over it rather than my misadventures. Then again, he'd been known to start out angry at the beginning of an all-star night and something about viewing the vastness of the universe would mellow him out. If I was lucky, maybe he'd already reached the growing-mellow stage.

I stepped out onto the roof, and sure enough, he had the telescope set up and was gazing at the wonders of the skies.

"Hi, Dad," I said softly.

He didn't even break away from the eyepiece. "Oh, you're home, Eve. Have a good time?"

So far, I couldn't figure out whether he was happy, was angry, or had passed into the mellow stage. "Pretty good."

He continued looking through the telescope. "C'mere." He motioned in my general direction. "Take a look at this."

Dutiful daughters—whether they're First Daughters or otherwise— know to always look through the telescope and show the appropriate amount of curiosity and appreciation. No matter what unintelligible blob appears there. I'd learned that when I was still in diapers.

I crossed the roof and stood next to him, bending down to look in the eyepiece he'd vacated. I was rewarded with a stunning view of a field of stars. It was beautiful—even if I didn't know why the heck it was special. "Okay, so exactly what am I looking for?"

"Dead center," he instructed. "A comet. It's hard to see because of the urban light clutter." He sighed. "Downtown D.C. is *not* the best place to view the stars."

I spotted the slight cloud trailing behind one of the stars. "Cool," I said.

"No, it's boring to you. I realize that." His laugh was small, but sincere. "But what will be cool, even for you, is the solar eclipse on the thirty-first of this month." He sighed. "Only problem is that the optimal place to view it will be the far North Atlantic. I don't think that the President can wangle a way to go to Iceland just to see a solar eclipse. The taxpayers would probably complain if I did too much of that."

The fact that Dad was chatting so amiably about astronomy was a very good sign. But just when I decided that I was safe, that he'd reached the mellow stage, he suddenly changed subjects.

"I missed you at dinner. Drew said you were going out with Michael and his friends."

"Yeah. We went to a place off the Beltway in the Virginia suburbs. It was nice—you'd like it. But the best part is that I'm finally convinced that they're not just Michael's friends. They've become mine as well."

That elicited a paternal smile. "I'm glad, Eve. I was afraid that by uprooting you and sticking you here, I'd make you lose all contact with your old friends and not give you a chance to make new ones." He paused. "But I was surprised you decided to go out." He caught me with the full power of his stare. "After our discussion, that is."

Uh-oh. The look on Dad's face . . . I swallowed hard. "I *had* to go out," I whispered. "I had to prove to myself that it was safe. That nothing would happen."

Dad remained silent, a useful technique for parents who want their child to spill his guts. It works beautifully on Drew, and I guess it still works on me.

I sighed. "If I hide here, then I'm admitting that I'm afraid and that I think the glider crash was no accident. And if I believe that, then I have to accept that someone died in my place. I refuse to do that." I tried to draw in a deep breath, but something—guilt?—clogged my efforts. "Call it self-protection. Call it denial. But until we get the facts, I can't allow myself to believe I was anybody's intended target, and that because of that, someone innocent died instead. I don't know how I could ever face, much less accept, that sort of guilt."

Dad looked me straight in the eyes. "It wouldn't be your fault. It'd be mine. I'd be the reason why you ever became anyone's target. So the ultimate blame would definitely be mine."

I leaned forward and kissed his cheek. "Good try, but I won't accept that. If someone was angry with your politics, why in the world would he decide to take it out on me?"

"Because getting to you would be a far more devastating blow to me than getting to me. I'd be destroyed, and yet still be alive to feel the pain of my destruction. And there's the tactical angle. It's probably a bit easier to get to you than to me." He pretended to glance down over the edge of the railing. "Eve, it's all I can do to not brick up the windows, dig a moat around the house, and install a drawbridge." He reached over and playfully tugged at a strand of my hair. "Rapunzel, Rapunzel . . ."

I managed to laugh, finding some humor in the mental image he'd created. "Mr. Wallerston might have a thing or two to say about unauthorized digging on the White House grounds."

"I suspect so." Dad remained quiet for several moments, then finally sighed. "But you can't blame me for being overprotective. From the day I took the oath of office, I knew, logically, even emotionally, that my life was, is, and always will be in danger. But it's even worse to think that I've placed you, Drew, and Patsy in a similarly tenuous position. I've been trying to deal with those fears the best way I can."

"I understand your problem," I said. "Danger's a part of your job. I know that. I've always accepted that. I guess that you're finally experiencing the same sort of fear that I've had to deal with since the day you told me you were going to run for the presidency. I really don't like knowing you're a constant target. Knowing that four other Presidents have died in office, and that there have been assassination attempts on every man who has held the office for the past forty years. How's it feel to have the shoe on the other foot?"

It was an unanswerable question. We could do little else but hug each other, finding reassurance and comfort in touch. And there was a bit more comfort in the thought that being aware of the dangers was the first step toward surviving them. After we broke apart, Dad turned his attention back to his telescope. "I understand that an old friend of yours came by today."

I managed to take the deep breath I couldn't earlier. I knew Dad wasn't being nosy; it's his business to know the comings and goings at the White House. I suspected he already knew who and why, and simply wanted to give me a chance to tell him. It was another variation on the "parent stays silent in hopes child tells all" gambit. Make a leading statement and stand back.

I cooperated. "Yeah. Megan Lassiter came by. I knew her in Denver. As it turns out, Ashley McCurdy—the girl who died in the glider—was Megan's half sister."

"Poor girl."

I wasn't sure which girl he meant. Both, probably. I continued. "Megan wanted reassurance from me that her family would be kept in the loop, no matter what the investigators find."

"That sounds like a reasonable request." He paused to stroke his chin. The gesture verged on looking staged. "But I'm not sure why she came to you, Eve. She's in the military, isn't she? There's a chain of command she can follow for getting information, especially since she's a member of the victim's family."

I shrugged. "She knows me. It was easier to start closer to the top. Maybe even with the source of the problem."

"Oh." It was a single word, but the message behind it was much more complicated.

He knew. And he knew I knew.

Dad continued to fiddle with his telescope, looking through the eyepiece and making small adjustments. "You know I feel guilty."

I thought we'd already covered this territory. I decided to pull the same technique he'd used earlier. I waited quietly for him to continue, but all I heard was the answering murmur of traffic noises from the streets beyond. In the distance, we both heard the faint echo of an ambulance siren.

He won the technique war.

I broke down and prompted him with a "Guilty about what?"

After a moment more of silence, he abandoned the stars and turned his full attention to me. "All kinds of things. For being President. For making you go in the first place. For playing the Daddy card and making you come home instead of continuing with your vacation plans. I know you're an adult. I do have faith in your ability to decide for yourself. You have the right to make up your own mind and not have your plans be overridden by an overly protective father."

I stepped closer and gave him a hug. "You didn't make me come

home. You advised me that you'd feel better if I did. There's a big difference between being asked and being ordered. At the time, I thought it was
a very clever move on your part."

"And now?"

I tried not to sigh too loudly. "I think you may have been right. I'd like
to get away for a while, but it looks like there are no vacations in my
immediate future. And I'm okay with that."

He stepped back, his hands resting on my shoulders. He smiled, and I
noticed a twinkle in his eyes that I hadn't seen in several days. "What
about taking a business trip with your aunt next week?"

"Really? Where?"

"San Antonio. Just imagine it—margaritas on the Riverwalk, all that
great Mexican food, and maybe a visit to a working ranch. Sounds like
fun, eh? Like a real vacation?"

The list was missing one key element. "And how many speeches?"

"For you, absolutely none. For Patsy, a big one." He winked at me.
"It'll be worth it. Your aunt wants to visit an old friend—one of the male
persuasion—and I think she'd like you along to act as a chaperone. I know
I'd feel better if you went."

I raised an eyebrow. "A chaperone? That's silly. This isn't the Middle
Ages. And it's not like she's a kid." The light slowly dawned. "Or are *you*
the one asking me to go?"

"Not me." Dad drew a solemn cross over his heart. "'Ask Eve if she'll
go with me.' Those were her exact words." He leaned closer, as if afraid
that Patsy, one floor down, would hear him. "I think she's a little apprehensive about seeing the old friend again. It's been a while since she's seen
him, and circumstances have changed. She said she'd be more comfortable if you were there. I really think she wants you to be a buffer. Apparently, they used to have *something*."

"Something . . . Something?" I repeated. "I don't remember her talking about any old beaux. So, who's the certain gentleman?"

He gave me his best inscrutable look. "Just someone she knew a long
time ago. I'll let her tell you all the details. You know, woman to woman."
Dad's grin was decidedly unpresidential. "So you'll agree to go?"

I didn't try to hide the second sigh.

"Why not? Maybe there are no journalists in San Antonio."

CHAPTER SIX

WASHINGTON POST: "THE RELIABLE SOURCE"

Only a day after her harrowing glider ride in Colorado, presidential offspring Eve Cooper was spotted making merry with a group of friends in a suburban Virginia bar. Evidently, her recent brush with death left her throat drier than usual.

Reporters . . . So my little voyage into a normal life had been observed after all. It was already on the news wires mere hours later. And not in a nice way, either. "Throat drier than usual." I stared at the words on my computer screen. I'd barely had enough to drink to even feel it—and I rarely drank at all. No point denying it—that'd make it look even worse. So much for scanning the news feeds to make myself feel better before I went to sleep. I shut down the paper's Web site. Before I crawled into bed, I decided I had enough energy left to check my E-mail. I sorted through various notes from friends, most of which were of the "Are you all right?" variety. Smack in the middle of it all was a note from slacker@suspense.net with the innocuous subject tag "for your information." I didn't recognize the address and wondered if it was spam or if maybe Drew was playing a trick on me as I clicked on it.

Luckily, Charlie knows better.

When I opened the E-mail, my virus-protection software started going into overdrive, flashing warnings that the attachment was infected, yada, yada, yada. . . .

But it was the text in the E-mail that shocked me far worse than the thought of a mere computer virus.

"DIE FIRST BITCH. NO MORE MISSES."

My throat threatened to close. My hands shook. Seybold had said that nobody had "owned up" to the glider's crash—it was a cornerstone of the current "This has nothing to do with Eve" theory of the crash. It appeared that had just changed, big-time. Was this proof that the crash was sabotage, or was someone simply trying to lay false claim to the accident just to stir up waters that were already troubled? People do things like that.

But why include an infected attachment?

Was it supposed to warn me, then erase itself so it couldn't be tracked? Well, if that was the case, then I had a big surprise for whoever had sent it. Evidently he or she didn't realize that I had a direct pipeline to one of the finest software geniuses on our end of the U. S. of A. My brother Charlie had made sure all of the family computers had the very best protection software available to man or machine—and it updated nightly.

With only a few keystrokes, I forwarded Charlie the E-mail, along with a warning that it was infected, and a note stating that it might have something to do with the glider crash. After a moment's hesitation to think, I also forwarded the E-mail, though without the attachment, to Peter Seybold's office. I burned him a copy of the attachment on a CD. I'd deliver it in person. The last thing I wanted to be accused of was inadvertently corrupting or crashing the computers in his office. God only knew what sort of sensitive stuff a virus could wipe out or scramble or send to an unauthorized address if it got into the White House system.

Once both of the E-mails were sent, I allowed myself to breathe. If anyone could trace something electronic back to its sender, it was Charlie. And the Secret Service would take this sort of threat seriously and take the appropriate actions.

But one thing really bothered me. How in the world had the sender gotten my very private E-mail address? The most likely answer was a bit unsettling.

It might be someone I knew. . . .

The next morning, bright and early, I hand delivered the CD-R to Peter Seybold. Too bright and too early, but I saw no need to stay in bed when I wasn't getting much sleep anyway.

So much for the sweet dreams Craig had wished me. Instead, I'd fought against nightmares all night long. But I guess, considering my last-minute-before-bedtime message, that's understandable. . . .

Besides wanting to sic Seybold on the security breach and subsequent threat, I had another reason to talk to him.

Megan . . .

He stood when I entered the room, something he'd never done before. His body language carried a bit less censure than usual.

Sympathy? *From him?* Perish the thought.

"Ah, Eve. I was about to call you," he said in his usual somber tone. "I read the E-mail you forwarded me. As you might expect, I find the whole situation highly disturbing."

"Tell me about it." I handed him the disk. "Here's the file that was attached to the note. Thanks to Charlie, my computer's fine. His antivirus program immediately recognized that the E-mail was infected and kept it from activating. The only reason I didn't forward the infected file to you along with the E-mail is that, though I have nothing against government-issued computers, I was afraid you might not have the same level of protection on your system that I have on mine. Budget constraints and all that. It pays to have a computer geek in the family."

Seybold contemplated the disk, then placed it gingerly on the center of his blotter, as if its infection might be communicable by touch alone. "Thank you. I appreciate that you decided to play to the side of caution."

"Me? Cautious? Try scared out of my shorts." My knees threatened to buckle but I refused to sit down. "You realize the implications here, don't you? 'No more misses' pretty much implies that someone considered that the glider crash was a failure. That they missed." I leaned forward. "Missed me."

"That's one interpretation," Seybold said, glancing at the CD.

Before, I was scared. Now I was getting just plain mad. "I'm glad you can be so cavalier with my safety."

He stiffened—if that was even possible considering how stiff he is on a normal basis. "I'm not being cavalier at all, Eve. The safety of the presidential family is second only to that of the President himself, as far as the Secret Service is concerned. We've increased all our security measures for all members of your family, you included."

I calmed down, some. After all, I try not to shoot the messenger. "I'm sorry. I know you're doing your best and that your best is awfully good. It's just that this is really bothering me. And we don't seem to be getting to the bottom of it."

"I understand. Apology accepted. We're all under additional pressure, you included. Have you mentioned this threat to your father yet?"

I shook my head. "Dad had a breakfast meeting, so I haven't had a chance to talk to him. But I did forward the whole thing to Charlie because I figure he's in the best position to help unravel what it is and where it came from. After all, it's his company's job to figure out what a virus does and how to build proper defenses against it. And since he's family, it wasn't like I was airing any laundry—dirty or otherwise—out in the open."

"That was a smart idea."

I swear I'd never heard him say that exact phrase in reference to me, much less come close to expressing such open support. I gaped at him. He seemed taken aback by my reaction.

"What's wrong?" He glanced over his shoulder as if expecting to discover the source of my attention hiding behind him.

"Who are you, and what have you done with the real Peter Seybold?" I demanded.

"Very amusing." He dropped into his high-backed leather chair. "Of course, I'll need a list of those people who have your E-mail address in order to properly investigate this situation."

"No." I added a silent, *Hell, no.*

He looked up, obviously shocked at my negative answer. "Pardon?"

So much for our momentary truce. "You heard me. No. My address book is private information, and it'll remain private."

"Don't misunderstand the reason behind my request. We don't think that one of *your* friends sent the E-mail, but it's quite possible someone may have given your address to someone else, quite innocently, or perhaps they inadvertently leaked the contact info without realizing it through a cc field or such. We merely want to investigate all of those possibilities."

I gave him my best "Drop dead" stare. "Then I'll send a broadcast mail and ask them myself. But I refuse to turn over my address book to you or anyone else. I can't expect my friends to value my privacy if I don't value theirs."

"I don't believe any of your friends are in situations quite as visible as yours. Or potentially as sensitive."

I remained stoically silent. But my body language screamed, *No way!*

Seybold leaned back in his chair and released a sigh that smacked of displeasure. "You don't make this easy for us, you know."

"I'm not trying to complicate an already complicated situation." I fought the instinct to start pacing in front of his desk. "And I'm not trying to stop you from doing your job. But we're talking about the last avenue of real privacy I have left in this fishbowl life of mine. Of ours," I corrected, feeling as if I were speaking for two of the three Cooper siblings.

I took one step closer to his desk, placed my palms on the smooth wood, and leaned toward him until we were parallel again. "Even you have to admit I've been very cooperative—allowing your security issues to rule my life, to determine where I go and when. And I suppose I don't have to remind you that, unlike some other First Kids who used to live here, I don't make it hard for you and yours to keep tabs on me."

Usually I'm the one who wants to avoid any comparison between my immediate predecessor, Willa McClaren, and myself, but every now and again I'm willing to use the contrast to my advantage.

After all, any comparison with Willa tends to make me come across like Miss Congeniality.

Seybold looked as if he were contemplating and maybe even categorizing the similarities between Willa and me. He finally released another annoyed sigh. "Point well taken."

Evidently, I'd pulled ahead of Willa in the Cooperation Poll.

He paused, then almost brightened as a thought struck him. "What about your brother, Charles? Would you feel comfortable letting him pursue this sort of investigation on our behalf as well as yours?"

Charlie? I took a moment to mull it over. Of course I trusted my brother. But wouldn't it be the same sort of compromise of my ethics to turn over my address book to anyone, even my own brother?

I had to draw a line in the sand.

I straightened to my full height. "I'll gladly work with Charlie, but I won't turn over the address book to him, or anyone else for that matter. I'll be glad to initiate the contact with my friends myself, and then I'll be equally glad to turn over any leads I receive to him or you or whoever ends up handling that part of the investigation. But my address book will remain private, no matter what."

Then he threw down his trump card, minus any triumphant smile. "I could force you. . . ." He stared at me and I stared back. "I could get a subpoena. . . ." More staring. Then Seybold remained quiet for an inordinately long time. "I've already spoken with your brother this morning," he said. "Charlie suggested practically the same thing to me that you just did—and he seems to think that your friends will be more honest with you than they would be with me. I hate to admit it, but he has a point."

I swear, if there hadn't been a security issue involved, I would probably have turned around and walked out right then and there. I don't like people who do end runs around me.

Then again, wasn't stomping out in a rage something that Willa would have done? I suppressed a sigh of exasperation (or was it frustration?) and stood my ground in silence.

"Okay. No subpoena." He stood, then walked around the end of his desk and perched near me in a vain attempt to make this little talk seem more informal. "So, despite the sensitive and private nature of this situation, I have no problem acknowledging your brother's expertise in this special field and am willing to accept his offer to work with our office as an outside computer expert, but to do it on your terms. I know you will cooperate with him to your fullest ability so that we can discover the identity of the person who sent you this E-mail. Once the sender is identified, we can determine the level of threat he or she might have, and take appropriate actions."

As God is my witness, Seybold's just as stuffy as he sounds. Mr. Speechmaker. I don't know if he's that way with everyone, or whether I just bring it out in him. I almost think he talks to me like that on purpose because he knows it weirds me out completely.

Go figure. . . .

But the important thing to realize was that we both accepted the fact that this investigation would be conducted on my terms. Essentially, I'd stood my ground and won the battle. As for the war, I had a feeling it would go on for the remainder of Dad's four-year term and—fingers crossed—the next four after that. However, I also had a feeling that no matter how long Dad was in office, Peter Seybold and I would always remain on opposite sides of the desk.

But despite that confrontational image, right now the two of us stood together in the middle of the room, our tentative truce holding. We even shook hands as if we hadn't butted heads only a few moments ago.

Ah, politics . . .

But as I tried to leave, Seybold motioned for me to stay. "There's one more thing."

"What?" I was starting to get really tired of this yo-yo conversation.

"It's a rather sensitive question, and I don't want you to think that I'm prying."

He paused as if wanting my consent.

"So?"

"Are you sure you don't have any past relationships that might have dissolved into something unpleasant, resulting in a threat such as this? After all, it did come through on your private E-mail."

Rather than fire back, I stopped to think. Really. I thought back over all the serious relationships I'd had in my life.

We won't dwell on the fact that I could count them on one hand.

"Honestly? I can't think of a soul who would do something like this. My few breakups have all been pretty low-key."

"What about new relationships?" He colored slightly, something I thought I'd never see in a million years. "I understand that you went out last night on a group event, but that you came home . . ." His voice trailed off.

I said it for him. "With one guy. For the first time since I moved to the White House." I shrugged. "And we kissed. For the first time. There's a first time for everything."

"And this gentleman . . . ?"

"Craig Bodansky. He's a close friend of Michael Cauffman, who I'm sure will vouch for him."

Seybold nodded. "I'm sure Mr. Cauffman will." He paused, then glanced down at his shoes for a moment before looking me straight in the eyes. "Eve, I don't intend to meddle with your private life—"

I finished his sentence for him. "Any more than you have to. I understand."

After a few more formalities, I was finally able to say good-bye to Peter Seybold, for the moment, anyway.

As soon as I escaped his office, I practically broke into a run. The one thing I wanted to do . . . that I *had* to do before Seybold could . . . was tell Dad exactly what was going on. It needed to come from me, so he could be assured that I took my safety seriously, but that I didn't believe that the E-mail I'd gotten was a true threat.

Now . . . if I could only believe it myself.

As I trotted toward the Oval Office, I tried to line up the facts as I knew them. My E-mail address was a fairly new one—a change I'd made around two months earlier, when the assortment of spam that landed in my old address started filling up with get-rich-quick schemes "refinance your home" messages and so on. None of the spam had ever seemed to be aimed strictly at me—for example, I'm hardly a prime candidate for Internet-supplied Viagra—nor had the volume changed once Dad became a public figure. I just felt uncomfortable with the content and I really thought that the spam conglomeration had been coincidental—my E-mail address had just ended up on the wrong mailing list somehow, somewhere. Most everybody else I knew had had the same complaint about their E-mail's spam content at some time or other.

Of course, it wouldn't have taken a genius to figure out that my old E-mail address, evecooper@prodigy.net, might have actually gone to the real, somewhat famous Eve Cooper at the White House. I'd hated losing such an easy-to-remember address. I'd had it for a while—years, in fact—since long before Dad's political aspirations had moved me from Denver to D.C.

So far, my new address had remained a closely guarded state secret, with only my innermost circle of friends privy to it. Up to now I'd never received a single piece of spam at that new address, or any messages from strangers.

So maybe it was a fluke. Maybe someone had sent the same threatening E-mail to every mailbox of every major Internet service provider that serves the D.C. area, and it happened to land in my mailbox at the same time it landed in several thousand others, coincidentally right about the time I was dealing with the fallout from a glider crash.

Yeah. I know. Lame.

But by the time I reached Dad's office, I'd almost convinced myself a widespread E-mail was a possible scenario. After all, the message was rather vague. Thanks to the lack of proper punctuation, it was even ambiguous. The first line could have substantially different meanings: "DIE, FIRST BITCH" versus "DIE FIRST, BITCH."

And "NO MORE MISSES"? Was that "misses" as in "hit or miss" or "misses" as in more than one "Miss So-and-So"?

As Aunt Patsy always says, rationalization is its own art form. . . .

Dad's secretary, Jeanne Seals, was on the phone when I hit the outer office. She gave me a fleeting smile of greeting and a silent gesture that said *Can you hang on for just a minute while I finish dealing with this fill-in-the-blank bureaucrat?*

A moment later, she hung up the phone and turned to me. "Good morning, Eve. How are you doing?"

Everyone had been asking me that for the last few days, from the ushers to the aides. Normally, these little inquiries would be a simple matter of White House types being well mannered and solicitous of this term's occupants, but after my recent misadventures, I was starting to wonder if the words reflected a higher level of concern for my safety.

"Pretty well," I said, not quite sure whether I was lying or not. I didn't see any need to prolong the pleasantries. "Is Dad free?"

She glanced to the inner office door. "He and Vice President O'Sullivan are in a meeting." She shifted her attention to the clock on her desk. "Let me check and see if they're finished. I suspect they are—they've been in there for a while."

As Dad's Vice President, Joseph O'Sullivan was supposed to bring certain elements to the political ticket to complement Dad's talents. Whereas Dad was considered a young President, being only in his early fifties, O'Sullivan was a robust seventy-six. Dad didn't come from a multigenerational political family, but O'Sullivan's roots were in New England, and screamed of old school, old family, and old politics. He was supposed to balance Dad's fresh new political viewpoint with a more stable, old-fashioned, old-party one. More than one political expert would tell you that the combination of O'Sullivan's qualities and Dad's own unique assortment of talents was what had put Dad into office.

In some very exclusive political circles, Mr. O'Sullivan, his wife, and their four strapping sons—Joe junior, Francis, Patrick, and Quinn—were touted as more suitable presidential material than we lowly Coopers, with our plebian tastes and mid-American values.

We were hamburger versus their filet mignon.

But, as we all know, especially in the arena of politics, public persona is frequently different from private reality.

I suppose it was a testament to the old-school code of brotherhood and silence that no one had publicly discussed Vice President O'Sullivan's many vices. For example, genetics ran strong, and similarly, in the males of the O'Sullivan clan—all the VP's sons looked very much alike, and very like their father. I'd noted immediately that the Vice President had at least two secretaries with strapping young sons who bore an eerie resemblance to the O'Sullivan boys. I had a pretty strong suspicion why that was the case. Out of respect for my father's running mate, I'd kept quiet about it.

O'Sullivan didn't return the favor. The Vice President was often critical in public because alcohol was sometimes served in the Cooper White House, at both official and unofficial functions. Dad likes an occasional glass of wine. So do I. So do our guests. But we're talking about very light social drinking here. I'll admit that I've never seen Vice President O'Sullivan drink alcohol, but I couldn't say that about his four boys. O'Sullivan had quietly dropped his vehement temperance stance recently after two of his sons—the underage twins Patrick and Quinn—had been arrested in a fight that broke out at their college watering hole over an unpaid bar tab.

I don't know which was more interesting—that the damage bill for the bar totaled only $150 (that said a whole lot about the engineering tolerances of modern college bar furnishings), or that the bar tab itself was almost twice that amount (at college prices, that's a whole *lot* of beer).

Frat boys . . . They learn so much at those exclusive private colleges.

In the press conference that followed the arrests, O'Sullivan blamed his sons' bad judgment on "youthful ignorance." He stopped just short of offering the classic "Boys will be boys" defense. Even he, doting parent that he is, figured the American public wouldn't buy that.

I know Mrs. O'Sullivan didn't buy it for one moment. Thanks to their mom, the boys were still paying for their "youthful ignorance." I doubted they'd drink again for a decade.

My opinion of Mrs. O'Sullivan was very different from my opinion of her husband.

I didn't think there were women like her anymore. In private, she was a sparkling, vibrant woman with elegant tastes, a wicked sense of humor, and an astounding intellect. Patsy and I had both been surprised and pleased when we had a chance to sit down with her. Eventually we broke through that outer shell of hers and got to know the real person inside. But in the public eye, Constance O'Sullivan was merely the lesser half of their old family union, a pale extension of her husband—a man who possessed only half her taste, a third of her personality, and a tenth of her intelligence. And what really got to me was that she seemed quite content to hide her light under a bushel, to remain in the background, concealing her true talents behind frumpy clothes, bad hair, and an unwillingness to speak in public.

Such a waste of true talent . . .

The only real saving grace of the political situation, as far as I could tell, was that although Joseph O'Sullivan was no great intellect, he was comfortable on camera, had undeniable presence, exuded authority, and knew how to make his wife's words sound like his own. And as long as he continued to repeat what his wife told him to say and didn't try to stray from the script, the world would view him as a highly effective politician rather than a highly talented actor. And his wife had enough good political sense for the both of them.

I suppose it's quite telling to say that Dad had started having more meetings with Mrs. O'Sullivan than with her husband. He quickly recognized and appreciated the source of the O'Sullivans' legendary strength, intelligence, and insight, and he wasn't afraid to acknowledge it in private so as to better utilize it in public.

But today it was just Dad and Mr. O'Sullivan. All of us, Jeanne and I included, knew that I wouldn't be interrupting anything of earth-shattering importance.

"Yes, Mr. President," Jeanne was saying into the phone. "I'll send her right in." She waved me toward the door. "Your dad says they're through and just shooting the breeze now."

When I walked into the Oval Office I was hit, as I always am, with the sudden and undeniable fact that my very own father was President of the United States. Now, I'm not stupid and this isn't a case where I forget this rather basic fact that affects every facet of my life. But there's just something about that rug with the presidential seal on it that always makes me stop for a moment in order to digest the reality of it all.

But I didn't have time to admire any rugs that morning. When I walked into the office, Dad was sitting on the couch that faces the door. He rose first.

He's got good manners, my dad does. Mr. O'Sullivan, seated on the opposite couch, turned around, recognized me, and got to his feet a few seconds later. His action was a case of manners at work as well, but I had a feeling his movement had more to do with Dad's standing than with acknowledging me.

I could have been wrong. With the exception of my father, I was having a real problem today dealing with male authority figures. . . .

"Good morning, doll." Dad stepped over briskly and planted a kiss on my cheek. "I really missed having breakfast with you this morning."

"It's just as well. I had a bad night and really wasn't fit for company," I offered.

Concern creased his face. "But I thought you had a good time with your friends last night."

"I did." I swallowed hard. "But something happened afterward. Once I got home. I'll tell you about it in private."

I couldn't help it. I glanced at Mr. O'Sullivan, hoping he'd get the message that this was something personal and that perhaps he ought to leave and let us have some face time alone. He remained standing, listening to us with undisguised interest.

Some people just can't take a hint.

Dad took my hand and looked me straight in the eye. "Honey?"

He didn't need a verbal response from me. Thanks to years of practice, the man could read me like a book. He understood with uncanny accuracy the look on my face. He turned to his Vice President. "Joe, I think I need to speak to my daughter privately."

Joseph O'Sullivan stared blankly at the two of us; then realization slowly dawned. "Oh. Yeah. Absolutely. We're through anyway." He moved woodenly toward the door. "I'll call you later if I receive any more details on"—he looked suddenly uncomfortable—"that certain problem."

"Thanks, Joe."

"Good to see you again, Evelyn."

I smiled nicely, trying not to wince at the use of my full name. Nobody who has any inkling of perception calls me Evelyn.

As soon as the door closed, Dad dropped to the couch and patted the cushion for me to join him. "Okay, Eve, what's wrong?"

I sat. After a few false starts, I blurted out the entire story about the E-mail. After I finished, Dad remained on the couch, not saying a word.

I felt compelled to fill the silence. "I sent everything to Charlie. Who knows that stuff better than him? And I made sure Mr. Seybold knows all about it. He has a copy of the E-mail and the infected file. We'll get to the bottom of it."

Some of the tension drained from his face. "I'm glad you're taking this seriously. I know I am."

"Seriously, yes, but I'm not completely convinced it's a legitimate threat. It's a bit . . ." I took a moment to search for the right word. "Theatrical," I declared. "It's just a little too theatrical to be real."

Dad nodded. "It feels like someone jumping on the virtual bandwagon, huh?" He stood and began to pace the floor. "So what's the next step? Do you hide? Do you thumb your nose at whoever did this? Do you simply go about your life as always? Or what?"

I contemplated my options. As much as a bit of nose thumbing would make me feel better, I knew I needed to make a more mature decision. "I'll take what's behind Door Number Three. Life goes on. I keep going as planned."

He reached over and kissed my forehead. "Good decision. That means you'll still go to San Antonio with Patsy?"

"Yes, sir." I stared out the windows into the Rose Garden, which was in full bloom. I was hit by a sudden urge to go outside and bask in the sunlight. You never know how many sunlit days you'll have to enjoy in your lifetime.

Maybe I *would* do some controlled nose thumbing. *(You can take your threats and shove them. . . . I'm going outside and I'm going to enjoy it.)*

I turned back to my father. "Are you okay with me going?"

"Yes," he said with resolution. "And no," he added with equal strength. He reached over and grabbed my hand. "Yes, I think it's important to get out and prove that you're not afraid of a few vague threats. And no, as your father, I'd just as soon know where you are at all times and be sure that you're completely safe. The idea of locking you up in a tower is starting to look good again. But"—he squeezed my hand—"you were about five years old when I accepted the fact that I couldn't wrap you in cotton and stick you on a shelf, no matter how much I wanted to. I think I gave up that illusion around the time when you jumped off your grandmother's shed with an umbrella, trying to emulate Mary Poppins."

Ouch. "You'll never let me forget that story, will you?"

He smiled. "Never. That's when I learned that my fragile little daughter was made of steel, and when you learned that a spoonful of sugar can only hide part of the medicine's bad taste." He pulled my hand up and gave it a quick kiss. "You go. You have a good time. But stay smart. Stay safe."

I gave him a hug. "Yes, sir."

After I walked out, I saw the Vice President lingering in the outer office. As soon as I stepped out, he rushed in, his voice booming: "Elliot, I just had an idea. . . ."

I glanced at Jeanne, who waited until he was out of sight before shaking her head. "He came up with the idea after talking to his wife."

We shared a *And we know who the brains are in that partnership* look.

But it started me thinking. Mrs. O'Sullivan had four sons around my age, all of whom had recently been in the public eye. Had any of them received threats, physical or otherwise? I could barely wait until I got back to my room to call her.

"Eve, darlin'," she said. "I've been wanting to talk you and see how you were doin', but I didn't want to intrude."

Mrs. O'Sullivan's husband might be a Bostonian with public virtues and private vices, but she was a steel magnolia from Atlanta who was far more than she seemed on the surface. I figured it proved that opposites attract.

"I'm fine, Mrs. O'Sullivan. Really."

"Now, sweetheart, I've told you a million times—Mrs. O'Sullivan is a ninety-three-year-old blue-haired harridan who is driving her nursing-home staff absolutely bonkers. I mean it when I say I want you to call me Connie."

I guess some habits are hard to break. "Yes, ma'am." I continued, pushing aside my reluctance. "If I may . . . uh . . . Connie, I have a rather . . . odd question to ask."

"Child, you know you can ask me anything," she said with the sort of warmth that would instill faith in a total stranger.

But she was no stranger. In the last few months, I'd gotten to know her pretty well, and I realized that her sense of compassion wasn't cosmetic. So I simply blurted out what I wanted. "Have any of your sons received any odd E-mails or anything you might consider . . . a threat . . . lately?"

There was a moment of silence; then she said in a low voice, "Eve . . . I'd be the last one to know. The older the boys get, the more private and the less . . . predictable they become. I tell myself it's college." She sighed. "So far, they haven't said anything to me about any threats beyond the usual fraternity high jinks." She hesitated. "This is about that glider crash, right? Do your agents think it might have been deliberate?"

"They don't know yet. But things . . . aren't looking too good."

"I'm so sorry, sweetheart. Listen, I'll talk to each of the boys today. If I learn anything, I'll call you immediately."

"Thank you, Mrs. O'Sul . . . er . . . Connie."

"No, darling," she said. "Thank you. I appreciate the heads-up. If it's happenin' to you, my boys could be next. Besides, it's always nice for a mother to have a legitimate reason to pry into her boys' lives and see if she can't talk some sense into them. Boys are so headstrong, but I suspect you know that just as well as I do. You just take care of yourself, Eve. Be smart, be careful, and don't take any unnecessary chances. Your father, your aunt, and your brothers need you more than you'll ever know."

And vice versa.

CHAPTER SEVEN

SAN ANTONIO EXPRESS-NEWS

AIR FORCE VILLAGE DEDICATES NEW WING

First Lady Patricia Davidson will cut the ribbon today at the dedication ceremonies for the new Lorilee Cosby Buckley Memorial Wing at the Air Force Village. The wing represents Phase Four of the Village's "Freedom House" program, part of the center's Alzheimer's Care and Research Center Foundation. The ceremony begins at 2 P.M., with a reception to follow.

Presidential First Daughter Eve Cooper will accompany her aunt. Despite the events of her recent trip to Colorado, White House officials have confirmed that she will attend the ceremony.

The moment we exited the plane, we were hit by a wave of heat that was almost staggering. Unbelievable as it sounds, I was pretty sure my shoes' soles were trying to melt to the asphalt as I stepped onto the tarmac.

Patsy waved at the reporters watching us arrive, then fanned herself with the file folder she'd been studying during the trip here. "My, but I'd forgotten how warm it can get in Texas."

Before we could give in to heatstroke, we needed to get through some formal introductions to local dignitaries while the reporters got their pictures. Finally, Patsy, our agents, and I were hustled by the natives into a couple of waiting air-conditioned town cars. The cool air in the passenger compartments felt like heaven as we shut the doors against the brutal Texas heat and the throng of journalists loitering just beyond a chain-link fence, packing up their cameras and stepladders.

"How'd we get out of answering questions out there?" I asked.

Patsy said, "I didn't think that you wanted to have to talk to a crowd like that coming right off the plane."

I sighed in agreement.

She continued. "So, in exchange for their good behavior today, I've promised the local press corps that we'll hold an informal press conference tomorrow afternoon. Both of us."

I swallowed hard. "Do I have to?"

Patsy reached over and patted my hand. "You don't have to do anything, but the sooner you get it over with, the sooner you can relax and enjoy yourself. You're going to have to talk to the press sometime. I know you were hoping to escape the entire situation by going away, but it doesn't work like that."

"I could hope, couldn't I?"

We headed out of the airport. As we drove by them, I watched as all the congregated reporters loaded into their various vehicles and sped away, most of them in an official press convoy to the hotel. Even with our police escort, it didn't take long until our progress slowed to a crawl and we plodded along like the other cars, stuck in traffic that was almost as bad as the Washington Beltway in rush hour.

As we crept along, our hostess, who'd been introduced to us as "Miz Betty-Jean Travis," chattered away ceaselessly. In the South, it's virtually impossible to tell the difference between Miss, Ms., or Mrs., unless you get it in writing. The spoken word "Miz" encompasses them all. "It's such an honor to have you here." Her hundred-watt smile nearly blinded us. "And I'm doubly honored to be your escort," Miz Betty-Jean added. "Out of so many people who offered to escort you, they picked little ol' me. Such an honor! Truly it is."

She might have sounded like a cartoon caricature of Texas womanhood when she spoke, but I had noticed that she'd seemed unfazed by the Secret Service agents, that the initial meet-and-greet had gone off flawlessly and on schedule, that she'd gotten us whisked into our transport along with our luggage in very short order, and that she'd managed to avoid having the press speak with us entirely. I was reasonably sure that there was a sharp, organized, and ruthless mind hiding out under that glossy former-beauty-queen exterior.

While the woman pointed out a building of "particular interest and great historical value," Patsy caught my eye.

"Junior League," she said quietly. "Certainly Daughters of the Texas Revolution—they're a big deal in San Antonio because they saved the Alamo. Probably DAR and United Daughters of the Confederacy, too. She's got an image to maintain."

I took a long look at the woman's electric blue designer suit and pumps, her slightly too big and too red hair, her tasteful and timeless pearls, not to mention the layers of flawless makeup, and I decided Patsy was right. That was a uniform. I nodded in agreement as I coughed away my laughter.

Unaware of our scrutiny, the woman reached into her designer briefcase (lizard skin dyed blue to match her suit) and pulled out a sheaf of papers, which she rustled through. I wondered if she had a briefcase dyed to match every outfit.

She held up one page in triumph. "Here's the updated itinerary. Now, ladies, if there are any changes you foresee, please let us know as soon as possible. We've scheduled a variety of entertainment and arranged for you to visit some of our more famous sights. There's the Alamo, the Hemisphere Plaza, the Institute of Texan Cul—"

Patsy cleared her throat, stopping the woman in midgush. "Miz Travis, I'm sure you've arranged a lovely and thorough schedule, but Eve and I thought we might take it easy on this trip."

Translation: *Don't plan every waking hour for us. We get enough of that in D.C.*

Patsy offered the woman her infectious smile, an expression that most people simply couldn't resist. That grin was a lethal weapon in my aunt's arsenal of charm. "I can't think of a better place to relax and play than San Antonio." At the sight of Miz Travis's crestfallen face, Patsy added, "Of course, it goes without saying that we will be fulfilling all the speaking engagements and meetings you've arranged. It's just the free time that we'd like to keep free."

Reassured, the woman brightened perceptibly and continued her running commentary about the sights along the way. By the time we reached the downtown hotel, my ears and eyes were tired. Besides being hot, San Antonio was incredibly sunny, and I'd forgotten to bring sunglasses.

But no amount of sun could fade away or burn out a journalist on the hunt for a story. Sure enough, even from a distance I could tell that there was a writhing knot of media waiting for us in front of the hotel. The TV vans' antennas made the hotel's front court look a bit like a weird metal forest.

"Never you mind, darlin's," our escort bubbled. "We have a contingency plan."

At her signal, our convoy veered off again into the downtown streets.

A few minutes later, after some tricky maneuvers by our drivers to thread our vehicles through back alleys clearly laid out before the advent of eighteen-wheelers and SUVs, we pulled up by the hotel's service entrance and were escorted into the building through a couple of nondescript hallways.

The only people who saw us arrive were some very surprised chefs and their staff in the hotel kitchen.

By the time we reached our suite, I was ready for a nap. But first I had to circumnavigate a gigantic bouquet of flowers that dominated the entranceway. They clearly weren't kidding when they said everything was bigger in Texas.

"That's huge." I strolled around it, wondering if its gravitational pull would suck me right into the jungle of baby's breath and fern. Who in the world would send such a mobile garden? "You don't think . . ." I stared into the lush foliage, swearing I could almost see clouds of oxygen rising from the plants. "Dad didn't send it, did he?"

"Coop? Not on your life." Patsy walked briskly toward the bouquet. She rustled through the greenery and unearthed a small envelope. "Aha, Watson . . . we have a clue!"

I reached for the card, but she deftly sidestepped me. "How about some privacy here? It says 'To Patsy' on the front. Not 'To Eve.'" She slipped out a small white card, held it at arm's length, and squinted at it.

"Where are your reading glasses?" I asked.

She shot me a dirty, slightly squinty look. "I don't need glasses." She tried to read the card again, glaring furiously at the little paper. "Or my arms are simply too short." After a few more seconds' worth of staring, she handed the card to me. "I surrender. Read it to me."

I took it, and was careful not to gloat. "'Dear Patsy, thanks so much for coming. It means the world to me. I'll contact you later. Love, Buck.'"

My aunt reached for the card, but I danced out of her way. "Buck?" I asked. "Buck? Exactly who is this 'Buck,' and what does he mean by 'love'?" I reread the card aloud in a breathy voice, putting emphasis in all the right places to sound like one of those late-night commercials for a 900 number.

Patsy held out her hand and shot me her sternest glare. "Card. Now."

"Okay, but you have to tell me who this Buck guy is," I said, handing over the card.

She slipped it into her jacket pocket, then patted the fabric. "He's just an old friend."

I pressed ahead, undaunted. I hadn't seen my aunt this flustered since one of the Senate's most notorious womanizers had made a pass at her at a fund-raiser. "How old? How good a friend?"

She leaned into the enormous mass of flowers and took in a deep breath, savoring the fragrance. I knew the air she was inhaling was fragrant, because I was standing at least five feet away from that mountain of flowers and it smelled like a perfume factory had exploded.

Patsy's voice was uncharacteristically soft. "Buck's just someone I knew before I met your uncle Herbert. He married my best friend, Lorilee."

"Lorilee?" I picked up the folder with the itinerary and consulted the second page. "As in the Lorilee Cosby Buckley Memorial Wing? The building you're dedicating?"

Patsy pulled out the card and consulted it again. I could only describe her look as dreamy. She looked like a junior high girl contemplating a photo of the newest teen idol. "One and the same."

I knew the name of the building we were dedicating, but I knew precious little else about it. Judging from Patsy's reaction, it was past time to remedy that. So once we were settled in our rooms in the suite, I grabbed a three-dollar can of Diet Coke. (I always wince when I look at hotel hospitality-fridge prices, but I knew that the Secret Service would prefer that I stay the heck out of public hallways when possible. If I want a cheaper Coke, these days I have to send a minion.) Then I cracked open the advance information file I was supposed to have read on the plane, but didn't.

I had slept on the plane instead. I haven't been sleeping well lately, so I'll take my shut-eye whenever I can.

As it turns out, the Lorilee Cosby Buckley Memorial Wing was a new addition to the Air Force Village, a retirement home for Air Force officers and their spouses. Evidently, Aunt Patsy's Buck was Brigadier General (Retired) Armond "Buck" Buckley. The man was not only a retired general, but also the newly retired CEO of a large San Antonio–based insurance company. He'd personally donated the money for the wing in memory of his dearly departed wife, Lorilee. Evidently Lorilee had worked tirelessly for that cause for many years before she passed away from a brain tumor.

The information included a picture of ol' Buck, and sure enough he turned out to be a very handsome and distinguished-looking gentleman— salt-and-pepper hair with solid white at the temples, a good strong chin, and the slightest hint of amusement in his eyes.

Hmm . . . Buck was certainly good-looking, he was quite clearly well off, and, judging by his donation for the building, he had a social con- science and he'd loved his wife. He looked far younger than his years. Reading between the lines, it also seemed that he was single. And he remembered my aunt Patsy quite fondly. That bouquet wasn't some simple nosegay. It was so large it filled the hall table and, I noted, showcased some of Patsy's favorite flowers (irises and orchids). Not only was it a showy gesture, he'd thought carefully about it and had evidently remem- bered, or at least thought to research, her tastes.

But best of all was the fleeting look on Patsy's face whenever I said Buck's name. What I'd seen in her eyes wasn't simple nostalgia. It was something far more intense. Something told me there could be more to this story than old memories. Aunt Patsy and Buck might be about to cre- ate new ones.

And I was ready to see what I could do to help that process along.

The dedication ceremony was at two, with a formal reception to be held immediately afterward.

The itinerary listed a dinner at the Towers of the Americas restaurant at eight. On the trip from the airport, our hostess had pointed the towering structure out to us as we hit the downtown area, and my stomach had clenched at the thought of eating dinner while sitting beside a window that looked out . . . no . . . directly down onto the city. I was hit with the memory of pressing my nose to the canopy of the glider and looking out and down at the world below. It wasn't that I possessed a fear of heights, but I was having a hard time keeping the aftermath of a certain situation from tainting new experiences.

What I'm trying to say is that I would much rather have had dinner somewhere on *terra firma* than *terror aloftus*. (I guess it's quite evident I never took Latin in school. But it sounds reasonable, doesn't it?) As I dressed for the ceremony, I planned my eventual escape. After all, I was willing to bet Patsy wouldn't mind having a romantic candlelit dinner with Good Ol' Buck, free of my distracting fifth-wheel presence.

The limousine picked us up promptly at 1:15 and our chatty Junior League hostess, Miz Travis, gave us a running commentary on all the interesting places we passed. Patsy and I took turns making polite noises in response. I could tell Patsy was preoccupied, and I wondered if it was in anticipation of hooking back up with Good Ol' Buck.

When our hostess turned her attention to the driver, giving him instructions, I leaned over to Patsy. "So, how long has it been since you've seen Buck?"

She blushed. "It's been a few years. At Lorilee's funeral." Her colored deepened. "But we've kept in contact since then with cards and E-mails." She turned toward the window as if fascinated with the passing scenery. I knew it was my cue to shut up.

But I had my answer. Yep, I smelled a romance blooming.

I spotted Good Ol' Buck, standing on the sidewalk. The picture hadn't done him justice; he was definitely a silver fox. When he spotted our convoy, his whole face brightened. It was like watching a teenage boy catch sight of his dressed-to-kill prom date for the first time.

We had barely rolled to a stop when he was at the curb, ready to open the door. Unfortunately, the Secret Service spoiled his fun. When we emerged, Good Ol' Buck looked as if he couldn't decide what to do—hug Patsy, shake her hand, or what.

Patsy made the decision for him. She immediately reached up, gave him a hug, and kissed him on the cheek. "It's so good to see you Buck."

"You, too, PittyPat."

PittyPat? I managed not to laugh out loud. But he noticed me nonetheless.

"Are you going to introduce me to your beautiful niece?" he asked, giving me his full attention, but not making me feel awkward about it.

Patsy turned to me. "Eve, allow me to introduce a very old friend of mine, Buck Buckley. Buck, this is my favorite niece, Eve."

I accepted his outstretched hand and received a firm shake. "And her only niece, I may add."

His eyes sparkled. "It's a delight to meet you, Eve. You remind me a lot of your aunt in her salad days."

I've always had a hard time with the phrase "salad days." All I can think of is an image of shredded lettuce—torn and wrinkled and green. Ugh—but I knew that's not how Buck meant it.

"I'll take that as a compliment," I said. "My aunt Patsy's pretty special." I offered him my best smile. That wasn't very hard. I could see why Patsy liked this man. "Dad says the same thing, especially when he overhears me bossing around my two younger brothers. He says it sounds just like the way Patsy used to treat him."

"Dear Patsy, it is so good to actually have you here." He took her hands in his. "So, now you're living in the White House. You're an ornament to it, I'm sure. And, may I add, the years have been very good to you, PittyPat. You look fabulous. Not a day older than when we all used to double-date."

I saw my aunt blush for the second time that day. Someone alert the folks at Guinness! This was definitely a world's record.

She added a smile to the flush. "Elliot's the one who deserves the credit for the political success. I'm just a tagalong."

The Junior Leaguer appeared at our elbows, her clipboard in her hand. Miz Travis shot Buck a sugar-couldn't-be-sweeter smile and inserted herself between him and Patsy. "I'm so sorry, General, but we do have a schedule to maintain. Miz Davidson, if you'll follow me."

Patsy gave us the "Save me!" look, but dutifully followed the woman toward the podium.

"It looks as if we've been abandoned." I decided his nickname was no longer Good Ol' Buck, but General Buck.

Clearly a gentleman, he offered his arm to me. "May I escort you to your seat?"

I accepted. We headed together toward the front of the small auditorium. He indicated the Junior Leaguer with a discreet nod of his head. "I've learned to be scared of women like that."

"Me, too," I whispered back. "Miz Travis gives me cold chills. I can tell she means well. But I feel like I could be sucked up in her wake and organized within an inch of my life before I knew what hit me."

"Women like that have their uses." He reached over and patted my hand. "They pretty well run Texas—and not always from behind the scenes anymore. If we had more people like her in the military, our costs would be down, our retention would be better, and our highly fashionable uniforms would change with every new season."

I laughed. He was probably right.

We reached our seats, not surprisingly in the center of the front row. Patsy had evidently been spirited away to be briefed on the chain of events. When the program started, it was the usual stuff. A local television newscaster was the master of ceremonies. He spoke. The head of the retirement facility spoke. General Buck threw in a couple of words, and then it was Patsy's turn.

Prior to Dad's campaign, the most public speaking Patsy had ever done was making announcements in church concerning the various projects being undertaken by her women's circle. When it came to asking for donations of baked goods or castoffs for the annual churchwide garage sale or even the PTA, she was a highly persuasive speaker. But you don't usually make requests for home-baked cupcakes while on the campaign trail.

In order to be an effective partner in Dad's campaign strategy, Patsy'd had to learn a whole new style of speaking while Dad stumped for office. What she lacked in political polish, she more than made up for in honest enthusiasm for her brother's talents and his fitness for high political office. Add my aunt's sense of humor and gracious manners, and she'd been a real plus for Dad on the campaign trail and during his presidency.

With three full months of being the First Lady under her belt, she'd gained more polish, but in my probably biased opinion, not at the cost of her warmth and enthusiasm. Maybe asking for funding from a national fast-food franchise or donations from the largest automotive company in the world isn't all that different from hitting up people for cakes and pies for the church's bake sale and folks to volunteer to run the PTA car wash. And the weird part about watching my aunt speak is that every time she does it, I learn things about her I've never known.

And this time was no exception.

Growing up, Patsy and Lorilee June Cosby had been inseparable, best friends since their first day of first grade. Their feats of mischief were legendary, growing in complexity as the girls grew older. When they were eight years old, they'd flown out of a second-story window on a purloined Persian rug, fully expecting to lift off, Aladdinlike, into the wild blue. They'd ended up instead in a prickly rose brier, scratched but unharmed—until Patsy's dad found out where his favorite Persian rug was. Patsy remembered the time that she and Lorilee went trick-or-treating with a big spare bag of costumes. They would rotate through the costumes, repeatedly hitting any house with a particularly good candy selection.

What that woman will do for chocolate . . .

One cold winter morning, they got up extremely early, sneaked up to their hilltop high school, and opened a fire hydrant, flooding the road that led up to the school. By the time the staff started arriving, the road was covered in a thin sheet of ice, and no teacher, much less any school bus, could get up that hill. School was canceled for two days.

I was beginning by then to see where Drew got his bent for mischief. God alone could help us if he decided the front drive of the White House should become an ice-skating rink next winter. I then remembered the plan of attack I'd given him to talk Dad into letting him host a school dance in the East Room.

Oops—that bit of advice might get ugly. I might just regret having given it. . . .

Patsy continued, explaining how, as punishment for their misdeeds, she and Lorilee were sentenced to work in the local nursing home. Patsy walked away from the experience a reformed prankster. Lorilee walked away from the experience with a career aspiration.

Their lives started on divergent paths from that moment on. They still remained best friends—they even roomed together in college—but their goals in life had changed. Patsy earned a business degree and planned to make a splash in the retail industry, and Lorilee majored in sociology with a specialty in gerontology.

Patsy gave the audience her usual infectious smile. "It's rare that you discover your life's calling while you're so young, but that's exactly what Lorilee did. She dedicated herself to improving the living conditions of others, to provide them with a safe, active, and healthy place to live in their later years. She was aware of the problems faced by Alzheimer's patients long before it became a common diagnosis. What we're here to celebrate today is her vision, her dream come true. And I want to thank everyone who worked so tirelessly to make her dream a reality."

Patsy named various staff members and charity coordinators, then looked at General Buck. "I've been standing up here talking about being Lorilee's best friend. But that's not entirely true. As close as we were as children and young women, distance crept between us as our lives took divergent paths. We were in college when we both met a man named Armond 'Call me Buck' Buckley." She turned and graced that man with a very special smile. "I'm sure you all know the story about how Buck and Lorilee met and fell in love at a college dance. But what most people don't know is that Buck's blind date for the evening was supposed to be me."

There was a light titter of laughter in the room. I looked over at General Buck, and he was nodding, substantiating her story.

She continued. "But I had a bad cold. I just felt too lousy to go out on a blind date. So I coerced Lorilee, my roommate, to go in my place." She laughed. "When she came back from the date, she was floating on air. She told me it was definitely love at first sight. You couldn't get a crowbar between those two from that moment on. And, trust me, I tried."

This elicited a big laugh.

"Buck always understood and respected Lorilee's vision for a facility like this. It's just a shame that she couldn't see its completion in her lifetime."

The speech grew sad at that point. Lorilee had died six years ago of a brain tumor, though she'd continued her work almost to the end of her life. We were all beginning to sniff and wipe our eyes when Patsy ended with more stories of her adventures with Lorilee—these from when the two women were supposed to be sober and responsible adults. Apparently, neither of them let that little detail get in the way of a good practical joke. By the end of Patsy's speech, our tears were from uncontrollable laughter.

After the thunderous applause, we trooped over to the new building, did the usual ribbon-cutting ceremony with the giant scissors (someone had been smart enough to build a nice, sharp pair of real scissors into the giant pair, so we didn't have the usual "It looks like a good idea, but these things won't cut" moment of panic), and then took a guided tour of the new facilities.

After all the tours had been given, all the pictures had been taken, all the hors d'oeuvres had been Hoovered, and all the hands had been shaken, we headed back to our limousine, this time accompanied by General Buck.

Feeling decidedly like a fifth wheel, I fell into step with Miz Travis. She chatted about our dinner plans, but I listened with only half an ear. Patsy and Buck were whispering and giggling, and I was dying to hear what they were saying, but was too polite to eavesdrop. Sometimes the good manners my parents had drummed into me were a real pain.

Patsy motioned for us to take a few steps forward and join them. It was then that she broke the bad news to the Junior Leaguer. "I'm afraid, Miz Travis, that we're going to make a change in your plans."

The woman consulted her clipboard as if searching for instructions for dealing with alterations to her printed schedule. "In what way?"

Patsy mirrored the woman's sugar-sweet smile. "I'm sure the restaurant you've selected has excellent food and the view is probably spectacular. But I think Eve and I would prefer something . . . a little more down-to-earth, figuratively and literally, just now." She nodded at me. "You understand, don't you?"

Underneath the layers of her makeup, the woman began to flush a shade of red that clashed with her hair. "Of . . . of course, how insensitive of me." She turned to me and began to pat my arm. "I'm so sorry, Evelyn. It never dawned on me that a tower restaurant would . . . I mean that . . ." She turned back to her stalwart clipboard. "I'm certain we can make different arrangements. No problem at all." She whipped out her cell phone and juggled it along with the board, trying to flip pages. "I have a few numbers here—"

"Don't worry," General Buck said, stepping forward. "I'll take care of this." He whipped out his own cell phone and dialed a number he apparently knew by heart. "Jorge? It's Buck Buckley. Any chance I can get the corner table tonight? Yeah? When?"

He covered the phone and consulted Patsy. "You two hungry now, or do you want to wait?"

Patsy glanced at me. We spoke simultaneously. "Starved."

He turned back to his cell phone. "In maybe about an hour or so. It's one of those high-profile things. No press. No leaks. Yeah. Sure." He covered the mouthpiece and turned to Patsy. "How many agents inside?"

She shrugged. "Two at least. Probably four."

He turned back to his phone. "Security will need a choice of four tables, two adjacent to ours and two with a clear view of our table and all the doors. We'll let them choose which they want to use. Yeah. *Gracias,* Jorge."

He flipped his phone closed. "Done."

After some deft sidestepping and quick talking, we ended up piling into Buck's car and leaving Miz Travis standing by the limousine with a very perplexed look on her perfectly painted face. Our agent-drivers stood by their cars, being briefed by Buck about the venue and directions to it.

"I feel guilty," Patsy said as she settled in the front seat of Buck's Mercedes. "She worked so hard."

"A bit too hard," Buck said, settling in behind the wheel. "It's her hallmark. I've known that woman for ten years. I know she means well, but I don't have a lot of patience with her. Besides dodging her amorous advances, I've learned through unfortunate experience that she overplans everything. Including her own life. I bet her lists start first thing in the morning: 'Oh-five-forty-five to oh-five-fifty, rise from bed. Find list. Then bathroom. Remember to not step on cat.'"

A picture of Miz Travis rising from the bed, suffering from amazing morning hair, not to mention morning breath, staggering around and searching for her list before she even brushed her teeth, ran through my mind. Some images are better not examined too closely. I wrenched my thoughts back to the matter at hand. "So, where are we going that's more down-to-earth?" I asked from the backseat. My sense of fifth wheelism would have been almost overpowering if one of Patsy's Secret Service agents hadn't been sitting next to me. At least there was a sixth wheel, too. And enough other wheels for a whole new 18-wheeler if you counted the agents in the cars in front of us and behind us. Maybe I could beg off with a headache and have somebody drop me off at the hotel. I almost said something, then kept my mouth shut. Did I really want to take my chances that there was something on pay-per-view I wanted to watch, or something on the room service menu that I wanted to eat?

As tasty as the hors d'oeuvres had been, I was major-league hungry.

Buck continued. "We're headed to a place that's not quite as fancy as the Tower of the Americas. In fact, most people describe it as a burger joint, but I promise you it's the finest burger joint in town. Maybe in the entire state of Texas."

My mouth started to water at the idea of eating a big ol' greasy hamburger. The White House kitchen produces a highly tasty but politically correct cheeseburger, lacking the proper amount of fat and gristle and salt for real perfection.

As we drove up to the restaurant and I could smell the fabulous scents wafting from it, I was convinced that Buck's idea had gastronomic merit. Now, just looking at the place, I would never have thought, Here's an interesting place to eat. It was a squatty orange metal building with white metal awnings over each of two doors, circa 1954. But I know from experience that great food often comes from such humble sources. Buck found a line of parking places that would hold our convoy, and we strolled in.

Eclectic didn't begin to describe the place.

Hole in the wall came closer. . . .

Buck took one look at my face and leaned over. "Trust me. You'll love Little Hipps."

He was right. I did.

Boy, had my imagination underestimated the size of the burger. Buck ordered for us, starting with something he called "shypoke eggs"—which were like the world's biggest nacho, a single huge chip smothered in cheese and jalapeños. Then Buck ordered us "Hippburgers," which, when they arrived, were the size of dinner plates. Our beer came in ice-cream-soda glasses.

It was delicious. I wondered if Buck's influence with the owner would extend to getting the recipes from this gem of a place for the White house chef. My arteries may never recover, but I'm young yet.

And despite the amount of cholesterol in her meal selection, it seemed to me that Aunt Patsy was growing younger right before my eyes as the evening progressed. I'd never seen her like that before. She wasn't exactly flirting. There's not a coy bone in her body. But something was passing through the air between Patsy and Buck. They regaled me with stories of their misspent youth, both misting up on occasions when they recalled things that Lorilee had said or done. I got the distinct feeling that Buck and Lorilee had had a wonderful and fulfilling marriage.

But I also got the feeling that both Patsy and Buck had been waiting for the right time to . . . reconnect. And in the midst of their big reunion, there I was—as I said, the proverbial fifth wheel. To their credit, they didn't make me feel unwanted.

Somehow the conversation worked itself around to grown children. The general talked about his two sons. One was finishing up his Ph.D. at MIT, and the other one had followed in his father's footsteps as a career officer in the Air Force, after graduating from . . . the Academy.

At the mention of the site of my recent troubles, our pleasant conversation ground to an awkward halt.

Aunt Patsy picked up the conversational ball after that moment of dead silence, talking once more about the good old days with Lorilee.

I hate it when people look at me, then blatantly change the subject. It's been happening a lot lately. I'm not a delicate person. In fact, I was starting to feel a burning desire to prove my lack of fragility.

While Buck and Patsy resumed rehashing their shared past, I began to contemplate just what to do next. Back home, when Dad had suggested that I should accompany Patsy on her speaking engagement to San Antonio, it had sounded like a good idea. I had wanted to get away and clear my head. I hadn't given much thought to why Dad had wanted me to go, beyond figuring that he wanted me out of Washington until things quieted down.

Now I was beginning to wonder if Dad had anticipated what might come of this reunion between his sister and General Buck. I was beginning to suspect that the reason Dad wanted me here was to serve as duenna.

I think Dad foresaw the "couple potential" between these two old friends. Perhaps, rather than Patsy wanting a chaperone along for the ride, it had been Dad who had decided I should accompany her, not wanting things between Patsy and Buck to go too far, too fast. Even though he's her younger brother, Dad has a protective streak a mile wide when it comes to his sister. But after looking at these two together, I was much more inclined to leave them alone and let nature take its course.

In any case, when I had agreed to go on this trip, I'd figured that maybe I could take a breather and think about what to do next. So maybe that's what I should do—leave these two lovebirds to it and work on my own agenda. I had to do something. I'd promised Megan I'd help. Though I really had no clear idea where to start.

There was one obvious loose end dangling that I could maybe do something about. It seemed to me that the best person to tell me what happened in that glider prior to the crash was the only survivor, Major Anthony Gaskell. He was probably still in that hospital back at the Air Force Academy. Maybe it was time to broach the subject of heading back to Colorado Springs.

I needed to find a reason as well as a way to go back to Colorado to talk to him. Since Texas was closer to Colorado than Washington, D.C., was, maybe I could persuade Patsy to let me take an unscheduled detour before heading home.

And this was my best opening.

I turned to Patsy. "You know," I said, interrupting her gentle flow of reminiscence, "speaking of the Academy, I wouldn't mind heading that way on the way home."

She looked aghast at me. "Good heavens, why?"

I shrugged. "Unfinished business." In response to her quizzical look, I said, "Don't you think it would be appropriate if I went to visit the injured pilot, see how he's doing? And maybe apologize? The prevailing theory is that he's hurt because of me."

"Surely you don't—"

Buck reached over and placed a hand on Patsy's arm. "Eve's right." He looked at me and added a quick aside. "I don't mean about your being responsible for the crash. From what I've heard, it hasn't even been established that the cause was sabotage. Even if it does turn out to be something like that, how could you have known? But it might be a great comfort to the man if you visited him even before any definitive report is made." He offered me and Patsy a small smile. "I don't know if it's good politics, but it's certainly good manners."

Patsy sighed. "Buck's right. You should go."

"And it's going to be easier to do than you think," he added.

Somehow I figured that was one of those little white lies that someone tells you to comfort you when you have a rather unpleasant task at hand. "Easier? I'm not too sure about that. I can just imagine what I'll say. Maybe, 'Hi, I'm Eve. I think you went down in a glider meant to kill/maim/injure me instead. I'm so sorry. Here's a get-well card.'"

Buck shook his head. "No, that's not what I meant. That part is going to be hard, no doubt about it. What I mean is that the injured pilot's no longer in Colorado Springs." He ducked his head and fiddled with his paper napkin. "I may be retired, but I still have my sources of information. And I keep track of the things that interest me, like you, Patsy, and your family. I get daily updates."

He glanced up at me. "Major Gaskell was recently transferred from the hospital on the Academy to the Air Force's top hospital. He's at Wilford Hall, here in San Antonio."

CHAPTER EIGHT

THE POLITICAL WATCHDOG ON-LINE:
"GUARDING YOUR FREEDOM"

First Lady Patricia Davidson was spotted in a San Antonio eatery yesterday, meeting unofficially with retired general Armond "Buck" Buckley. This merely adds more fuel to speculation that President Cooper is contemplating an illegal militarization of the White House and isn't below using family members to further his cause. Last week, his daughter visited the USAF Academy, where her presence and behavior were described as "disruptive." If Cooper doesn't pull back from his current course, the USA and its citizens are in grave danger of being placed under military law. Help us stop him. Send your donations to . . .

A chill ran up my spine when I spotted the sign that read "Wilford Hall Medical Center." I can't help it. I don't like hospitals.

They remind me of those long months when Mom was trying to battle cancer. A visit to a hospital forces me to relive those days when we all secretly wondered if the debilitating effects of the chemo cure weren't actually worse than the disease.

When we'd make our daily trek to her hospital room, she'd try to remain upbeat for all of us kids. But as soon as the door closed behind us and we headed for home, I was sure her big, reassuring smile collapsed and her show of strength would be over for another day.

Then one day, exactly one month after my twelfth birthday, she couldn't even muster the energy for her usual sunny smile when we showed up. I don't know what was worse—watching her deal with what she considered her body's betrayal of her family, or watching Dad try to keep up the pretenses that she couldn't maintain.

It was only a matter of days after that before we lost her.

So at a very tender and impressionable age, I learned to associate hospitals with death and dying rather than recovery and life. Now, as a rational adult, I know better, but it's still hard to get over the initial concept that going to a hospital as a visitor is an unpleasant task and going as a patient is a far worse fate.

I had to remind myself that instead of exploratory surgery, this was an exploratory mission. Thanks to Buck's influence, I had a good plan of attack. First we dropped Patsy and Buck off at the main entrance. A mob of military and hospital personnel had been waiting for their chance to meet the First Lady, and Patsy didn't disappoint.

However, I was being a bit more antisocial than usual, hiding in the eclipse created by John Kingston's massive form. He sat by the limousine door, essentially shielding me from view. I didn't make the grand entrance with Patsy and Buck, but instead was taken to a less public entrance where I could be spirited upstairs without any fanfare. Thank to John's bulk, no one even knew I was in the car.

And my aunt's entrance was grand indeed. Patsy is a sight to behold when she gets into First Lady mode. She has a way of making everyone around her feel special that seems to endear her even to Dad's most vehement critics. She looked especially chipper this morning, wearing her favorite suit, one that was almost the same shade of light blue as her eyes.

Staying safely in the shadows of the car, I watched Buck as he stood to one side and watched Patsy work the crowd. That man had his eye on my aunt, big-time. But I noticed he was working the crowd in his own quiet way. Buck was no slouch at that either. Since we were headed to an Air Force base, I'd almost expected him to show up in something vaguely military in cut, but instead he wore a pair of light khaki Dockers and a white polo shirt and carried a navy blazer slung over one shoulder.

I also noted that his retirement from the military and his thriving insurance business hadn't reduced him to sitting on the porch, whiling away his hours in a rocking chair. Somewhere in his life, he found time for a serious daily exercise regimen. He had a healthy tan and a rather impressive physique. I knew several guys far younger than Buck who would probably kill to look that good.

Anyway, back to the story. Buck might be retired, but he still had an inordinate amount of "The general wants this" influence over the current Military Powers That Be. Thanks to Buck's sway, Patsy was going to perform a fairly quick dash-in, dash-out red-carpet visit to the hospital, drawing all attention away from me as John Kingston and I snuck up to Major Gaskell's room. That was Buck's plan.

And that's exactly what happened.

Kingston and I entered by a side entrance, unnoticed except by a few tight-lipped guards. We took the stairs. By the time we reached the fifth-floor landing, I was doing my best to hide my labored breathing. Dad and I used to play tennis for our regular exercise, but his duties had been eating into his court time lately. I made a promise to myself that as soon as I got home, I'd drag him out to the court for a couple of sets. Or at least take up running or something.

It was a bit awkward to realize that despite how big John was (big, as in muscle and height, not slobby big), he hadn't even broken a sweat, much less gasped for breath.

Of course, being fit is part of Kingston's job requirement. My job description places more emphasis on my ornamental qualities and a certain diplomatic reticence than on my aerobic conditioning. It was time to hit the gym more often, for my own good. Not that I could outrun John at the best of times. Of course, I've never given any of my agents a real run for their money, but I know if he put his mind to it, Drew sure could, especially when he's eaten enough sugar and caffeine.

The hallway was conspicuously empty except for another agent at the far end who nodded at us. He had evidently secured the area. That gave me time to pause at the door to the major's room, catching both my breath and my thoughts. After a moment, I gathered my courage and my wind and knocked on the door.

Someone answered, "Come in."

John stuck his head in first, and after he deemed it safe, I stepped in, spotting a dark-haired doctor type dressed in a white jacket over light blue scrubs. He stood at the foot of a bed, consulting a clipboard.

When he turned and saw me, his face flared in recognition. "Miss Cooper, it's an honor to meet you," he said in a soft voice. "I'm Major Bud Trichey, Orthopedic Trauma. I was told you were coming."

"Pleased to meet you . . . sir." I wasn't sure whether to address him by his rank or as "Doctor." "How's Major Gaskell doing?" I whispered.

The doctor tucked the clipboard under his arm. "It was touch and go there for a while. He had us all worried, but Tony's much better now. It's still going to take some recovery time, but he'll be good as new."

A groggy voice emanated from the bed. "Bud? That you? What's going on?"

Major Trichey glanced toward the patient. "Ah, Tony, you're awake. Good timing. You have a special visitor."

We stepped closer to the bed, and the doctor turned to me. "Miss Cooper, allow me to introduce our patient, who—as it happens—is an old friend of mine. Major Anthony 'Gadget' Gaskell. Tony, this is Eve Cooper, President Cooper's daughter."

If I hang around these Air Force types much longer, I think I'm going to have to come up with a spiffy nickname for myself—something more action-oriented than my rather lame Secret Service name, "Apple."

"*The* P-President?" Gaskell straightened in bed, then winced.

"No, just his daughter," I offered in apology.

"Hold on for a sec', Gadg." The doctor reached down, found the bed controls, and ran the head of the bed up so Gaskell could see me comfortably but still be reclined. "There. I bet that's better." He replaced the clipboard at the foot of the bed and then took a few steps toward the door. "I'll give you two some privacy." He shot me what I suspected was his best bedside manner. "It's very nice to meet you, Miss Cooper."

"You, too, sir," I echoed out of rote. I turned back to the man in the bed and was struck with a sudden sense of "I really hate hospitals and I don't want to be here" awkwardness. I tried to cover my moment of panic. "Uh . . . I'd shake your hand, but it looks like you're all tied up right now." I pointed to the tangle of tubes and wires that were hooked to his right arm. His left arm was encased in a plaster cast, as was one leg, which was also in traction. "Can I take a rain check?"

"Sorry." He managed a weak laugh. "I'm afraid I'm off of the hand-shaking detail for the next few weeks. But it's a real honor to meet you." He looked as if he was searching for the proper thing to say next. After a moment of silence, he added, "I . . . I voted for your dad."

"Thanks." It's the best response I've learned since the election. I don't expect people to volunteer details about what is meant to be their secret ballot, but since so many people tell me, I've found that acknowledging the existence of the vote is the best course of action.

After all, these *are* the people who put my dad in office.

I gave the patient my best "I know you're going to recover" look of confidence. "I was in town, and I wanted to meet you and to see how you were doing after the crash."

"Better. Much better. Thank you."

The opening pleasantries were over; now came the hard part. I drew a deep breath. "So far, the investigators haven't figured out what caused the crash. But there's a theory that it might have been a result of sabotage, with me as the intended victim. If that's true, then the only reason you're here is because of me. For that, I am truly sorry."

"No apology necessary." He tried to smile again, but his bruised face wasn't cooperating. "I'm not so sure about your theory." He seemed to fade out for a moment; then he picked up the threads of our conversation. "Like I told the investigators, there's another theory they ought to consider. It might be a dead end, but they won't know until they look."

I felt the hairs on the back of my neck stand up. "What theory?"

His eyes glazed over momentarily, and then his gaze sharpened again. "I wasn't s'posed to be soaring that day. Only reason why I did was 'cause the cadet who was supposed to take . . ." His face grew suddenly pale, and he took a moment to muster his strength and regain his train of thought. "Keith Rydell was supposed to take Ashley up, but was called away and I stepped in. Last-moment substitution." The major closed his eyes and winced.

Was he saying what I thought he was saying?

"Are you saying this cadet pilot might have been the target, rather than me?"

"Possible, though now hearing it said aloud, it sounds pretty unlikely." His voice grew scratchy. "Keith's had a hard time adjusting to the Academy life."

He swallowed hard and made a weak gesture toward a plastic pitcher on the bedside table. I found a glass, poured the water, and held it so he could sip from the protruding straw.

"Thanks." He did look a little rejuvenated.

"What sort of problems has Cadet Rydell been having?" I prompted, not wanting him to lose the thought.

"Academic probation, disciplinary actions." He paused. "And then there was the big scandal."

My politician's-daughter training kicked in. When I hear the word "scandal," I sit down, shut up, and take notes. I never know what I'll hear. Or how hard I need to brace myself. But I do know that it's always better to be fully informed. I looked behind me, found a chair, and dragged it over to the side of the bed. "What scandal?"

It took a while for him to get going, but once he started, it came out like a flood. Apparently Keith Rydell had had a hard time adjusting to military life from the moment he stepped foot on Academy grounds. He almost washed out of basic training his first summer there. And once the semester started, his academic troubles mounted quickly.

"The smarts that had helped him sail through high school without trying didn't cut it when it came to the Academy's tougher academic structure," Gaskell explained. "It took him a while to realize that native intelligence wasn't enough to get by anymore. Keith needed to study, and he'd never really learned how to do that."

I nodded. I remembered how hard I'd found it to transition between high school and college, how my method of last-minute cramming for one didn't work for the other. I'd hit that wall myself as a freshman before I found my feet as a college student.

"Despite great high school grades, not to mention strong test scores, Keith began to struggle in almost all his academic classes."

I asked the obvious question. "So did he start cheating?"

Major Gaskell sighed. "No. For all Keith's troubles, he never cheated. He and I had several long discussions about that. One of my duties to him and to the rest of the cadets in my squadron is to act as a mentor, to help them discover their own inner strengths, and to lead them to choose the right path for themselves. But I couldn't protect Keith from his own insecurities. As his troubles mounted, his self-confidence plummeted."

"A vicious circle," I supplied. I'd been there, done that. You fail and you feel bad about yourself, and then because you feel bad about yourself, you fail even worse.

"Exactly. And since he was in such a vulnerable position, it was easy for him to become an unwitting pawn for a couple of upperclassmen who were involved in running illegal substances."

"Drugs?"

"Yeah. Unfortunately." He managed a small nod. "But Keith didn't know that drugs were involved until the ring was busted. He thought he was running a black market in comparatively harmless stuff, things that would be legal outside the Academy environs, like cigarettes and porn magazines, to the other cadets."

"And you believed him?"

"Oh yeah. You spend hours mentoring a kid and you get to know that kid pretty well. I never once saw any signs that Keith believed drugs might provide any sort of solution to his problems, much less any short-term relief from them. He's always been staunchly against drugs. I think he was guilty of stupidity, and maybe naïveté. It was stupid of him to agree to transport unknown items, naïve to believe that they were harmless. But his self-worth was so lousy that when his fellow cadets offered to pay him to bring the stuff from off base, it was easy for him to believe that making money was the only thing he could do right. As it turned out, his so-called friends were using him to transport an entire pharmacy under the administration's nose."

"Ouch."

"Nasty stuff, too. You name it, they had it."

He gestured for the water again and I held it for him. After a long sip and an even longer sigh, he continued. "When everything broke open, it looked like Keith was going to take the fall along with the others. That is, until one of the accused cadets admitted Keith's real role was nothing more than an uninformed mule. It put Keith and his testimony in a better light. Because of Keith's testimony, the entire ring was identified and eventually court-martialed."

"But Keith wasn't court-martialed himself, was he?" He couldn't be and still be at the Academy, I thought.

"No. He was disciplined, but he remained as a cadet. Keith received much milder punishment in comparison to the others, and was able to stay at the Academy. He hopes to finish his degree and perform his active-duty commitment as an officer." His face darkened. "Something the other cadets will never be allowed to do."

Aha! I smelled the potential for revenge. *Let's get the guy who narked on us.* "So you think the other cadets may have been—for the lack of a better word—gunning for Keith because he testified against them?"

"It's certainly possible." Gaskell took a moment to contemplate the concept. "It'd be a reasonable explanation for the crash, except that, in all honesty, I don't see how they could pull it off. All of the former cadets are serving time in Leavenworth right now. I sincerely doubt they have any friends left in the cadet corps, and certainly none who'd be willing to exact that sort of revenge on their behalf. Those boys were an embarrassment to everyone at the Academy, especially their fellow cadets." He made a face, then shifted uncomfortably in his bed.

" 'We will not lie, cheat, or steal, nor tolerate among us anyone who does,' " I stated, repeating the cadet honor code that I'd seen written in a dozen places and heard a dozen times during my Academy visit.

"Exactly. Keith didn't have many supporters during his trial. Everybody wanted to keep plenty of distance between themselves and any mention of drugs or contact with those accused. Keith had no supporters, except for Ashley." Gaskell's expression softened. "Poor kid. She was loyal, and she believed in his innocence when a lot of us weren't so sure, me included. She was the one who really helped him get through all this."

He heaved a painful sigh. "If someone wanted to get revenge on Keith as a payback for damning testimony, killing her was the most effective way to destroy his life. With her gone, I'm afraid Keith is going to fall apart again."

"The worst kind of revenge," I whispered. Strike all around the victim, but don't hit him directly. That kind of revenge leaves the target alive to witness all the destruction wreaked because of him. Like trying to get at Dad by targeting me. Hurt a man where it scars the most—by hitting those he loves.

Effective and efficient terrorism.

Gaskell closed his eyes. I thought I saw a tear forming in the corner of his eye. "Poor Ashley," he said. "Such a sweet girl. Hated drugs. I spent a lot of time with her. I supported her. She supported Keith. Such a sweet girl. Too bad I . . ."

I waited for him to finish his statement, but he said nothing else.

"You said Rydell was bringing the packages from off base. Does that mean someone off base, some nonmilitary type, also might have been involved?"

He didn't reply. From his breathing pattern, it was evident he'd fallen asleep.

I shifted in my chair, figuring it was time to leave, but Gaskell roused, blinking awake. He stared at me blankly at first; recognition followed a moment later. "You know . . . I don't really remember," he said, as if confessing something.

"Remember if anyone from town was involved?" I inquired gently.

"No. Member wha' happened. How it happened." He opened his eyes and extended his fingers as if to mimic an airplane, diving slowly into a bedsheet mountain. "Could be everyone's fav'rite explanation."

"What's that?"

He appeared to drift away again.

"Major Gaskell, what's everybody's favorite explanation?" I repeated, hoping that he would respond to his name and rank.

He roused again. "Pilot . . ." His next word was muffled.

I leaned closer. "Pilot what?" My mind raced ahead. Another pilot? I tried to think of words that would follow pilot, but the only thing that came to my mind was "pilot light."

He didn't even open his eyes. "Error," he muttered. "Always try to call it pilot error. It's never the equipment. Always blame the pilot. . . ." His voice trailed off. He had obviously fallen asleep again.

After a few more moments of silence, I replaced the chair as quietly as I could and tiptoed toward the door. Just as I was reaching for the handle, it swung in slowly. John was opening it for Major-Doctor (or was that Doctor-Major?) Trichey. The doctor took one quick glance inside, saw that his patient was sleep, then motioned for me to follow him into the hallway. We shifted into the hallway, under John's watchful eye.

The doctor thumbed over his shoulder. "I should have warned you. Sorry. Tony can't help nodding off. He's on some pretty strong painkillers. Did he make much sense?"

I shrugged. "Pretty much. He told me stuff about a drug scandal at the

Academy, his fears of being blamed for the crash, and other things. I'll need to go back to the hotel to sort it all out."

He gave me the doctor-knows-best nod and consulted his clipboard. "I'm sure he appreciates the visit."

"If he remembers it."

Trichey looked up and grinned. "I doubt he'll forget you. He likes pretty women. And I know he voted for your father." He tucked the clipboard under his arm and held out his hand. "It was a pleasure, Miss Cooper. If Tony wasn't lucid enough to remember to thank you for this visit, then please allow me to do so. Thank you."

"You're very welcome." I shook his hand. "When he wakes up again, please tell him I said to get well soon."

We excused ourselves and headed our separate directions. Flanked by John Kingston and another agent, I prayed that the trip down the stairs wouldn't leave me panting for breath again. Going up, it was understandable, but if I did it going down, I was going to completely embarrass myself.

As we all trotted down the stairs at a ruthless speed, John radioed ahead to the driver of our car. By the time we all reached the first floor, the car was just pulling up to the exit. It was such a smooth operation that I doubt anyone in the area noticed me.

One, two, three.

The car pulled up, we slid in, and the car pulled away. But, to my dismay, I realized that the car had picked up an unexpected passenger during our absence—our Junior League escort, Miz Betty-Jean Travis. Today she was dressed in a flaming red power suit with lizard-skin shoes and briefcase dyed to match. I was beginning to wonder how many briefcases the woman had. Hadn't she ever heard of the theory that basic black went with everything? All that red clothing made her hair look even redder. And bigger.

She opened her mouth to speak, but Patsy cut in first. "How'd it go?"

I sighed, though more to catch my breath than because I felt the need emotionally. "Pretty good. I think I learned a lot."

Buck leaned forward to see me better. "Such as?"

"Such as the cadet who was supposed to be flying the glider had been involved in some big drug scandal at the Academy, along with a bunch of other cadets and maybe some civilians."

Buck stroked his chin thoughtfully. "You know, I remember hearing about that. They court-martialed five or six cadets for possession and distribution."

"Oh mah goodness," Miz Travis said with a gasp.

We all ignored her.

"And Rydell, the cadet pilot who was supposed to have taken Ashley up? Turns out he'd been used as a mule—" Patsy elbowed me. I looked at Patsy and elaborated. "As a drug runner. He ended up supplying key information that convicted his fellow cadets."

Patsy thought about that. "Then you think all this trouble was intended to affect this cadet instead of you?"

I shrugged. "Maybe. It's possible."

"It makes sense," Buck weighed in. He turned to John. "Your folks did a complete check of the glider before you let Eve get in, right?"

"Yes, sir."

"And you found nothing?"

"Nothing at all, sir. Nor did the Air Force personnel."

Buck turned back to me. "Then, if your suspicions are correct, it stands to reason that any sabotage was done between the time you landed and the time it was flown again. I'd bet that, once your flight was over, the glider was under somewhat less-intense scrutiny. The security was probably a lot laxer."

"True, we just walked off and left it parked in its spot. I don't remember anybody staying behind to watch it."

Patsy brightened perceptibly. "Well, that's a relief. Maybe all this worry was over nothing."

I wasn't quite ready to believe that. I saw no harm in letting Patsy feel better. But I wasn't completely convinced that I'd found the answer. That E-mail still bothered me.

I offered her my best smile. "Yeah, maybe you're right."

A cell phone interrupted us and we all dove into various purses and pockets to find the culprit.

"It's mine," Buck announced. "Buckley here," he said into the phone. "Yes?" He glanced at us, primarily at Patsy, and smiled. "Definitely busy." Turning back to the phone, he lowered his voice. "Yes? Can't you handle this yourself? Oh . . . I see. . . . Well, wait a moment." He covered the phone and shot us a rueful grin. "Retirement isn't what it's cracked up to be. This is the office and there's a paper that I have to sign. It'll only take a few minutes and it's only a couple of blocks off the route back to the hotel. Would it be an imposition to stop there for a moment?"

The Junior Leaguer pulled out her clipboard. "Well, we are scheduled to go to the Institute of Texan Cul—"

"Not at all," Patsy burbled, effectively cutting the woman off. "We'd love to see where Buck works, wouldn't we, Eve?"

"Worked," he corrected. "I'm merely an adviser these days." He glared at his phone. "Or so I keep telling them."

Blame the matchmaker in me.

Here I had two perfectly lovely people, one I loved to distraction and one I already truly liked. Only an idiot couldn't see the sparks between them. What we had here was a prime example of two people with extraordinary chemistry.

Why not help them with their laboratory work?

"I have an idea." I turned to John Kingston. "How much trouble would it be to split ranks? Buck and Patsy head on off to his office and I head back to the hotel?"

He grunted. "We have the manpower. And the vehicles." The unspoken message was *We don't even try to outguess you people, so we come prepared for all contingencies.*

I turned back to Patsy. "Then why don't we do that? I have this headache," I lied.

"Oh, sweetie. Do you want some aspirin?" Patsy started digging into her purse.

Miz Travis reached into her briefcase and pulled out a plastic bag full of pill bottles. "I bet I have something even stronger. . . ."

Her voice trailed off as we gaped at her medical stash. "It's all right," she said in a small voice. "I have prescriptions for them all." She shriveled before our eyes in the face of our universal disapproval.

I decided to be kind and simply waved away her effort on my behalf. "No, thank you. That's okay. If I can simply go lie down for a while, I'll be fine."

"I'll head back with you . . ." Patsy started, her sense of duty putting messy footprints all over my matchmaking plans.

"No, I'll be fine. You two head to Buck's office, and John here"—I glanced at him, already busy on his radio making preparations—"will see to me. Right?"

John nodded toward the window, where we saw a car pulling up next to us in the parking lot.

"Are you sure you wouldn't rather have me come back to the hotel with you?" Patsy wore the right expression and her words were full of that honest concern that pseudoparents have for their children, but I knew that somewhere in the back of her head, she was realizing exactly what I was doing. That woman knew me far too well.

"I'm sure." I leaned past her and gave Buck a quick kiss on the cheek. "I'm sorry to duck out like this, General Buck. I'm sure I'll regret missing the"—I glanced at the schedule—"Institute of Cultures."

"I understand completely." And judging by the twinkle in his eyes, I'm sure he did.

As I climbed out of the limousine, Patsy called out, "We'll meet you back at the hotel for lunch around one, okay?"

"Perfect." And it was. It'd give me a couple hours to myself and, more important, give them a couple of hours to themselves.

I had no fear that they could shake Miz Travis off their tail somehow.

I waved good-bye as they drove off, and then settled myself in the second car. It was far smaller than the limousine. I was getting spoiled, I guess. Now I was thinking of a Lincoln Town Car as a subcompact. "So it's just us, then," I announced to the crew.

"Where to?" the driver asked.

"The hotel."

Although he was a Secret Service agent, the driver seemed a lot more laid-back than most of the agents I knew well. "Hot date, eh?" he kidded.

"Not me." I pointed to the limousine driving away from us, safely nestled in its own caravan. "Them. I hope."

"I thought maybe you wanted to go shopping or something," John said.

"It's tempting, but no. All I want is for my aunt Patsy to enjoy herself. It'll be nice to go back to my hotel room where it's quiet and cool. Besides, I want a chance to digest all the things Major Gaskell told me." What I didn't tell all the Secret Service guys was that I was hoping I'd get up enough courage to make a few phone calls to see if Seybold and the Investigative Powers That Be had anything they'd share with me.

What I needed to do was go back and reexamine everything that had happened so far. Had we all been wrong? Maybe I wasn't the intended victim and Rydell was. Maybe the threatening E-mail was a crackpot who wanted to shake me up. I wished that Diana had been assigned to me on this trip, but she was on vacation. She's always been a great sounding board when I have something I want to talk through. She doesn't merely echo what I say, but helps me look at all the facts of a situation from different angles.

I don't have that sort of relationship with John. John's a great agent, but he's not much of a talker.

But that gave me an idea. I reached into my purse and pulled out my cell phone. I did have that sort of relationship with someone else. Someone who can think rings around just about everyone.

I dialed, it rang, and I made my way through the answering hierarchy in mere moments. "Charlie, it's Eve. Got a moment?"

"Sure. Hey, aren't you still in Texas? How is it?"

"Hot." I thought about Patsy and Buck. "And possibly getting hotter."

"You learn anything from the pilot?"

"Yeah. That's why I called. I want someone to help me think through this. You find out anything interesting on your end yet?"

"No, not yet. A guy who works for me is building a program that will go back and trace the IP address of the person who opened the anonymous account."

"Is that legal?"

"Don't ask."

"Okay." I scrounged around in my purse, looking for a pen and something to write on. No sign of them, though I distinctly remembered putting them in my bag. They'd vanished into thin air. It's as if a portal to another universe lives in the bottom of my purse, probably connected to the one in the washer back home that used to eat my socks. After one last try, in disgust I quit rooting around in my purse. "Can you take notes of this conversation, then E-mail them to me? I can't find a pen."

"Where's the Palm Pilot I gave you for Christmas?"

I gulped. "At home. I'm too afraid of losing it to bring it on trips."

"You? Afraid? Yeah, right. There aren't too many people bold enough to ask presidents of billion-dollar companies to act as their private secretary," he complained.

"I bet their big sisters do."

"Good point. Shoot."

"Number one: I need to know if the NTSB has determined definitively that the glider crashed because of pilot error or because it was sabotaged."

"Okay," Charlie said. "Examination of glider: pilot error or sabotage?" he read back in his usual word-saving version.

"Number two: Has anyone associated with the drug scandal—military or otherwise—threatened Cadet Keith Rydell?"

"What drug scandal?" Charlie said. "This is the first that I've heard of a drug scandal."

"That's what I found out from Gaskell. There was a big one at the Academy. Rydell, the guy who ratted out the rest of the cadet conspirators, was supposed to be flying that glider during the flight that crashed. The scandal involved cadets and maybe some nonmilitary types. Given Rydell's past, the scandal might provide a motive to make that glider crash. Would you pull up some information on it, please? That'll be number three."

"Sure. Rydell with two Ls?"

"I think so. Evidently, some fellow cadets used him as a mule to bring drugs onto Academy grounds. Rydell testified at their court-martial. Could you also check to see if the authorities, both civil and military, think they caught everyone involved? Maybe there's one cadet or someone from town who escaped the dragnet and is now trying to get revenge or something."

"Okay. Drug scandal at Academy, all players. Number four?"

It took me a while to formulate the right words for this one. "Did anyone blame Major Gaskell for persuading Rydell to testify against the others? Could be one of the guilty parties or maybe someone totally different."

"Good one. Number five?"

"Check to see if my pilot, Taylor Dobbs, has or had any connection with anything unusual or unexplained. Maybe even the drug scandal. Maybe he was the intended victim, instead of me or Gaskell or Rydell."

"Any other potential victims? You're getting a long list there, Eve."

I thought about my "We always hurt the ones we love" theory. "Ashley McCurdy. Maybe by killing her, they were hoping to shut Rydell up."

"After the fact? Not likely. Revenge, retribution, I'll buy that. But he's already talked. It's too late for a preemptive strike."

"Keep her on the list—"

I heard a sudden loud pop and the car swerved hard to the right. I fell across the seat and smacked my head against the door. The phone flew out of my hand.

The driver swore viciously, and my immediate reaction was to sit up and see what idiot had hit us. John, sitting in the passenger side of the front seat, reached over and shoved me back down. Hard.

"Stay down!" he shouted. "Gunfire!"

CHAPTER NINE

SECRET SERVICE RADIO TRANSCRIPT

"Shots fired. I repeat, shots fired. One, maybe two direct hits. Apple undamaged. I repeat, Apple undamaged. Taking evasive maneuvers."

"Hang on," the driver commanded through gritted teeth. He was obviously fighting the steering wheel. I could feel us skidding across the asphalt, and I prayed that it was onto the shoulder of the road and not into the lanes of oncoming traffic. Cars honked, brakes screeched, and I had the distinct feeling people were making uncouth gestures in our direction. But I couldn't see them. I was smashed facedown into the leather upholstery.

I heard some more popping sounds, then an odd thud. I turned enough to look up at where I'd been sitting. A web of cracks now covered the back windshield. They seemed to emanate from one place, a spot that by my calculations was directly behind where my head had been when I was sitting up in the backseat a second or two ago.

Not a good sign.

Self-preservation kicked in. I rolled from the seat to the floorboards. It seemed safer down there. I wondered if the car was armored. And bulletproofed. And, if so, how well.

When the car started slowing down, a little voice in my head began screaming, *Don't stop! Get us the hell out of here!* I was the only one who heard that little voice. My real voice was clogged up somewhere in my throat, which was threatening to squeeze closed. Which was bad, because the contents of my stomach were threatening to make a reappearance.

We lurched to a stop.

Evidently, John Kingston thought I might surrender to the temptation to pop up and ask, "What's wrong, guys?" He placed a meaty hand on my back, pushing me down into the floorboards, putting some muscle into it.

"Stay down," he said.

"Don't worry," I said in a muffled voice. I was pleased that I didn't sound too shaky. It surprised me, because I was feeling like panicking might be a good idea.

I could hear someone pull up behind us. For one perilous, almost James Bondian moment, I wondered if some sort of assassin had caught up with us. Kingston would give James Bond a run for his money, I told myself. At least the bullets had stopped flying. I huddled deeper into the floorboards, trying to make myself the smallest target possible. If there were bad guys out there, I knew that the good guys don't always win.

But rather than bad guys, it was the cavalry. I soon realized from the things that John was saying either to our driver or into his radio that the vehicles that had pulled up next to us were more parts of our detail.

I had the feeling they were literally circling the wagons.

I felt suddenly self-conscious for cowering like a scared rabbit on the floorboards. On the other hand, I was pretty sure that the Secret Service approved of my lying low. As a compromise, I turned over on my side so that I could at least see something other than the floor mats. Of course, that meant getting another stunning view of the spiderwebbed glass and the well-placed hole at my head level.

Maybe cowering wasn't such a bad idea after all.

But I swallowed hard and studied the shattered glass, realizing that it had merely cracked and that there was no resulting hole on the interior surface.

What do you know . . . bulletproof glass actually works.

Outside, I could hear people shouting orders.

John leaned over from the front seat, his weapon drawn. He was scanning the area while talking into his radio. Although it wasn't the first time

I'd ever seen one of my agents with gun in hand, I must admit the sight always shook me up.

Armed and dangerous, and all to protect me. In fact, I was pretty sure they'd sworn to take a bullet for me. It frightened me that they might yet have to today. I wasn't sure we were out of the woods yet.

Judging by the intense look on John's face, he was receiving orders from a higher-up via his earpiece. "Yes, sir," he said. "She's fine." He glanced down at me. "No injuries and absolutely calm, sir. Handled herself like a trooper."

Yes, I agreed silently. *That's me. Calm on the outside and completely liquefied on the inside.* I gave John a smile that was probably shaky and a thumbs-up which definitely was.

After a series of brusque grunts, John looked down at me. "Okay, here's the plan. The other car is going to pull up next to us, but they're going to turn around so that they're facing the other direction."

"So we can see who's shooting at us?" Can you blame me for being a little dense when I'm under great stress?

John didn't get mad at my evident lack of understanding. "No. We lost both back tires back there and the rear windshield has been compromised. We have to move you to another car."

I wasn't too sure what his plan was, but I had enough faith in those whose job was to protect me to blindly follow orders.

"Okay," I said. "Tell me what you want me to do."

I shifted back to the seat, being careful to keep all my body parts below the top of the seat. A compromised rear windshield—that didn't sound too good.

"I'm going to count to five. On three, the doors on both cars will open. I'll get out on four. Once I'm in position, I'll call five, and I want you to move as quickly as possible into the other car."

"I move on five. Not three, not four, but five."

"Yes, ma'am."

"Then let's do it."

At this point, I think I was working on survival instinct alone. "Flight" had clearly won any struggle against the concept of "fight."

On "five," I threw myself into the other car. As it turned out, the bulletproof doors on both sides of me weren't my only protection. John used his body as a shield, literally putting himself between me and whoever had been shooting at us.

I was sprawled across the backseat of the other car. I'd barely landed before the door slammed behind me and we peeled out of there.

In seconds, two screaming squad cars pulled out of traffic and in front of our entourage. I've traveled in motorcades before, but never doing twenty or thirty miles an hour above the speed limit. Sanctioned speeding. That seemed funny to me at that moment, but I wasn't really firing on all cylinders.

But some instincts are ingrained, no matter how much stress you're under. As soon as I got myself sort of upright, I automatically reached for my seat belt and put it on.

"Ma'am, it might be better if you remain reclined."

I realized then that there was another male agent sitting in the backseat with me.

I shook my head. "Not unless you want me to get carsick." My stomach was queasy enough in reaction to all the hoopla. "I'll keep my head down, but I'd rather not lie down just now."

He grimaced at me and started to say something, but John shook his head. "If she wants to sit up, she sits up." He glanced at me. "But you really do need to stay below the level of the seat back. Okay, Eve?"

He'd called me by my first name. Very unusual for him. Even under these circumstances, I found it comforting.

"No problem," I said. "Good plan. Wouldn't want to do in another windshield."

Holding on to the door handle for support, I slouched down in my seat.

"How far are we from the hotel?" I asked. At the speeds we were driving, I doubted it was going to take very long to get there.

The agent sitting next to me kept a sharp watch out the back window. Evidently he was not too worried about being mistaken for me. Or he figured the glass would hold if somebody took a shot. "Ten minutes with the escort."

I could see the flashing lights of several approaching squad cars. They moved in, essentially putting us in the center—sort of the meat in a police car sandwich. My heart thundered along with the wailing sirens and pulsating lights. A few basic truths commanded all my attention.

Somebody was shooting at my car.

Somebody was shooting at me.

Somebody was trying to kill me.

One of the agents consulted his radio, then leaned over to the driver and gave him some terse instructions.

"What?" I demanded. "What'd they say?" I wanted to know everything. If anyone didn't understand that, after the turmoil I'd gone through in the last few minutes, then he just wasn't human.

"Don't worry," the man whose name I didn't know assured me. "We were just getting instructions on where to go once when we reach the hotel."

"Okay." I settled back in my seat. I drew in a deep breath and tried to regain control. I turned to the agent beside me and held out my hand. "Hi, I'm Eve Cooper. Who are you?"

The man looked a bit startled.

"I thought we should introduce ourselves. It seems to me that I ought to know the names of the people who just saved my life." No response. Just more staring. I pressed on. "I'm scared to death. If someone doesn't start talking to me, about anything, even about what just happened, I think I could go crazy." I stared at him. "Let's try this again. What's your name?"

The look he gave me was one an airport screener would give a package marked "Weapon of Mass Destruction." "Barry Delaney."

"You live in San Antonio?"

He shook his head. "Dallas."

"D-Dallas," I said. I was *not* going to start shaking. "I—I went to Dallas on assignment once."

And I continued to chatter, unable to keep track of the stupid things I was probably saying. Somehow, I felt compelled to use the mundane, inconsequential words to try to regain my control and my sanity. I was going to hold it together and pretend that something earth-shattering hadn't just happened to me.

It was John Kingston who came to my rescue, starting some very un–Secret Service chatter.

"So how long did you work for the wire service?"

"Not long enough." There. That was a suitably safe topic. I tried to remember a couple of the better stories about my adventures behind the lens. I went blank.

John filled in the silence, telling me about his wife, her family, his family, anything to help me pretend all was well.

We weren't fooling anyone, but it helped.

Once the two new agents realized what was going on, they relaxed a tiny bit—at least they stopped looking at me as if I were going to shatter, or crack up like the other car's windshield.

The promised ten minutes crawled by. Our shield of cop cars got thicker. Finally, we got within sight of the hotel, but instead of pulling into the hotel's garage entrance, we took a detour, turned into a back alley, and headed toward a loading dock. Once we pulled in, a large overhead door rattled shut behind us. The big space reverberated with the clank of its closing.

I found the sound quite disconcerting. Somehow, it sounded like the ominous clang of a jail door, marking the end of my already limited freedom. Blinking in the sudden gloom, I squinted through the tinted glass of the Lincoln into the relative darkness beyond. In the shadows, I could see a whole cadre of personnel waiting for us on the loading dock. Some wore the bland nonuniforms of the Secret Service. Others wore burgundy red blazers and were obviously members of hotel security. There was a cop or two sprinkled in there as well.

As soon as the driver shut off the engine, the security folks spread out, creating a cordon leading inside. I wondered if it led all the way from the loading dock up to our suite.

This is probably overkill, I thought, then immediately chastised myself for my extremely poor word choice.

And I was expected to walk that long mile, not in disgrace, but certainly fighting a big case of fear, with a nasty undercurrent of embarrassment.

I figured I had two options. I could let everyone know exactly how scared I really was, or I could pretend that people shot at me every day and I could handle it.

If I'd ever wanted to channel Aunt Patsy and her ability to retain grace under high stress, this was it. I closed my eyes. I took several shallow breaths and then one big deep one. Then I opened my eyes.

Time to see if I could deliver that Oscar-winning performance.

Before I got out of the car, I held out my hand and shook the hands of both Agent Delaney and the driver, thanking them for the ride and for their superb handling of the situation. Just like Aunt Patsy would do. Then I reached over and patted John Kingston's massive arm. "Thanks, John. You can ride with me any day."

He looked somewhat taken aback. "Just doing my job, ma'am."

I noticed he'd dropped "Eve" and gone back into his "ma'am" routine. Then he smiled at me. I felt as if I'd just passed some kind of test.

As soon as the car door opened, I was hit with the sharp aroma coming from the large garbage Dumpsters that lined the loading dock. My already unquiet stomach lurched in response and sweat beaded my upper lip. *Lovely.* I swallowed hard. I wasn't going to puke in front of this audience. I tried to hide my reaction to the odor, which was made worse by the hot, unmoving air, but the agent helping me out of the car noticed.

"Sorry about the stench," he offered in apology. "We wanted a secure area to unload you, and this was the best alternative."

I shrugged. "I appreciate that. Don't worry about it. This is a loading dock. It's Texas. It's hot. That sort of smell just comes with the territory. I'll be fine."

A hotel official appeared by my elbow and started to escort me up the chipped concrete stairs that led to the dock and what I assumed was yet another back entrance into the hotel proper. "Miss Cooper, I'm so sorry we couldn't provide you a secure entrance that wasn't so—"

"Memorable?" I managed to laugh without choking on the fetid air or my churning stomach. "I really will be fine." Maybe if I said it enough, I would begin to believe it. "Trust me, I've smelled worse in my day. In fact, once, I fell into a Dumpster in the back of a Japanese restaurant when taking a picture of their loading dock. Their specialty was sushi. It was even more memorable." I conjured up the best smile I could, considering the situation. "Thanks for arranging the private entrance."

What I'd neglected to mention to this audience about my previous Dumpster experience was that I didn't fall in. An irate restaurant owner had pushed me in. He didn't want anyone getting photographic evidence of the empty crates that proved his "fresh" fish came from frozen sources. I had to remember the moral of my own story; I'd faced trouble before and survived. Maybe not trouble like this, but certainly serious trouble. I'd made it through. I'd do it again.

"I'm Jonathan Mattey," the man said. "I'm the day manager for this hotel, and I just want you to know that we're more than willing to take whatever steps are necessary to make sure your stay at the McAllister remains safe as well as pleasant. My staff has worked and will continue to work diligently with your security people to assure your stay here is enjoyable as well as totally secure."

I acknowledged his promise with a nod. "I appreciate your assurance, and I can promise you . . ." I paused and looked around at the loading dock and all its many and varied personnel. "I feel safer already." I felt compelled to continue with the obligatory "We've been very impressed and very pleased with the hotel and its staff. This is a lovely facility." There, I'd said it. Aunt Patsy couldn't have done it better.

Mattey straightened and his tentative smile grew wide with pride. "Thank you very much, Miss Cooper."

Maybe there really was something to this manners stuff.

With the pleasantries over and before my stomach could rebel on me, we finally left the dock and its robust aromas behind and headed through a set of heavy double utility doors. Mattey guided my entourage of agents (many still with guns drawn) through a labyrinth of back hallways, proving that even the most glamorous of hotels had some extremely unglamorous areas.

However, it wasn't all dingy corridors. Our tour through the bowels of the hotel included a quick trip through the kitchen. By this time my agents had holstered their weapons, though their hands still looked twitchy and stayed close to their jackets. A pastry chef brightened when I commented nicely on the dessert he was plating as I walked by. It seemed the right thing to do at the moment. My reward for my observation was an éclair that under any other circumstances I'd have wolfed down. But I couldn't stop—my escorts would be furious with me. Besides, between my nerves and the last lingering traces of the loading dock stench still circulating in my sinuses, I couldn't have swallowed a bite.

But before the chef's face could fall, I asked if I could take the prize to my room, where I could savor it properly. The chef beamed and gave it to me.

I took it and thanked him—I'd learned a lot about how to talk to chefs at the White House. Thank-yous are always appropriate. I got out of there with my dignity intact and my escort relieved. And a big honking éclair.

But I wasn't hungry. I wasn't sure I'd ever be hungry again. My Aunt Patsy mask was starting to fail, and I was hit with an overwhelming desire to give in to the inner child who wanted to scream "I was scared," curl up in a corner, and have everyone comfort me and tell me everything would be better.

But that wouldn't happen. It was my duty to remain gracious and in control and to make everyone around me feel as if this were a simple change in plans rather than a measured response to confirmed danger. I owed it to my dad to pull it off.

As we rode up in the freight elevator, I noticed the main advantage of using freight elevators: no elevator music. Clearly I was getting a little punchy. Once we reached our floor, we trooped down the hallway and I was delivered to my suite door.

An agent opened it for me. I didn't get one good step inside before finding myself smothered in Aunt Patsy's embrace. What she lacked in size, she more than made up for in enthusiasm and strength. And thank heavens, I recognized her grip before my overactive imagination took control.

"Oh, sweetheart, I was so worried when they told me what happened. We headed straight back here as soon as we heard. Are you all right, sweetheart? Your father said for you to call him the moment you got back to the room."

I tried to respond to her questions, but my answers were muffled by her death grip.

"Air," I gasped, trying to extricate myself.

She loosened her hold and switched to holding my hand. "I couldn't stop worrying. I knew we shouldn't have separated."

"How could you have known? How could anyone have known?"

Buck stepped into view. "The town car is being flatbedded back to the police garage so their forensic people can look at it."

"You mean look at the bullet holes?" The sense of calm control I'd managed to work up earlier started flow away in their presence. I dropped into the nearest chair, my legs growing suddenly too rubbery to support me.

Patsy knelt beside me. "Sweetheart, are you all right?"

"No." Before I could surrender to every emotion that had been churning inside my gut, I uttered the words I'd been wanting to say since the car made that fateful lurch to the right. I looked up at her, at Buck, then back to her.

"I want to go home."

"Of course." Patsy shoved a cell phone in my hand. "Call your father. I've already started packing our things."

Okay. I'll admit it.

I almost started crying when I spoke with Dad.

Almost.

We're not talking a case of hysterical waterworks or those gulpy sobs that make it hard to understand what a person is saying. But just those unpleasant hot tears that sting your eyes and roll down your cheeks, leaving salty streaks.

"Eve, are you all right?" His voice was unusually calm and quiet—the tone he uses when he's really upset.

"Not a scratch on me," I said. My voice never wavered. I never lost control, but I couldn't stop the tears. "I'm okay, Dad."

"It's scary, eh?"

"Yeah." It was the only word I could manage around the sudden flood of emotion making my knees start to quiver. "Yeah," I repeated.

"This time, it's unmistakable. Somebody's out to get you."

"I know," I whispered. "But I don't know why."

"Right now, we don't need to know why. Right now, we simply need to get you home." He paused. "I need to know you're going to be safe, Eve. Please, be careful."

I've never heard my father sound quite so . . . desperate. Hearing his anguish was eating a hole through me. "I will, Dad," I assured him. "Everyone is on double-triple alert. It would take an army to reach me right now. And you're the only one with an army handy."

I heard him release a sigh.

"Okay, if you're able to crack a bad joke, then I know you're okay for now. Can I talk to Patsy?"

I handed over the phone and headed to the bedroom. Then it hit me—Charlie! What in heaven was he thinking! The last thing he'd heard from me was gunshots being fired and a thump! My cell phone was back on the floor of the car being towed for forensic examination. I wasn't sure that using the house phone was a good idea. Finally, I asked the nearest Secret Service agent to fill in my brother on what had gone on, and to tell him that I'd call him as soon as I could. I wasn't up to talking to him just yet. I was pretty sure I'd lose it if I tried.

I finished the packing job Patsy had begun. As I folded my unmentionables, I decided that for once, I wasn't upset that another vacation had been shot to hell.

Better the vacation than me . . .

Packing took only moments, which was unfortunate because I had to kill—another bad choice of words—almost an hour before we could head to the airport. I tried to interest myself in television, but the only channel that didn't have a running news crawl describing my newest misadventures was HBO. I didn't want to watch *The Sixth Sense* for the sixteenth time.

I didn't want to see dead people.

Finally, we got word that the flight and escort arrangements were completed and we could leave. I was relieved, even if it meant entering yet another car, hopefully this one with its back windshield intact.

If it'd been solely up to me, I might have seriously considered renting a car and driving myself to the airport. I know how foolish that sounds, but half the time, I wonder if riding around in large entourages with limousines, chase cars, and police escorts isn't tantamount to painting a target on my back with the words "High-Profile Victim, Aim Here."

All those vehicles had sure come in handy today, though. That brought up another thought. If I was indeed someone's target, then the last thing I wanted to do was draw Patsy into the path of any potential danger . . . or bullets.

Who would notice another blond tourist in sunglasses in a rented subcompact heading to the airport? Heck, why not?

But nobody liked that plan, especially the Secret Service. And I couldn't really blame them. Their collective butts were on the line when it came to taking responsibility for my safety.

So instead, we—meaning me, Patsy, Buck, and our litter of agents—traveled in a highly recognizable entourage through the streets of downtown San Antonio. Though I tried to insist that Buck and Patsy get in a different car from the one I was riding in, Patsy overruled me. As luck would have it, the driver took a slight detour so that we passed by the Alamo.

You know, I'd always pictured it as a lone outpost in the middle of nowhere, a quiet testament to the brave souls who had fought and died there.

And that's just what it had been, back in the days of that brave but forlorn last stand. It was now a tourist attraction, located smack in the middle of downtown San Antonio, nestled between tall buildings and surrounded by busy streets.

Somewhat like the White House . . .

Buck sat in the back of the car on the other side of Patsy. "Next time you two come, we'll go to Dirty Nelly's on the Riverwalk and we'll see just how many Irish drinking songs you know."

He wasn't being obtuse, ignoring what'd happened. He was trying to distract us, making the assumption that our next trip would be totally normal. In fact, in the last desperate hour he'd been a pillar of support for both Patsy and me, not only distracting us, but even sometimes making us laugh. It was thanks to him that we were making a speedy trip back home. He'd arranged for us to use his corporate jet, rather than flying on a commercial flight.

As we rode along, I wondered if there was a hidden agenda in his offer. Because we were using his jet, it was only natural for him to ride with us to the airport, and maybe even on the ride back to D.C. to be with Patsy for as long as humanly possible. Patsy certainly wouldn't mind.

Trust me, I don't mind that sort of hidden agenda. After all, who am I to stand in the way of true love? Or at least the potential for true love. Just contemplating it was a wonderful distraction in the midst of the horror.

When we reached the airport, we took a turn just short of the road marked "Terminal" and headed instead toward a series of small hangars. I could tell which one contained our plane by the number of unmarked cars parked around it. As we approached, the hangar doors slowly pushed open until the space was just wide enough for us to drive right in.

Moments later, we were ushered on board Buck's private jet. It might have been smaller than a commercial plane, but not by much. Buck and Patsy chose seats toward the rear of the plane. To assure them maximum privacy, I chose one near the front.

"You aren't going to sit by us?" Patsy asked, her look of innocence not quite reaching her eyes.

"No, no . . . I thought I'd sit up here and maybe get a nap. Or read." *Or anything else I can think of to give you two a little quiet time together.*

One of our agents started down the aisle to shadow them, but I grabbed his sleeve. "Let's give them a little privacy. Sit up here with me."

He looked a bit shocked, but nodded. "Yes, ma'am."

I smiled at him. "Do you know Diana Gates? The agent usually assigned to my detail?"

He nodded again.

"You ever play poker with her?"

The man's mouth twitched.

"I take it that's a yes. Here's the important question. After playing her, you ever walk away with any money left in your pocket?"

His twitch developed into his version of a small smile. "Rarely."

"Good." I patted the seat across from me. "Then I stand a chance. I've got some cards and it's your task to find some peanuts." He took a few steps back up the aisle. I added, "And see if anybody else wants to play."

Our poker game, played for wildly high though imaginary stakes, proved to be a perfect distraction from my overwhelming memory of screeching tires and shattering glass. It also kept me from trying to find a reflective surface and take sneak peeks to see how Buck was comforting Patsy.

Very nicely, I hoped.

Once we landed, I felt it was safe to turn around. When I did, I saw Buck lean over and place a very chaste kiss on Patsy's cheek. I was almost disappointed. Of course, even I knew that my mental image of the two of them necking during the entire flight like high schoolers in the back row of a movie theater was absurd.

They wandered up the aisle toward me as we all waited for the ground crew to open the door.

"We appreciate the ride home, Buck," Patsy said, displaying her usual impeccable manners.

I followed her lead. "It was a pleasure meeting you. All you've done for me and Patsy really was beyond the call of duty, General Buck. Thanks."

His smile was aimed toward me, but his gaze didn't quite leave Patsy's face. "But not beyond the call of friendship," he said softly.

Friendship.

Yeah. I should have a *friend* that looked at me like that.

Patsy placed a hand on his arm. "You aren't heading back right away, are you, Buck? Surely you can stay for a while."

He ducked his head. If I wasn't mistaken, he actually blushed. "Well, I'd planned to do a quick turnaround—"

"Nonsense. You could at least stay for dinner. If I know Elliot, he'd love to thank you in person for all you've done for me and Eve."

He took her hands in his and sighed. "Patsy, I'd love to stay, but I really can't. I have to get home to Annabella."

Huh? Who's Annabella?

To my surprise, Patsy merely nodded. "Oh, of course. I understand."

He smiled. "You always did." He leaned over and gave her a kiss on the cheek, his lips lingering just a bit longer than I expected. "You take care, you hear me, Patricia?"

I've seen Patsy adapt to almost every situation. It's been a long, winding road from being an adoring aunt to a substitute mother to a substitute First Lady. She's borne every bend in that road with grace and courage.

But judging by the look in Buck's eyes, he didn't see her as a substitute anything.

It was beautiful. I swallowed hard. I would have stood there and openly gawked if Patsy hadn't looked over and given me an obvious "How about some privacy, here?" look.

Buck tore his gaze away from her long enough to give me a quick buss on the cheek. "It was a pleasure to meet you, Eve."

I felt comfortable enough to give him a hug. "You, too, General Buck. Thanks so much for everything. You're my hero."

I climbed into the waiting car and tried not to watch the two of them say their good-byes. I felt like a doting parent watching a kid on a date. Finally, I saw daylight between them. After they separated, Patsy wandered toward the car. I understood that sort of postkiss daze; I'd felt it once or twice myself in my limited lifetime. I hoped her knees held out as she walked to the car.

Once she slipped into the seat beside me, I pointed to Buck and his pilot, who were walking slowly back to their plane. "You know what he's saying right now?"

Patsy watched his retreat with entirely too much attention and appreciation for a woman her age. "What?"

I spoke in a low growl. " 'Louis, I think this is the beginning of a beautiful relationship.' "

"You rat." Patsy made a face. "In *Casablanca,* Ilsa was the one who left on the plane. And it was 'friendship,' not 'relationship.' "

"Then maybe it's time for a sequel. *Return to Casablanca*?"

Patsy didn't even dignify that with a response, much less laughter. Okay, so it was weak. But I wanted her to concentrate on the wonderful part of her trip, not my scary adventure. And she did. She stared out the opposite window from the plane, as if not wanting to watch Buck fade away as we pulled away.

I wanted to distract her, but the one thing that had me burning with curiosity might not be the best topic to bring up. On the other hand, I was sure it didn't have anything to do with me. I decided to throw caution to the four winds.

"Okay, one more question. No, two more."

She faced me, still careful not to look in the direction of the plane. "What?"

"Who is this Annabella? And why is Buck so hot to get back to her?"

I expected several possible reactions from her; anger, anguish, concern . . .

But I didn't expect her to grin.

"Because she's pregnant."

Pregnant? My mind jumped to a cascade of unsavory explanations. I knew from his discussion about his kids that Buck had no daughters, or even daughters-in-law for that matter. So who was this pregnant Annabella? His housekeeper? His girlfriend?

His second, third, or fourth wife? Or mistress?

"That's the answer to my second question." I swallowed hard. "And the answer to the first question—who is Annabella?"

"His"—Patsy paused, shaking with laughter—"dog. She's a registered golden retriever who is ready to drop her litter any day now." Her mirth faded and she had a rather thoughtful expression. "He's offered us a puppy when they're weaned. Think Drew's ready for the responsibility of caring for a dog? The White House needs an official pet."

Until it pees on some priceless antique rug . . . On the other hand . . .

"Yeah," I said. "It's high time somebody who is more trouble than Drew moved in to take the heat off him."

We both grinned.

CHAPTER TEN

NATIONAL WIRE ASSOCIATION

Presidential First Daughter Eve Cooper suffered another scare today when the car in which she was riding had a blowout as it was moving down a San Antonio freeway. The Secret Service agent driving the vehicle momentarily lost control, but regained it seconds later without impacting any other cars or the railing. Ms. Cooper and the other occupants of the car were uninjured. Ms. Cooper, along with First Lady Patricia Davidson, has curtailed her Texas trip and returned to Washington, D.C. This accident comes after another close call for the First Daughter, a glider crash at the United States Air Force Academy. . . .

We settled around the same kitchen table we'd been using for years. It was part of the furnishings we'd brought with us when we moved into the White House. The table wasn't an antique by any means, but it did have a great deal of sentimental value, and a lot of family history behind it. It was the first piece of furniture Dad and Mom bought when they got married. Although they could have afforded a better table years later, they held on to it because neither of them could bear to part with it.

We'd held many serious discussions while sitting around this table as a family. I remember our collective joy and surprise when Mom told us she was pregnant with Drew. At age nine, I was old enough to understand the excitement, as well as, I hoped, to be a help to her.

I remember the night when we all sat around the table, watching her remain dry-eyed as she told us about her newly diagnosed cancer. She promised to do everything she could to beat it. She told us not to worry.

We'd all sat around this same table, Drew in his high chair, when Dad explained to us that Mom was losing the battle. He told us that night that she was dying.

But we were lucky. This table had seen many, many more happy discussions than sad ones. And it'd had its share of historic ones, as well. We'd been seated around this same table when Dad announced his decision to make a presidential bid. Drew, Charlie, Patsy, and I were sitting around this table, nursing mugs of hot chocolate, when the network news anchors declared Dad the official winner of the election in the wee hours of election night.

The discussion we were about to have might just fall into all three categories, I thought. Happy because I was unharmed. Sad—well, that goes without saying. And historic, too. Assassination attempts on presidential family members make the history books. Dad handed me the report he'd received while we were flying back home. The look in his eyes scared me, even though his face was perfectly controlled.

I suppose it was encouraging that he didn't make me sit there and listen to him read it aloud, but it was no fun to read it silently to myself, knowing that he was awaiting my comment. Essentially, the report said that the police, aided by the Secret Service, had pulled a fragment of a single bullet out of the town car's rear right tire. Investigators were scouring the highway in hopes of finding the other bullet, the one which had struck the rear windshield but hadn't penetrated. They assumed it had bounced harmlessly to the roadside. Forensic tests were still being conducted on the one bullet they had, but their experts were willing to say that the bullet had most likely come from a high-powered rifle.

Think sniper.

That's what the Secret Service was doing, anyway. Taking into account the entrance angle of the bullet into the tire and the location on the road, plus details from the shattered windshield, the agents had examined several buildings in the vicinity and had zeroed in on the most likely location, based on height and line of sight: Wilford Hall Medical Center.

That was scary.

I put down the papers and wrapped my chilled hands around the cup of hot chocolate Patsy had placed in front of me. I couldn't bring myself to drink any, and I noticed that neither she nor Dad had touched any of theirs either.

There are some things that hot chocolate simply can't fix.

Dad glanced at the paper. "Did you get to the part about the hospital roof?"

"Yes, sir."

He spoke in a low voice. "They've fingerprinted the area that was used as the staging area by the shooter, as well as the spent casings they found up there. They're running the prints right now. We should learn something. Soon."

I stared blankly at the file on the table. "Soon," I echoed.

Something finally flared in his face, and his voice cracked. "Eve, I can't go on like this."

"What?" My stomach did a big flip-flop. "Dad?" I reached out and touched his arm. "What are you talking about?"

"You." He looked up, dry-eyed, but the fear he felt was palpable. "I can't go on pretending that this isn't scaring me to death. You know how much you mean to me. If my being President is going to put you in this sort of jeopardy, then the obvious answer is to do whatever it takes to remove you from the public eye."

I had a sudden vision of me living out the rest of his White House tenure in some underground bunker. The prospect made my frayed nerves unravel even more.

My father reached across the same table where we'd celebrated his election win and looked me straight in the eye. "And the only realistic way to remove you from the public eye is to remove myself."

Was he saying what I thought he was saying?

He gave me his most resolute stare. "I'll resign, if that's what it takes to keep you and your brothers safe."

I couldn't speak. But I had to. I had to stop him.

"No," I managed to say between gritted teeth. "I won't let you do it."

Dad waved a hand in protest. "Eve, don't—"

"I won't let you," I repeated, interrupting him. "At the risk of sounding like a movie cliché, America needs you. The world needs you."

He slammed his fist against the table. "Damn what they need. My family comes first. Always has, always will."

This was no political rhetoric. This was love, pure and simple. No question. Have I mentioned how much I love my dad?

It took me a moment to find my voice. "I know that, Dad. All of us know that." My hand didn't tremble when I placed it on top of his. "I need you too, Dad, but even more important, I need you in office."

"Eve . . ." He looked as if he wanted to say something else but couldn't.

But I could. "It's the truth, Dad. If you step down from office, then the bad guys win. How do you think that would make me feel? Something like that would haunt me for the rest of my life. I'm not going to let them get away with it. I'll do what I have to do to keep myself safe. If that means staying holed up in the White House for the rest of your term, then so be it. Or maybe I'll move in with Charlie. He's got a fortress up there. Heck, I'll go live in a nunnery if necessary, but there's no way in hell I'm going to let you resign."

Patsy had been uncharacteristically quiet up to now, but it was evident that she could no longer contain her thoughts.

"She's right, Elliot. If you resign, then you're bowing to undue, unwarranted, unlawful pressure." She gave him her best big-sister glare. "Coopers don't quit."

He sat back in his chair and folded his hands across his stomach. He appeared to be contemplating our unanimous stance against resignation. After a few moments of stony silence, he spoke. "Okay. No early departures. But I do reserve the right to rethink my decision at any point. And I'll certainly have a better idea of what to do when we learn more about what is happening to Eve."

Patsy and I sighed in unison. Another presidential crisis averted.

Dad looked at both of us and then managed a small grin. "I have a distinct feeling I've been double-teamed."

"Maybe," I said.

Patsy and I looked at each other. "Great minds think alike," she offered.

Dad pushed away from the table and gestured for both Patsy and me to do the same. We ended up in a big three-way hug. After a moment or two, he whispered, "You'd hate living with Charlie in the middle of nowhere, wouldn't you?"

"Detest it," I said in complete honesty. "But I'll gladly do it if it means keeping you in office. I'm willing to put my faith in the people whose job is to keep me safe. If you think about it, so far they've done a pretty good job of it. I'm here. And I'm safe. Right?"

He tightened his embrace and said nothing. After a while, he offered a sigh. "We do have the best security teams in the world protecting all of us. They'll be even sharper than usual until we get to the bottom of this. And we have the finest investigators in the world determined to find out who the people are who are behind this." He pulled back and gave me his finest "I really believe what I'm saying" smile. "It's just a matter of time before we figure this all out."

A matter of time.

Those words continued to haunt me. Seybold had repeated them to me later that day. The same words ended virtually every security report I read. Everybody continually promised it was just a matter of time before they unraveled the entire plot and discovered the who, what, how, when, and why behind the shooting incident. The initial reports never used the word "attack" even though I definitely felt attacked. What I'd endured was an "incident."

So far, our crack security team had no suspects, no witnesses, no fingerprints, and no real leads.

Seybold had already put forward his pet theories in print. He was the first one to suggest that, yes, the glider crash had most likely been an accident. But he felt that the publicity and attention the incident had generated had put the spotlight on me, something we'd luckily avoided so far during Dad's tenure.

In Seybold's little scenario, some nutcase had watched all the media concern over my safety and decided that if he made a couple of threats against me, he might be recognized for his efforts and immortalized in the history books.

It'd been done before.

Essentially, Seybold theorized that the reason behind the attack in San Antonio wasn't over any deep-seated hatred for me or what I might stand for. He even suggested that the attack probably didn't reflect anyone's anger over Dad's politics in the past, present, or future.

I was simply a convenient way for some lunatic to achieve his goal of getting worldwide attention.

Talk about a sense of irony; I was both the most important part of the equation as the potential target, and the least important, since I was merely the means to some madman's end.

At least if this was over politics, it would make a nasty, evil sort of sense.

Selfish bastard.

I'm referring to the shooter here—not Seybold.

Seybold's theory was only one among many—it was merely the explanation that angered me the most. That sense of anger had lingered through the night, ruining my sleep. Unwilling to face anyone the next morning, I remained upstairs and scrounged up breakfast from my dwindling personal supplies.

Toast and Diet Coke—breakfast of champions.

But it was all my stomach could tolerate. I'd finished the first piece of toast when I glanced over and saw my answering-machine light flashing.

For a moment, I considered pretending I hadn't seen it. I was getting good at the ostrich-in-the-sand routine. But my conscience nagged me.

I finally hit the playback button.

The first message was from Megan Lassiter, saying she had some news and asking me to please call her back at my earliest convenience. I noted it was a request, not a demand or an order, so our truce must still have been in force.

The second call was from Peter Seybold. He didn't fool around with pleasantries such as "please" or "earliest convenience." And because he brings out some of my worst juvenile traits, I decided to place him second on my list of things to do this morning. I called Megan first.

"It's Eve. You called?"

"Thanks. That was fast." She sounded almost grateful. "Do you think we could get together sometime today and talk? There are a couple of things that happened, stuff I've learned that I think you need to know." This was quite a different Megan from the one who had invited herself over the last time, ready to read me the riot act. I wondered what exclusive news she had that wouldn't filter to me through official sources.

"News like what?"

She paused, and I heard a decidedly watery sniff.

"I can't discuss it over the phone. Can I come there? Sometime this morning?"

I could just hear the words "or sooner" in her voice. "Sure, Megan." I glanced at my desk calendar. "I'm clear all morning long, and into the early afternoon."

"How about eleven?"

"Great. I'll clear you through security."

After we hung up, I sat down, wondering what her new revelations could be. Her fierceness was gone. Now she sounded shaken. It was unlikely she knew much about my latest adventures, since the real story had been kept out of the press. We wouldn't want any more crazies wanting the world's attention to get any bright ideas, after all.

Then again, maybe Megan had Air Force contacts at Wilford Hall who'd mentioned Patsy's impromptu visit, my little mishap, and later the joint efforts of the security forces and Secret Service and their inordinate interest in the roof of the building.

Two plus two . . .

But in any case, I didn't think my safety was her chief concern.

It *was* one of Peter Seybold's many responsibilities, and I knew I needed to go ahead and get dealing with him out of the way.

Rather than call him, I headed straight to his office, telling myself I could use the exercise to get my mind clear and my blood flowing. His secretary told me he was busy, but swore he'd be free "in just a minute."

And four and one half minutes later, he was.

I stepped into his inner office. "You have news?"

He motioned for me to close the door. I did, and then I approached his desk. I didn't like the look on his face, but then again, when have I ever?

He tapped a folder on his desk. "We just learned that there was an unplayed voice mail left for you at the hotel."

I raised my eyebrows in response. He continued.

"Typically, when a guest checks out, the system is automatically purged. But one of my junior investigators had the bright idea of checking the backup files."

Voice mail?

Offhand, I couldn't remember. Had I gotten any messages while I was there? I didn't think so. But in any case, who gave a junior G-man permission to listen in on any of my private messages? Just as I was about to give in to my basic instinct to complain, I realized two important facts: one—as far as I knew, I'd received no voice mail while in San Antonio, so I had no personal mail to be reviewed/snickered at/pried into; and two—it's not smart to make life difficult for the folks whose job is to find the person or persons who want to do me harm.

Sometimes, I need to put my privacy rules aside if I want to save my hide.

Seybold continued. "Unfortunately, there was no way to trace the incoming number. But we do have a copy of the message." He reached into a drawer and pulled out a small tape recorder, placing it at the center of the desk. "The message isn't as . . . unsavory as the E-mail you received, but it's a threat nonetheless. What I want you to do is pay less attention to what is said, and instead, listen to the voice to see if you recognize it."

I stared at the tape recorder, my heart going into overdrive. At this point, I'd be lucky to hear anything over the rushing of blood in my ears.

He pushed a button and the machine started.

At first, there was static. And then an obviously prerecorded female voice said "One message, left today, at two-oh-four P.M."

There was a bit more static, and then I heard what sounded to be a male voice, almost growling. "That was your only warning. Next time, I won't miss."

I stared at the tape recorder. "This makes absolutely no sense at all. If that was my only warning, then what in heck does he call the E-mail I received? Just a friendly little reminder?"

Seybold pushed the stop button. "First things first. Do you recognize the voice?"

I dismissed his question with a rather unladylike snort. "Of course not. He was growling. I don't know anybody who growls on a regular basis. It was obvious he was trying to disguise his voice. It could have been anybody." I tapped the recorder with my forefinger. "Let's go back. What's with this 'only warning' bit?"

Seybold rested his elbows on his desk and formed a temple with his fingers. "There's a rather obvious difference in vernacular between this voice message and the rather coarsely worded E-mail you received. That suggests they may have come from two different sources. Plus, the time stamp of the voice mail indicates that the call was made just moments after your car was hit. The background noise suggests the caller was outside rather than inside when the call was placed. We feel it was much too well timed to be merely coincidental."

That made sense to me. I received the E-mail only after the glider crash became a front-page story, and even then, the sender took his sweet time to draw inspiration from the publicity before he sent his message. But if the phone call came moments after the incident, only the shooter or maybe a confederate could have made the call. After all, only they knew when and where it had happened, and who was in the car.

I summed up our mutual theories in the fewest possible words. "So it all boils down to this. E-mail: hoax. Phone call: real."

He nodded. "Yeah. It looks that way."

"So what am I being warned against? Asking questions? Getting involved?" I tried not to sigh. "For simply being my father's daughter?"

Seybold held out his empty palms in a rare gesture of emptiness. "In all honesty, we have no idea. But we're working on it."

"That's not very reassuring."

"Perhaps this will reassure you a bit more." He reached into his desk drawer and pulled out a thick folder. "I thought you might like to review these. They're copies of the reports I've received so far concerning this case—much more in-depth than the initial reports you've seen. A few names have been omitted, but in those cases the investigation has reached a dead end, and we're merely preserving the privacy of the investigated individual, who didn't contribute anything useful to the information gathered." He held the file out for me.

"Thank you." I accepted the file, stunned. In fact, I was completely incredulous. I'd never expected quite this amount of cooperation from him or his office.

"Let me know if you see any new avenues to pursue," he said, sounding sincere.

I walked out both amazed and awed by this sudden change in his tactics. Why he'd changed his mind, I didn't know. But I didn't care. I tucked the file under my arm and headed back to my quarters at a trot, anxious to dive into the material and to see if the reports held any answers to my questions. Or even better, if they would help me come up with new "avenues." But the minute I sat down, ready to start reading, I got the call from downstairs that Megan Lassiter had arrived.

I gritted my teeth at the bad timing, gave the folder one last loving look, and slipped it into my desk drawer. I reached the elevator door just as it opened and Megan stepped out.

The first thing I noticed was that she'd been crying. No surprise there. The second thing was that she was carrying her own file folder, hers only slightly thinner than the one Seybold had given me. We dispensed with the pleasantries, and instead I led her to my sitting room, where she took a seat and promptly began crying. She wasn't hysterical or anything like that. She just kept making little hiccupy sobs. Every time she tried to speak, the sobs got in her way.

Finally, she simply held out the folder and managed to squeeze out one word: "Read."

I examined the first page on top and realized it was a printed copy of an E-mail sent the previous summer from Ashley McCurdy to cadet, second class Keith Rydell. Rather than quote it verbatim here, the quick synopsis was that she was thanking him for understanding and respecting why she wouldn't have sex with him.

I stared at Megan, the words "invasion of privacy" echoing through my mind. "These are private notes, Megan. Very private notes. Are you sure you want me to look at them?"

She sniffed, then managed a hoarse whisper. "Yes. I talked to my parents and they agreed." I shrugged, then started scanning through the other sheets of paper. They all seemed to be love notes sent between the two of them—very "just between the two of us" private stuff. Not to mention somewhat steamy. Just because Ashley wasn't actively engaging in sex didn't mean they didn't talk about it.

While reading these notes, I decided it was about time I cleaned up my own E-mailbox. Delete some things. Maybe password-protect a couple of areas . . .

I turned back to the file, and after reviewing all the letters, I held out the folder to Megan. "Okay. I read them." I shifted uncomfortably. "I can see why they upset you. I feel like some kind of voyeur. I'm not used to reading other people's private mail."

Especially that of the recently dead. Who maybe died in my place.

Megan nodded, gave one final sniff. She faced me, resolute, her control regained. "I understand. I didn't like it either, but I wanted you to understand what sort of girl Ashley was. She had standards, and Keith apparently respected them. They were both young, but their relationship really appears to have been strong, built on love, trust, and loyalty." She dug into the file folder and turned to a page flagged with a bright pink sticky note. "Here's the start of when things went wrong for Keith with the drug stuff. Ashley stuck by him. She truly believed he was innocent. She even offered to testify on his behalf."

"Did she?"

"No. The only thing she could have done was act as a character witness. She knew nothing about what he had been doing. The only useful testimony she could offer would be that to the best of her knowledge, he'd never done any drugs. And his blood test substantiated that anyway."

I stared at the files, promising myself not only that I would password-protect some areas, but that I'd double delete some of my older E-mails as soon as I had time.

Of course, it wasn't like I had any steamy love letters to hide. Insert my long mental sigh here.

I redirected my attention from inward to outward. "So why did you want me to read these?" I suppressed a shiver. "Where did you get them?"

She colored slightly. "I found printouts of some of the E-mails she sent to Keith, hidden in a file under her mattress."

"Did you check her computer for the rest of them?"

She shook her head. "Nothing. She'd wiped her E-mail program clean." Her momentary flush of color faded as Megan nervously tapped the folder with her forefinger. "Something happened to my sister about two months ago. You can see it reflected in the tone of her E-mail to Keith. Now, after the fact, I realize I noticed it, too, when talking to her on the phone. None of us in the family figured it out at the time. We thought maybe it was the aftermath of the investigation, taking a toll on her. That, combined with the usual pressures from college. She was trying to keep her grades up, despite all the time she spent dealing with Keith."

She paused and drew in a shaky breath. "Reading her E-mails, I think you'll agree that despite some ups and downs, their relationship still appeared as strong as ever. Keith seemed somewhat confused by the emotional roller coaster she was going through, but he was apparently dealing with it."

"I assume that you've now got some idea of what caused that . . . roller coaster."

Megan's face crumbled. "We just got back the results from her autopsy. The medical examiner said Ashley was six weeks pregnant when she died."

CHAPTER ELEVEN

El Paso County Coroner's Office
Subject: Ashley Jessica McCurdy
Age: 19
Cause of death: High-velocity impact with ground, compres-
sion injuries to the torso and blunt head trauma consistent with a
small-craft impact with rocky terrain.
Note: Subject was six weeks pregnant.

After Megan left, I still couldn't figure out why she'd felt such a press-ing need to share such personal information with me. Unless maybe she wanted me to know that now two people had died in my place. But to her credit, Megan hadn't seemed vindictive. I think she simply needed to tell someone, and it wasn't the sort of news you broke to your average mourner. She needed a safe outlet. Evidently, I fit the bill.

As for me, the news hit like a brick. Coming on top of the shooting in San Antonio, the discovery that an unborn child was a victim in all this was devastating. And I wasn't sure what to do about it.

One thing I could do was call for help. Given that I was related to a computer whiz, I figured I should probably take advantage of it. Ashley's E-mail messages might be one thread to pull as I tried to find some answers. Megan had given me all the information she could, in the hopes that it would help me find out what had happened to her sister. I E-mailed Charlie and asked him to check into the E-mails Ashley had sent. I faxed him copies, but noted that most of them didn't have full outgoing information. That might stop him before he could get started. But I doubted it—I knew my brother.

Still, I felt like a rat when I picked up the telephone and called Seybold's office. Megan hadn't sworn me to any secrecy, but I still felt as if I were telling tales out of school.

He answered with a curt, "Yes?"

"It's Eve Cooper. I've just had an interesting conversation with Megan Lassiter."

"And?" The man doesn't waste time on such frivolities as sympathy.

I plunged ahead. "Megan informed me of something that may have some bearing on her sister's role in this situation."

"Indeed?"

"Ashley's family just learned that she was six weeks pregnant when she died."

I was spared from any one-word assessment of that piece of information. Most men would have at least essayed a short voyage into the vernacular.

Seybold, as controlled as ever, snapped straight into analytical mode. "I appreciate the detail. It's possible that the revelation may alter some of our interpretations of the facts."

"I thought so too. I'm going to go over the reports you gave me, keeping this in the back of my mind. I may be coming back to you with some questions, if that's all right."

"I'd expect no less." There was an awkward pause. "Eve, thank you."

"You're welcome," I said automatically, then hung up. Then it hit me. What? He thought I'd keep this sort of stuff to myself? Not share? So far, hadn't I been the soul of cooperation?

Of course, you might say my life depended on it.

Sobering thought . . .

I shook off the impending mental meltdown and decided to tackle Seybold's stack of investigative reports with Megan's revelation in mind. But first, I had a call to make.

Normally, Charlie and I communicate via instant messenger. It's quick and easy, but sometimes I just need to hear a human voice.

This was one of those times.

I called his private number.

"It's about time," he grumbled. "You okay?"

"I've been better."

"You're not going to want to move in with me or anything like that, are you?"

I couldn't help but smile. My brother. Ever the curmudgeon. "You've been talking to Patsy."

"Yeah. She wants me to put in a moat around this place and fill it with alligators."

"Don't use just alligators. Piranhas are good too."

"I'll keep that in mind. So, do you need to bunk here for a while?"

"I'll take my chances here."

We were playing verbal Ping-Pong, just as usual, never quite saying soppy things like "I'm worried about you" or "I love you." Still, the message was clear. Charlie might hate having company in his sanctuary of solitude, but if I needed a place to stay, I had one. That's love.

But what I needed this instant was information. "Listen, remember that list of things we were talking about in the car before we were so rudely interrupted?"

"Yeah. Ready for it now?"

"If you don't mind."

"I'll E-mail it to you this instant." He paused. "Eve, if things get too hot for you in town . . ." His voice trailed off.

"I know. Thanks."

"By the way, those faxes you sent? Without all the headers to parse, I can't do much with them. But I checked out what headers there were and they went to studly@hottmail.com. Hottmail is one of those free 'read your mail on-line' services that anyone can use, even if he provides completely bogus sign-up information. A dead end."

"Maybe the cadet set it up because he was afraid of getting love letters sent through military mail."

"Possibly."

My computer announced I'd received new mail, and sitting in my in box was a note from Charlie with the subject line "List". "Got the list. Thanks. Let me know if you find anything else interesting."

We both said our good-byes.

I quickly learned my desk wasn't big enough for the pages and pages of reports. I had to spread them out on the floor in order to group them in some chronological order and by chief subject, using the E-mailed list as a basis. That way, I could go through the list and match each question with answers from the various reports.

1. Examination of glider: pilot error or sabotage?

I found reports from the National Transportation Safety Board, the chief agency in charge of investigating all airplane crashes, motorized or not. According to the investigators, the glider had hit the mountain with such force as to rip through the various cowlings that protected the plane's controls and tear up parts inside. The extent of damage had made it difficult for the investigators to determine if the only likely area for mechanical failure, the elevator controls, had been meddled with prior to the crash. The wreckage had been brought to the FBI labs in Quantico, just south of here, and had several aeronautical and metallurgical specialists working on the wreckage. They were attempting to reconstruct the glider in order to determine if they could "establish control continuity from control stick to the ailerons, rudder, and elevators."

Whatever that meant . . .

The report also included a history of that particular model of glider, a "Schweizer SGS 2-33A," which in the past six years had had no history of mechanical failures, and no fatalities up to now. All the crashes of that particular model glider in the past had been credited to pilot error or weather problems.

Summing up, I was pretty sure the data meant: It's never happened before and we don't yet know why this one crashed.

2. Keith Rydell—was he the intended victim because of the drug scandal?

3. And what about the scandal, anyway?

The investigation had indeed included a very thorough and frank look at the Academy's drug scandal. According to the Air Force's Office of Special

Investigation reports, Keith Rydell had initially been considered a suspect, but charges were eventually dropped when his drug test came out clean and he agreed to testify against everyone else involved. One of the cadets who was charged with drug trafficking admitted in court that Rydell had been duped into playing packhorse and had had no knowledge that he was actually transporting drugs from an off-base mail drop to the Academy.

There were no records of threats against Rydell's life by anyone military or otherwise, and a follow-up note from his AOC, the now-hospitalized Major Anthony Gaskell, mentioned that Cadet Rydell was recovering from the stigma of the scandal and making significant strides in both his academic and military studies.

But now I guess the new question was: How well was he handling Ashley's death? And did he know anything about her pregnancy?

> 4. Drug bust—how many cadets were involved? Where are they now? Did they catch everybody?

The reports stated that six cadets from the same squadron were charged with drug trafficking and were eventually court-martialed. Currently, all six were serving sentences of various lengths at the Leavenworth Disciplinary Barracks at Fort Leavenworth, Kansas. Investigators described the drug ring as highly organized and very centralized, and also stated that they believed they'd caught everyone involved. Because Rydell had belonged to a different squadron, that had helped to substantiate his minor role in the process.

According to Rydell, he'd receive a call from a legitimate off-base private mailbox place telling him that he'd received a package. Essentially, he had no contact with or knowledge of the actual source of the drugs, just the otherwise innocuous mailbox place.

> 5. Major Gaskell—did someone blame him for convincing Rydell to testify? Could someone want revenge?

Other than the report I just mentioned, Major Anthony Gaskell's name came up only one other time in the investigation. That was a statement in which he displayed shock over the actions of the six accused cadets, whose actions, he said, had come as a complete and total surprise to him. Although the six cadets weren't in his squadron, he knew of them, but he'd had no suspicions they were involved in any illegal activities or had coerced one of his charges into joining them, even peripherally.

Although, once aware of the problem, the major had encouraged Rydell to testify against the six, it didn't appear that Gaskell's influence was the cadet's sole impetus for being a witness for the prosecution. Another supporter of the absolute truth was Ashley, but she wasn't next on my list. Taylor Dobbs was.

> 6. Potential victim: Taylor "the Jokeman" Dobbs—
> any connection with the drug scandal?

According to the investigation, Dobbs had a squeaky-clean record. He wasn't in the same squadron as either Rydell or the court-martialed cadets. Dobbs even lived in a completely different dorm. He had no disciplinary marks in his records, and a solid academic record; the only negative comment in any of the reports was a remark from a superior officer that, while off-duty, Dobbs had a propensity for horseplay and considered himself "quite the ladies' man."

I could substantiate that. . . .

> 7. Potential victim: Me

Of the three incidents, I could believe that both the glider crash and the tire incident might have an instigator or culprit in common, because of the amount of planning necessary to make either happen. But the E-mailed threat didn't take any great intelligence, accessibility, or arcane knowlege other than knowing how to send an E-mail to me. As far as that analysis went, the blasted thing didn't even have proper punctuation. Any idiot could have done it, if he got lucky at guessing my E-mail address.

So if we discounted the E-mail threat, it meant that the voice-mail message that suggested that I was being warned for the first time was right. But warned against what?

I really hadn't done anything, so far. Butting into the investigation seemed so . . . so . . . Nancy Drew–like to me. Despite my adventures of last February involving the body we found in the Rose Garden, as far as this case went, I really hadn't even tried to play amateur sleuth. I'd only asked a few questions of a few people. These attempts on my life seemed much too serious. This was a matter for the pros.

Which isn't to say I hadn't found out as much as possible without actually pulling a Miss Marple. In the case of Megan, she came to me. And in the case of Major Gaskell, it was strictly good manners to apologize if I was indeed the reason why he'd been hurt.

After all, there was a whole team of professionals doing an in-depth investigation of this mess. And as far as I knew, no one had taken a shot at any of them. So maybe my own crime was that I'd asked the wrong question of the wrong person.

Or better yet, someone thought I had.

And now, the person who was growing in importance as the best possibility:

8. Intended victim: Ashley McCurdy

The investigators had come up with nothing that would point to Ashley as a likely candidate for being targeted for death other than her unwavering support of her boyfriend, Keith Rydell. An insufficient reason in my book, but hey, I'm not a drug dealer, nor do I know how they think.

Ashley's only role in the drug scandal was strictly tangential. Her statements were ones that simply testified to her boyfriend's character from her limited point of view. She'd certainly never witnessed anything illegal and had added nothing to that side of the case.

But you could consider her a chink in Rydell's armor. If you wanted to get to him, getting to her, in my opinion, would destroy him. At least, that's the impression I'd gotten from those E-mails and every person I'd discussed their relationship with. So maybe somebody who wanted to get at Rydell had decided to get at him through his weak point. . . .

Conversely, I wondered if the news of her pregnancy might mean that the investigators needed to take a second look at Ashley and Rydell and their relationship. I was pretty sure that there were rules that said cadets couldn't get married. Was there some similar rule on the books about them fathering a child? Would her pregnancy interrupt or even destroy Keith Rydell's military aspirations? Had her value to him been switched from asset to liability because of their unborn child? My impression was that it was very unlikely, that Rydell truly loved Ashley, but it was a plausible motivation. It was pretty thin, but we had so few leads that even thin ones needed to be checked out. Still, I was going to hold that one close to my chest until all the other possible leads played out.

9. Who wrote the threatening E-mail?

I was pretty sure it was a hoax. So I didn't think I cared. Unless Charlie came up with something that connected the E-mail to someone involved with the glider or car incidents, I was more than willing to believe it was just some nutcase capitalizing on the unfortunate situation for the sheer publicity of it all. But the question still remained: How did a nutcase get my E-mail address? So far, those folks who knew my current E-mail address had all sworn they'd not given it to anyone else, and I had no reason not to believe them. Besides, my E-mail address was based on my own name. Which meant it was simple enough to be guessable—yet another thing about my E-mail that I was going to have to address in the near future, when I got the time and focus.

Though, if people kept taking potshots at me, that might take a while. . . .

Having reached the end of my list, I sat down and surveyed the wreckage, all the papers strewn across the floor in an order incomprehensible to anyone but me.

My in-depth study had answered few if any of the questions I had. Instead, it had led me to start a new list of questions. That, and it had given me a whopper of a headache. To quote an old Monty Python skit, "My brain hurts. . . ."

My head wasn't the only thing hurting, I realized when my stomach growled audibly. I was hungry, which might be adding some nice throbbing action to my current headache. I glanced at my watch and was stunned to learn that it was almost three o'clock, well past lunchtime. My big breakfast had finally given out on me, leaving me famished.

I left the papers stacked in organized chaos on the carpet and tiptoed through the carnage into my snack kitchen. I had little more than peanut butter and jelly to eat. In the chaos of my life lately, I hadn't arranged to restock.

The phone rang. I hesitated a second before answering it.

But it wasn't a caller with a growling voice and an urge to kill me. It was Craig. My heart took an unexpected extra beat.

That call was a lifeline back to the normal world. The first few minutes we talked were full of awkward "How are you, I'm fine" phrases, and then he finally got down to business.

"I was wondering if you'd like to go out Friday night."

A date?

"You mean everybody or . . . just us."

"Just us."

I was about to say yes when I looked at the calendar and saw the big circle drawn around the date. Drew's dance. Damn. I kicked the leg of the nearest chair. "I can't. I agreed to chaperon the dance Drew's class is holding here." Revelation struck hard and fast. "Why don't you come and help me?"

He laughed. "I don't know if I'm chaperon material. Don't we have to set an example for all those impressionable young minds?"

"Yeah." My mind raced ahead on an evil path. "Then again, there's always reverse psychology."

"You mean show them how they shouldn't act?"

And so we danced around what might be. Don't get me wrong—our call never reached even an R rating. But we talked about ourselves, each other, and vague possibilities. By the end of the call, we were laughing, feeling comfortable with each other, and looking forward to Friday night's freshman dance.

I was happy.

I had barely hung up the phone before it rang again. Thinking it was probably Craig calling to discuss some detail I'd forgotten—getting into the White House as a personal guest of the First Family isn't like going to a party at a suburban home—I picked it up and nearly said Craig's name. I was lucky I stopped myself in time. It was Michael.

"Where are you?" I demanded. "I'm dying to see a friendly face."

"Downstairs."

My stomach growled again. "You hungry?"

"Not very. If you are, I think I have a couple of Lifesavers covered in lint in my jacket pocket."

"Thanks. I'll pass." I sighed. "Come on up anyway. I want to get your opinion on something."

"Okay."

I ran to the kitchen and threw a plate of sandwiches together and grabbed a couple of soft drinks. Given the state of my room, I didn't want to call downstairs and order something. They'd send a minion up with food if I asked for it, but I didn't want to have to explain the mass of paper I had spread all over the floor and every other flat surface to any of the staff. So I decided that peanut butter and jelly would have to suffice.

A few minutes later, Michael stepped in and looked around. "What's with the paper carpet?"

"That's what I want you to look at. It's everything I can get on the investigation so far. I wanted your take on it." I held up a peanut butter and jelly sandwich. "Can I fix you one?"

"No, thanks. Too late for lunch and too early for supper."

"The story of my life." I motioned for him to follow me into the sitting room, picking a path so as not to disturb the papers. I handed him my list of questions. "Each pile of papers corresponds to the questions, starting here"—I pointed to the first pile—"and going clockwise."

"How very organized of you." He glanced at the piles. "I think."

Michael dropped his camera bag in a chair and sat in the best spot on the floor to reach the various piles. At first I tried to watch him, to read his expression, but that served no real purpose other than to irritate him and frustrate me. So I took deliberate refuge in the kitchen, where I made two more sandwiches, ate one of them, and then cleaned up behind my culinary expedition. Once I finished the cleanup, I piddled around the kitchen, straightening this and policing that, trying to find busywork to occupy my hands as well as my mind. And trying not to eat that last peanut butter sandwich. (I'd used the last of the jelly before I made it.)

Not sure I had the willpower to resist, I carried the sandwich to my bedroom and tried to distract myself from eating it by alphabetizing my paperback collection. In the other room, I heard Michael say something I couldn't quite make out.

"What?" I called out. "Find something?"

He stood in the door to my room, my list in his hand. "I'm not sure. Maybe. Mostly, though, I think I've come to the same conclusions as you."

I held out the last sandwich as an offering, but he waved away my generosity.

"No, thanks. Really." He held up a piece of paper. "The girl's pregnancy opens up some new motivations."

"I thought so too."

"And there are some scenarios you don't cover."

"Like what?"

He reached into his jacket pocket and pulled out a pen, scribbling as he spoke. "For instance, what if the cadet was trying to get rid of her and her baby, and in order to do that, he sabotaged the glider himself."

"I thought of that, but it didn't quite ring true for me. I can believe that Rydell would be desperate enough to do something rash to preserve his military career. But he doesn't strike me as the kind of guy to try murder. And to potentially kill two people, one of them a girl I think he loved? Plus his own child? And from what I've read, Rydell really liked Major Gaskell. Even if he decided to murder Ashley to save his military career, which I doubt, wouldn't he do it in a way that wouldn't take out an innocent bystander? It doesn't make sense."

Michael shrugged. "Maybe he didn't anticipate the major taking the flight, and couldn't risk stopping it without exposing his own role in the sabotage."

Possible, I thought. "But wouldn't it eventually come out that she was pregnant, regardless of who took her up? Given that he was the scheduled pilot, and in a relationship with her, he would be the most likely suspect."

Michael chewed on the end of his pen. "Good point." He started to scratch out what he'd written, but then shrugged. "We consider all possibilities, right?"

He had a point. I nodded in agreement.

"Then try this concept. What if the child wasn't his?"

I rolled my eyes. "Didn't you read those letters? It's obvious she was crazy in love with him. Absolutely. There's no way that the baby wasn't his."

"True, true."

I stepped closer and gestured to question number four on my list, trying not to get peanut butter on the paper. "What about the part of the drug ring they didn't catch?"

Michael thumbed through the appropriate pile. "But I thought the report said that all the cadets involved were identified and prosecuted."

"They were, but someone was sending the drugs to the mail drop. Who?"

Michael examined the summary report again. "There's not much about that. Says here that the mail drop was opened by an unidentified man who paid for the services by money order, using false personal information."

"Essentially leaving no paper trail."

"Exactly. The investigator called it a dead end."

"More like a loose thread." I contemplated the paper for a moment or two. "Or a loose cannon. Maybe this guy was afraid that Rydell had figured out who he was. Killing Rydell would eliminate that situation."

Michael's forehead creased in concentration. "Why would he have waited to do something like that now and not do it when the case was still being tried?"

I took a bite of my sandwich. Since I wasn't going to talk with my mouth full, I had a few moments to think while I ate. "What if Rydell was trying to protect someone like himself, someone else who was duped by the bad guys? Or maybe Rydell was trying to protect Ashley by keeping the secret? Or maybe he didn't realize there were others involved until long after the fact? Maybe he was preparing to go to the Academy authorities with these new revelations."

Michael dropped into the nearest chair. "And the bad guys knew if they did anything to him directly, the authorities would reopen the drug case and start looking harder. But instead, they might have decided to teach Rydell a lesson by killing or at least injuring his girlfriend in an 'unfortunate accident.'"

"Threatening a loved one is a tricky tactic." I shrugged. "It might shut him up or it might have the reverse effect. With Ashley gone, Rydell might decide he had nothing to lose, and spill his guts. Then again, it's possible they were gunning for Rydell and had decided that Ashley could be considered an . . . an . . . ." I searched for the right phrase.

"An acceptable loss?" Michael supplied.

"Yeah. Rydell was supposed to be flying the glider. Maybe the major and Ashley were both simply innocent victims, accidental targets." I shivered. There was nothing acceptable about murder, but I'd spent a lot of time wondering if Ashley, and now her unborn child, had died for no other reason than that she was in the wrong place at the wrong time, merely standing in the line of fire between the killer (or killers) and their intended victim.

My appetite for peanut butter (or anything else, for that matter) disappeared, and I placed the remainder of the sandwich back on the plate.

"It's certainly one possible scenario," I said, fighting the sinking feeling in my stomach. "Then, when the plans changed at the last moment, and the major stepped in to fly the glider in the cadet's place, the bad guys couldn't risk stopping the flight, because then that would have turned attention and suspicion toward them."

Michael leaned back in the chair. "So, if there are other—for the lack of a better word—other gang members, is anyone actively looking for them?"

I dropped to my hands and knees to consult the stacks of papers on the floor, finding the report about the investigation and court-martial. "In the court-martial summation, the report states that they felt certain that all guilty parties at the Academy had been identified and duly punished for their crimes. But it doesn't mention anything about nonmilitary guilty parties."

"No one is going to admit that there are any loose strings." Michael punctuated his remark with an unattractive snort. "The whole case might just unravel."

"Unravel . . . ," I echoed. My mind started racing ahead, and evidently whenever that happens, I get a glazed look on my face.

"What, Eve?" Michael prompted.

I continued my plot hatching in silence.

"Eve?" he said in a warning tone.

"What if . . . ," I started.

"What if what?"

"What if someone could go to the prison and speak with the six cadets? Do you think we might learn more?"

"You thinking about going?"

I took a sudden interest in my bare feet. "I can't. Dad would probably implode if I even suggested doing something like that."

"That's putting it mildly," Michael said with a bark of laughter. "So what if I go instead?"

He had caught me by surprise. "Wh-what?" I stuttered.

"I volunteer to go to Leavenworth and talk to the cadets."

I stopped and stared at him in amazement. Of course that was what I had wanted, but I had never expected him to agree without some coaxing, wheedling, and maybe even a bit of whining. I gave him my most critical look. "That was entirely too easy."

He shrugged. "Not really. I'm headed home this weekend for a quick visit with the parents. They live close by. It'd be no problem at all to head over to the barracks, take some pictures, ask some questions."

"Leavenworth. Okay, I know that's in Kansas, but aren't you from Missouri?" At least that'd been his explanation for the trivia expertise that had resulted in our second-place finish at the bar. Then again, my sense of direction often failed me, which probably accounted for my lousy grades in geography.

"I did grow up in Missouri." He smiled. "In the thriving metropolis of Weston, to be exact. It's just north of Kansas City. As the crow flies, it's about ten miles from Leavenworth, just across the Missouri River. So getting there is no problem. But what *will* be a problem is getting all the permissions and clearances set so I can visit the prison." His grin grew. "But I imagine that you know somebody who can pull a few strings on my behalf. I'll leave that up to you and all your high-placed connections."

I contemplated a possible line of attack as we walked back to the living room. "I guess I could ask Mr. Seybold to make the arrangements."

Michael snorted. "Don't bet on it. He doesn't like me very much."

I pictured Peter Seybold at his desk, his hands folded neatly and a haughty look on his face. "I'm not so sure he likes me, either. Hell, I'm not sure he likes anybody. But he *is* the one who gave me copies of the various investigations and reports . . . *without* my even asking him about them."

Michael scanned the assortment of papers still scattered across the floor. "Then he must be slipping in his old age—or maybe he's desperate. Never mind. Maybe the best way to cut the red tape is to start through your dad and let him ask Seybold to work out the details."

"And you truly don't mind doing it?"

He shook his head. "It's nice going back home, but there's really not much I can do other than visit my parents. None of my sisters and their families live in the area, and most of my friends have moved away. And after you've sat around the supper table, eaten a mountain of food, and then caught up on who's done what and who died and all the regular gossip, we seem to run out of things to say. I'll appreciate having something else to do while I'm there."

He glanced at a calendar that I had hanging beside my desk. "But you'll have to work fast. My flight leaves tomorrow from Reagan around three." He glanced at his watch. "And I have to head back to my apartment now because this is the only time I have to pack. I'm working straight up until flight time tomorrow."

"Okay, it's a deal, then. I'll get to work on Dad and call you later with the details."

"Great." Michael picked up his camera bag and plotted a path to the door through the piles of paper. He paused at the door. "Drew's party is tomorrow night, right?"

I nodded, neglecting to mention my new partner in crime.

"Good luck. You're going to need it. I remember what it was like to be a fifteen-year-old boy. Good thing you'll have company."

"The Secret Service? Yeah, they should come in handy. Every high school party could use armed and martial-arts-trained chaperons."

"No. Craig."

I gaped at him. "What? Did Craig call you right after he talked to me?"

Michael grinned. "Caught me on the way up the stairs. He *is* my best friend, you know." His expression took on a wicked gleam. "We have no secrets. Bye."

Oh, great. I'd never live this down.

After he left, I turned back to the problem at hand, staring at the paper carnage. I decided that as long as I kept things organized, I could work as efficiently from the table as from the floor. Grabbing a pad of sticky notes, I started flagging each stack on its edge so that the flag stuck out, then stacking the piles one on another. If I could consolidate my stuff into a single big pile, I could sit in a chair or on my bed like a civilized person.

When I reached the papers that Megan had left, I stopped what I was doing. I forgot my desire to be civilized, grabbed a cushion from the couch, got comfortable on the floor, and began to reread them.

Six weeks pregnant. I couldn't help but sigh.

Ashley wouldn't have been showing. I'd had a roommate in college who managed to hide her pregnancy from me and everyone else until she was seven months along, and then went into premature labor. Then again, she was what Patsy likes to describe as "big boned." If Ashley looked anything like Megan, she was model thin and had no hopes of hiding her condition for long.

I knew Ashley hadn't told her family about the pregnancy. But had she told anyone else? Like her boyfriend? Of course, it was totally possible that at that early stage, she didn't even know about it herself.

I stared at the autopsy report, which gave me an eerie amount of detail about the pregnancy, even the blood type of the unborn child. It was a sobering piece of information because it suddenly made me realize that we truly were talking about the loss of two lives. Ashley had been O-positive, and the baby A-positive.

Two blood types, two lives, two deaths.

Hazy college-level biology class memories rose to the surface. If Ashley was O-positive and her baby was A-positive, then Rydell's blood type must be A-positive.

I searched through the pile of medical reports, realizing I had nothing about him other than the summary tox screen that had been used as evidence at the court-martial trial that stated he had no drugs in his system.

It didn't mention his blood type.

In fact, none of the papers I had in my horde of documents mentioned it, and I had a sudden urge to know, to be sure. Call it curiosity run rampant, but I wanted to know.

For sure.

The trouble was, I didn't want to overestimate my benefactor's largesse. I'd already decided not to bother Dad. I was planning to go directly to Mr. Seybold to arrange the proper Leavenworth permissions for Michael. Color me brave. But could I also hit the man up for even more data over and beyond what he'd already given me?

I'd ask him if I needed to, but there was no reason I couldn't check using my own sources right now.

So I turned to my computer, logged on, saw that Charlie was on-line. (No surprise there. He lives on-line.) I sent him an instant message.

"How EZ would it be to get into military medical records and get information on someone's blood type?"

His reply: "2EZ."

CHAPTER TWELVE

PARTY, PARTY, PARTY!

> You're invited to the Altamont School's end-of-the-year 'Good-bye Freshmen, Hello World' bash to be held in the East Room at the White House, 1600 Pennsylvania Avenue. All students must provide their Social Security number to the school office by the Tuesday prior to the party in order to obtain security clearance. You must show your picture ID (school ID or driver's license/permit) to enter the White House grounds. You must arrive between 7 and 7:30 P.M. Late arrivals will not be permitted to enter. Parents are welcome to attend as long as they provide like information to the office. The party will end promptly at 11:30. Please refer to the attached map for pickup, delivery, and parking instructions. No alcohol will be served, chaperons and security personnel will be in attendance, and there is no smoking whatsoever in the White House or on its grounds.

The next morning, Drew barged into my room and woke me much too early and insisted that I come downstairs and lend my decorating expertise to him and a few classmates who were charged with making the East Room into Party World USA.

Evidently, he'd mistaken me for Martha Stewart.

I'm not responsible for anything I say when woken out of a dead sleep. But, luckily, I don't think Drew could understand my gibberish. Once I fully woke up, I grumbled at him, making sure to clearly enunciate my theory that the ushers were perfectly capable of removing all the valuable antiques and paintings from the room and rendering it suitable for a bunch of party-crazed teenage hoodlums.

It was the hoodlum part that got him.

After listening to a five—no, make that ten-minute diatribe about the excellence of his school, the magnificent pedigree of his loyal friends, and as far as that went, his own set of values, I unilaterally surrendered.

He was right, I was wrong. And sleepy. And grumpy.

I apologized for my bad choice of words and promised to come down and join the "fun" in a half hour or so. Of course, secretly, I was still stewing. Wasn't it enough that I'd agreed to chaperon the stupid thing? Evidently not. Now I had to help set things up. That was not in my contract.

I grabbed my rattiest college sweatshirt—not from my college, but from that of an ex-boyfriend—and the most comfortable pair of barely presentable jeans I owned, nuked a cup of superstrong tea, and headed downstairs, hoping none of Drew's friends had thought to bring a camera. Or, if they had, praying they didn't want to immortalize my new look on film.

I love being behind the camera, but not in front of it. Especially when I'm wearing my fuzzy pink bunny slippers and morning face.

When I got downstairs, most of the breakables had already been removed from the room. I also noticed that the usual valuable and historic paintings were gone and others, much less distinguished, hung in their places as substitutes. That was good. I sided with Mr. O'Connor about taking no chances with a room full of celebrating fifteen-year-olds. If it'd been my responsibility, I would've removed the carpet, the curtains, and every stick of furniture, then covered every leftover surface in the same sort of cheesy plastic my great-aunt Honoria always used on her dining-room chairs and lampshades.

I spotted Drew, huddled in the corner with three girls and two other boys, evidently the lucky members of the party committee, tasked to handle decorations, food, and music. They were kneeling on the floor, consulting a large piece of butcher paper that I realized was a blueprint of sorts, drawn with what looked to be purple crayon. I stifled a laugh as I approached. *Watch out, Harold—there's no drawing on the White House walls*. But I soon realized that I'd done the teenage planners a disservice. This group could have planned a major military maneuver with no other tools than butcher paper and a box of Crayolas.

Everyone had assigned tasks. Mine turned out to be the dangerous task of filling balloons. So I manned the helium tank and found that the most important part of my job was being forced to constantly swat Drew and his friends away from stealing my finished product. Evidently they all thought it was great fun to recite Shakespeare while under the influence of the helium. I didn't know whether I should be impressed that they could recite any Shakespeare at all, or appalled that they wanted to inhale the stuff, even if its sole purpose was to make them sound funny, not act funny.

By eleven o'clock, the decorations were finished; I think I must have filled every balloon within a two-mile radius of the White House. The balloons were grouped into bouquets at strategic points, as well as floating free against the ceiling, dangling their jewel-toned ribbons above our heads. Crepe paper had been strung in a complicated pattern all over the ceiling, adding a crazed but festive air to the entire room. (Mr. O'Connor put a stop to their plans to hang mirror balls from the chandelier arms. Who could blame him?)

Prevented from causing any permanent damage to the fixtures, the committee called it quits and headed their separate ways to get ready for the Big Dance. As they wandered past me, I overheard the girls talking about their facial and hair appointments and what color they were having their nails done.

Once they passed out of hearing range, I turned to Drew and whispered, "I just thought this was an end-of-year dance. What's with the facials and stuff? It sounds more like a prom or something."

Drew shrugged. "Everything's fancy with them. You should have heard them all planning for picture day. Special makeup, pose practicing. It was ridiculous. From what the guys tell me, the end-of-year party is normally a laid-back gig, but I think the girls are ramping up a little because the party's being held here instead of the school gym. Can you believe it? Most of the kids told me they'd never even been here before," he said, as if he couldn't comprehend the absurdity of that idea.

I remembered his reaction the day we moved in—after the inauguration. He'd been struck speechless—not Drew's usual mode of operation. He'd made up for it the next day, when he practically burst into tears, swearing he could never call "this monster museum" a home.

How far he'd come since that cold, snowy day in January. . . .

"I'm glad we're having the party here. Not just because this is the only place we could get, but"—Drew glanced around—"I sorta feel safe here."

A chill went up my back. "What do you mean . . . safe? Have you felt not-safe other places?"

He shrugged. "Not really. It's just that with all this going on with you, I can't help but wonder . . ." His voice trailed off as he ducked his head.

I finished his statement for him. "If you're just as likely to be a target as me?"

"Yeah." He shrugged. "I'm probably being paranoid, huh?"

It was my turn to shrug. "Honestly? I have no idea. So far, everything seems to have been strictly aimed at me."

"I know. And that worries me too."

When Drew looked up, I no longer saw the callous, self-absorbed look of youth in his eyes, but mature familial concern. For once, Drew didn't resist my effort to hug him. As I pulled him into an embrace, I said, "You don't have to worry that I'm going to do anything stupid. I'm sticking to the rules and to my agents like glue."

"Promise?"

"Yeah." I pulled back and crossed my heart with my forefinger, then poked him in the chest. "But you have to promise to be just as careful."

"Definitely." He glanced toward a window. I guess I have time to blade for a while before I have to get ready for the party."

"Just don't break anything." *Like yourself.*

Funny that his definition of remaining safe didn't include staying away from Rollerblades, skateboards, and other hazardous activities. It could have been worse. At least no previous administrations had installed bungee-jumping facilities. Knowing Drew, he'd spend the rest of the day working off his worries through physical activities. An hour before the dance, he'd take a fifty minute hot shower, and then he'd use the last ten minutes to decide what to wear.

Drew and the others guys in his class had it easy—pants, shirt, matching socks, and they were ready to party. But girls? We're not so lucky.

As I headed back to my room, I decided to push all my very real worries out of my mind and try to enjoy the party. It seemed a safe distraction. With all the talk I'd overheard about the girls getting facials and such, the last thing I wanted to do was get nailed by a bunch of teenage fashion police.

Of course, I knew that less was more—that is, in terms of fashion accessories, as opposed to lack of clothing. If this dance was going to be Prom Night Redux, then I'd be smart to go the simple but classic route with a little black dress. Given that this was D.C., I figured half the girls would make the same choice. I'd fit right in.

If I stuck out, it would be *so* embarrassing. . . . For Drew, if not me.

But my plans to immerse myself in party doings took a backseat to the real world once I got back to my room. An interoffice memo file had been slid under my door. The note attached to the outside said, "Didn't want to disturb you while you were with your brother." I didn't recognize the handwriting, but any qualms I had about anonymous notes were instantly squashed when I saw the initials at the bottom—"P.S."

Not "P.S." as "postscript," but as in "Peter Seybold."

The envelope held another report, this time an in-depth look into the life and times of Taylor "the Jokeman" Dobbs, my pilot. As I read, I learned a lot more than I needed to about him, including the results of a standard security investigation into his family (widowed mother on a fixed income; four sisters, two of whom still lived at home—one brother-in-law in jail for domestic abuse); his academic records (pretty impressive, with only one slightly lower-than-usual grade—a B instead of an A in Biology 360: Cell and Molecular Biology); and such a list of academic and military achievements that it made me wonder if I'd done nothing but play around in college.

I hadn't, of course, but Dobbs had the sort of record that made me wonder if he wore blue tights and a red cape beneath his Air Force blues.

All in all, it drew the picture of a boy who had risen from humble roots to become a man who was making something great out of himself. The investigator concluded that Dobbs was very astute, very smart, and very determined. He was the sort of guy who used jokes to soften some of his more straitlaced edges. Although the report didn't state it per se, I concluded that Dobbs wouldn't risk the success he'd achieved so far by doing something stupid like be involved in any conspiracy against me or anyone else. It simply wasn't in his nature.

So . . . one suspect down? Or had he ever really been a suspect at all?

My stomach churned as I stared at the other pile of papers on my desk—the one that posed questions without answers. I needed to get to the bottom of them if I was ever going to get out of the White House again. But tonight I should be safe. I could forget about the attacks while I was home, I figured. Throwing myself into Drew's party seemed like a decent way to distract myself from the problems at hand.

At least in theory.

As to practice, I spent the rest of the day not getting my hair or nails done, but reading through every piece of information I'd been given. Finally, determined to put it behind me for at least one day, I dealt with the necessary evil of catching up with my E-mail.

I'd heard back from every person I'd written, asking if they'd given out my E-mail address, and every single one of them had sworn that he'd not passed on my E-mail address to anyone.

Period.

I pulled off the "For Your Eyes Only" note on the Dobbs file and faxed it to Charlie. Speaking of Charlie, he hadn't sent me any purloined information yet, but then again, I suppose it does take time to hack into government databases—especially military ones.

My churning stomach calmed down enough so that I could eat a light lunch. Afterward, I planned on taking a well-deserved nap, but the phone interrupted those plans. I grabbed the phone and threw myself on the bed.

"Hello?"

"Eve? It's Craig."

Aha! My date for the evening. The blood rushed to my face, leaving me feeling just a bit flushed.

"Everything still good for tonight?" I asked, trying not to sound too anxious. I guess I'd been hanging around too many teenagers. Their ways were starting to rub off on me.

There was a telltale hesitation before he spoke. I gripped the phone a bit tighter than necessary.

"That's why I'm calling. Something's come up." He paused, then sighed. "Eve, I'm so sorry, but I can't help you chaperon your brother's party tonight."

My stomach settled somewhere in the vicinity of my knees. What was

I supposed to say or do? Throw a fit? Demand a reason? The most innocuous thing I could think of was, "I hope nothing's wrong."

"It's my dad. He's had a mild heart attack."

My self-pity instantly transformed to honest concern. "Oh, no! Craig. I'm so sorry. Is he going to be all right?"

"Yeah, the doctors say he'll be okay, but my mother's a complete basket case. I have to go keep her from killing him with kindness. She tends to overreact in situations like this, and I don't want Dad to be irritated into another attack."

I'd been hearing noises in the background of the call, sounding like announcements being made over a loudspeaker, and I decided he wasn't home—and that this wasn't a local emergency. "I understand. Completely. Where do your parents live? Can you get a flight all right?"

"They're just in Philadelphia. I'm catching the Metroliner, so I'll be home in a couple of hours. Hopefully, Mom won't drive Dad completely crazy between now and then."

"I hope everything turns out all right."

"Don't worry. It will," he said with only the slightest bit of reluctance. "This might be the wakeup call Dad's needed to realize he has to cut back on the cigars and the beer and the time in front of the TV. In any case, I'm really sorry to miss the dance tonight. I was hoping it could be considered our first real date. Will you give me a rain check? Please?"

"Absolutely. I'm not sure you should feel so sorry about missing a high school dance, though. It has all the earmarks of being extraordinarily painful." At least it did now that I didn't have a partner in crime with whom to share that pain.

"Okay, a raincheck for an adult night out on the town, just the two of us. Deal?"

The two of us and my dawgs . . .

"Deal."

There was a loud noise in the background. "I think they just announced my train. I'll probably get back too late Sunday night to call. If it's okay, I'll call you Monday and you can tell me how the dance went."

"I'll share every boring detail. Don't worry about me. You go home and protect your father from your mother."

"I will. And Eve? Thanks for being so understanding. Bye."

"Bye."

I hung up the phone and allowed myself one very long, very exasperated sigh. Okay, so I'd go to the party stag. What was the harm in that?

Worse things could happen.

. . . Like watching the place I call my home, which is also a national treasure, be destroyed from within . . .

The head-banging music was so loud I was afraid the plaster would shake loose from the walls and we might see parts of the White House that had not been seen since the days of Dolley Madison.

I leaned over to Diana Gates, now back on my detail after her long-deserved vacation. "Remind me to apologize to my dad when he gets back. I now have new insight into his role as a parent."

"How so?"

"This." I waved my hand at the milling crowd. "I don't like the music, there are girls who are wearing clothes more suitable for cheap hookers than high school students, and I'm sure someone's going to try to spike the punch any minute now." I sighed. "Listen to me! When did I get to be so . . . so old?"

She offered me a rare smile. "You're not old. It's a matter of filling an obvious void. Your dad's not here, so you're channeling him. If he were here, he'd be in charge of making those complaints and you could simply be you."

"I'm not too sure about that." I stared at the stack of CDs that the student disc jockey had lined up on the table for eventual play. "I can't imagine liking some of this music under any circumstances."

The kids hadn't been able to afford a DJ, much less a band, so everyone had brought their favorite CDs and one of the techno geeks had set up a rather involved sound system to play them, and volunteered his services. Mr. O'Connor, the White House's head usher, had mentioned during the decoration phase that there was a professional-quality sound system and mixing board, should they want to use it. Drew and the guys had turned it down, on the theory that they'd rather use equipment they were familiar with.

Thank God . . .

Between the sound system they'd cobbled together and natural teenage behavior, the noise level was frightening enough as it was.

I tried to hang out in a quieter corner where I could observe the crowd but hopefully not command any attention. I wanted to be a proper chaperone: unseen until my services were needed. I was a success at preserving my hearing. However, I failed utterly at remaining in the background, unnoticed.

Several of Drew's freshmen-excuse me-sophomore friends insisted on hanging around me, laughing at my feeble jokes, some of them trying to get a look down my modest neckline.

Boys will be boys. . . .

I danced with a couple of the kids who approached me with the sort of behavior I didn't mind encouraging. You know the type; the ones who have been standing by themselves, trying to work up enough nerve, practicing what to say to ask a girl to dance, probably for the very first time in their lives. I figured that they approached me because they felt safer getting a rejection from an older woman rather than from one of their female peers. When they did finally ask me, they were nervous, they stumbled over their words, but they were quite polite.

Those boys I danced with.

The ones I brushed off were the cocky types who stood in large groups, laughing, making fun of their lesser brethren. They'd swagger up to me as if it were my duty to entertain them because isn't that what hostesses are supposed to do? Or worse, assuming that if I danced with someone they considered a dork, then wouldn't I be thrilled to dance with one of the cool jocks?

I had no problem giving them my best "Go away, little boy" stare, along with a simple "No."

However, a couple of them were persistent and wouldn't take "No" for an answer.

Or "Go away."

Or "Get lost."

Or "No, you're fifteen and not in a million years. Now go away unless you want me to call security."

Those two boys were going to have a short talk with a Secret Service agent pretty soon if they didn't back off.

There was one particular knot of boys who, although they weren't exactly obnoxious, also wouldn't leave me alone. It's not that they were being bad, but they were being entirely too attentive. As a result, I was the recipient of several heated glares from a band of girls who obviously thought I was deliberately usurping attention that should be paid solely to them.

And I agreed wholeheartedly.

You can have them, girls. Honest.

I tried to shift the attention to anyone but myself, but nothing seemed to work. I looked over at my agent, Diana Gates, standing a discreet distance away, and mouthed the words "Help me."

Instead of trotting over with a convenient excuse to extricate me from Hormone Central, she spoke into her small radio. I wasn't sure what sort of rescue to expect, if any. My always overactive imagination conjured up a platoon of Army Rangers, with green-and-black-painted faces, rappelling down ropes to land around me in a circle and then spirit me away.

Maybe that wouldn't be so bad. Army Rangers are usually older than fifteen, right?

My thoughts of a fantasy rescue intensified as I watched the faces of the kids around me. The boys stiffened perceptibly and the girls adopted rather vapid smiles. For one wild moment, I wondered if those Army Rangers had materialized.

I turned around to discover that their headmaster, Mr. Lendon, was approaching. That explained the sudden change in the air.

The first time I saw Mr. Lendon was at Drew's school play. As the story went, he'd bet the students they couldn't raise one thousand dollars for charity. When they managed to raise the money, losing the bet meant Mr. Lendon had to take a role in the school play, a role that resulted in him singing and dancing onstage, complete with tight jeans and Elvis-like moves. I remember remarking to Patsy at the time that I'd never had a headmaster who looked anything like him.

Yum . . .

So actually, this was the first time I'd ever seen him in street clothes and not dressed up like an extra from a Broadway touring company of *Grease.* He wore a nice tweed jacket with leather-patched elbows and some not-so-tight pants. He might not have appeared as Bad-Boy Exciting as he had dancing onstage, but he still looked much too good to be a teacher, much less the headmaster of some stuffy private school.

He gave the boys a smile that I'd describe as bordering on stunning.

Of course, the boys didn't seem to appreciate his expression at all. "Enjoying yourselves, gentlemen?" He stressed the last word as if reminding them that they were expected to comport themselves properly. He acknowledged the girls with a polite nod, his smile dimming a few hundred watts for propriety's sake. "Ladies. You all look lovely tonight."

I swear they all giggled.

Every last one of them.

He turned to me and turned the wattage back up, gracing me with a smile that almost made my knees grow weak. "And you, too, Miss Cooper. I'm sure the students would like to join me in thanking you and your family for your generosity for extending such hospitality and letting us stage this party in your home. As impressive as it is from the outside, it's even more so inside."

If I'd thought the girls disliked me for usurping the boys' attention, I could see that now they positively hated me for being the sole recipient of Mr. Lendon's attention. Not to mention his enticing smile.

I tried to keep my response as formal and as innocuous as possible. "You know what they say, Mr. Lendon. 'It's America's White House.' We're merely the temporary tenants."

He laughed politely. "If I may steal you away for a moment, I wanted to ask you a couple questions about the history of the building." He gave the kids an all-encompassing look. "Students, I'm sure you won't mind if I talk with Miss Cooper for a few moments. Alone." He placed a hand on my elbow and steered me away from the group.

He sounded almost earnest as we walked away. "Now, I was wondering about the Grand Staircase. I've always heard stories about it, and I wonder, is it true that . . ." His voice trailed off as we got out of earshot of the group. Unfortunately, it wasn't out of their view—I could feel the girls continue to skewer me with rapier-sharp looks. I was lucky they couldn't maim or possibly kill someone of their own species with a mere glance. I'd developed a pretty tough skin against those sorts of barbs years ago, during the latter parts of my own teen years. It was either that or die of the slings and arrows of outrageous pubescent insults.

"There." Mr. Lendon released my arm. "I believe we're beyond their range now. Consider yourself rescued," he said with a rather pleasant laugh.

I glanced at Diana, playing sentry in the corner. She shot me a silent thumbs-up. I had to remember to thank her later for her choice of rescuers. She had excellent taste.

"Thanks." The slight nod of appreciation was meant for him as well as Diana. "I was starting to wonder which of the groups would attack first, the boys or the girls, and who was going to be handy to try to gather up the pieces."

"No telling." He glanced over at the two swarms of teenagers, who now seemed united by a common goal. The girls hated me because I'd slipped away with their beloved headmaster. And now the guys hated the headmaster for having spirited away the only single "real" woman in the place likely to give them the time of day, namely me.

Some days, you simply can't win, kids. But maybe I can. . . .

Mr. Lendon lifted one shoulder in a shrug. "They'll get over the disappointment in a couple of minutes. Teenagers are remarkably resilient. And by providing them with a common enemy, we've actually given them the tools to start breaking the ice. We may actually get to see some dancing."

I watched the two self-segregated groups. "Right now, that doesn't seem likely."

"I know what you mean." He glanced at the makeshift sound system. "I'm not sure why they call it a dance when it takes them a good hour or so before everybody warms up enough to meet anywhere near the middle of the room, much less actually dance. And these are the same kids we can't pry apart in the school hallways. Suddenly, in a purely social situation, they act like they don't know each other."

He pointed to one side of the room (nearest the bathroom and the mirrors) that was predominantly female and the other side (nearest the food) that was predominately male. "But watch. I think our nefarious ice-breaking plan is starting to work."

We watched the two groups we'd just left as they started to abandon their gender-specific sides, comingle, and pair off.

"And the ice begins to melt," he said in his best *National Geographic* announcer voice.

"I suppose that's when the chaperoning duties really start," I said, remembering one or two unchaperoned parties in my past.

He eyed the slow migration to the middle of the room. "We still have about another half hour before the gap closes completely, and then our jobs will turn into somewhat ineffective efforts to keep them apart by decent distances." He glanced at the DJ. "You know what will happen. Someone will hand him a CD with something other than a frantic back-beat, so that you can actually make out the lyrics, and that's when we all have to go on red alert."

Mr. Lendon paused, then shot me a smile that could probably turn every female student into quivering Jell-O. However, I remained upright and in a semisolid form, thanks to years of conditioning. "Actually, I don't know that we've ever been formally introduced." He held out his hand. "I'm Rob Lendon."

"Eve Cooper," I said automatically, realizing my faux pas a second or two later. I still haven't gotten used to the realization that there are total strangers who know exactly who I am, who my father is, where I live, what I eat, where I sleep. . . .

I tried to joke my way past my gaffe. "But I guess you know that."

He had the sort of smile that not only reached his eyes, but made them twinkle. It was a highly attractive look on an already highly attractive man. What an old friend of mine would have called a "double whammy."

"The political fishbowl aside, I feel like I know you because Drew talks about you a lot. Your brother is quite a character."

Talking about Drew seemed a nice, innocuous subject. "That's putting it mildly. Take it from me; you can't believe half of what he says."

"Don't worry. He says some rather nice things about you. I think he appreciates the stability you're trying to keep in his life. I realize from what he's said that your father's political career really hadn't affected the family until the presidential election and the win. Drew's lucky that up till then your family always lived in the same house and that he's always attended the neighborhood school. Considering the big changes that have been thrust on a boy his age in a relatively short amount of time, I think he's handling it pretty well."

I had to agree. "We Coopers come from pretty hardy stock. We've learned to be flexible. Then again, I wonder if I would've been able to handle the upheaval and the change nearly as well as Drew has if all this"—I indicated the room, meaning the White House, with a sweep of my hand—"had happened to me right as I was entering high school. I sort of doubt it."

Mr. Lendon's expression changed to one of concern. "Considering all that's happened to you lately, I think you're doing pretty well. Drew's been worried about you."

"He's not the only one." I couldn't help from sighing.

Mr. Lendon continued. "We may be out of school for the summer but the kids know they can call me anytime they need to talk. And Drew's called more than once already."

"I didn't know that." On the one hand, I wanted to feel bad that Drew hadn't come to me to talk things out. On the other hand, I couldn't help but approve of the person he did choose as a sounding board. "Do you think he's handling it . . . okay?"

"Sure. Don't worry. He may feel somewhat frustrated and even a bit worried, but those are appropriate feelings, considering the circumstances. He's mostly concerned about your safety. He's been hit in the face with the reality of what almost happened to you. Because of that, he can't deny the somewhat tenuous situation that all of you are in. Besides being worried about you, he's feeling a bit less secure about everything—his own safety and that of your father and your aunt. He needs a safe outlet to express those fears, and I'm more than willing to offer it."

My, my. Handsome, brilliant, and caring.

He glanced across the room. "Damn." He turned back to me. "Sorry. I see trouble brewing. If I act now, maybe I can break up a skirmish before it starts." He reached over, squeezed my hand, and gave me a grin that made me completely forget he was the headmaster of a stuffy private school. "Can we talk more later?"

"Sure."

He took a few steps toward the offenders, who did look as if they were spoiling for a fight; then he stopped and turned toward me once more. "And save a dance for me. The kids aren't the only ones who brought their favorite music. They'll hate my contribution, but I think you'll like it."

I wandered around, trying not to look besotted as I performed basic chaperoning duties. I spoke with a few stray parents, answering a few questions about the house ("Yes, it is the biggest place I've ever lived in"), about my dad ("No, Dad and Aunt Patsy are in Manhattan tonight at a charity event"), about my unfortunate adventures of late ("I'd rather not talk about that, if you don't mind"), and about a variety of disjointed topics ("I never discuss politics at high school dances").

Or anywhere else, as far as that was concerned. I don't do politics, which is harder than you imagine, considering it's been Dad's lifelong career.

Wandering over to the refreshment table, I sampled the punch, pleased to see that no one had spiked it. Of course, it was little more than red sugar water, and the kids had passed it up for canned soft drinks. I watched the surface of the liquid in the bowl react to the driving beat of the current song.

So far, the music had been on the loud and pounding side—definitely not my favorite style of music. But when I heard the melodious wail of a saxophone, I knew someone entirely different (and probably older) had commandeered the CD player. I turned and saw Rob Lendon walking my way.

"Now this is what I call music. May I have this dance?" He held out his hand and I accepted it. We danced. It was a long, slow song, and the man knew what he was doing on a dance floor. Rather than go into every little detail, suffice it to say that I enjoyed myself.

Immensely.

Of course, the credit for that goes to Rob, who not only was a good dancer, but was funny and interesting and managed to strike just the right chord between familiarity and respect. That's not easy to do when you're slow dancing in front of a hundred kids who are staring at you because you've taken over their moment with your stupid slow music and touchy-feely dancing.

That is until some of the more intrepid teenage couples decided that touchy-feely dancing looked like it might be fun. More important, if their chaperones were busy dancing, no one would be paying attention to what else might transpire on the dance floor.

Wrong. Like most teachers, Rob had eyes in the back of his head.

"Let's see some daylight, there, Granger," he said to a couple of kids off the starboard bow. They shifted appropriately, unsticking themselves from each other.

"Mr. Cason, you and Miss Marshall too."

Another couple of kids shifted so that a thin sliver of light was visible between them.

"Is there daylight between us?" I asked innocently.

His voice brushed against my ear. "I sincerely doubt it."

We swayed together in perfect unison.

He continued. "Then again, there doesn't have to be. We're adults and they're not. It's not a fair world. The sooner they learn it in small, manageable doses, the better adjusted they will become. After all, there are simply some privileges that come with age—like the right to drink responsibly, the right to vote, the right to not-too-dirty dance, and . . ." He paused, obviously trying to expand his list.

"The right to lower insurance rates?" I supplied.

He laughed. "Definitely one of the perks that comes with age and experience."

The music ended too soon. Rather than selecting another cut from Rob's CD, the student DJ played something loud and raucous and not conducive to the sort of dancing I wished we could continue.

Rob said something I couldn't hear over the racket. Taking my hand, he led me through the jungle of gyrating dancers to the door leading to the Cross Hall. (Did I mention that the males and females had finally abandoned their sides of the rooms? Like when a warm front and a cold front meet, the center of the room was doing its best impression of a hurricane.)

We wandered out. Rob was still holding my hand, even though it wasn't necessary to, once we got out of the throng and closer to the door. And I must say that it felt both comfortable and right to be holding hands. We ended up passing up the ornate red seats and benches that lined the Cross Hall and sitting on the flight of stairs above the first landing of the Grand Staircase. The music still blared loudly, but we were far enough away and sheltered by a couple walls, so we could at least hear each other.

We spoke simultaneously. "Thanks for the dance."

We laughed.

He saluted smartly. "Yes, ma'am."

I glanced through the railing in the direction of the East Room. "Shouldn't we be back in there on chaperon duty?"

"I think they can handle one dance with the other chaperons in attendance, don't you?" He placed his hand on the stair tread, the beat of the music thrumming through the floorboards. "No one could possibly be slow dancing to this."

I've probably not mentioned it before, but there were also several teachers from the school, including a husband-and-wife team, attending the party as chaperons. It would simply be their turn to monitor the crowd and keep them off the walls. Literally.

Suddenly I couldn't think of anything appropriate to say. After all, this wasn't just some nice guy I'd met on the dance floor; this was Drew's principal. There had to be a conflict of interest in there somewhere. It would be totally inappropriate of me to start inquiring about his marital status, his outlook on life, and all the other things I wanted to know.

But I didn't have to ask.

He volunteered.

CHAPTER THIRTEEN

About Altamont

The mission of the Altamont School is to improve society by nurturing compassionate, educated individuals capable of independent thinking and innovative ideas. To this end, the school employs faculty members who are committed to truth, knowledge, and honor in order to attract, nurture, challenge, and prepare their students not only for the most rigorous college programs, but also for productive lives. Altamont's faculty is led by Headmaster Dr. Robert W. Lendon. . . .

Rob started by clearing his throat. "I'm thirty-two. I was born and raised in Chattanooga, Tennessee. I graduated from the University of Oklahoma with a bachelor's degree in history and then a master's in secondary education. I worked for a while as a teacher at the Altamont School, then went back to school and earned my Ph.D. in educational theory and policy from the University of Pennsylvania. I came back to Altamont as the headmaster two years ago. I've never been married, but I came close a couple of years ago. We didn't make it past the engagement. I'm in excellent health, I have good job security, and no, I don't have a history of trying to pick up my students' parents or, in your case, my students' siblings." He paused to drag in a deep breath as if his admission had winded him.

"Through?" I asked.

He nodded. "You?"

I drew a similar deep breath. "I'm twenty-five, soon to be twenty-six, and I have a news-editorial journalism degree from the University of Colorado, Boulder. No close calls when it comes to marriage, but I've been a bridesmaid six times. I have six of the most dreadful bridesmaid dresses in existence in my closet to prove it. They will never see the light of day again. I worked for a while with NPS—the wire service—and was a year into working on my master's when Dad decided to run for President. So after he won, I dropped out of school and quit my job in order to play substitute mom for Drew, since we all figured Patsy would be up to her eyebrows in her First Lady responsibilities. I've never looked twice at any of Drew's teachers, much less danced with any of them. So I guess you can sum it all up by saying I'm single, unattached, and out of work. I'm a graduate school dropout and I live with my parents."

It's the last part of that list that always gives me a problem. Even though there is a very good reason why I live with my family, it always sounds to me as if I do it because I'm a big fat failure.

Rob leaned back and gave me a highly quizzical look, pausing to scratch his chin. "Isn't that a rather harsh assessment?"

I knew what was coming. At least, I knew the usual response.

But to my surprise, Rob went on to say, "You honestly mean to say that none of those dresses can ever be worn again in a social setting? Not one of them?"

I laughed at the unexpected absurdity of it. How could I not? He'd disarmed the situation in the best possible way. No wonder he was such a success in his position. I could see why Drew felt comfortable calling him to talk over his problems.

"You have a nice laugh and a nice smile, Eve Cooper. For someone's big sister, that is."

We were now doing a different sort of dance, one I felt a little more competent when performing. "You do, too, Headmaster Lendon. For a school principal, that is."

"Come, now," he said with a sigh, "you know principals never smile. We're supposed to stalk the school hallways, yell at the students, and sit in the teachers' lounge to stifle discussion. We're all supposed to be old and grouchy and we're definitely supposed to make the lives of every student and half the teachers absolutely miserable."

I shook my head. "Don't forget. I saw you at the school program, dancing and singing on stage like a young John Travolta. I also saw the looks on the faces of the various females in the audience. And back there at the dance? I saw the same look in the faces of the girls when you approached. That wasn't misery. They looked totally besotted."

"Ah, yes . . ." He winced, wrinkling his nose until his eyes closed. "That's probably the most difficult part of my job."

"Being the sole recipient of their adoration?" I batted my lashes, but the effect was lost since his eyes were still closed.

"I have to present myself as a bit older, a bit stodgier, than I really am in order to keep up the illusion of age and respect." He opened his eyes and pointed to his jacket. "Thus the scholarly attire."

"How very professorial of you," I offered.

"You can laugh, but it's not easy finding that delicate balance between responding to them on an intellectual level but not necessarily an emotional one."

"Ah, yes." I held up my hand in a classic Vulcan salute. "The Mr. Spock syndrome."

He snorted at my gesture. "It's not a matter of being afraid to demonstrate any emotions. It's more a matter of making sure that nobody, especially the girls, can possibly misinterpret those emotions and infer any response other than the innocent one I intended to deliver. You know, it's not easy being a mentor to young people."

I glanced through the railing and spotted a couple of kids who had evidently thought they could sneak away and find a quiet place in the hallway where they could neck. But when they realized we were sitting on the stairs, they wheeled away and walked hand in hand back toward the party.

"I can imagine," I whispered as I pointed at the girl whose mature figure and form-fitting dress made her look twice her age. "Some of those girls in your school look a lot like women, even to me."

"They dress like women, and they act like women, and they desperately want to be treated like women. By me. Personally. That's the most difficult part—discouraging their advances without crushing their spirit. It's not easy to get into their heads but avoid their hearts."

He glanced at a nymphet who was obviously enjoying the discomfort of the very nervous young man she was talking to. "Some students want to turn fantasy into reality. Or at least they end up getting the two confused. They'll do anything and everything to have the two merge. Some teaching professionals are more successful than others at staving off their advances."

He shook his head as if trying to shake away unpleasant thoughts. "I don't want to talk about Lolitas and their victims. I'd rather talk about you." He glanced toward the hallway and made a face. "But I'm afraid we probably need to wander back in there and do some chaperoning. It's gotten very quiet in there."

"Too quiet," we said simultaneously.

And we were right. The blaring music had stopped, which was good for the plaster, but might signal an unexpected change in the party.

Rob stood and offered me a hand to help me up from the stairs. Rising as best I could, considering my dress and high-heeled sandals, I teetered a bit once I was upright. He steadied me.

The courage built in me. After all, he seemed nice, was obviously intelligent, appeared quite thoughtful, and Lord knows, he was gorgeous.

Best of all, I was no dreamy-eyed coed.

"This might not be exactly appropriate, considering what we've been talking about, but . . ." I leaned over and kissed him.

He met me halfway, which I considered a good signal that I wasn't acting rash or strictly on my own accord. Whether my heart was racing because it'd taken a good deal of courage to make the first move or because I was reacting to the sheer excitement of it all, I'm not sure.

Why waste my time trying to analyze the situation? He was enjoying it. I was enjoying it. After a few more tingling seconds, we broke apart, his arms still around my waist and our faces only inches apart.

"That was probably a bad example for us to set as chaperons. I hope no one saw this," I said, feeling the flush of embarrassment on my cheeks. Or was that attraction? Honestly, I couldn't tell.

"Maybe. But if they saw us, I won't have as much trouble with the female students anymore," he said.

"Though if Drew sees us like this, he'll kill me."

Rob squeezed my hand. "Brothers do tend to be a bit protective of their sisters, big or otherwise. But it's their right, I suppose."

I tried to wipe away a small, telltale smudge of lipstick at the corner of his mouth. "They don't expect their sisters to kiss their teachers."

"Headmaster," he corrected.

"Even worse."

"Longer hours, but better pay."

We didn't move, standing close together for a moment more. Then we sighed and broke apart.

Heading back into the party, we made a point of not holding hands. Why invite rumor, speculation, or trouble? I'd removed the smudge of lipstick on him, and he had no other telltale signs of that kiss that I could see.

As we filtered through the milling crowd of teenagers, we were separated, and I felt someone pulling on my arm; it was Drew.

He dragged me toward the refreshment table. "Eve, did you tell the staff to keep the table full of food?" He almost knocked off a bowl of chips as he swung his hand toward the table. He pulled back his hand and lowered his voice, practically hissing at me. "If so, then you gotta pay for it. We don't have enough money in the kitty to repay the cost."

Contrary to popular belief, the presidential family doesn't eat for free in the White House. We pay for every meal that is prepared for us in the White House, with the exception of state dinners. We even pay for all food served to our private guests. Essentially, Dad's position gets us the room, but not the board. Though, thankfully, we're not responsible for the labor costs. The White House staff, chefs and all, come with the house.

Plus, it's become a sort of captured-market situation. Since I can't just run out to the grocery store anytime I want, if I want specialty foods beyond the meals provided for me, I have to request that certain things be bought on my behalf, and then I pay for the purchase out of my own funds.

It's complicated, but fair.

As a minor child, with no monetary support other than the allowance he gets from Dad, all of Drew's food costs are completely covered by Dad. And trust me, that's one big bill. The kid would eat us out of house and home if we let him.

So I was totally astounded that Mr. Usually Oblivious of What and How Much He Eats actually had noticed the secret replenishments of party foods. I'm not used to him being quite this observant or fiscally responsible.

Maybe there's hope for him after all. . . .

I motioned for him to come closer. "Don't worry," I whispered. "Patsy okayed the extras. Dad'll pay the food bill." I turned in time to see one of the chefs roll out a big cart that had a large flat cake on it. It was decorated like a brick wall with graffiti sprayed on it, saying "Sophomores Rule!"

I pointed to the cake. "And I think that's courtesy of Aunt Patsy and Dad too. Consider it a present for having survived your freshman year in a new school."

Drew appeared visibly relieved for only a moment before he stiffened again. "Whatever you do, don't let Mr. Lendon know that Dad and Patsy kicked in a little extra food. He'll make us have a bake sale or a car wash or something to make up the difference."

I thought I hid my reaction to that well, but some little brothers know their big sisters all too well. Drew narrowed his eyes and gave me a long, critical stare. "You two were out there in the hallway talking for a while. A long while, in fact." His stare turned into a glare. "Was it about me?"

"Uh . . . no," I said truthfully.

He continued to glare, and then his eyes opened wide. "Oh my God, you kissed him." For the second time that night, he pulled me by my arm to a less populated corner of the room. Once there, he started shaking his finger in my face. "Don't deny it. It's written all over your face." He began to stomp around in a circle, flapping his arms. "Man, if anyone finds out, I'll be the laughingstock of the class, of the entire school."

"You look like a chicken. If you don't stop, you'll draw the attention of everybody in the room and then they'll know something's wrong."

He crossed his arms tightly, as if that were the only way he could stop himself from gesturing. "Do you know how long it took me to fit in at school? Do you know the sort of grief I'll get if anyone learns about you and"—he made a face—"Mr. Lendon?"

I folded my hands and stood still while he threw his modified fit (designed to berate me in relative privacy but not to pique the curiosity of his classmates). When Drew finally wore out, I leaned forward and whispered rather sweetly in his ear, "We kissed. And I liked it." I paused for emphasis. "*We* liked it."

What can I say? Sometimes, I just can't help but give in to my baser self.

Despite what Drew considered to be a major, unwanted complication on my part, the party was a hit. When 11:30 rolled around, the kids were still going strong and we had to break their collective hearts and inform them that the party was officially over. Enough kids had the presence of mind and manners to thank me on the way out to make me feel good about the younger generation.

Now exactly how old does that statement make me sound?

Old enough to possibly date their headmaster?

And speaking of Rob, he stayed until the last straggler was safely tucked in the last parent's car and had headed for home before he approached me. Unfortunately, Drew decided he needed to observe the entire conversation. Closely. So I felt a bit awkward as Rob and I brazenly exchanged telephone numbers and E-mail addresses.

"Drew's not going to give us any privacy, is he?" Rob whispered.

"You could order him to back off, but he probably minds you about as well as he does me."

"Drew? Nah, he's a good kid."

"He's a nosy, opinionated kid," I countered.

Rob took my hand. "Then rather than let him speculate about the possibilities, let's give him something definite to talk about after I leave." He leaned over and gave me a kiss that shot a bolt of electricity down to my toes and back up again, hovering in the places where you can really appreciate shivers the most.

When he finally broke away, his eyes were twinkling again. "Nice party. Nice house."

"Nice kiss," I managed to say once I caught my breath again.

The moment Rob left our sight, Drew said in a huff, "What the hell was that?"

"A kiss," I said in a dreamy voice, one designed to dig the knife in just a little deeper.

"Yeah, a kiss with the headmaster of my school." He crossed his arms. In fact, he was a hair's breath away from pouting. "Isn't that illegal or immoral? Or something?"

"Only if you're a student. Lucky for me, I'm not one." I reached up and ruffled his hair, an action he tolerates only from Aunt Patsy.

Just like usual, he batted my arm away. "Quit it."

I continued nonetheless. "Rob and I are—"

"You call him Rob?" Drew looked absolutely incredulous and some-what insulted. He kicked the edge of the sidewalk. "Aw, man . . ."

"As I was saying before I was so rudely interrupted, we're two con-senting adults who—"

Drew covered his ears with his palms. "I don't want to hear it. It's bad enough that I'll probably have nightmares after seeing you two . . . kiss." He wore his fiercest look. "For God's sake, please tell me no one saw you two earlier out in the hallway where you two were necking."

I shook a finger in his face. "First, we weren't necking. It was only one kiss." I contemplated the memory a second or too longer than necessary for art's sake. "A really good kiss, but only one. And second, I don't think anyone saw us."

"Don't *think*?" he echoed sarcastically. "You're not sure?" He said something totally unprintable and headed for the stairs. "If anyone learns about this . . . ," he continued to mumble as he walked out of sight.

I tried to go back and help with the cleanup, but the butlers waved me away. So instead, I glided up the stairs to my room. Once there I was hit with a sudden sense of guilt. I was supposed to have gone to the party with Craig. But how fast had I forgotten about him and become entranced by another man?

Much too fast.

How fickle of me . . .

Then again, maybe I deserved a chance to celebrate my sudden change in fortune. After having a very long dry spell with little or no social contact with anybody beyond the political kind (and trust me, political friendships don't count at all), to suddenly have enjoyed two rather intoxicating kisses from two different men in the space of a week?

It was definitely a personal record.

I decided that, rather than feel guilty, I ought to celebrate my good luck. Both Craig and Rob were nice guys with stable lives and good futures. And Lord knows, they were both great kissers. Sure, I'd known Craig longer. We'd started purely as acquaintances and the relationship had grown slowly but steadily from there. But, then again, between Rob and me there was that undeniable appeal and excitement of an unexpected and sudden whirlwind-type attraction between two people who are essentially strangers.

I looked at the slip of paper with his phone number.

There was nothing wrong with having two guys interested in you, right? Or with being interested in two guys, at least at this tingly, first-date stage of a relationship. Right?

I sat down at my computer and decided to write a note of condolence to Craig and a note of thanks to Rob for chaperoning.

See? I was learning how to balance this situation already.

But as soon as I got on-line, Charlie popped up with an instant message.

"Where have you been? It's late."

"Drew's party," I typed. "Just ended."

"Fun?" He added a ";-p". It was supposed to be a sideways smiley face, winking and sticking out his tongue.

"Actually, yes. I met someone."

"Not a student! =:–o" That was the smiley face, now gaping in surprise with his hair standing on end. Charlie's got a million of these things. You almost need a program to keep track of them.

"Not a student. The headmaster. Very yummy. Good kisser."

"My condolences to Drew. He must be crazed by this."

"<g>" Charlie's not the only one who knows emoticons and E-mailisms. I "grinned" at his remark. After all, Drew is the youngest kid, and has spent his short life trying to find ways to bedevil both Charlie and me. Turnabout is fair play.

Charlie continued. "Got that info you asked for."

"And?"

There was a long pause before he answered. "Hard to hack into Academy computers. Must have too many bright computer science majors there. Extra firewalls. But got into regular military records and came up with Rydell's blood type."

"So?"

"O+"

O-positive?

"BRB," I typed. *Be right back.* I scrambled through the papers that I'd moved from the floor to neater stacks on my desk before I'd gone to bed the night before. Finally, finding the autopsy report, I verified that just as I remembered, Ashley McCurdy was O-positive as well, but the unborn baby had typed out as A-positive.

"Charlie, correct me if I'm wrong, but an O-positive father and O-positive mother can't have an A-positive child. Right?"

"Not if I remember my freshman biology class."

My mind raced ahead a hundred miles an hour. If Keith Rydell couldn't be the father of Ashley's baby, then who was? Another boyfriend? An acquaintance? A stranger? Had Ashley been attacked by someone? That would have tracked with her early letters that talked about her desire for celibacy and then the sudden change in tone. Maybe someone really had been trying to get at her boyfriend in the most painful possible way, and had found the perfect way to hurt him.

Through her.

"Can you get back into the military records?" I knew from discussions over the years with Charlie that sometimes the holes in systems closed up after you entered them, when system operators realized someone unauthorized had visited their databases and how he'd done it. Then again, since Charlie's business was closing the holes, he knew more about opening them than anyone else in the industry.

"No problem. Need more?"

I found the sheet of paper that listed the six cadets currently serving sentences at Leavenworth and was about to give him their names, ranks, and serial numbers, but I scratched that thought before I even had Charlie check it out. If Ashley was only six weeks pregnant, the father couldn't have been any of the six former cadets because they'd been put on house arrest for the duration of the trial and then bundled off to Fort Leavenworth shortly afterward to start their prison terms.

They'd been in the slammer a whole six weeks before that crash.

I tapped my desk, trying to figure out what to do next. On a whim, or maybe it was more of a hunch, I typed, "Major Anthony Gaskell. Don't know his middle name, but his nickname is Gadget and I think he's still assigned to the Academy. Currently at Wilford Hall in San Antonio."

"BRB."

That meant Charlie was probably going fishing right then and there for the information, using his newly discovered hole in the military computer system. Although he has the skills of a world-class hacker, he's never had a hacker's need to augment or destroy data just to prove he's been there. His only goal is to learn how to get into a system so he can close up the holes behind him.

That's why he sits in a multimillion-dollar compound in Vermont, living the happy lifestyle of a Net hermit and making a zillion bucks writing software to catch people just like him.

It takes one to know one. . . .

Ten to one, he'd contact the military sysop after this and offer the government some free repair services in hopes of getting yet another government contract.

"We have a winner," he typed.

"What?"

"Gaskell, Anthony A. Major, USAF. Current assignment: USAF position: Air officer commanding, Cadet Squadron Twenty-three. Born 21 April 1964. No dependents. Currently hospitalized at Wilford Hall Medical Center suffering from injuries sustained in a soar plane accident."

"Blood type?"

I waited for a few seconds. Then the answer popped up: "A-positive."

CHAPTER FOURTEEN

BIOLOGY 101 TEXT

Mendel's third principle: Each inherited characteristic is determined by two heredity factors/genes, one from each parent, which determine whether a gene will be dominant or recessive.

It wasn't a smoking gun. And it wasn't sufficient evidence that could be used in a court of law to prove that Major Gaskell was the father of Ashley's child. I fully understood that.

But it *was* a beginning.

A-positive is a very common blood type. Both Dad and I are A-positive. Millions of people are.

But the important thing here was that Keith Rydell wasn't.

So the only thing we could be certain about right now was that the baby that his girlfriend had been carrying wasn't his.

I thought back to what Major Gaskell had told me in the hospital . . . how he'd tried to support Ashley as she supported Keith. Did he mean he was trying to act as a mentor to her, just as he would the cadets in his own squadron? Or was his brand of consolation different when it came to an impressionable young girl, frantic about her boyfriend.

A vulnerable, confused young girl . . .

What had Rob said about the difficulties and responsibilities of those who mentored the young as a part of their profession? He even had a Ph.D.

in the area, and he still said it was difficult to achieve the right balance.

Had Major Gaskell, a pilot, not a professional educator, stepped beyond the boundaries of good taste and allowed his efforts to console an upset young girl to turn into something much less savory?

I went back to the stack of E-mails that Megan had pulled off her sister's computer. Several of them lacked headers, so you couldn't tell whom they were sent to other than the salutation of "Hey, Babe."

That could be Keith Rydell or it could be a million other young men.

Or not-so-young men.

I began to examine the letters and came across several inconsistencies. All the letters addressed to "Babe" lacked headers. But all the ones obviously addressed to Keith included his name or other identifying information in the text of the letter. That substantiated the two-boyfriend theory.

The letters to Babe were written somewhat differently. She talked about the excitement of their relationship and the quick moments they had to find to be together, and I couldn't help but wonder if that was due to the relationship's forbidden nature.

It all began to fall into place for me.

She talked about ignoring the differences between them, about the fact that they lived in different worlds. The more I read, the more I could believe that she was talking to someone other than Keith Rydell, someone of a different age level and position. I noticed simple things, like her mentioning something about where they'd go when it was time for him to move.

Not when it was time for Keith to graduate.

At no time did she mention Major Gaskell's name, or anything that would directly connect her with him, but I couldn't help but believe that's exactly to whom she was sending these messages. It wasn't the sort of stuff a girl her age sent a young man the same age.

But then again, I was merely speculating. I had no proof. The evidence I was working with wasn't even strong enough to be called circumstantial. It was all a tissue of suppositions, thinner than a cheap sock. I was no expert, had no advanced degrees in educational psychology. But it wasn't that long ago that I'd been a nineteen-year-old girl. I could see why it might have happened.

Before I could decide to pursue the mentor avenue, I needed a real expert to look at the letters. But it was late, too late to drag anybody out of bed to take a look at the letters and make any sort of analysis of them. And I wasn't about to take this to Peter Seybold until I had something more than a gut feeling to go on. The man had a fondness for cold, hard facts. I didn't have even a whisper of one to give him.

The next morning, I waited until a decent hour before calling the best person I could think of who understood the relationship between the older mentor and the younger protégée: Rob.

He sounded surprised, but rather pleased that I had called, and even intrigued by my odd request. He had a busy day already scheduled but said he could squeeze in a lunch. Since lunches out aren't all that quick when you have a couple of Secret Service agents in tow, he agreed to come to the White House.

With a little cooperation from the staff, I had a very simple rooftop lunch planned. I found a sundress that I'd forgotten about in my closet, one that looked nice without making it evident I was dressing up for him. The weather cooperated, with the midmorning clouds dissipating to a clear blue sky. Rob arrived promptly at high noon and was escorted up to the family quarters.

"Nice view," he commented, looking out across the South Lawn. "I didn't even know there was a balcony up here. I thought the only people on the roof of the White House were the guys with the handheld missile launchers."

"Oh, them . . . they hide whenever we have company out here," I joked. "Hungry?" I indicated the table I'd stocked with simple sandwich makings. I wasn't about to hit him with a seven-course meal.

"Honestly? I'm almost more intrigued than hungry. Tell me about these letters you want me to look at."

I motioned him toward the table. "I'll explain while we eat. Two birds, one stone."

We made sandwiches and got drinks, and while we ate, I gave him the abbreviated, somewhat sterilized version of all the events that had happened to me so far.

By the time I got to the part about the hospital visit in San Antonio, he'd stopped eating completely. When I got to the part about the sniper fire, he reached over and placed his hand over mine.

"My God, Eve. I had no idea. Drew didn't tell me that part. Are you okay?"

His concern was touching and reassuring and maybe just a bit thrilling at the same time. "I'm fine," I said. "The Secret Service takes particularly good care of all of us. But, please, don't say a word about what happened. We were able to keep it out of the press."

"Sure. But still . . . a sniper." His hand tightened on mine. "It must be difficult for even the Secret Service to protect someone from that sort of danger." He looked around. "I think you can tell the guys with the missile launchers to come out of hiding. I'd feel better if they had a clear shot at any incoming artillery."

I continued with my story, leaving out the part about having obtained some of the medical data from less than legal sources. (What Charlie does and how he does it will remain a secret between just him and me.)

I pointed to the file folder on the table. "What I need is your opinion about a series of letters between the girl who died and one, or maybe two, men."

"Private letters?"

"Yeah. E-mail that her family gave me in the hope it would help with the investigation. When we talked about your experiences as a high school headmaster, I had no idea that I would need to pick your brain about this. But I don't know anyone else who has such insight into and experience with the mentor-student relationship. More important, I think you have a pretty good suspicion of what might go wrong if either party overstepped the boundaries of good taste."

What I didn't tell him was that I hoped his assessment, based on experience and interpretation, substantiated my less than educated one, based on intuition and hunches.

"I'll do anything I can to help."

Despite my protests that he could do it after lunch, he pushed aside his half-eaten sandwich and asked for the letters. Now, please.

I handed him the file, which contained a single stack of paper. I'd deliberately mixed up the two piles I'd created when I'd initially separated them as those "to Keith" and those "to someone else." But as Rob read through them, he started sorting them into two piles, making the same sort of assignments I had.

After he finished, he took a long swig of his soda and released a long sigh. "After reading this much of someone else's private mail, I'm starting to feel . . . like a voyeur or something."

"Me, too." He'd hit it dead on the nose. That's exactly what I'd felt. "You're right. Prying into the affairs—and I do mean affairs—of another person is a dirty business. But, as I said, I got those letters from Ashley's sister and with her family's permission. Her parents and her older sister are just as confused as we are."

"You're a good friend."

I shrugged. "It's not all altruism. I have a feeling that if I can help figure out what happened to Ashley and why, then my own problems might disappear too." I paused, trying to fight a different type of shiver—the unpleasant kind. "Then maybe the threats will stop."

Rob reached over and grabbed my hand for a quick squeeze. It was exactly what I needed at the moment.

"Thanks." I drew a deep breath. "So what about the letters?"

He straightened the two piles of papers. "I've separated these based on to whom I think they were intended, judging by content. This group"—he tapped the one on the right—"has letters that I believe were sent to a male who was most likely a peer to her. There are lots of references to 'we' and 'our,' which implies a sense of equality in age and experience. The language is very informal, as if she was assured they had similar vocabularies and frames of reference."

"In this group"—he indicated the pile on the left—"she uses the words 'you' and 'I,' as if there wasn't an implied understanding of a we or any sense of unity or equity between the two of them. That would substantiate the idea she was talking to someone older and with a wider variety of life experiences, far beyond what she considered her own limited accomplishments. She speaks of things like your music rather than our music, which also might imply a difference in taste based on a difference in years."

"Like the music last night. I knew that jazz CD was yours the moment I heard it. It's a favorite of mine, too."

He nodded. "Each generation is possessive of what they believe to be their exclusive music, as well as a bit disdainful of music they believe belongs to another generation or decade. Her word choices are more formal and even her sentence structure is more proper, as if wanting to impress someone with her sense of maturity and her wisdom beyond her limited years. Simply put, they're love letters to two men, one around her age, and one most likely older than her by more than ten years, more like twenty."

I stared at the papers, then at him. "You got all that? Just from those?" I asked in absolute awe.

He ducked his head. "I have a minor in adolescent psychology. I figured it'd be useful as a school administrator."

"Wow."

He looked up, looking more like an eager schoolboy than the venerable headmaster of an exclusive Washington, D.C., private school. "So did I tell you anything new, or had you figured this out on your own and simply wanted a second opinion."

I shrugged. "I'd come to most of the same conclusions, but mine were based only on intuition and speculation. What you said goes a lot further to substantiate the concept of two lovers."

"Don't shortchange yourself." He looked deep into my eyes. "Intuition and instinct can be powerful weapons in the right hands."

For a moment, I wasn't sure whether he was talking about my assessment of the letters or something else entirely. I could have sat there staring at him all day. But I didn't have that luxury.

I had to choose to believe we were still talking about the case. "Rob," I said softly, "all of this has been confidential, but what I'm about to tell you really needs to stay strictly between us. Okay?"

He drew a solemn cross over his shirt pocket. "Promise."

"What if I told you that we just learned that the girl who wrote these letters was pregnant when she died?"

"Poor girl." He winced in sympathy. "And you want to know which of these two men is likely to be the father?"

"Something like that."

"Well, based on the contents of the letters, she didn't sleep with the younger man. She talks about him respecting her wishes and enough of it rings true to make me think they hadn't had sex. But the older guy . . . I'd almost say that these letters were written right before and right after they had sex. There's an almost desperate tone starting in about the third letter, as if she's trying to justify her actions. As if, having enjoyed herself, she wants to keep him interested so that the relationship will continue. She may have made love to him only once or twice at the most, but she seems quite anxious to prove herself worthy for additional contact."

His expression grew somewhat somber. "If this relationship had gone on much longer without a continuation of their physical contact, I think she would have segued from a 'See how interesting and mature I am' stage to a 'Why don't you love me?' stage to a 'You're a bastard' stage to an 'I'm turning you in to the authorities' stage."

"And I suspect the 'I'm pregnant' stage falls somewhere between 'Why don't you love me?' and 'You're a bastard,' right?"

He nodded. "In most cases."

"I thought so."

Rob stayed only a short while after that because he had an appointment at one of the area universities. Evidently, even headmasters of ritzy private schools need temporary jobs to tide them over the summer, when there was no school in session. And to think what Dad pays for Drew's fancy school. . . .

I messed around the rest of the day, trying to let all the facts and theories work in my subconscious rather than my conscious mind. I was getting a bit depressed, thinking about Ashley, her unrequited love, the baby that would never be, the letters. The only bright side to it was that thinking about her woes made me forget most of mine.

Until Michael called, that is.

"Lieutenant Cauffman reporting in, ma'am."

"Very funny. What'd you find out?"

"Not 'How was the trip?' or 'How's the family?' but right down to business?"

"How was the trip?"

"Uneventful."

"How's the family?"

"Doing fine. How was the party? Did you and Craig act as proper chaperons, or did you two need a chaperon yourselves?"

"Craig couldn't make it. His father had a heart attack and he had to go home to be with his mother."

Michael sounded appropriately shocked. "Is his dad all right?"

"Craig thought he'd be okay. He wasn't as worried about his dad's recovery as he was about his mother's reaction. He said she was apt to smother his father in attention and cause another heart attack."

Michael harrumphed. "I've met his father. He's a big teddy bear of a man. A real nice guy. His mom? Well, let's just say she's a little high-strung. I can imagine she might take the news a bit hard."

"That's what I gathered. So what did you learn at the prison?"

"Not prison. Barracks." He sighed. "But you're basically right. The disciplinary barracks aren't quite like maximum-security prisons, but they're definitely jails. For the most part, the inmates are better behaved. There's less inmate-on-inmate crime, fewer problems with drugs, more inmate discipline. You don't feel as if you're taking your life in your hands when you enter, but there are still armed guards everywhere and some prisoners you don't want to turn your back on."

"What about the Academy Six?"

"If I'd met them on the street, I never would have picked them out as pushers, much less any sort of criminals. They were polite and respectful, and even seemed to want to help."

"So?" I asked in my best get-to-the-point voice.

"None of them seemed to have the least amount of resentment or anger toward Keith Rydell. They admitted they'd duped him, but every last one of them said he thought they would've been convicted just the same with or without Keith's testimony. If anything, five of them are angry at the sixth one, who pretty much ratted out the rest of them. He's kept in a different wing of the prison from the others. He says it's for his safety. They say it's because he wants special treatment."

"Nice. What about Ashley McCurdy?"

"Every one of them admitted to knowing Ashley, but only because she was Keith's girlfriend. If we're to believe them, they have nothing but sympathy over her untimely death. They swear they have no vendettas or reasons to put out a hit on her, on Keith, or on anyone else at the Academy."

"Do you believe them?"

I could hear some hesitation in his voice. "I do. Sort of."

"What is it?"

He sighed into the phone. "The few times I've talked to guys in prison, they always swear they're innocent. Every blasted time. But these guys are freely admitting their guilt. They use words like 'greedy' and 'stupid,' not 'misguided' and 'misled.' They're bright enough to realize they got caught and that denying it would simply make them look ridiculous. But they're not ridiculous. If they did have something to do with the glider crash—no matter if it was meant for Rydell or maybe both Rydell and his girl—they wouldn't admit to it or say anything that would implicate themselves. They got caught once, but I have a distinct feeling it might not happen again."

"So you're saying you think they *did* have something to do with it?"

"No, I'm saying that I can't possibly tell. We're not dealing with the typical dumb bad guy who wants to show you how big and bad he is and brags to his cellmates or to the guards about what he's done or is going to do. They're too smart for that."

It made sense, I guess. After all, if not for their brief detour into the world of crime, those six cadets would eventually have graduated and become Air Force officers.

A sobering thought.

And it led me to my next sobering thought.

I need to go back to San Antonio.

CHAPTER **FIFTEEN**

Job Description—Air Officer Commanding: Primary role model
in the formation of cadet leadership and professional qualities.
Guides the cadet chain of command in maintaining high standards
of discipline, developing unit esprit de corps, and implementing
squadron training programs. Counsels individual cadets, resolves
attitude and conduct problems, and makes recommendations con-
cerning the fitness of candidates for commissioned service.

Instead of trying to convince Patsy and Dad not only that I needed to
return to San Antonio but that I could do so safely, I took some of the
same advice that I've given Drew in the past.

I took a page out of my own Parent's Handbook and called General
Buck.

"Eve!" His voice was big and booming through the receiver. "Good to
hear from you. How's your aunt Patsy?" He meant it to sound off-the-cuff,
but he couldn't fool me.

"Fine, sir. She and Dad were in New York last night at a big charity
event."

"I know. I saw them on the news. Patsy looked as lovely as ever."

My God, but that man has it bad for my aunt. I didn't intend to trade
on his affection, but I figured it wouldn't hurt, given the situation.

"I have a favor to ask, General."

"Anything, my dear. And call me Buck, please."

"I need to come back and talk to Major Gaskell again. I have some new questions. But considering what happened last time, I don't think either Dad or Patsy is going to be too enthusiastic about my returning to San Antonio."

"I can't say that I blame them. After what happened last time, they have the right to feel protective. After all, you're your father's little girl, no matter how old you are."

"I realize that, sir. And I also know I'm an adult and I should be able to go anywhere I want, within reason."

I could hear him laugh on the other end.

"It's that 'within reason' part that is tripping you up, isn't it?" Not only was General Buck in love with my aunt, but he was an extremely perceptive man.

He continued. "So you want my help in putting together a military strategy?"

"Something like that. Maybe more strategy than military."

"Let's see what we come up with if we put our heads together."

The man was also a master strategist. The result of our little meeting was a fairly straightforward plan on how to approach Dad and Patsy, and how to convince them that my safety could be guaranteed because of the level of added protection we'd planned.

The trick? There'd be no advance notice to the press or any military personnel. The only persons who would know I was in San Antonio would be handpicked staff members, selected by General Buck himself, who evidently had deep connections within all areas of security in San Antonio, including the Secret Service. We'd be picked up by his private jet and flown to a small but secure airfield on the outskirts of town, and we'd stay in his very large gated home, which could also meet basic Secret Service needs for security, both inside and out of the house.

And the key to this entire mission was the word "we." Buck was anxious to invite Patsy to accompany me, for what I suspected were his own reasons as well as mine.

And to my utter surprise, when properly executed, General Buck's plan worked. After a very long and heated discussion, Patsy and Dad agreed. Patsy was able to rearrange her schedule to get her Sunday and Monday free to accompany me to San Antonio.

I know what you're saying. *My God, Eve, you're twenty-five years old.*

You have the right to go where you want, when you want, and not play
these sorts of games just to please your parents.

I agree.

If I were any person other than the President's daughter, living any life other than the one I do, with such strict security needs, and living in any place other than the White House, I'd be able to control my own life without hopping through so many hoops.

At some point, probably sooner rather than later, I will have to take a stand and reclaim my independence. But this wasn't the time. Not with so many questions unanswered, about the glider crash, the shooting, and everything else. I'd like to make sure that people aren't going to be shooting at me when I decide to assert my independence.

I honestly believed that my visit to Major Gaskell might provide some very necessary answers that might allow me to regain some of the limited freedom I'd recently lost.

So, the next morning, Patsy and I slipped out in a nondescript motorcade and headed to Andrews AFB. About a half hour after we arrived, Buck's private jet landed, unfortunately without Buck. He'd stayed back in San Antonio to coordinate with the Secret Service agents from the local field office. Five of us got on the plane, Patsy and me and our three agents, including Diana Gates. That had been at my request. I've seen Diana under fire. She was definitely the person I wanted at my side in case we ran into trouble.

As soon as we got in the air, Diana reached into her jacket pocket and pulled out her ever-present deck of cards. She said nothing, but the invitation was there.

Patsy looked at her and gave her a demure smile. "No, thanks. Your reputation precedes you, Ms. Gates."

I swear Diana actually blushed.

But she did find two willing card players (or, rather, victims) in the other two agents, which left Patsy and me some privacy to talk.

"I don't know what to think about you and Buck double-teaming me. It was either a brilliant masterstroke or you both play dirty. I'm not sure which."

I hadn't been looking forward to this conversation, but at least she hadn't made up her mind yet. "I vote for brilliant masterstroke," I offered.

She contemplated her answer for much too long, then rewarded me with a sigh. "I reserve the right to cast my vote at a later date. Like on the trip home." A steward approached, bearing a tray of enticing appetizers. Patsy sighed once more, but this time with far less exasperation. "Isn't it just like Buck to do something like this?" She picked out a few morsels and thanked the steward. I declined the tray. My stomach was too tied up in knots from my worrying about what I planned to do once I got there.

Buck's theory was that we should hit our quarry hard and fast, then retreat to a neutral corner. No one at Wilford Hall outside of one of Buck's most trusted cronies knew I was coming. The man was making no preparations for my arrival and would simply grease the wheels just ahead of me. I'd head there with my detail just as soon as we reached San Antonio. The local agents had been given a blind assignment and had no idea who was supposed to step off the private plane, just that it was their mission to guard that person or persons. Diana would be in charge of my detail with local support while Patsy's two agents would coordinate her protection with the local agents.

By the time we landed, Diana had won twenty dollars off of each of the other agents. I wonder if, as a duly deputized member of the Department of the Treasury, she'd ever admit that she plays with marked cards. . . .

The local agents managed to suppress their momentary look of surprise when the door opened and who but the First Lady and her entourage strolled off the plane. They even kept their poker faces when Buck walked up and planted a kiss on Patsy that lasted longer than either of my kisses with Craig or Rob.

After his liplock with Patsy, he turned to me and gave me a fatherly kiss on the cheek. "Everything's on schedule, General Cooper." He laughed as he turned to Patsy. "Mighty smart niece you have here, PittyPat. Takes after her aunt."

She graced me with a maternal smile. "I agree—at least about the smart part. Sometimes a little headstrong, but always bright."

Our plan was to split up at the landing strip. Buck and Patsy were going to head to his ranch house, north of town in what he called the Hill Country. He'd told me the house would be easily securable because of its location, the amount of open space surrounding the house, and the sophisticated alarm system he'd had installed some time ago. He'd admitted that five years before, a disgruntled ex-employee with a drug problem had made threats against his life, necessitating the alarm system and backup security plans.

Considering how thoroughly he'd helped me plan my return visit, I suspected the house security ranked right up there with that of the White House itself.

I kissed Aunt Patsy good-bye, assuring her that I would follow Buck's plan to the letter and not let my security detail out of my sight.

"I'm just glad Diana's back on the job and with you," Patsy whispered. "And it's not that I don't trust and appreciate the other agents. I know they're dedicated to their job, but Diana . . ."

"Has already proven herself," I supplied. Diana had utilized both her smarts and her strength to extricate me from a rather difficult, even dangerous, position early in her assignment to protect me. Although she remained somewhat aloof personally, I knew her well enough to understand her sense of humor, admire her card-shark abilities, be in awe of her physical conditioning, and be totally assured that protecting me was her highest priority at all times.

Aunt Patsy gave me one more kiss, then released my hands. I slid into the car the local field office had provided. Instead of a limo or a town car, both of which screamed, "Attention: VIP inside," they'd provided us with a dark blue Saab with windows tinted just enough not to let anyone see who was sitting in the backseat.

"She's big enough for four of you, fast enough to get you out of a tight squeeze, and she has military stickers so you can drive right onto base without anyone stopping you."

I reached over and hugged him. "Thanks, Buck. I owe you one."

He reddened slightly as he darted a glance toward Patsy, who was being helped into another car. "I'll think of a way for you to pay me back. Count on it."

And so we left.

The landing strip was little more than a runway and a couple of hangars. The trip to San Antonio started on a two-lane blacktop highway that eventually widened to four lanes as we started to see more signs of civilization. A short while later, we went over a very small rise, and suddenly we were surrounded by residential neighborhoods. Suspiciously similar houses stretched for as far as the eye could see. Traffic started picking up, and soon we had joined a moderate lunchtime throng. When we passed by a sign pointing to "Wilford Hall Medical Center" at the bottom of a freeway ramp, the driver explained that we wouldn't be taking the interstate. Instead, we'd use back roads to get us there. Considering my last adventure on the interstate near the hospital, I was glad to take the planned detour.

Thanks to Buck's stickers, once there we passed through the guard point with absolutely no fanfare. The gate guard snapped a salute which the driver, a local agent, returned with equal precision.

"Former military?" I asked.

"Yes, ma'am. I used to work security for the general until he retired."

"And then you joined the Secret Service?"

"Yes, ma'am. On his recommendation. Best job I've ever had besides working for the general. Nice to be able to finally combine the two. Just like old times."

So it seemed Buck was right when he said he had connections into the various areas that might impact our little plan. I guess I shouldn't have been so surprised. . . .

Buck had also provided a few pieces of what he called "camouflage" for us. At his request, I'd dressed rather informally, in jeans and a shirt. And, after great thought, I'd not put on any makeup and had pulled my hair back in a simple ponytail. America had never seen me looking quite so . . . au naturel. Anyone looking for the President's daughter would be looking for someone dressed like a visiting dignitary, with full makeup, a power suit, high heels, and hose. I looked in the rearview mirror and decided I'd given new meaning to the phrase "hide in plain sight."

As we pulled into the parking lot, the agent in front handed me a San Antonio Spurs ball cap and a bushy houseplant. He reached into the plant and fished out a small radio. "Backup, if you have any trouble. Otherwise, we have agents stationed inside along our route."

Buck must have known that Diana couldn't afford to be quite as casual, since her suit jackets are designed to cover the fact that she's always armed and dangerous. The driver agent provided her with a white lab coat, complete with appropriate badges and IDs hanging from the front pocket. With her short hair and ramrod bearing, she could pass for military medical personnel without question.

Now I understood why she'd worn a navy blue suit and pale blue shirt. It wasn't an Air Force uniform, but with the white jacket and proper add-ons, it would pass on fairly close inspection.

I turned to her. "You knew about this, right?"

Her face remained impassive. "I do what I'm told to do."

We climbed out of the car and walked into the hospital through the front door, just like any other visitors. As we walked along, I played "Guess who's an agent?" as we passed various people in the hallways—patients, visitors, doctors, nurses. No one paid any attention to me, which was a good sign for two reasons: all of the agents knew how to stay in the background and not tip their hands, and nobody else had recognized me.

It was almost like a choreographed dance that resulted in us commandeering an elevator by ourselves. It involved a janitor, a mop, and a well-placed cleaning cart. As soon as we entered the suspiciously empty elevator, the janitor managed to clumsily block the entrance so that none of the other passengers could enter along with us. The doors slid shut and off we went, alone and secure.

As we ascended, I turned to Diana. "The janitor. One of ours?"

Her lips quirked, signaling the acknowledgment.

"That was cool. Did he have to practice it a couple of times so that it looked so realistic?"

"I heard he worked on it a couple hours at the elevator at their office, yesterday afternoon. Pissed off lots of fellow agents trying to get home," she said in a deadpan voice.

You never know when she's pulling a fast one. "You're kidding, right?"

Her lips quirked once more. I wonder if that's how you can tell if she's bluffing at poker.

Major Gaskell had been moved to a different room just that morning. We were even on a different floor than the last visit, and the room was on the opposite side of the building. Whether it was in anticipation of the meeting or just happenstance, I don't know. But I was told that the new room location was nearer the stairs for what I assumed was a quick and easy exit.

As we walked down the long hallway, I still played "Who's an agent?" Was the tall man standing at the nurse's station delivering flowers an agent? Did he have a radio stuffed down in the center of the bouquet like the radio in the plant I carried?

Or was it the woman sitting in the wheelchair? She didn't look all that sick to me.

Or the janitor on the ladder, working on something in the ceiling?

Or the doctor standing near the window, consulting a medical chart?

I'd have to ask Diana later. If she'd even tell me.

I realized what I was doing—trying to distract myself from the task at hand. In just a minute, I was going to march into the major's room and start asking him some very difficult questions—uncomfortable for me to ask and equally so for him to answer. I had no authority to demand any answers, so I was going to have to draw them out by whatever means available to me, short of threat and torture. But lacking those two avenues, I would certainly use guile and misassumption to my fullest advantage.

When I realized that the janitor's ladder was standing next to the door to Gaskell's room, I decided that the man was definitely an agent. He gave Diana a nod that could have been taken as simply a friendly gesture. I assumed it was something far more important, but I studiously ignored him as I opened the door to Gaskell's room.

This was going to be a no-knock raid of sorts.

He was awake and a bit startled by our sudden entrance. He squinted at me; then recognition slowly flooded his face. "Miss Cooper! I didn't expect another visit from you."

To misquote a famous skit, "No one ever expects the Spanish Inquisition!"

Buck and I had discussed my interview technique and had agreed that making it radically different from the previous visits might catch him off guard.

I stomped into his room, pulled off my ball cap and tossed it on the foot of his bed, and allowed the plant to clatter onto a nearby table, knocking over the get-well cards that had been carefully placed there. Diana remained behind me with her back against the wall. She flipped back her medical jacket to reveal her shoulder holster, then stood at parade rest, looking cool, calm, and decidedly lethal.

What a card that Agent Gates is.

I turned to my intended victim. "We have to talk, Gaskell." In our strategy meeting, Buck had instructed me not to use first names or any ranks. I said "Gaskell" with the same intonation I would use when saying "vermin," "scum," or "pedophile."

The good major looked somewhat alarmed. "Is there something wrong?"

"Yes, there is. A girl is dead. People are pointing fingers at me. The NTSB investigators still aren't sure whether it was sabotage or pilot error. And I don't think I had anything to do with any of it. So I want the truth from you."

"B-but I told you. I don't remember the crash."

"Like hell you don't. You and Ashley McCurdy went up in that glider together and something happened. What was it? Did the controls suddenly stop working? Did you get hit by a gust of wind? Hit an unexpected thermal?" I paused artfully. "Or did Ashley tell you something you didn't want to hear?"

"I t-told you," he stuttered. "I don't remember. The doctors said that—"

"I don't care what the doctors said. I want to know what Ashley told you. I want to hear the words from you, because she's dead and can't tell us herself."

He grew decidedly paler. "I don't know what you mean. She didn't tell me anything."

"Are you sure about that?"

He had started to regain some self-control, which was bad. It meant I needed to hit him with something new—keep him off balance.

"Wait. Before you say anything, I have to admit I just told you a lie." I gave him my best "I'm in control here" smile.

He now looked totally confused. "Excuse me?"

I walked around the end of his bed so that I was on the other side now, forcing him to move to a more awkward position in order to maintain eye contact with me. "I said that Ashley couldn't tell us what she said to you up in the glider. But actually she can." I didn't look behind me as I held out my palm. "File," I commanded.

Diana slapped the file folder into my hand as if I were a doctor and she were in charge of handing out the surgical instruments. That file was my scalpel, so to speak, and I was hoping to use it to open up the man in front of me.

"Isn't it true that Ashley McCurdy told you that she was pregnant?"

CHAPTER SIXTEEN

COMMISSIONING OATH OF THE UNITED STATES ARMED FORCES

. . . I do solemnly swear that I will support and defend the Constitution of the United States against all enemies, foreign and domestic, that I will bear true faith and allegiance to the same; that I take this obligation freely, without any mental reservation or purpose of evasion, and that I will well and faithfully discharge the duties of the office upon which I am about to enter. So help me God.

He gaped at me. Whether it was out of shock or guilt, I couldn't tell. But I was going to assume it was the latter, and act on it. Perry Mason had nothing on me.

"Don't even try to lie to me. Her autopsy records indicated that she was six weeks pregnant when she was killed. So when you crashed that glider into the mountain, you didn't just kill her, you killed her unborn baby, too."

He fought for control. "She told me no such thing."

"Yeah, right. How do you know?" I countered. "I thought you said you didn't remember anything about the crash. So what is it? You remember nothing or you remember everything? You can't have it both ways!"

He took entirely too long to think about his answer, making a show of trying to draw out some long-suppressed memories. But I knew what he was actually doing: gauging whether he could use her revelation as a suitable, even believable, reason for the crash.

He drew in a deep breath and winced in pain. I made sure to show him absolutely no sympathy at all.

"Okay . . . you're right," he confessed. "I do remember some things. Ashley did tell me she was pregnant. It was a real shock to me. I knew she and Keith were getting serious and I'd counseled them both more than once about not doing anything to jeopardize Keith's future career in the military. Cadets can't be married, or get married, and they're not supposed to be fathers, either."

"And so, on hearing this stunning revelation, you became so upset that you crashed?"

"Not quite like that. When Ashley admitted she was pregnant, she said she hadn't told Keith yet and didn't know how. I told her not to tell him. He'd had enough grief with the drug-ring trial. He didn't need this, too. We argued because I told her that if she had the baby, Keith couldn't acknowledge it. She couldn't even claim him as the father on the birth certificate. I told her that the best thing would be for her to either go away, have the kid, and then give it up for adoption, or to end the pregnancy now. But that she couldn't have the baby and Keith. Not yet."

He sighed, shifting uncomfortably in the hospital bed, continuing the story while staring straight ahead as if inundated with horrible images flashing through his memory.

A likely story.

He continued. "The poor kid got hysterical. Ashley started screaming and trying to hit me. So there I was, trying to calm her down and fly at the same time. Then we hit a thermal." He closed his eyes artfully, as if trying to shut out the memories. "I couldn't react in time and I lost control of the glider and we crashed." He opened his eyes and turned to me, a tear glistening on his cheek. "So you see why I couldn't tell anyone what happened? I had to protect Ashley, even after she died. And Keith, too. If he'd found out . . ."

I stared back at him, keeping all emotion out of my face. We stood there, gazes locked, and I said nothing for a full fifteen seconds. I just stared at him. Finally, he turned away.

I'd won.

I tucked the file under my arm and started to clap. "Bravo. Excellent performance. Worthy of an Oscar. Or maybe a Tony." I released an ugly bark of laughter. "Get it? A Tony for Tony?"

I stepped closer, all laughter gone from my face and voice. I spoke in a soft voice. "You almost had me believing you really were a miserable mentor who saw his sage advice and heartfelt guidance ignored, and to what end? The death of two innocent souls." I sighed. "What a crock."

He blinked.

"There's only one problem with your story. But it's a *major* problem, if you'll pardon the pun. You see"—I pulled out the file folder—"Ashley McCurdy wasn't pregnant with Keith Rydell's child. Both of them have . . . had . . . O-positive blood type. The autopsy showed that the baby had A-positive blood."

I reached down and plucked the chart from the hook at the end of his bed, flipping through some pages. I didn't necessarily see his blood type listed anywhere on the chart, but that didn't matter. I knew it already. And my goal was to give the revelation as much drama as I could.

As I glanced through the pages, I added, "If you remember your high school biology class, you'll probably remember that two O-positive parents will produce only O-positive offspring. In order to have a child with A-positive blood, you have to have at least one A-positive parent."

I paused to stab a random page in his chart. "And guess who, in their little circle of close friends, just happens to be A-positive? Well, looky here. Your medical records says that you have A-positive blood. How interesting." I dropped the metal chart on the bed, perilously close to his injured foot. "Care to amend your story, *sir*?" I infused as much sarcasm as I could into the word "sir."

He stared at me, all his pretenses slipping from his face until I saw the real Major Anthony A. Gaskell.

And I didn't like what I saw.

His face became a cold, calculating mask.

"Ashley told me she was pregnant and the baby was mine. I didn't believe her. I figured there was just as good a chance of it being Keith's. But she told me they'd never slept together. I didn't believe her. The rest of the story—well, I told you what happened. She got hysterical, started trying to hit me, we hit a thermal, I lost control, we crashed." He looked up with no pretense of warmth or sympathy, challenging me to deconstruct the last part of his excuse. "It was still an accident, no matter whose baby it is."

"Was," I corrected. "Your baby is dead."

Apparently that was the pivotal tactic to take, because tears started to fill his eyes and his dead expression turned into a grieving one.

"I know," he said in a strained voice. "And I can never forgive myself for that."

Buck had warned me that he might try to play on my sympathies. The tears looked real and the voice sounded like that of a truly miserable man. It was hard, but I retained my "Don't mess with me" attitude.

"Nor should you. You should never have been in the position to have fathered her child. Why did you sleep with her in the first place? Why did you sleep with a nineteen-year-old girl? The girlfriend of one of your students?"

He closed his eyes and new tears cascaded down his cheeks, creating dark splotches on the pillowcase. "She was scared. She thought there was something I could do to help Keith, to stop the case from going to trial, to save him from the prosecution. She was beside herself, upset, and she needed someone."

I remained unmoved. "To talk to, maybe, but not to go to bed with."

He looked up, pain filling his features. "You never met her, did you?"

I shook my head. "I saw pictures of her. She was pretty."

"Not just pretty. She was beautiful. And she had a beautiful soul to match. She was the sweetest, kindest girl you could imagine. She was desperate to help Keith, to do anything she could do to try to help him."

"So you're trying to say she seduced you?"

"Yes . . . no . . . ." He reached up with his good arm and covered his face with his hand. "It sounds so sordid now. But it wasn't then. She felt like she needed to do something to help. She came to visit me in my apartment, just to talk about Keith. She broke down, I comforted her, and one thing led to another. . . ."

"And you had sex with her."

"We made love," he corrected me. "Yes, it was wrong. Yes, I realize now that it wasn't the right thing for me to do. But at the time it seemed so natural. She wanted it. I couldn't resist her. And it seemed to help. It calmed her fears, let her regain some control. It helped her find some hope, made her feel as if she was helping."

I didn't believe a word he said. I wasn't falling for his cock-and-bull story. He was blaming the girl and the heat of the moment for his faulty judgment and misguided reasoning. It was the oldest trick in the book—blame it on the woman. "She tempted me!" Men since Adam have used that excuse to cover every sort of misconduct. But this was nothing more than a desperate attempt to justify a very, very bad decision.

A career-ending decision, I suspected.

"So, tell me about the crash."

"I did already."

"Again, please," I said.

"I lost control while trying to deal with her hysteria. We hit a thermal, I lost control, and then we hit the mountainside. When I woke up, I realized Ashley was dead and I panicked. I knew you'd just gone up in the same glider—Dobbs had bragged about it before I agreed to step in for Keith and take her up."

"Keith asked you?"

"He had no reason not to. He had no idea that Ashley and I . . ." He stumbled for the word.

I could have supplied several crude ones to describe his actions.

He glanced at me. "And he still doesn't know, right?"

I smiled sweetly. "Not yet. Whether the situation stays that way depends on how convincing you are. Go on."

Resignation filled his face. "I figured that if I could make people believe it was possibly a case of sabotage, meant for you, then no one would look closely at either me or Ashley."

"You thought wrong." I crossed my arms. "I have very strong motivations to look at those motivations. So you're admitting that I was never in danger? That all this concern was over nothing more than a horrible accident compounded by your attempt to cover it up?"

He hesitated, then answered, "Yes," in a flat voice.

My sense of relief was fleeting. I might have cleared up the glider incident. But the sniper fire that took out the tire of the car I was in? I couldn't accept simple coincidence as an explanation for that. Especially since this jerk was in the hospital the shots were fired from.

"When I was here last week, what did you do after I left?"

"Do?" He looked truly puzzled. "I slept I guess. Up to yesterday, I was on some pretty strong painkillers." He lowered his voice. "And I wish I was on some right now."

"Can you walk?"

He grunted, reaching with his free hand and tugging at the sheets that covered his legs. One was encased in plaster with metal rods sticking out of it in several places. "It'll be a while before that comes off, and then I have about a year of physical therapy, they say. So the simple answer is no. Not yet."

I persisted. "Are you right-handed or left-handed?"

"Right-handed." He was starting to regain control, becoming irritated by my questions. "But I don't see why in hell I should answer any more of your questions. You're not a cop."

I pointed over my shoulder. "No, but she's a federal agent and overheard every word you said. Right, Diana?"

"Yes, ma'am, Miss Cooper. Every word."

He glared at her. "You didn't read me my rights. You have to Mirandize me in order to use any of this in a court of law."

I tucked the sheet back around his legs. "But like you said, I'm not a cop. I'm a private citizen. And at no point during your confession did you address her. You said everything to me, not her. But she can substantiate anything I say I heard in a court of law. It's a neat loophole. I guarantee that both civilian and military lawyers checked to make sure it would hold up in either court. I think Ashley's family will be pressing charges any day now. Manslaughter, reckless endangerment of a minor—who knows what they'll dream up?"

"She was no minor," he sneered.

"No, but her baby was. You killed your child, too, remember?" I moved toward the door. "Good-bye, Major Gaskell. And good luck. You're going to need it."

Good riddance, I added silently.

As Diana and I left, we heard him mutter something that sounded suspiciously like "bitch" to us.

No matter . . .

I'd gotten what I'd come for: a confession. The bit about it holding up in court might be pure baloney. Maybe it would, maybe it wouldn't. But since he was no lawyer, maybe it would keep him off balance for a while.

And the more pain and consternation I could cause that wretched man, the better.

I was pretty sure that he'd caused me more than a fair share of it.

Our trip back to Buck's house was uneventful. No sniper fire, no blowouts. Nothing but the usual problems with big-city traffic. That was no big deal. Since I now lived in Washington, D.C., I knew Beltway traffic would beat this traffic hands down. It took almost an hour to cross the town, using the smaller traffic arteries. Although I didn't think lightning would strike twice, the agents driving us stuck to the smaller roads, making sure that no one was following us. I appreciated their sense of caution, considering I'd essentially returned to the scene of the crime.

Although it would have been a good time to dissect everything Major Gaskell had said and to deconstruct his confession, I didn't want to talk about it. Not quite yet. I needed to let his words soak in for a while before starting to analyze them. Plus I wanted to keep the pool of people in the know about this as small as possible for now—though I had a feeling that I'd have to go through the entire recitation for Buck and Patsy as soon as I got to his house, not to mention make a phone call to Peter Seybold.

Thanks to Buck and his instructions on how to grill a military suspect, I felt that the session had been a complete success. Now if I could simply find the last few missing pieces, like who shot at my tires and why, then I could put this whole mess behind me. The tragedy would never go away—Ashley and her unborn child were gone forever. But I was now convinced that absolutely none of it was my fault. I could grieve for the fallen without that horrible, pressing sense of guilt at causing their deaths.

Once we were beyond the outskirts of town, we drove for another half hour past fields that were green only beneath the semicircles etched by the irrigation system. We passed at least two herds of longhorn cattle. I'd never seen them before in their natural element. The only longhorn I'd ever set eyes on previously had been a college mascot for a football team—and the Cotton Bowl doesn't exactly count as natural terrain for a bovine. The so-called Hill Country looked more like Rolling Pasture Country to me, but I guess this part of Texas doesn't have much in the way of mountains in comparison to the Colorado Rockies.

Finally, we pulled up to a large wrought-iron gate. Overhead, the sign read "The Buckin' B Ranch," with both Bs sitting at a cockeyed angle. The

driver paused to announce our presence into the gate's speaker grille. An
agent appeared from nowhere, acknowledged the two agents in the front
seat, demanded Diana's ID, reviewed it, and then acknowledged both of
us with a friendly nod.

"Welcome to the Buckin' B, Miss Cooper, Agent Gates."

"Thank you," I answered for both of us.

The gate swung open automatically and the agent waved us through.
The wrought-iron structure started to close behind us the moment our
back bumper cleared the opening. I figured we'd see the house just over the
next rise, but instead we continued driving for at least ten more minutes.

I leaned forward to address the driver. "Just how much land does General Buckley have?"

"Just shy of two hundred fifty acres, ma'am."

I knew Buck'd said he had a small ranch, but I'd forgotten that the
Texan definition of small differed from the rest of the world's. I thought he
meant a nice ranch-style house on the outskirts of San Antonio's ritzier
suburban neighborhoods. "Two hundred fifty acres? That's huge!"

"Not really. Not by local standards. LBJ had roughly six hundred acres
at his ranch in Johnson City. And the King Ranch down south of the state
is over eight hundred thousand acres. Larger than the state of Rhode
Island."

I'm such a city girl. Live and learn.

We went over another small rise (though they call them hills in Texas),
and then we could see the house. It was three stories high, with stucco
walls and a terra-cotta tile roof, pretty standard for houses in this area,
judging by some of the other houses we'd seen on the way out. But what
made this house different was the landscape. It was a perfect jewel in a
perfect setting. A blue lake peeked out from behind the house, and an
abundance of greenery sprang out around it like an oasis in the desert. I
hadn't seen this many trees anywhere else in San Antonio except for a few
city parks we'd driven by.

After passing through yet another gate, complete with guards who
dutifully checked all our IDs, we drove a couple hundred feet more and
pulled up in the circular drive, stopping at the front door. I noticed an
agent standing there guarding the door, his dark shoulder holster in stark
contrast against his white shirt.

Buck had been right about the house having adequate security for visiting dignitaries. Having run this much of a gauntlet and not even gotten inside yet, I felt that our safety had been placed in very good hands indeed.

After passing muster, we entered the front foyer, where one of Patsy's agents sat, munching on a plate of burritos. On seeing me, he tried to stand, but had a hard time balancing his plate.

"Don't bother standing," I said, waving my hand at him. "Eat. Be happy. Where's Aunt Patsy?"

I heard a voice from another part of the house. "Eve? That you? We're in the kitchen."

The driver was evidently familiar with the house, because he motioned for me to follow. Diana reached down and snagged a burrito from the other agent's loaded plate as I started off.

"I'll stay here and get a status report," she said with a casual air.

I eyed the burrito. "That hungry?"

"Famished."

The driver led me through a comfortable-looking living room that had a masculine feel to it, though not to the point of having dead animals staring at me from every wall, and pieces of furniture made from horns. There were the obligatory bits of military memorabilia here and there, but the room gave you the idea that the Air Force had been only one part of Buck's illustrious career.

I passed several pictures of him shaking hands with a variety of famous people. Besides the "I love me" shots, there were photos of him and the late Lorilee. One, fairly recent, was of the two of them on horseback. I stopped at their wedding photo, seeing a much younger, but very dashing, Buck in uniform and a blushing Lorilee in a veil and satin gown. To her right, a very young Patsy beamed into the camera, clutching her maid of honor bouquet with both hands. I'd had no idea Patsy had even been part of the wedding party. Or that she'd been such a total knockout in her youth.

We continued through a rather formal dining room and into a large gourmet kitchen, where I found Patsy up to her elbows in flour.

She looked up and smiled, looking at least ten years younger than just this morning. "Hi, sweetie. Buck's teaching me how to make sopaipillas."

I spotted him by the stove, wearing a chef's apron. He turned around with a plate in his hand. "Good timing, Eve. I just finished this batch." He placed the plate on the counter, pulled out a stool, and patted the seat. "Sit. Try your aunt's newest culinary triumph."

I'll admit it: I was hungry, and willing to be sidetracked. I guess play-ing bad cop can really take a toll on a person. Maybe that explains why cops always gorge on doughnuts. Right now, eating sounded like an awfully good idea. I plopped down on the stool and juggled the Mexican version of the doughnut, a hot sopaipilla which had been dusted very lib-erally with powdered sugar and cinnamon. Tearing off a corner of the pil-low of bread, I filled it with honey from the plastic squeeze bottle sitting on the counter.

"Well?" Patsy demanded.

"Hang on, I haven't put it in mouth yet. It's too hot." I blew on it, then finally took a tentative bite.

Ambrosia. A minute late the treat was gone and I was licking pow-dered sugar and honey from my slightly singed fingertips.

"Well?" she asked again.

I held out my plate and said in my best Oliver Twist voice, "More, please?"

They laughed and I gorged myself, eating my lunch in reverse—dessert, then the main meal, and finally an appetizer of chips and salsa.

Having witnessed Buck's kitchen, I was beginning to wonder if Patsy's lifelong obsession with and love of salsa, which she'd passed on to all of us younger Coopers, might not have its roots in her taco-salad days with Buck and Lorilee. . . .

Some day I'd ask.

But as we moved to the back porch to admire the view across the spring-fed lake, it became my turn to answer their questions.

I was more than anxious to spill my guts about the visit with Major Gaskell. I wanted to share all the tidbits I'd learned. I knew what my inter-pretation of what he'd said was, and now I wanted theirs.

After I spilled my guts, Patsy sat back in her chair, shaking her head. "A man of his age and a vulnerable young girl like that. I don't know what he was thinking."

I shook my head. "He wasn't thinking. That's the problem. Or worse," I added, "he was thinking with the wrong part of his body."

Buck shifted to the edge of his seat. "I can tell you one thing. That sort of behavior is not tolerated by the Academy administration, nor is it at all representative of how they operate or the high standards they maintain.

The man is an abomination, a disgrace to the uniform. And I'll do everything in my power to see that he's punished for conduct unbecoming an
officer and a gentleman."

I'd never seen Buck quite so fired up. He was red in the face and his
left hand was tightened into a fist. I guess you never know what a person's
hot-button issue might be. Then again, it wasn't hard to believe that a former general officer would remain very connected to the military and
would expect a certain minimum level of behavior from its members of all
rank.

Patsy reached over and patted his shoulder. "He'll get what's coming
to him, Buck. You don't have to worry about that." She turned to me. "But
what I don't understand is what the girl thought she'd possibly gain by
sleeping with the man. Especially if she'd been that adamant about waiting
until marriage to sleep with her boyfriend."

I sighed. "That bothers me, too. Gaskell wasn't connected to the case.
Or at least, his only connection was being the cadet's squadron com-
mander and mentor. What did she think she'd gain by sleeping with him?
What purpose would it serve?"

Buck settled back in his seat, his momentary wave of anger now under
control. "She must have thought he had some sort of influence on, or
knowledge about, the case."

Diana lounged in the doorway. She'd obviously overheard our discussion. She remained silent until I motioned for her to enter and speak.

"What do you think, Diana? You heard him too."

She remained in the doorway. "It's possible that he merely led her to
believe he had some sort of influence. Some men will say or do anything to
get a young and attractive girl into their bed."

Buck, Patsy, and I all started to speak at once. Diana held up a hand to
stop us. "Some men, I said. I'm not saying all men, just a select few."

"She's right," Buck said. "You heard everything Gaskell said, right?"
"Yes, sir."

"Then you definitely need to join us in this conversation. Get in here
and sit down. What's your opinion about Gaskell and the young lady?"

Diana took the offered seat. "Either he had no influence in the case,
and he merely made Ashley believe she could skew the results by sleeping
with him, or he's involved somehow on a level that we and the Academy

haven't discovered. If that's so, maybe Ashley realized it, and hoped that by sacrificing herself to him, he would do something to protect her boyfriend."

"Succinct and precise. I agree. I think you're right on the money. You would have made an excellent officer, Miss . . ."

"Gates, sir. And I did make an excellent officer. I served four years in the Marines."

I gaped at her. "Really? How come I never knew that?"

She smiled sweetly at me. "You never asked."

I made a brief call to Seybold. I told him what I'd found out. His responses were so terse, there's no use reiterating the conversation here. After giving me a restrained chewing out for going to San Antonio without discussing my plans with him, he acknowledged my input in his usual "I don't tip my hand" fashion.

Patsy, Buck, Diana, and I continued talking for several hours, until we all got tired of hashing and rehashing every little detail. So, finally, we all went our separate ways to clear our heads. Well, not completely separate. Patsy and Buck decided to paddle around his lake for a while. I decided to take a nap. I think Diana went looking for more food.

Seeing that I really was tired, Buck left Patsy and gave me a quick tour of the house as he led me to one of the guest rooms. The place was enormous—six bedrooms, seven baths, a hot tub, a Jacuzzi, a sauna, stables, the private lake, and probably a dozen other amenities that would make it some real estate agent's dream.

Buck led me to a room that was larger than my room at the White House. And the view out the window was spectacular—a beautiful view of the lake, the winding stream beyond the lake's causeway, a garden gazebo across the lake, and bright blue sky.

Not a monument or a tourist in sight . . .

Maybe I could persuade Dad to come up with his own summer White House—someplace nice—like so many other Presidents before him. Johnson had his Texas White House not so far from here. The Bushes had Kennebunkport, Maine, or Crawford, Texas, depending on generation. The Carters had Plains, Georgia. The Kennedys had their compound in Massachusetts. The Fords hung out in Vail, Colorado.

I'd work on Dad when we got back to D.C. Maybe we could do the Vail thing too.

After taking a long soak in the Jacuzzi, I curled up on the bed and fell deep asleep. If I dreamed, I don't remember. That meant no nightmares, either. Which was fine with me. The responsibility for that crash had finally rolled off my back, and I had the first undisturbed sleep I'd had since I got off the plane in Colorado Springs.

When I awoke, I felt better than I had in weeks. Maybe it was my clear conscience. After all, I'd gotten sufficient proof in my mind to exonerate me for being the cause of Ashley's death. As unfortunate as that had been, I now believed that it had had absolutely nothing to do with me.

But then again . . . why hadn't I felt compelled to call Megan with the "good" news?

I knew the answer.

Because my good news wasn't necessarily her good news.

Informing Megan that I'd determined that I wasn't responsible for Ashley's death, directly or indirectly, wouldn't help her situation, especially since I would be delivering a second whopping load of bad news. ("Oh, by the way? Ashley wasn't carrying her boyfriend's child, but that of the boyfriend's command officer. Who says she seduced him and attacked him in the plane, causing the crash that led to her death.") Her sister would still be dead, her family's grief would still be palpable, and they'd still have no comforting answers as to why this tragedy happened in the first place.

Would it really hurt to wait until Monday to talk to Megan face-to-face and explain what I'd learned? After all, both Buck and Diana had some interesting theories. I didn't think it was unreasonable for me to wait twenty-four hours in order to pursue those theories before calling Megan and setting up a meeting with her. I wanted to be sure that I had my facts in place and a final summation of what went wrong before I passed on the bad news.

Now fully awake, I heard voices and followed the sound until I arrived at what was evidently Buck's study. Diana sat at a computer, and Buck stood over her shoulder, directing her. He turned and spotted me just as I was covering my yawn.

"Good, you're up. Diana and I have been working on a theory. I just sent out some feelers to see if I can't get some information from a couple of old buddies of mine."

"On a Sunday afternoon?"

"Officers are on duty twenty-four seven. Plus, these are some very close friends. They'll do it for me."

"What sort of theories?"

"That Ashley must have thought there was some sort of evidence against her boyfriend that she could get quashed if she slept with the major."

I nodded. "Good theory."

"Any ideas what that evidence might have been?"

Something nagged at the back of my mind. "I remember Megan saying something about Keith having taken a drug test, but that he passed. It was in a summary report I read. But what if someone futzed with the paperwork? What if he didn't really pass?"

Diana and Buck gave each other a look. She sat down at the computer. "I'll write the letter," she said. "You figure out who it goes to."

What a team.

I yawned again. "Where's Aunt Patsy?"

Buck pointed toward the door behind him. "In the kitchen. I think she misses having a real kitchen of her own. She wanted to make supper for everyone."

As much as Patsy might have missed having a kitchen, we'd all missed eating her food. Patsy's a great cook, and I was pretty sure that if she'd been turned loose with a decent pantry, we were in for a smorgasbord of her favorite recipes. She does a fried chicken that puts the Colonel and his seven secret herbs and spices to shame.

I left Buck and Diana to their theories and headed for the kitchen. Familiar aromas hit me before I got into the room. I looked around, but Patsy wasn't there. I figured that gave me free rein to check out our menu for the evening.

A pot of homemade chili simmered on one burner and a pot full of potatoes boiled on another. I looked in the oven and saw my favorite "Pork Chop à la Patsy" bubbling on the bottom rack. On the counter sat her scratch biscuits, all ready to pop in the oven for the last ten minutes left on the pork chops.

Judging by the smell, the chicken had already been fried and was waiting for some sneak thief like me to sample it.

"Hmm," I said. "I wonder where Patsy put the chicken."

"Keep your cotton-pickin' hands off of my dinner," came a voice from
another room.

"Where are you?" I moved toward the sound of her voice.

"Here, visiting a friend."

I discovered her in a large pantry, sitting on the floor, next to a large
box with a cutout side. "What in the world are you doing down there?"

"Talking to my new best friend, Annabella. And her babies."

I stepped around her and saw a beautiful golden retriever lying in the
box on a red plaid blanket. Curled up next to her were several squirmy,
squealing bundles of fur. Puppies. Six or seven of them at least.

I knelt beside Patsy. "How old are they?" I asked in a soft voice. You
never know whether new mothers will become aggressive or not when it
comes to strangers being around new offspring. That perfectly understandable reaction crosses all species boundaries.

"Two days. Aren't they gorgeous?"

Annabella thumped her tail like a proud mother.

"Beautiful. So this was the Annabella that Buck didn't want to leave
by herself. I can see why. She's a beauty."

Patsy reached up and scratched Annabella's ears. "You can pat her. It's
okay. She's a very calm mother."

I allowed Annabella to sniff my hand first; then, once she seemed to
approve, I scratched the wide spot between her ears. Her tail continued to
thump in appreciation.

"Purebred?"

Patsy nodded. "One of Buck's neighbors owns the sire. It was a
good breeding. Annabella's doing fine, the puppies all seem healthy."
Patsy paused for a moment. "Buck's already said we can have one if we
want."

I eased back to a sitting position. "You really think the Cooper White
House is ready for a puppy?"

She shrugged. "I don't see why not. Buck said he'd wean, then paper-
train, the puppies. We'd probably have to keep the puppy upstairs with
you at first, of course."

"Until she or he gets out of the chewing stage?"

Patsy nodded. "I can just imagine the fit Mr. O'Connor and Mr. Wallerston would have if she decided to gnaw the legs of one of the antique chairs."

The mental image of the two men screaming in fright made me laugh. "Actually, I was more worried about a puppy christening one of the expensive rugs."

"You can clean that up. It's the teeth marks that are permanent." Patsy sighed. "Still, maybe a dog isn't such a great idea."

I remembered another family dog we'd had, also a golden. "Having a dog is a fine idea. It's dealing with a puppy that might cause everyone so much work."

One of the puppies, eyes still closed, had stumbled away from the others. Patsy reached in gently and nudged him closer to a teat. "This one keeps wandering away, trying to strike out on his own."

"Does he have a name?"

"None of them do."

"Then if it were up to me, I'd christen him Columbus."

"Perfect name," rumbled a deep voice behind us. Buck stood in the doorway and smiled at his pet. "How you doing, Belly?" The dog's tail started a new and invigorated rhythm, canine for "Better now that you're here."

"Belly?" I asked.

"It's just her nickname. Her full registered name is Queen Annabella of Buckingham. And I bet my Annabella is hungry. Aren't you, girl?"

Patsy and I moved out of the room so he could prepare her food. I ended up helping Patsy finish dinner, and we both swore we'd try to cook at least once a month when we got back home.

Home.

Buck's place looked and felt like a home. It was warm and inviting, with comfortable furniture and family mementos everywhere. The White House still didn't have that homelike quality. At least most of it didn't. But I was starting to consider the third floor more or less my home. Having my friends over had helped make it become my space. But the rest of the house?

Most of it was still somewhat foreign to me.

Maybe having a dog would help.

Certainly the White House has survived many other dogs. But the thought of the look on Burton O'Connor's face when he saw a me with a puppy in tow....

A crate-trained dog who didn't like chewing on antique furniture.

Yeah. Right.

Our dinner reminded me of the old days when we were never quite sure how many extra guests we would have at the table. Patsy set up the food buffet-style in Buck's kitchen, which allowed everyone to eat at their leisure, to sit at the dining-room table, to sit outside on the porch, to take their food back to their command post or wherever they wanted to eat.

Diana didn't usually eat when and where I did, so I understood when she wandered into another room with her plate. But later on we arrived in the kitchen at the same time for seconds.

I hoped and prayed as we both made a beeline to the chili pot that there were two servings left. Diana reached it first, looked in, and said, "Just enough for two."

"Good." She held the lid while I ladled out the remaining chili, dividing it between our two bowls. "By the way, please tell your aunt how much the agents are in total awe at having the First Lady cook for them. And she's a great cook."

"Thanks. I'll tell her. But if you think this is good, just wait until dessert. I think she made her 'Death by Chocolate' cake. It's so good, you'll think you've died and gone to heaven."

Diana's eyes brightened.

It seemed chocolate was Diana's only weakness. I'd have to remember that. Instead of playing poker with peanuts, perhaps we should switch to peanut M&M's to keep her distracted. If nothing else, she'd be tempted to eat her ante rather than raise it.

After dinner and all the "I can't believe I ate that much" groans, Buck, Patsy, and I performed a familiar ritual for American families—trying to find something fit to watch on TV on a Sunday night.

Bereft of anything that interested any, much less all, of us, Buck turned Patsy and me loose in his DVD collection, and we found a spy thriller we hadn't seen yet.

So we all sat on Buck's big leather couch, Patsy in the middle, and watched a movie. As it played, I fought the feeling I was a fifth wheel. I stuck it out through the entire movie, not excusing myself until the very end.

Maybe I should have felt guilty. After all, Buck had been the one to help me figure how to get to San Antonio. Didn't he deserve a little reward? Like some private time with Patsy? So I didn't even stick around for the closing credits. Instead, I excused myself with little fanfare and simply left.

With any luck at all, Buck knew exactly what to do from there.

As I walked past Buck's office, I saw Diana huddled over the computer. "Checking your E-mail?" I asked.

"Checking to see if any of the general's buddies have responded. He cc'd all the inquiries to my account so I could monitor things."

"Anything yet?"

"Just one note from a friend of his at the Academy, about the drug screen test. He said he'd fax the original results once he got ahold of them." She glanced toward the door. "Are they . . . alone?"

"Yeah. Sitting on the couch. We just got through with a movie, and the fifth wheel here is going to bed."

"Good. My relief is already here. I thought I'd stay up and see if any responses come back from our inquiries."

I nodded toward the living room. "If anything comes in that he needs to see, why not wait until later, unless it's urgent? They're probably in there necking right now."

Diana raised one eyebrow. "Isn't that taking 'Kiss the cook' a little seriously?"

"Yeah. But I'm pretty sure he's been wanting to kiss her since long before he got her in the kitchen."

At the sight of my stifled yawn, she sighed. "In any case, there's no use for you to stay up. Good night. We'll all be outside, with an internal sweep on the hour."

"Good night." I shuffled off to my bedroom, where I contemplated one more soak in the big Jacuzzi. But I really didn't need it to feel sleepy. A big supper, lots of inactivity watching the tube, and I was ready for bed.

But as much as I appreciated my deep, dreamless nap earlier that afternoon, I sincerely hoped I might have a couple good make-you-wake-up smiling dreams, reliving or perhaps allowing fantasy to go beyond those very happy moments with Rob at the dance. Though I've never had much luck directing my dreams.

In the middle of the night, instead of waking up with a smile on my face, I woke up hungry. That was totally absurd because I'd stuffed myself silly with Patsy's cooking. Maybe I woke up because it'd been a very long time since there had been any pieces of Patsy's homemade chicken sitting in a refrigerator ready to be raided. It wasn't as much hunger but a need to fulfill my nostalgic curiosity. There was nothing that said home to me quite as loudly as a midnight snack of a leftover drumstick or thigh.

I stood, stretched, and hoped that there weren't any agents who might assume any movement in the house signaled an intruder. I didn't need some local guy who had orders to shoot first and ask questions later to finish what Major Gaskell had started. Then I remembered what Diana had said, that the agents would be stationed outside the house and would make quiet indoor sweeps only on the hour. I found my watch and, thanks to its glowing dial, learned it was 2:15 in the morning. I should be safe from being mistaken for a prowler.

I still had to worry whether the agents performing the one or two o'clock security sweeps had had the bright idea of raiding the refrigerator and beating me to one of those last delicious pieces of cold fried chicken.

I don't normally assume that my guest privileges include fridge-raiding rights, but since Patsy was the one who had cooked the food, I figured I had some built-in leniency.

The house was dark but I remembered my way around fairly well. The glow dial of my watch actually added enough illumination to keep me from tripping over coffee tables and such. I made it without incident to the kitchen, found the chicken in the fridge, still wrapped in plastic wrap the way Patsy had left it. I helped myself to the only leg still uneaten. I also decided to appropriate a glass of milk. I found a clean glass in the drain board, which saved me from having to prowl through the kitchen cabinets to find a glass.

I was just settling down to enjoy my snack when I heard Annabella whine from her bed in the pantry.

"It's okay, Annabella, sweetie. It's just Eve, getting a snack."

She continued making a plaintive sound, increasing from a whine to almost a wail. Any louder and she'd wake the whole house. I wasn't about to share my chicken leg with her, but I could give her a few nuggets of dog food, since I'd noticed where Buck kept it.

I headed into the pantry and my foot hit something solid. At first I thought I'd stepped on Annabella; then I realized that whatever it was, it was too large to be a dog.

She continued to whine.

I fumbled along the wall, trying to find a light switch. I accidentally found it the hard way, the light flaring suddenly and blinding me for a moment. I shielded my eyes and squinted down, making out the figure of a man sitting on the floor and leaning against the wall.

Buck . . .

CHAPTER SEVENTEEN

First Aid Instructions

1. *If unconscious, check victim's breathing first, then the pulse.*
2. *If no pulse exists, start CPR.*
3. *If pulse exists but not breathing, begin rescue breathing.*

Each of us under Secret Service protection has a personal alarm that we can hit and get help in minutes, if not seconds, depending on where we are. I'd left mine on the bedside table and simply hadn't thought about picking it up for what I had anticipated would be a quick and safe trip to the kitchen. After all, the house was supposed to be secure.

But while sitting on the couch watching the DVD, I'd spotted an alarm panel for the house, nestled behind the door that led to the porch. Like most alarm systems, this one had a big red button marked "Panic."

And this was definitely the time for a big red panic.

I ran to the back door and slammed the button, starting a cacophony of Klaxons, then ran back to Buck. He wasn't conscious, so I checked to learn that, yes, he was indeed breathing, but his pulse wasn't strong enough to give me too much assurance. I didn't remember him mentioning any heart trouble, but there was always a first time, I guessed.

Agents thundered into the house, and I shouted out, leading them to my location. Poor Annabella did her part as well by barking, which made her puppies whimper. She seemed quite torn between caring for them and caring for her master.

Diana was the first to reach me. "What's—damn!" She immediately shouted orders into her radio.

"I think he's had a heart attack or something." I moved out of the way because I knew she'd had more first aid training than I. Trapped in the corner by the dog box, I tried to calm Annabella down by talking softly to her.

"It's all right. Buck's going to be fine. Calm down. . . ."

She stopped barking and started whimpering again, which was at least easier on the ears. By this time three other agents had arrived on the scene, as well as Patsy, who pushed her way past one of them and spotted Buck on the floor.

The anguish in her voice as she called out his name almost reduced me to tears.

It's true. She does love him.

The agents were right on the ball. Since it was evident Buck hadn't actually fallen, but done a controlled slide down the wall, they assumed they weren't dealing with spinal injuries. They carried him to the couch. Diana and another agent stayed with Buck while the other two agents started arranging immediate medical support. Someone produced a blood-pressure cuff, and Diana got on the radio again, this time relaying Buck's vital signs—heart rate, respiration, and blood pressure.

I supposed we had to take comfort in the fact that he had all three. Patsy found a suitable position by his side but out of the administering agents' way. When Buck opened his eyes, her name was the first word he uttered.

And he loves Patsy.

Although it'd been a good half-hour drive from the outskirts of town just to his front gate, an ambulance arrived in less than fifteen minutes. During that time, the agents had been instructed to give him aspirin and to continue to monitor his vitals. The fact that he was conscious, alert, and in only a moderate amount of pain was encouraging. But we all knew that only hospital tests could tell if he'd had any damage from the probable heart attack, whether he was in danger of having another, or whether something else was involved in his collapse.

As they loaded him onto the ambulance, Patsy was beside herself. "It's all my fault. I should never have fixed so much rich food."

I gave her a mild shake. "Don't be ridiculous. One rich meal isn't going to give a man a heart attack. Has he ever had heart trouble before?"

"I . . . I don't know. I don't think so." She drew in a shaky breath. "I hope not."

They started to close the ambulance doors, but Patsy stepped forward. "I'm riding with him."

Her lead agent stepped forward and placed himself between her and the ambulance door. "Ma'am, that's not a good idea. You can't go by yourself, and there's not enough room for you and an agent without compromising the care these professionals might need to give to the general."

She remained uncharacteristically belligerent. "Well I'm not going to stay here," she said through clenched teeth.

"No, ma'am. I understand that. You go get some clothes on and I'll have the car pulled around. I'll drive you to the hospital myself."

I stepped forward. "Count me in." Diana stepped behind me like a shadow. Whither I go, so goes she.

The agent nodded as if it was a foregone conclusion. "Yes, ma'am."

I grabbed Patsy's arm and started pulling her back inside. "Come on. You can't show up at the hospital looking like that." I turned to the agent while still pulling Patsy toward the front door. "We'll be ready in less than five minutes." I'm not necessarily a poster girl for Proper Decorum, but I knew Patsy didn't want the First Lady to be seen wearing her favorite bathrobe, fuzzy slippers, and bed hair.

Diana helped me get Patsy moving. Once we got to her bedroom, Patsy had regained most of her usual control, and about half of her usual composure. She changed clothes quickly, as did I, pulling on the same jeans and shirt I'd worn the day before.

Good to our word, we were changed and out the door in less than five minutes. We all crawled into the Saab, Patsy's agent and Diana in the front seat, Patsy and me in the back. Two other cars would go with us, one in front and the other in back, each with two agents. Two agents would remain in the house to maintain its security.

I rolled down the window and called out to the agent by the door, "Make sure to go talk to the dog. She's pretty upset."

He trotted over to the car. "Yes, ma'am. Don't worry. I know Belly really well. I'll pay her some attention, calm her down, and make sure her puppies are okay. You just take care of General Buckley, ma'am."

And off we went.

As soon as we hit the smooth blacktop, Diana turned around and handed Patsy a small bag. "Here. I thought you might need this."

Patsy opened the bag, revealing a small cache of her makeup. Nothing fancy, just the basics and a small hairbrush.

Diana shrugged. "You never know when someone with a camera will show up. And you are the First Lady."

Agents take care us in sometimes unexpected ways. . . .

The lead car in our entourage had a police bubble light, which excused our running red lights and exceeding the speed limit. Because it was the wee hours of the morning, there was a stunning lack of traffic, and it took us only about ten minutes to catch up with the ambulance. Diana stayed on the radio, giving us periodic updates. The medical technician said Buck was in stable condition, and because of that he was going to be taken to Wilford Hall instead of a smaller hospital along the way.

"Are they sure it's safe?" Patsy asked.

The driver answered quickly. "Yes, ma'am. Wilford Hall is one of the best cardiac-emergency facilities in the city. If he's stable, then it's to his advantage to go there. They'll be able to take care of him better than anywhere else in town."

Ten minutes later, we pulled up at what was now becoming a very familiar sight: Wilford Hall Medical Center. We were out of the car and at the ambulance door before they could even open it. A group of doctors waited while the ambulance crew pulled Buck's gurney out. I recognized one face, that of Doctor-Major Trichey, whom I'd met in Gaskell's room the first time. Standing in the back of the knot of medical personnel, he abandoned them and came to us.

"Miss Cooper, are you all right?" He looked up and was stunned when he recognized Patsy. "Ma'am! Are you . . . is everything okay?"

"Neither of us is hurt," I said. "It's our friend, General Buckley. We think he had a heart attack."

"General Buck? Oh, then that's why we were all called." His face tightened even more, signaling that in military eyes, the general ranked equal to if not higher than the First Lady.

"What do you mean?"

"We only knew it was a code-one emergency. That means all hands to the ER. I was afraid it was a train wreck or a major fire or something. They didn't give us any details."

"The Secret Service probably wouldn't let them."

Diana listened to her radio, then tapped me on the shoulder. "We need to go inside. They have a secure waiting room for you."

We learned that local agents had arrived before we did and, working with the base police, had secured the emergency room and its waiting area. I hated to think of what other emergency cases had been shuttled off to other areas of the hospital or made to detour en route to other hospitals because of us. I didn't need any more guilt.

We dutifully followed Diana and ended up in a nondescript but serviceable waiting room, plenty big enough for Patsy and me and our security detail, which was growing in size as the minutes passed. Buck had been wheeled into their cardiac treatment room and was being tended to.

Patsy couldn't sit still. She paced the room, trying to distract herself by learning the names of the various local agents. She's one of those rare people who never forget a name. If we ever came back to San Antonio, she'd remember not only their names, but whatever details she wheedled out of them, like the number of kids they had, their spouses' names. . . .

It's just part of her charm and the reason why the Secret Service agents all seem to adore her.

After about fifteen minutes, a doctor came into the waiting room. "Mrs. Davidson? I'm Colonel Johnson. I'm a cardiac specialist. I just wanted to let you know that the general is quite stable, awake, talkative, and in quite good spirits."

Patsy grabbed my hand. "Oh, thank God."

The doctor continued. "This was essentially a very mild angina attack. He has no prior history of heart problems, so we are going to monitor him for a while and run some tests later. But in all honesty, we expect to discover little, if any, damage. For the most part, he's a very healthy man, and I fully expect him to stay that way for a very long time."

Patsy gave him a hug. "Thank you, Doctor. May I see him now?"

He smiled. "Yes, ma'am, just as long as you can keep him quiet. But"— he turned to me, a rather concerned look on his face—"the general has asked if he could speak to Miss Cooper first."

Patsy and I looked at each other.

"Me?"

The doctor nodded. "That's what he said. Quite clearly."

Unsure why I was getting the first visitor's slot and not Patsy, all I could do was turn to her and apologize. "I'm really sorry, Aunt Patsy. I have no idea why he wants to talk to me."

She gave me a hug. "That's perfectly fine, Eve. He has his reasons, whatever they are."

"I promise I won't stay long."

Her smile was simple but reassuring. "Don't worry, sweetheart."

I followed the doctor out of the waiting room (with Diana trailing me) and into the treatment room, where Buck was stretched out in a bed that rivaled something from *Star Trek*. The only difference was that a tangle of wires had been fixed to Buck's chest in several places and led to the machinery behind him, which displayed his various vitals.

He gave me a weak smile. "I must have scared you to death. I'm so sorry, Eve. I was up checking on Annabella when the pain hit."

I patted his hand. "Don't apologize to me. I'm just glad that I got the munchies in the middle of the night or I might not have found you."

"There was a different reason why I got up. I heard the fax machine in my office." He raised up slightly and looked around. "Where's my robe? I think I shoved the papers in the pocket."

I looked around, saw nothing, then waved over a nearby nurse. "Excuse me, but the general needs something that was in his robe. Do you know where it might be?"

"Sure." She reached under the bed, pulled out a plastic bag, and handed it to me. "Here you go." She turned to the general, her face reflecting a mixture of concern for his health and respect for his rank. "How are you feeling, sir?"

"Much better, thank you, Captain."

"If you need anything, just hit your buzzer." She indicated the unit by his hand. "I'll break the land-speed record to get to you."

She headed out the door.

I pulled the robe out of the bag and patted around until I found a pocket containing several folded sheets of paper. "These papers?"

"That's it. I didn't even have a chance to read them because I heard Belly whining. I shoved them in my pocket and went to see what was wrong with her. Then"—he pointed to his chest—"whammy." He lifted slightly, resting on one elbow to get a look at the papers. "So who are they from and what do they say?"

I wagged my finger at him. "Down. I'm not supposed to get you excited."

He settled himself back into a reclining position. "I'm down. I'm calm. I'm the picture of serenity. Now what do they say?"

I studied the papers. "They look like medical records." It was like looking at a foreign language, but I spotted enough keywords to realize what I was looking at. "It's . . . a tox screen from the Academy hospital. For Cadet Second Class Keith Rydell." I found all the blocks checked "negative."

I held the paper so that Buck could see it. "It looks like it's the drug screening test that proved he had no illegal substances in his system."

Buck sighed. "Then I guess he really was innocent."

I shrugged. "I guess so. Then there must be another reason why Ashley slept with Gaskell. Maybe there was some other piece of evidence she was trying to suppress."

"Or maybe it's the other way around. Maybe she was trying to entice information out of the major."

We'd touched on that possibility in our discussion last night, but not the reason behind it. "Like what information?"

The general shrugged, which wasn't easy to do with all those wires attached. "Something she thought the major knew but wasn't telling about the case. Who knows? Maybe he'd discovered the drug ring and turned a blind eye after being sufficiently bribed. After learning he slept with that girl, I wouldn't put any other illicit behavior past him."

I glanced out the door and saw Patsy waiting patiently for her turn. "I think I'd better go. There's somebody out there who really wants to see you. Bad."

He grinned, bringing some very needed color to his face, and making me think that maybe, just maybe, he was going to be all right after all.

Once I stepped back into the waiting room, I gave Patsy a hug and a quick kiss. "He looks and sounds good. He wants to talk to you now." Patsy headed into the treatment room and I took her chair in the waiting room.

Okay, so the tox screen was negative. Or so it appeared to the inexperienced eye. Ashley hadn't slept with Gaskell to suppress a report that further exonerated her boyfriend.

Then why did she sleep with him in the first place? Lust? Infatuation?

That didn't track with what I knew about her. Then again, it did explain the somewhat breathlessly naive tone of her subsequent E-mails to him— at least E-mails that had been sent to the anonymous studly@hottmail.com who I'd initially thought was Keith Rydell, but now realized was probably Major Gaskell.

Had he seduced her so that he had leverage he could use against Rydell? Had the pregnancy been an accident or a carefully orchestrated way to control or even destroy Rydell?

Boy . . . talk about going off on wild tangents. That's what you get trying to brainstorm in the wee hours of the morning.

I tried to study the fax, only recognizing about a third of the medical terms, but assuming that the word "negative" was a good thing when discussing possible drug use. But, hey, I was in the middle of Medical Terminology Central with plenty of people who could interpret.

I snagged a nearby nurse, the same one who had helped us. "Can I ask you a question?"

"Sure, Miss Cooper." She leaned forward as if she had a confession to make. "By the way, I just wanted you to know that I voted for your dad. Everybody around here did."

Ah, yes, another unsolicited confession about a secret ballot. See? People do it to me all the time.

I gave her the obligatory smile of thanks, then turned to business. "Are you familiar with tox screens?"

"Sure." She nodded enthusiastically. "We do them all the time in the ER." Her face suddenly went pale. "You don't think . . . the General . . ."

"No, absolutely not," I said in a hurry, wanting to correct her misassumption. "It has nothing to do with the general." I unfolded the papers and smoothed out the wrinkles, making sure to fold them so the name couldn't be seen. "Could you look at this and tell me what it says? I mean, what it really means?"

She consulted the paper. "It's a standard tox screen, a toxicology screening test done on urine to test for drug use." She laughed. "Around here, folks call it Project Golden Flow."

"So what would it screen for?"

"Oh, lots of things." She pointed to one column. "This column shows you what drugs they're screening for and the second column gives you the length of time. Like here. Amphetamine. If you've taken any in the last one or two days, you'll test positive. If you took them three days ago, you may or may not test positive. Any longer than that and the test probably won't catch it."

I looked at the first few drugs:

Alcohol-Positive: 3 to 10 hours: Negative
Amphetamines-Positive: 1 to 2 days: Negative
Barbiturates-Positive: 2 to 6 weeks: Negative
Benzodiazepines: 3 to 6 weeks: Negative

The list went on from there, covering every sort of common drug abuse, the range of time it measured, and Rydell's negative results. I turned to the nurse. "So you're saying that the guy this tox screen was done on tested negative for any and all drug use?"

She glanced over the list. "They were pretty thorough. They even tested for possible steroid drug use." She ran her finger down the list. "Wait a minute. You said this test was done on a male?"

"That's what I was told."

She shook her head. "This part of the test looks into possible anabolic steroid abuse, and to do that it has to measure testosterone levels. This urine came from either a female or a really delicate-looking guy with the highest voice you could possibly imagine. The doctor who requested the test would know. He had to witness the patient actually producing the sample. Chain of evidence, you know."

I had a sudden flash of insight. Ashley had provided the urine sample for her boyfriend, who possibly couldn't have passed a drug test. Somehow, they must have made a switch right under the doctor's nose. Gaskell found out, and in exchange for his silence, Ashley slept with him. What was bad was that she evidently liked sleeping with him, perhaps lured by his maturity, his experience, and quite possibly the forbidden nature of it all. And the very worst of all? She'd ended up pregnant.

God, it had been staring us in the face.

The nurse pointed to the name of the doctor who had ordered the test. To me it was just an illegible scribble. "Talk about being lucky. The doctor who requested this is assigned here, Major Trichey. Maybe he remembers more about it." She looked around. "In fact, he was just down here a minute ago. Let me find him and maybe he can clear up this mystery." She headed off down a side hallway.

I don't expect my brain to work well in the middle of the night, especially in the emergency room. But lucky for me, all the cylinders were firing in order right now.

Trichey was Gaskell's best friend. Certainly, he'd realized that the urine sample hadn't come from Rydell. The test required that he witness the whole thing.

Now it made even more sense. Maybe Ashley slept with Gaskell in order to secure his help in Keith's case. But what help could he possibly give? How about making sure that results of the drug test that Keith failed are changed so he miraculously passes? So Gaskell turns to his old friend Trichey, who is in the perfect position to make the switch. But why would Trichey risk his career doing this for a friend?

There had to be a stronger reason. Trichey had to have a personal stake in this. Did Gaskell have something on Trichey? Did he force him to change the drug test? Or were Trichey and Gaskell so buddy-buddy that the doctor had no qualms violating his medical and military oaths to do something illegal, immoral, and unethical?

If Ashley hadn't supplied the sample, then why didn't Trichey substitute male urine. Surely he knew someone who knew medicine could catch the inconsistency. . . . Like himself . . .

Unless his urine wouldn't pass the test either.

As I said, nighttime brainstorming is less about logic and more about creative inspiration.

But this was all making sense to me, sleep-addled brains or not.

Simple answer: Maybe Trichey was protecting himself as well as his best buddy. After all, where there is a doctor, there are drugs.

Maybe it was a student drug ring, but it could have had officers involved, including a doctor who could get his hands on the drugs.

As to Gaskell's role, I could only speculate. Maybe he was able to grease the path of distribution by creating reasons why the cadets under his command had to go certain places at certain times. Or maybe he studied their personalities to find those cadets who might be tempted to involve themselves in such illegalities.

Had he been right about Keith Rydell, but not factored in Ashley's influence for truth, justice, and the American way?

If I'd been associated with the military and wanted to hide my involvement, I would've mailed the drugs to an innocuous off-base mailbox place, making it appear as if the source were civilian.

God, was I onto something? Or was I just so sleepy I couldn't think straight? Maybe Patsy and Buck could help me straighten this out.

I glanced into the ER proper. To my horror, I saw Trichey standing next to Buck's bed, talking to him and Patsy. My first instinct was to scream for him to get away from them. I knew that was a dangerous reaction and quite possibly one born of a wild imagination.

Innocent until proven guilty . . .

But I didn't want to take any chances.

I had to keep my cool, get him away from them, then get help. After all, I had no real proof of any of my speculations. All I had was theory and a bunch of unanswered questions.

But every instinct I had said that he was guilty. Very guilty.

I swallowed hard. The first thing I had to do was get the doctor away from Patsy and Buck and move him into the safest place I could think: a waiting room that was filled with Secret Service agents. I took one step into the treatment room, unwilling to stray any farther into what might be enemy territory. "Uh, Dr. Trichey, can I ask you a question?"

He looked up from his discussion with Patsy. "Just a moment."

"It's really important."

Patsy looked up quizzically. "Honey? Is something wrong?"

"No, no," I said too quickly. "I just need to talk to Dr. Trichey. Out here."

He had started to make his apologies to Patsy when the nurse I'd been talking to walked into the room, coming in behind Trichey. "Pardon me, Major, but Miss Cooper is in the waiting room and has some questions about a tox screen it appears you ordered while at the Academy." She looked up and spotted me. "Oh, there you are. I thought you were still in the waiting room."

I'm not sure what tipped him. It could have been the amount of detail the nurse gave him. Or maybe it was the look on my face. He moved like lightning. One moment, he was talking with Patsy; the next moment, he'd grabbed her by the arm and pulled her in front of him. He wrapped his arm around her waist, pinning her arms to her side, and reached over to a nearby tray of instruments and knocked some of them to the ground with a metallic clatter as he snatched one particular item. A scalpel.

He held it to Patsy's neck. Although it wasn't a big knife, it looked all too lethal as it gleamed in the artificial light. "Don't move," he ordered.

"Yes, sir." I rested my hand above my jeans pocket, felt the outline of my personal panic button, and pushed, hoping I could activate the unit through the material. At least I'd remembered to grab it off my bedside table this time.

"Everybody just stay calm," he ordered. "No one has to get hurt."

I gently put the papers down. "I'm calm. Patsy's calm. Nobody is going to do anything rash, Dr. Trichey." Out of the corner of my eye I could see Diana standing just beyond the doorway, gun drawn and ready to charge in.

"Doctor, can you take that thing away from my aunt's throat? It looks sharp." I hoped that by identifying the assailant plus the type of threat, Diana and the other agents could act faster.

She nodded, and I could see her relaying the information into her radio.

"Major?" The nurse made the mistake of stepping toward him.

"Get back," he screamed. He took the scalpel away from Patsy's neck for a moment, just long enough to take a wild slice at the nurse. She shrieked and leaped back out of the way. She reached for a phone, but pulled her hand back when she saw the knife once again at Patsy's throat.

To her credit, Patsy didn't scream, flinch, struggle, or do anything other than stand there, looking poised.

"Give me those papers," he demanded.

"Absolutely." I held them out. "They're yours." What I neglected to tell him was that they were merely plain paper faxes. Someone somewhere at the Academy had the originals. But maybe he might not notice that at first glance. Considering how irrational he was, I wasn't sure he hadn't dipped into a pill bottle or two today.

"Bring them to me," he demanded.

I could see Diana shaking her head furiously. *Don't go to him.*

"I'm not too sure that's a good idea," I said. "Why don't I bring them halfway there?"

"Put them . . ." He looked around the room. "Put them there." He nodded to an empty gurney about halfway between us. I took a couple of steps forward, reached out and dropped them on the edge of the bed, and moved backward.

He pushed Patsy forward to the bed. The moment he pulled the knife from her throat to reach for the papers, there was a loud howl from the machines monitoring Buck.

"Oh my God, the general's having another heart attack," I shouted.

It was enough of a distraction to allow Patsy to stomp down on her assailant's instep and knock his arm so hard that the scalpel clattered to the floor.

But the pièce de résistance was that Buck wasn't having a heart attack. I'd seen him choose his weapon, then get a fistful of the wires that were not merely attached to his chest, but that held him hostage to the bed. He jerked them loose, causing the machines to go crazy. Between the noise of the machines and my shout, it'd given Buck the time he needed to react.

The clang of the metal bedpan hitting Trichey's head had to be the sweetest sound I've ever heard. A split second later, the Secret Service swarmed the room and Trichey learned a very important lesson: No one, and I mean no one, messes with the First Lady.

EPILOGUE

When Patsy and I returned to the White House on Monday, Dad spent almost an hour yelling at us. It was the usual sort of rant—about pulling boneheaded stunts, not letting the Secret Service do their job—but instead of yelling at me, he aimed most of his tirade at Patsy. I didn't come away completely unscathed, because I was the bright one who had decided to go back to San Antonio, but she caught the brunt of it because she was "the adult and should have known better."

Dad sometimes forgets I'm an adult too.

He also seemed to forget that he'd agreed to my plan to go to San Antonio the second time.

After he finally paused to catch his breath, Patsy gave him her sweetest smile and asked, "Are you quite through, Elliot?"

He glared at both of us. "For now, but I reserve the right to pick up the thread where I left off at a later time."

Of course, he never did. It was simply his way of telling us that he was worried about us, that he loved us, and that if anything ever happened to us, he didn't know what he'd do.

So instead of picking up the argument again, we ended up having a rather nice family dinner. Patsy actually cooked. And afterward, the family did the sit-together-in-front-of-the-TV thing. All of us, Drew included. Just like the old days. We even agreed on the program to watch.

Will wonders never cease?

I had two phone calls to return, one from Craig and one from Rob. I had to make the difficult decision as to which call I was going to return first.

Someday I might even tell you whom I called. Though not what I said . . .

But about all the missing pieces to the puzzle . . .

It wasn't until Wednesday that we started getting those pieces. After Trichey was arrested on Sunday for attacking Patsy, all sorts of law enforcement types went through his desk at the hospital, his locker, and his house, but found nothing incriminating. However, one very bright investigator started wondering how Trichey got back and forth between work and home, since according to base records, he'd never registered a car with them.

That's when they found Gaskell's car parked in the reserved lot at Wilford Hall. And inside it they discovered a set of golf clubs in the trunk. Nestled between irons and woods sat a high-powered rifle with a scope. A ballistics test proved it was the gun used to shoot out my tire.

But did it belong to Gaskell? Or was it Trichey's? Without any telltale fingerprints, it was a hard call. That was because Gaskell's injuries turned out to be not as severe as everyone had been led to believe. He was in far better shape than either he or his personal physician, Trichey, had let on. Evidently, Trichey had even overprescribed medications for Gaskell's nonexistent pain, a stunt he'd developed while at the Academy. He'd prescribed strong painkillers for injured patients, then given them nonnarcotic substitutes instead and pocketed the unused medication.

When questioned, Trichey insisted that the meds had been strictly for his own misuse and that he was merely a "man with a monkey on his back" and in need of drying out, not capital punishment.

But there is never honor among thieves. When questioned separately, Gaskell admitted that the misdirection of medication had provided the kernel of inspiration that eventually spawned the Academy drug ring. They'd eventually expanded their crimes beyond the simple substitution idea and had supplemented the prescription drugs with some illicit contributions obtained from a downtown dealer.

So who had shot at me?

When the two men turned on each other, it got real ugly, real fast.

Trichey said Gaskell was the shooter. Gaskell said Trichey did it.

So who was telling the truth?

Since Trichey's assessment of his patient's condition was now deemed unreliable, Gaskell was examined by two independent doctors, who verified that he was unable to walk because of his compound leg fracture. That meant he couldn't have climbed the stairs to the roof to the shooter's perch, much less have walked to the car to stash the gun. Lucky for him, his room was on the opposite side of the building too.

So we had our smoking gun, so to speak, and the probable shooter, but not the real reason behind the attack.

After all, what had I done wrong?

Gaskell suggested that Trichey had panicked, unsure of how much the doped-up major had told me about the drug ring. (Evidently, an eager nurse had actually followed the instruction on the chart and actually given Gaskell the heavy doses of drugs he'd been prescribed after he complained of some pain.) It was hours after the tire incident before Gaskell regained his senses enough to assure his partner he'd told me nothing of significance. But by then, the damage had already been done. And who was to say his memory was all that accurate, under the haze of heavy doses of narcotics?

Things unraveled so much that Gaskell swore that Trichey had admitted he hadn't been trying to hit the tire, but that I had been his true target, and the only reason why he'd gotten the tire instead of me was that he was such a lousy shot.

In return, Trichey's defense was to proudly call attention to his marksman ribbon, which damned him as much as it exonerated him. It certainly explained his ability to hit a moving vehicle from such distance. In return, he started talking about Gaskell's ill-fated glider crash. He suggested that Ashley hadn't just surprised Gaskell with the news of the pregnancy but had threatened to tell the authorities about his involvement in the cover-up, destroying his military career.

That part we'd figured out. But his next jab was the kicker.

Trichey said that his friend had confessed to him that Ashley hadn't died on impact but that, despite his moderate injuries, Gaskell had managed to pull himself out of the cockpit, crawl over to where she lay, still alive, and bash her head with a rock.

You can bet some military investigators swarmed back to the scene of the crime in search of the murder weapon.

Gaskell countered by swearing that he couldn't have done anything that physical after the crash, because his injuries had been quite severe. Evidently he'd forgotten he'd told me that he'd been well enough to try making the crash look like sabotage.

All his protests became moot when investigators actually found the rock—complete with fingerprints, blood, bits of brain matter, and all—tossed off the ridge into the trees below.

We had our smoking gun and our bloody rock.

The case is in court now, and lucky for me, I don't have to go to court to testify. As it turns out, my little bluff about Diana being able to testify was actually true.

Who knew?

Unfortunately, Keith Rydell will likely face a new military tribunal now that there is wide speculation that his toxicology test results were tampered with. I have a feeling he'll be joining his comrades at the disciplinary barracks.

Speaking of Leavenworth, Michael's visit back home lasted a couple days longer than he expected. His mother decided to celebrate the return of the prodigal son by serving the fatted calf.

They all got food poisoning.

He's scheduled to return next week. While he's on the injured list, I agreed to fill in as an unofficial official White House photographer.

Not that I have any joy at all in his misfortune, but it's been awfully nice to have a purpose these days, albeit a temporary one.

As for Megan and her family, although they were stunned at the new revelations about Ashley—that she'd been murdered by the father of her unborn child—they seemed to honestly appreciate the efforts I made to uncover the truth, especially in light of the danger to me and to Aunt Patsy.

I don't know if Peter Seybold appreciated those same efforts. He's not real happy with me right now.

But, then again, when is he ever?

Drew seems excited at the prospect of getting a dog. Buck has promised that we can adopt Columbus just as soon as he's weaned. The staff assures us that they've dealt with a variety of animals in the White House. They tell us a golden retriever puppy won't be any worse a challenge than any of the other White House pets.

And, speaking of Buck . . .

He's fine. He's more than fine. He had no lasting damage from his minor heart attack, or further complications from the brouhaha in the emergency room. And his little brush with mortality seems to have built a fire beneath him. He's been courting Patsy daily, sending her flowers, candy, gifts, calling her. . . .

He's a persistent suitor.

What I'm afraid is that he's going to ask her to marry him.

And that she'll say yes.

And you know what that means, don't you? It'll be up to *me* to become the new freakin' First Lady.

Oh, brother . . .